D1068289

THE UNIVERSITY OF VIRGINIA EDITION OF
THE WORKS OF STEPHEN CRANE

VOLUME X

POEMS AND LITERARY REMAINS

Editorial expenses for this volume have been met in part by grants from the National Endowment for the Humanities administered through the Center for Editions of American Authors of the Modern Language Association.

First published 1975

The University Press of Virginia

ISBN: 0-8139-0610-5
Library of Congress Catalog Card Number: 68-8536
Printed in the United States of America

I'd Rather Have—

Last Christmas they gave me a sweater,
And a nice warm suit of wool,
But I'd rather be cold and have a dog,
To watch when I come from school.

Father gave me a bicycle,
But that isn't much of a treat,
Unless you have a dog at your heels
Racing away down the street

They bought me a camping outfit,
But a bonfire by a log
Is all the outfit I would ask,
If I only had a dog.

They seem to think a little dog
Is a killer of all earth's joys;
But oh, that "pesky little dog"
Means hours of joy to the boys.

Manuscript of Crane's earliest preserved poem (Cmdr. Melvin H. Schoberlin, USN [Ret.])

STEPHEN CRANE

POEMS AND LITERARY REMAINS

EDITED BY
FREDSON BOWERS
LINDEN KENT PROFESSOR OF ENGLISH AT THE UNIVERSITY OF VIRGINIA

WITH AN INTRODUCTION BY
JAMES B. COLVERT
PROFESSOR OF ENGLISH AT THE UNIVERSITY OF GEORGIA

THE UNIVERSITY PRESS OF VIRGINIA
CHARLOTTESVILLE

To

Clifton Waller Barrett

FOREWORD

THE tenth and last volume of *The Works of Stephen Crane* contains all of his known poetry and all of his known independent unfinished manuscripts. Manuscript drafts of published works are not included since these have been provided in earlier volumes in connection with the final texts. The literary remains have been printed substantially in diplomatic-transcript form with a minimum of editing: their interest lies precisely in the rough state in which Crane left them.

One previously unknown juvenile poem is included by courtesy of the owner of the manuscript, Commander Melvin H. Schoberlin USN (Ret.). A few unrecorded versions of known poems have been turned up to add details to the record of their publishing history. Of some importance, however, is the previously unnoticed appearance of a facsimile of the printer's-copy manuscript for no. 69, *Do not weep, maiden, for war is kind*, which at last establishes the authoritative form of this text. On the basis of a bibliographical analysis of the paper of the manuscripts and typescripts, as well as a fresh ordering of the publishing history assisted by a few unprinted letters, the editor has been able to redate or to assign more precise dates to a number of the poems. The editor's "The Text: History and Analysis" discusses the publishing history and the evidence for dating and in the section "The Dates of the Poems" offers a chronological arrangement of the poems by year of composition.

In the present edition the two collections *The Black Riders and Other Lines* and *War is Kind* are printed first, in the order in which they were originally published. After *War is Kind* appear all of the uncollected poems, whether published in Crane's lifetime or not, arranged in chronological order as precisely as the evidence permits. The apparatus for each poem lists the basic documents from which the text has been established and records emendations to the selected copy-text made from other sources as well as all alterations in any preserved manuscript; a table of variant readings, both substantive and accidental, from the established text is provided, as is a description of any manuscript or typescript. Notes discuss problems in the transmission of the text. In the printed copy-texts the typography does not distinguish between parenthetical dashes of about one em and terminal dashes of about two ems which mark broken-off syntax. The extension of short to long dashes in such texts has been treated as a matter of emendation. In the manuscripts, on the other hand, the length of dashes can seldom be determined with any certainty; hence in these texts the editor has silently adjusted the lengths according to the sense.

This volume also contains a newly discovered addition to the canon in a piece of syndicated journalism previously known only from its title "Kellar Turns Medium" in Crane's inventory lists of 1897. This would have appeared in Volume VIII if discovered earlier. A few addenda record further appearances in print of Crane's syndicated stories to help piece out a more complete record of his publications. Finally, a comprehensive title index to the ten volumes of this edition is provided for the reader's assistance as a finding list.

The expenses of the preparation of this volume with its textual analyses and apparatus have been subsidized by a grant from the National Endowment for the Humanities administered through the Modern Language Association of America and its Center for Editions of American Authors, but with support, as well, from the University of Virginia.

The editor is much indebted for assistance and various courtesies to Professors Matthew J. Bruccoli and Joseph Katz of the University of South Carolina and to his colleague Professor J. C. Levenson of the University of Virginia. Mr. Kenneth Lohf, Librarian of Rare Books and Manuscripts of the Columbia University Libraries, has been of unfailing and particular assistance, the more valuable because of the wealth of poetic manuscript material in the Special Collections. Miss Carolyn Ann Davis, Manuscript Librarian of the George Arents Research Library at Syracuse University, helpfully answered a number of questions, as did Lawrence F. London, Curator of Rare Books at the University of

North Carolina Library, Chapel Hill; Josiah Q. Bennett of the Lilly Library, Indiana University; and Brooke Whiting, Literary Manuscripts Librarian of the University Library, University of California at Los Angeles. The editor is grateful to the libraries of Columbia University, the librarians at Syracuse University, the Berg Collection at the New York Public Library, Astor and Tilden Foundation, Indiana University, University of California at Los Angeles, University of North Carolina at Chapel Hill, Dartmouth College, and the University of Virginia, as well as to Alfred A. Knopf, Inc., holder of residual Crane copyrights, for permission to print manuscript and typescript material. The British Museum, the London Library, and Harvard University courteously made printed material available. The constant assistance of the custodians of the Barrett Collection at the University of Virginia has been invaluable. The expert and scrupulous attentions of the volume's Chief Research Assistant, Miss Gillian G. M. Kyles, and her assistants, Mrs. Malcolm Craig, Mrs. Alan Buster, Miss Carolinda Hales, Mrs. Kathy Armstrong and Judith Nelson, have been essential and appreciated beyond the possibility of simple acknowledgment, for in these days of relatively rapid editorial publication no single scholar can hope to assume the burden of the repeated checking for accuracy of collation, reproduction, and notation enforced by the standards of the CEAA editions. Miss Joan St. C. Crane kindly checked the bibliographical descriptions and supplied the color coding. Professor Don L. Cook of Indiana University, who inspected this volume for the seal of the Center for Editions of American Authors, made various valuable queries and suggestions.

The editor's personal debt to Mr. Clifton Waller Barrett and his magnificent collection at the University of Virginia remains constant and can be expressed only by the dedication of each volume of this edition to him. The illustrations have been included by permission of Commander Schoberlin, USN (Ret.) and of the University of Virginia Libraries.

F.B.

Charlottesville, Virginia
August 1974

CONTENTS

Literary Remains

INTRODUCTION

According to C. K. Linson—the artist whose New York studio Stephen Crane frequented in the early nineties—"In the Depths of a Coal Mine" was written in a hotel room in Scranton, Pennsylvania, where Crane and Linson journeyed in June, 1894, on commission to produce an illustrated article on the mines for the McClure Syndicate. Linson, writing an account of the adventures in his memoir of Crane, quotes the opening paragraph of the first draft of this piece (the manuscript of which was given to him by Crane) as an example of the writer's remarkable sense of composition and color:

> The breakers squatted upon the hillsides and in the valley like enormous preying monsters eating of the sunshine, the grass, the green leaves. The smoke and dust from their nostrils had devastated the atmosphere. All that remained of the vegetation looked dark, miserable, half-strangled. Along the summit-line of the mountain a few unhappy trees were etched upon the clouds. Overhead stretched a sky of imperial blue, incredibly faraway from the sombre land.[1]

Like Hamlin Garland, Linson was much impressed by Crane's compositional facility,[2] and hints that he composed the passage effortlessly, "sitting at a hotel window in Scranton," shortly after their first descent into the mines. Both Linson and John Raught, another artist who admired Crane's striking visual effects, thought it a remarkable painting. "It suggests," Linson wrote, "a great canvas of a dramatic solemnity. Painters have marveled at the grim impressiveness of the landscape, and John Raught has

[1] Quoted in C. K. Linson, *My Stephen Crane*, ed. Edwin H. Cady (Syracuse University Press, 1958), p. 67. See Tales, Sketches, and Reports, *Works*, viii (1973), 600.20–26. Crane revised the whole manuscript and the opening passage of the printed version differs somewhat (cf. *Works*, viii, 590.24–31).

[2] See "The Text: History and Analysis" below, p. 190.

painted it, but none has pictured it better than Crane in the few words of that paragraph." [3]

Linson was not likely aware that this swiftly composed passage is a variant of a pattern of image and symbol which Crane had already worked out long before and had ready at hand, as it were, to render his inevitable impression of the latent menace of the landscape surrounding the infernolike mine. We recognize the characteristic figures and images: the grass-green valley, the terrible monsters of prey, the blasted vegetation, the blighted atmosphere, the cloud-muffled mountains in the middle distance, and over all the serene and poignantly remote sky of "imperial blue"—Crane's major symbols, arranged in characteristic compositional pattern. They recur in various forms and adaptations almost obsessively in the *Sullivan County Sketches*, in *The Red Badge of Courage*, in the poems of *The Black Riders* and *War is Kind*, in "The Open Boat," "The Blue Hotel," and indeed in most of his work, including some of the most casual of his journalism.

In *The Red Badge of Courage*, for example, when Henry Fleming is oppressed by his dread of mysterious threats which seem to him at times to emanate from nature itself, Crane renders this description of the landscape:

> When the sun-rays at last struck full and mellowingly upon the earth, the youth saw that the landscape was streaked with two long, thin, black columns which disappeared on the brow of a hill in front and rearward vanished in a wood. They were like two serpents crawling from the cavern of the night. . . .
>
> . . . the long serpents crawled slowly from hill to hill without bluster of smoke. A dun-colored cloud of dust floated away to the right. The sky over-head was of a fairy blue.[4]

Again, the mellow earth blighted by monsters, the vaguely animistic hill, the obscuring clouds, and the ironic counterimage of the serene blue sky. The specific imagery of the pattern appears in a wide range of variation and is ingeniously adapted to describe a variety of events and circumstances, as shown by this example from an account of a night in the trenches at Guantanamo, selected almost at random from Crane's war dispatches:

[3] Linson, *My Stephen Crane*, p. 67.

[4] The Red Badge of Courage, *Works*, II (1974), 16.11–16, 16.32–34.

These times on the hill resembled, in some ways, those terrible scenes on the stage—scenes of intense gloom, blinding lightning, with a cloaked devil or assassin or other appropriate character muttering deeply amid the awful roll of the thunder-drums. It was theatric beyond words; one felt like a leaf in this booming chaos, this prolonged tragedy of the night. Amid it all one could see from time to time the yellow light on the face of a preoccupied signalman.

Possibly no man who was there ever before understood the true eloquence of the breaking of the day. . . .

Then there would come into the sky a patch of faint blue light. It was like a piece of moonshine.[5]

Although the hill here is not clearly the animistic hill of the basic symbolic pattern, it is even so not merely naturalistic. Like the hills of Scranton as Crane saw them, and at Chancellorsville as he imagined them, it bears something monstrous—devil or assassin—and in the cloaking darkness the observer feels the weight of some terrible meaning apparently beyond this time and place, "a prolonged tragedy of the night" relieved, though tenuously here, by the patch of faint blue light.

It is not possible to demonstrate here the full range of variants in Crane's use of this pattern, but the figures recur constantly in some form or other, sometimes as a metaphor expanded into a whole composition, as in the early fable "The Mesmeric Mountain," sometimes in fleeting allusions scarcely distinguishable as metaphors at all, as illustrated by this passage, to give one last example, from "The Little Regiment," again selected nearly at random:

Regiment after regiment swung rapidly into the streets that faced the sinister ridge. . . .

The little sober-hued village had been like the cloak which disguises the king of drama. It was now put aside, and an army, splendid thing of steel and blue, stood forth in the sun-light.[6]

Symbolic overtones are severely muted in this version, but references to elements of the familiar pattern are faintly discernible in the epithets, figures, and general drift of meaning. The animistic mountain has become a "sinister ridge," the sense of obscurity has been transferred from the usual clouds (or darkness)

[5] "Marines Signaling under Fire at Guantanamo," TALES OF WAR, *Works*, VI (1970), 196.7–16, 196.22–23.

[6] *Works*, VI, 15.32–38.

to the cloaking village, the feeling of violence and menace has been shifted from monsters and demons to the army, "splendid thing of steel and blue." But even at this naturalistic remove the impression of menacing powers dramatically revealed, of some mysterious relation between human depredation and demonic nature, suggests the character of the imagination which conceived them.[7]

The major terms of this pattern of metaphors consolidate a variety of associated images and symbols. The imagery of demonic nature evokes dragons, serpents, ravaged and menacing landscapes, vacant deserts, empty seascapes—visions of a world fallen and cursed which derive clearly from Crane's heritage as a minister's son and descendant of a long line of Methodist preachers. One of them was the Reverend Jesse Peck, bishop of Syracuse and author of *What Must I Do to Be Saved?*, a forbidding treatise on the universality of sin and the irresistibility of divine retribution. It was this heritage which Crane thought he repudiated when he abandoned his father's parsonage for the studios of bohemian New York, but clearly, as the persistent recurrence of religious allusion, imagery, and motif in his fiction and as the anguished speculation about God in the poetry of *The Black Riders* and *War is Kind* show, it was a heritage he could not deny. The bleak doctrines of his ancestors lingered in his imagination as apocalyptic visions of ruin, depravity, and destruction in a devil-haunted world ruled over by a violent and vengeful God.

In Crane, as in Hawthorne, nature is the battleground of God and the Devil, and the awesome powers of these Adversaries are obliquely revealed in nature's delusionary and uncertain signs. The wrath of the hateful God of vengeance and the malice of the Devil, major subjects in the poetry, seem to merge in ambiguous aspects of the landscape. Out of the sea rush the primeval riders of sin:

> Black riders came from the sea.
> There was clang and clang of spear and shield,
> And clash and clash of hoof and heel,
> Wild shouts and the wave of hair
> In the rush upon the wind:
> Thus the ride of sin. [3.1–6]

[7] This argument is elaborated in my introductions to *Works*, VI and IX.

Majestic mountains, arrayed godlike on the horizon, menace the little men of the earth:

> On the horizon the peaks assembled;
> And as I looked,
> The march of the mountains began.
> As they marched, they sang,
> "Aye! We come! We come!" [21.16–20]

In a hopeful vision it appears that the little man might prevail against this threatened assault by nature:

> Once I saw mountains angry,
> And ranged in battle-front.
> Against them stood a little man;
> Aye, he was no bigger than my finger.
> I laughed, and spoke to one near me,
> "Will he prevail?"
> "Surely," replied this other;
> "His grandfathers beat them many times."
> Then did I see much virtue in grandfathers,—
> At least, for the little man
> Who stood against the mountains. [13.16–26]

But as we know from his futile encounter with haunted caves, demonic tarns, and wrathful hills in Sullivan County, the little man's expected victory is likely a delusion of wish and vanity. The full development of the metaphor in "The Mesmeric Mountain" makes clear that the hostility of nature, represented ambiguously as a projection of the little man's religious anxiety, cannot be prevailed against, since nature (and by extension, God, as the poem suggests) may be after all merely indifferent. The hero gains the summit of the wrathful hill in a mad rush of defiance, and once there strikes a victor's pose as he gazes complacently over the familiar valley lying far below. But the story ends: "The mountain under his feet was motionless." [8] Henry Fleming's presumption at one point in *The Red Badge of Courage* that he had "climbed a peak of wisdom from which he could perceive himself as a very wee thing" is represented as a grand delusion, as is his conviction that dragons "were not so hideous as he imagined them" and his poignantly self-congratulatory belief that mountains which had

[8] *Works*, VIII, 271.34.

lately threatened him had fallen to his courageous defiance "like paper peaks." [9]

Still, as several of the poems and these passages from the fiction show, the meaning of the mountain symbol is by no means fixed or consistent. Mountains—or variant images of lofty things —appear sometimes as possible links between the fallen world of the little man and the poignantly yearned for God of tenderness and compassion whom Crane celebrates in many of the poems as a foil to the bullying, wrathful God of vengeance:

> In the night
> Grey heavy clouds muffled the valleys
> And the peaks looked toward God, alone.
>   "Oh, Master that movest the wind with a finger
>   "Humble, idle, futile peaks are we.
>   "Grant that we may run swiftly across the world
>   "To huddle in worship at Thy feet."
>
> In the morning
> A noise of men at work came the clear blue miles
> And the little black cities were apparent.
>   "Oh, Master that knowest the meaning of rain-drops
>   "Humble, idle, futile peaks are we.
>   "Give voice to us we pray oh, Lord
>   "That we may sing Thy goodness to the sun."
>
> In the evening
> The far valleys were sprinkled with tiny lights.
>   "Oh, Master
>   "Thou that knowest the value of kings and birds
>   "Thou has made us humble, idle, futile peaks.
>   "Thou only, needest eternal patience;
>   "We bow to Thy wisdom, oh, Lord——
>   "Humble, idle, futile peaks."
>
> In the night
> Grey heavy clouds muffled the valleys
> And the peaks looked toward God, alone. [55.1–25]

The sense of this, considered in the context of the angry mountain, is clearly ambiguous. The refrain "And the peaks looked toward God, alone" may mean that only majestic mountains, not the noisy men of the "little black cities," can talk to God. But then

[9] *Works,* II, 82.19–20, 86.36, 97.25.

they are after all "idle, futile peaks" and there is no hint, except perhaps in the implications of the moving piety of their prayers, that the heedless God they implore is accessible to them, even if He exists at all. In any case these are not the angry peaks that threaten the little men of the "muffled valleys"; they seem to be as poignantly alienated from God as the world of men over which they tower so majestically. Another poem, in which appears a variant of the mountain image, suggests that perhaps God answers only peremptory challenges, not prayers, and then in the guise of the vengeful God of Bishop Peck:

> Once a man clambering to the house-tops
> Appealed to the heavens.
> With strong voice he called to the deaf spheres;
> A warrior's shout he raised to the suns.
> Lo, at last, there was a dot on the clouds,
> And—at last and at last—
> —God—the sky was filled with armies. [53.14–20]

But still again, the mountain appears in "The Blue Battalions" as a way to a God who does indeed exist:

> When a people reach the top of a hill
> Then does God lean toward them,
> Shortens tongues, lengthens arms. [82.1–3]

Even as He does not, apparently, in still another, where the speaker, "musing in a black world," sees suddenly in the far sky "a radiance"

> Ineffable, divine,—
> A vision painted upon a pall;
> And sometimes it was,
> And sometimes it was not. [29.14–17]

Like the hero of the fable "The Mesmeric Mountain," the speaker scrambles desperately up a hill:

> The hard hills tore my flesh;
> The ways bit my feet.
> At last I looked again.
> No radiance in the far sky,
> Ineffable, divine;
> No vision painted upon a pall. [29.27–30.3]

These examples trace the major lines of Crane's anguished thoughts about God as they can be inferred from the constant play of his characteristic metaphors over the surface of his prose writings and from his direct attack on the subject in nearly one-fourth of the poems in *The Black Riders* and *War is Kind.* God may be, so the speculation goes, a brutal and violent ally of the Adversary himself, shadowed forth in the ambiguous aspects of a menacing nature. But on the other hand, such a view of nature may be merely delusionary, a projection of the observer's turbulent spiritual anxieties; nature may be neutral and indifferent and God—perhaps—dead. Or perhaps in some world lying at impossible distances dwells a God of love and compassion, accessible only to the true believer—if accessible at all. It is a mistake to assume, as Daniel Hoffman does in his generally excellent study of Crane's poetry, that "there is in Crane's treatment of God and of religion a progress from the utter denial 'Well, then, I hate Thee' to an affirmation of faith in the 'interior pitying God.' " [10] Fortunately perhaps for his art, if not fortunately for Crane himself, he never resolved these warring concepts. These three possibilities he entertained about the nature of God—as malevolent, pitying, or indifferent—examined obsessively in the poems, are mutely orchestrated in the magnificent imagery of "The Open Boat," surely the most poignant religious story in American literature.

The devastated mountain, the preying monsters, and the obscured landscape imaged in the opening paragraph of the piece on the Scranton coal mine are developed and elaborated in a major group of poems in *The Black Riders* and *War is Kind.* The scarred mountain extends to a general image of the ruined world —the desertlike, "reptile swarming place," violence-ridden world of darkness and terror which is Crane's version of the ruin of Eden, a subject sardonically treated in the posthumously published "A God came to a man." A concommitant theme, the universality of sin, is treated specifically in still another group, one of which, the title poem of *The Black Riders*, has already been cited. These poems obviously derive from an imagination pro-

[10] Daniel Hoffman, *The Poetry of Stephen Crane* (New York: Columbia University Press, 1957), p. 48.

foundly influenced by the bleak fundamentalism of Crane's Methodist heritage.

Another set of poems, extending from the recurring image of the sky which Crane characteristically sets in ironic juxtaposition to the monster-haunted landscape, is as complex and ambiguous in the meaning of its imagery as is the group structured on images of ruin and devastation. Like the image of the animistic mountain, the recurrent image of the "fairy blue sky," "the sky of imperial blue," or the "vast blue sky" is related also to a group of associated images. These refer variously to an amorphous transcendental order or to a dreamlike vision of the ideal, out of space and out of time, as inaccessible to the little men on the "black landscape" as is the yearned-for God of compassion and love:

Places among the stars,
Soft gardens near the sun,
Keep your distant beauty;
Shed no beams upon my weak heart.
Since she is here
In a place of blackness,
Not your golden days
Nor your silver nights
Can call me to you.
Since she is here
In a place of blackness,
Here I stay and wait. [14.1–12]

In the fiction they dramatically counterpoint images of the demonic landscape. Henry Fleming looks up from the blistered battleground and feels a "flash of astonishment at the blue, pure sky and the sun-gleamings on the trees and fields." [11] Associated images range from pastoral and idyllic (purling streams, fertile plains, golden fields, and rich, benevolent sunlight), to images of a serene and passionless Christian heaven, to images of a cold and forbidding cosmic order lying almost beyond the reach of human thought. Edenic imagery may dramatize ironically the ruin of the fallen world, as in the allusion to the "preying monsters eating of the sunshine, the grass, the green leaves" in the opening paragraph of "In the Depths of a Coal Mine." But it may also be associated with the self-serving sentimentality of the ob-

[11] *Works*, II, 38.32–34.

server, as it so often is in Crane's ironic commentary on his heroes' distorted views of the harsh realities of a god-abandoned world. Or it may represent the innocence of the observer, as in the following poem, where a maiden's vision of a fairylike seascape is counterpointed against a wrecked sailor's chilling perception:

> To the maiden
> The sea was blue meadow
> Alive with little froth-people
> Singing.
>
> To the sailor, wrecked,
> The sea was dead grey walls
> Superlative in vacancy
> Upon which nevertheless at fateful time,
> Was written
> The grim hatred of nature. [47.1–10]

The apparently contradictory perception of the sea as "superlative" in its indifference and at the same time the epitome of hatred is resolved dramatically by the shift in point of view in the phrase "at fateful time." Seen objectively the sea is indifferent, but seen subjectively at the crucial moment of drowning it wears an aspect of hatred, an example of ambiguity which Crane constantly attributes to the shifting—and normless—perceptions of the observer.

The structure of some of the poems is based on contrasts between the serene order of an envisioned, but inaccessible, heaven and the "cluttered incoherency" of the fallen world:

> A slant of sun on dull brown walls
> A forgotten sky of bashful blue.
>
> Toward God a mighty hymn
> A song of collisions and cries
> Rumbling wheels, hoof-beats, bells,
> Welcomes, farewells, love-calls, final moans,
> Voices of joy, idiocy, warning, despair,
> The unknown appeals of brutes,
> The chanting of flowers
> The screams of cut trees,
> The senseless babble of hens and wise men——
> A cluttered incoherency that says at the stars:
> "O God, save us!" [53.1–13]

In another, the "mighty hill," which out of context of the metaphor fully elaborated elsewhere is merely a version of the conventional Christian trial of passage, is set in tension with the lost and unrecoverable Eden, or perhaps Christian heaven.

> There was set before me a mighty hill,
> And long days I climbed
> Through regions of snow.
> When I had before me the summit-view,
> It seemed that my labor
> Had been to see gardens
> Lying at impossible distances. [15.13–19]

But in another the transcendental vision is of the "superlative" vacancy perceived by the forsaken sailor:

> If I should cast off this tattered coat,
> And go free into the mighty sky;
> If I should find nothing there
> But a vast blue,
> Echoless, ignorant,—
> What then? [41.1–6]

The image of the "imperial blue sky" over the ravaged hill at the Scranton mine, considered in the context of the fully developed metaphor, is invested with ambiguous meaning. It may refer to the edenic order glimpsed fitfully in the associated pastoral imagery, or it may suggest a tenuous promise of heaven for the little men of the bedeviled world, like the black-faced miners who, as Crane observes, were "symbols of a grim, strange war that was being waged in the sunless depths of the earth." [12] Or it may symbolize, this "imperial" sky, the silent mockery of a vacant and heedless cosmos. In these unresolved allusions one finds the measure of Crane's profound spiritual uncertainty. For even if, on balance, he seems to opt for a god-abandoned universe, still visions of a Methodist heaven and a lost Eden crowd upon his imagination, and no certain choice among them seems possible.

Crane's reputation rests lightly on his poetry, and justly so. The myth of the little man on the black landscape, bewildered by the ambiguous signs perceived or imagined from an unknowable or

[12] "In the Depths of a Coal Mine," *Works*, VIII, 591.10–11.

nonexistent God, is not suitable matter for abbreviated parables, epigrams, and gnomic utterances. No single poem conveys effectively the implication of the myth, and some cannot be clearly understood out of the context of the full development of the metaphor in the fiction. Many of them read curiously like exercises in which the aim is to reduce the symbols elaborately orchestrated in the fiction to their simplest possible forms, where they tend to become resonantless abstractions of the complex play of meaning in the prose work. "Personally," he wrote a couple of years after the publication of *The Black Riders*, "I like my little book of poems . . . better than I do 'The Red Badge of Courage.' The reason is, I suppose, that the former is the more ambitious effort. In it I aim to give my ideas of life as a whole, so far as I know it, and the latter is a mere episode, or rather an amplification." [13] The poems of both volumes do seem often to be curiously personal, as if Crane's motive in writing them might have been to try to clarify for himself the vision "amplified" in the fiction. This seems especially true in the poems about God, where the Deity appears stripped of cloaking metaphor and symbol and is confronted directly as principal in Crane's anguished religious speculation.

Still, the poetry is important, not only because it concentrates certain tendencies in the evolution of style and method toward the "new" poetry of the early twentieth century, but because it illustrates clearly the response of a brilliant literary imagination to the turbulent and contrary flow of thought and feeling of the American nineties. The poetry and fiction arise from an imagination profoundly affected by the historical breakdown of Protestant authority and the decline of romantic idealism. If in the times of Emerson and Hawthorne the assimilation of transcendental idealism to American Protestantism provided, as Bernard Duffey has said, a coherent world view in which the "assumption of quest and celebration of openness were ready at hand as daylight ideals" and in which "emotions and grandly simple ideas were resolvable in intuitions of a spiritual order, consubstantial with nature," [14] no such view was accessible to Crane. Under the influence of

[13] To John Northern Hilliard, [1897?], in R. W. Stallman and Lillian Gilkes, eds., *Stephen Crane: Letters* (New York University Press, 1960), p. 159.

[14] Bernard Duffey, "Romantic Coherence and Romantic Incoherence in American Poetry," *Centennial Review*, VII (1963), 223.

scientism, the Higher Criticism, and the demonstrated fallibility of social institutions, these assumptions were no longer articles of faith on which might rest a serene acceptance of what might lie beyond the limits of the knowable. The premises of this older vision could no longer in Crane's time support a coherent view of existence. In his poetry and fiction they linger as discrete propositions, without cohering center, appearing in his symbolic landscapes as uncertain and antithetical possibilities, incapable of resolution.

J.B.C.

POEMS

The Black Riders and Other Lines

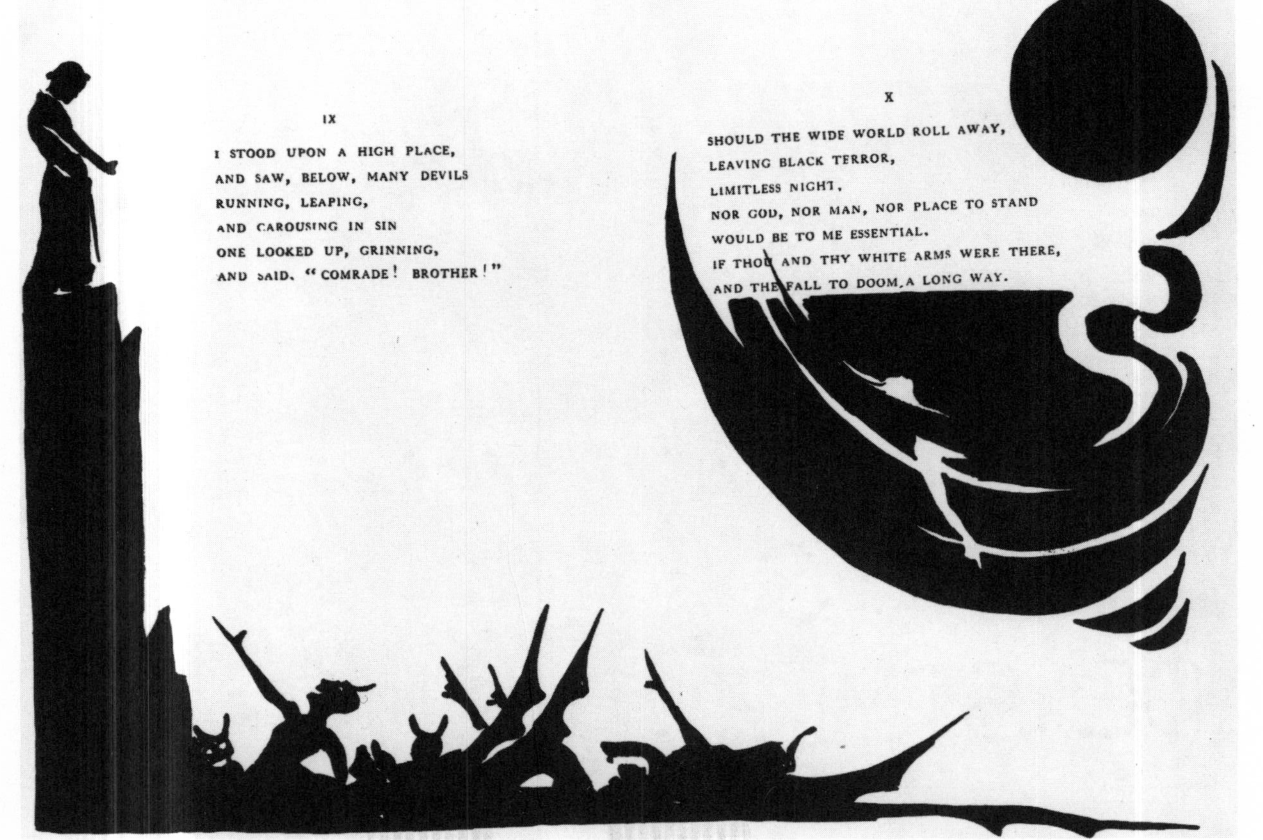
IX
I STOOD UPON A HIGH PLACE,
AND SAW, BELOW, MANY DEVILS
RUNNING, LEAPING,
AND CAROUSING IN SIN
ONE LOOKED UP, GRINNING,
AND SAID, "COMRADE! BROTHER!"
X
SHOULD THE WIDE WORLD ROLL AWAY,
LEAVING BLACK TERROR,
LIMITLESS NIGHT,
NOR GOD, NOR MAN, NOR PLACE TO STAND
WOULD BE TO ME ESSENTIAL.
IF THOU AND THY WHITE ARMS WERE THERE,
AND THE FALL TO DOOM, A LONG WAY.

Bookman's proof of Melanie Norton's illustrations for *Black Riders*, nos. 9 and 10 (University of Virginia—Barrett)

Reject front cover design for the first American edition, possibly by Frederick Gordon (University of Virginia—Barrett)

I

1 Black riders came from the sea.
There was clang and clang of spear and shield,
And clash and clash of hoof and heel,
Wild shouts and the wave of hair
In the rush upon the wind:
Thus the ride of sin.

II

2 Three little birds in a row
Sat musing.
A man passed near that place
Then did the little birds nudge each other.

They said: "He thinks he can sing."
They threw back their heads to laugh.
With quaint countenances
They regarded him.
They were very curious
Those three little birds in a row.

III

3 In the desert
I saw a creature, naked, bestial,
Who, squatting upon the ground,
Held his heart in his hands,
And ate of it.
I said, "Is it good, friend?"
"It is bitter—bitter," he answered;
"But I like it
"Because it is bitter,
"And because it is my heart."

IV

4 Yes, I have a thousand tongues,
And nine and ninety-nine lie.
Though I strive to use the one,
It will make no melody at my will,
But is dead in my mouth.

V

5 Once there came a man
Who said,
"Range me all men of the world in rows."
And instantly
There was terrific clamor among the people
Against being ranged in rows.
There was a loud quarrel, world-wide.
It endured for ages;
And blood was shed
By those who would not stand in rows,
And by those who pined to stand in rows.
Eventually, the man went to death, weeping.
And those who staid in bloody scuffle
Knew not the great simplicity.

VI

6 God fashioned the ship of the world carefully.
With the infinite skill of an all-master
Made He the hull and the sails,
Held He the rudder
Ready for adjustment.
Erect stood He, scanning His work proudly.
Then—at fateful time—a wrong called,
And God turned, heeding.
Lo, the ship, at this opportunity, slipped slyly,
Making cunning noiseless travel down the ways.
So that, forever rudderless, it went upon the seas
Going ridiculous voyages,
Making quaint progress,
Turning as with serious purpose
Before stupid winds.
And there were many in the sky
Who laughed at this thing.

VII

7 Mystic shadow, bending near me,
Who art thou?
Whence come ye?
And—tell me—is it fair
Or is the truth bitter as eaten fire?
Tell me!
Fear not that I should quaver,
For I dare—I dare.
Then, tell me!

VIII

8 I looked here
I looked there
No where could I see my love.
And—this time—
She was in my heart.
Truly then I have no complaint
For 'though she be fair and fairer
She is none so fair as she
In my heart.

IX

9 I stood upon a high place,
And saw, below, many devils
Running, leaping,
And carousing in sin.
One looked up, grinning,
And said, "Comrade! Brother!"

X

10 Should the wide world roll away
Leaving black terror
Limitless night,
Nor God, nor man, nor place to stand
Would be to me essential
If thou and thy white arms were there
And the fall to doom a long way.

XI

11 In a lonely place,
I encountered a sage
Who sat, all still,
Regarding a newspaper.
He accosted me:
"Sir, what is this?"
Then I saw that I was greater,
Aye, greater than this sage.
I answered him at once,
"Old, old man, it is the wisdom of the age."
The sage looked upon me with admiration.

XII

12 "And the sins of the fathers shall be visited upon the heads of the children, even unto the third and fourth generation of them that hate me."

Well, then, I hate Thee, unrighteous picture;
Wicked image, I hate Thee;
So, strike with Thy vengeance
The heads of those little men
Who come blindly.
It will be a brave thing.

XIII

13 If there is a witness to my little life,
To my tiny throes and struggles,
He sees a fool;
And it is not fine for gods to menace fools.

XIV

14 There was crimson clash of war.
Lands turned black and bare;
Women wept;
Babes ran, wondering.
There came one who understood not these things.
He said, "Why is this?"
Whereupon a million strove to answer him.
There was such intricate clamor of tongues,
That still the reason was not.

XV

15 "Tell brave deeds of war."

Then they recounted tales,—
"There were stern stands
"And bitter runs for glory."

Ah, I think there were braver deeds.

XVI

16 Charity, thou art a lie,
A toy of women,
A pleasure of certain men.
In the presence of justice,
Lo, the walls of the temple
Are visible
Through thy form of sudden shadows.

XVII

17 There were many who went in huddled procession,
They knew not whither;
But, at any rate, success or calamity
Would attend all in equality.

There was one who sought a new road.
He went into direful thickets,
And ultimately he died thus, alone;
But they said he had courage.

XVIII

18 In Heaven,
Some little blades of grass
Stood before God.
"What did you do?"
Then all save one of the little blades
Began eagerly to relate
The merits of their lives.
This one stayed a small way behind
Ashamed.
Presently God said:
"And what did you do?"
The little blade answered: "Oh, my lord,
"Memory is bitter to me
"For if I did good deeds
"I know not of them."
Then God in all His splendor
Arose from His throne.
"Oh, best little blade of grass," He said.

XIX

19 A god in wrath
Was beating a man;
He cuffed him loudly
With thunderous blows
That rang and rolled over the earth.
All people came running.
The man screamed and struggled,
And bit madly at the feet of the god.
The people cried,
"Ah, what a wicked man!"
And—
"Ah, what a redoubtable god!"

XX

20 A learned man came to me once.
He said, "I know the way,—come."
And I was overjoyed at this.
Together we hastened.
Soon, too soon, were we
Where my eyes were useless,
And I knew not the ways of my feet.
I clung to the hand of my friend;
But at last he cried, "I am lost."

XXI

21 There was, before me,
Mile upon mile
Of snow, ice, burning sand.
And yet I could look beyond all this,
To a place of infinite beauty;
And I could see the loveliness of her
Who walked in the shade of the trees.
When I gazed,
All was lost
But this place of beauty and her.
When I gazed,
And in my gazing, desired,
Then came again
Mile upon mile,
Of snow, ice, burning sand.

XXII

22 Once I saw mountains angry,
And ranged in battle-front.
Against them stood a little man;
Aye, he was no bigger than my finger.
I laughed, and spoke to one near me,
"Will he prevail?"
"Surely," replied this other;
"His grandfathers beat them many times."
Then did I see much virtue in grandfathers,—
At least, for the little man
Who stood against the mountains.

XXIII

23 Places among the stars,
Soft gardens near the sun,
Keep your distant beauty;
Shed no beams upon my weak heart.
Since she is here
In a place of blackness,
Not your golden days
Nor your silver nights
Can call me to you.
Since she is here
In a place of blackness,
Here I stay and wait.

XXIV

24 I saw a man pursuing the horizon;
Round and round they sped.
I was disturbed at this;
I accosted the man.
"It is futile," I said,
"You can never——"

"You lie," he cried,
And ran on.

XXV

25 Behold, the grave of a wicked man,
And near it, a stern spirit.

There came a drooping maid with violets,
But the spirit grasped her arm.
"No flowers for him," he said.
The maid wept:
"Ah, I loved him."
But the spirit, grim and frowning:
"No flowers for him."

Now, this is it——
If the spirit was just,
Why did the maid weep?

XXVI

26 There was set before me a mighty hill,
And long days I climbed
Through regions of snow.
When I had before me the summit-view,
It seemed that my labor
Had been to see gardens
Lying at impossible distances.

XXVII

27 A youth in apparel that glittered
Went to walk in a grim forest.
There he met an assassin
Attired all in garb of old days;
He, scowling through the thickets,
And dagger poised quivering,
Rushed upon the youth.
"Sir," said this latter,
"I am enchanted, believe me,
"To die, thus,
"In this medieval fashion,
"According to the best legends;
"Ah, what joy!"
Then took he the wound, smiling,
And died, content.

XXVIII

28 "Truth," said a traveller,
"Is a rock, a mighty fortress;
"Often have I been to it,
"Even to its highest tower,
"From whence the world looks black."

"Truth," said a traveller,
"Is a breath, a wind,
"A shadow, a phantom;
"Long have I pursued it,
"But never have I touched
"The hem of its garment."

And I believed the second traveller;
For truth was to me
A breath, a wind,
A shadow, a phantom,
And never had I touched
The hem of its garment.

XXIX

29 Behold, from the land of the farther suns
I returned.
And I was in a reptile-swarming place,
Peopled, otherwise, with grimaces,
Shrouded above in black impenetrableness.
I shrank, loathing,
Sick with it.
And I said to him,
"What is this?"
He made answer slowly,
"Spirit, this is a world;
"This was your home."

XXX

30 Supposing that I should have the courage
To let a red sword of virtue
Plunge into my heart,
Letting to the weeds of the ground
My sinful blood,
What can you offer me?
A gardened castle?
A flowery kingdom?

What? A hope?
Then hence with your red sword of virtue.

XXXI

31 Many workmen
Built a huge ball of masonry
Upon a mountain-top.
Then they went to the valley below,
And turned to behold their work.
"It is grand," they said;
They loved the thing.

Of a sudden, it moved:
It came upon them swiftly;
It crushed them all to blood.
But some had opportunity to squeal.

XXXII

32 Two or three angels
Came near to the earth.
They saw a fat church.
Little black streams of people
Came and went in continually.
And the angels were puzzled
To know why the people went thus,
And why they stayed so long within.

XXXIII

33 There was One I met upon the road
Who looked at me with kind eyes.
He said: "Show me of your wares."
And this I did
Holding forth one.
He said: "It is a sin."
Then held I forth another.
He said: "It is a sin."
Then held I forth another.
He said: "It is a sin."
And so to the end
Always He said: "It is a sin."
And, finally, I cried out:
"But I have none other."
Then did He look at me
With kinder eyes.
"Poor soul," He said.

XXXIV

34 I stood upon a highway,
And, behold, there came
Many strange pedlers.
To me each one made gestures,
Holding forth little images, saying,
"This is my pattern of God.
"Now this is the God I prefer."

But I said, "Hence!
"Leave me with mine own,
"And take you yours away;
"I can't buy of your patterns of God,
"The little gods you may rightly prefer."

XXXV

35 A man saw a ball of gold in the sky;
He climbed for it,
And eventually he achieved it——
It was clay.

Now this is the strange part:
When the man went to the earth
And looked again,
Lo, there was the ball of gold.
Now this is the strange part:
It was a ball of gold.
Aye, by the heavens, it was a ball of gold.

XXXVI

36 I met a seer.
He held in his hands
The book of wisdom.
"Sir," I addressed him,
"Let me read."
"Child——" he began.
"Sir," I said,
"Think not that I am a child,
"For already I know much
"Of that which you hold.
"Aye, much."

He smiled.
Then he opened the book
And held it before me.—
Strange that I should have grown so suddenly blind.

XXXVII

37 On the horizon the peaks assembled;
And as I looked,
The march of the mountains began.
As they marched, they sang,
"Aye! We come! We come!"

XXXVIII

38 The ocean said to me once,
"Look!
"Yonder on the shore
"Is a woman, weeping.
"I have watched her.
"Go you and tell her this,—
"Her lover I have laid
"In cool green hall.
"There is wealth of golden sand
"And pillars, coral-red;
"Two white fish stand guard at his bier.

"Tell her this
"And more,—
"That the king of the seas
"Weeps too, old, helpless man.
"The bustling fates
"Heap his hands with corpses
"Until he stands like a child
"With surplus of toys."

XXXIX

39 The livid lightnings flashed in the clouds;
The leaden thunders crashed.
A worshipper raised his arm.
"Hearken! Hearken! The voice of God!"

"Not so," said a man.
"The voice of God whispers in the heart
"So softly
"That the soul pauses,
"Making no noise,
"And strives for these melodies,
"Distant, sighing, like faintest breath,
"And all the being is still to hear."

XL

And you love me?

I love you.

You are, then, cold coward.

Aye; but, beloved,
When I strive to come to you,
Man's opinions, a thousand thickets,
My interwoven existence,
My life,
Caught in the stubble of the world
Like a tender veil,—
This stays me.
No strange move can I make
Without noise of tearing.
I dare not.

If love loves,
There is no world
Nor word.
All is lost
Save thought of love
And place to dream.
You love me?

I love you.

You are, then, cold coward.

Aye; but, beloved——

XLI

41 Love walked alone.
The rocks cut her tender feet,
And the brambles tore her fair limbs.
There came a companion to her,
But, alas, he was no help,
For his name was Heart's Pain.

XLII

42 I walked in a desert.
And I cried,
"Ah, God, take me from this place!"
A voice said, "It is no desert."
I cried, "Well, but——
"The sand, the heat, the vacant horizon."
A voice said, "It is no desert."

XLIII

43 There came whisperings in the winds:
"Good-bye! Good-bye!"
Little voices called in the darkness:
"Good-bye! Good-bye!"
Then I stretched forth my arms.
"No— No——"
There came whisperings in the wind:
"Good-bye! Good-bye!"
Little voices called in the darkness:
"Good-bye! Good-bye!"

XLIV

44 I was in the darkness;
I could not see my words
Nor the wishes of my heart.
Then suddenly there was a great light——

"Let me into the darkness again."

XLV

45 Tradition, thou art for suckling children,
Thou art the enlivening milk for babes;
But no meat for men is in thee.
Then——
But, alas, we all are babes.

XLVI

46 Many red devils ran from my heart
And out upon the page.
They were so tiny
The pen could mash them.
And many struggled in the ink.
It was strange
To write in this red muck
Of things from my heart.

XLVII

47 "Think as I think," said a man,
"Or you are abominably wicked;
"You are a toad."

And after I had thought of it,
I said, "I will, then, be a toad."

XLVIII

48 Once there was a man,—
Oh, so wise!
In all drink
He detected the bitter,
And in all touch
He found the sting.
At last he cried thus:
"There is nothing,—
"No life,
"No joy,
"No pain,—
"There is nothing save opinion,
"And opinion be damned."

XLIX

49 I stood musing in a black world,
Not knowing where to direct my feet.
And I saw the quick stream of men
Pouring ceaselessly,
Filled with eager faces,
A torrent of desire.
I called to them,
"Where do you go? What do you see?"
A thousand voices called to me.
A thousand fingers pointed.
"Look! Look! There!"

I know not of it.
But, lo! in the far sky shone a radiance
Ineffable, divine,—
A vision painted upon a pall;
And sometimes it was,
And sometimes it was not.
I hesitated.
Then from the stream
Came roaring voices,
Impatient:
"Look! Look! There!"

So again I saw,
And leaped, unhesitant,
And struggled and fumed
With outspread clutching fingers.
The hard hills tore my flesh;
The ways bit my feet.
At last I looked again.

No radiance in the far sky,
Ineffable, divine;
No vision painted upon a pall;
And always my eyes ached for the light.
Then I cried in despair,
"I see nothing! Oh, where do I go?"
The torrent turned again its faces:
"Look! Look! There!"

And at the blindness of my spirit
They screamed,
"Fool! Fool! Fool!"

L

50 You say you are holy,
And that
Because I have not seen you sin.
Aye, but there are those
Who see you sin, my friend.

LI

51 A man went before a strange god,—
The god of many men, sadly wise.
And the deity thundered loudly,
Fat with rage, and puffing,
"Kneel, mortal, and cringe
"And grovel and do homage
"To my particularly sublime majesty."

The man fled.

Then the man went to another god,—
The god of his inner thoughts.
And this one looked at him
With soft eyes
Lit with infinite comprehension,
And said, "My poor child!"

LII

52 Why do you strive for greatness, fool?
Go pluck a bough and wear it.
It is as sufficing.

My lord, there are certain barbarians
Who tilt their noses
As if the stars were flowers,
And thy servant is lost among their shoe-buckles.
Fain would I have mine eyes even with their eyes.

Fool, go pluck a bough and wear it.

LIII

I

53 Blustering god,
Stamping across the sky
With loud swagger,
I fear you not.
No, though from your highest heaven
You plunge your spear at my heart,
I fear you not.
No, not if the blow
Is as the lightning blasting a tree,
I fear you not, puffing braggart.

II

If thou can see into my heart
That I fear thee not,
Thou wilt see why I fear thee not,
And why it is right.
So threaten not, thou, with thy bloody spears,
Else thy sublime ears shall hear curses.

III

Withal, there is one whom I fear;
I fear to see grief upon that face.
Perchance, friend, he is not your god;
If so, spit upon him.
By it you will do no profanity.
But I——
Ah, sooner would I die
Than see tears in those eyes of my soul.

LIV

54 "It was wrong to do this," said the angel.
"You should live like a flower,
"Holding malice like a puppy,
"Waging war like a lambkin."

"Not so," quoth the man
Who had no fear of spirits;
"It is only wrong for angels
"Who can live like the flowers,
"Holding malice like the puppies,
"Waging war like the lambkins."

LV

55 A man toiled on a burning road,
Never resting.
Once he saw a fat, stupid ass
Grinning at him from a green place.
The man cried out in rage,
"Ah! do not deride me, fool!
"I know you——
"All day stuffing your belly,
"Burying your heart
"In grass and tender sprouts:
"It will not suffice you."
But the ass only grinned at him from the green place.

Rejected back cover design for the first American edition of *Black Riders*, possibly by Gordon (University of Virginia—Barrett)

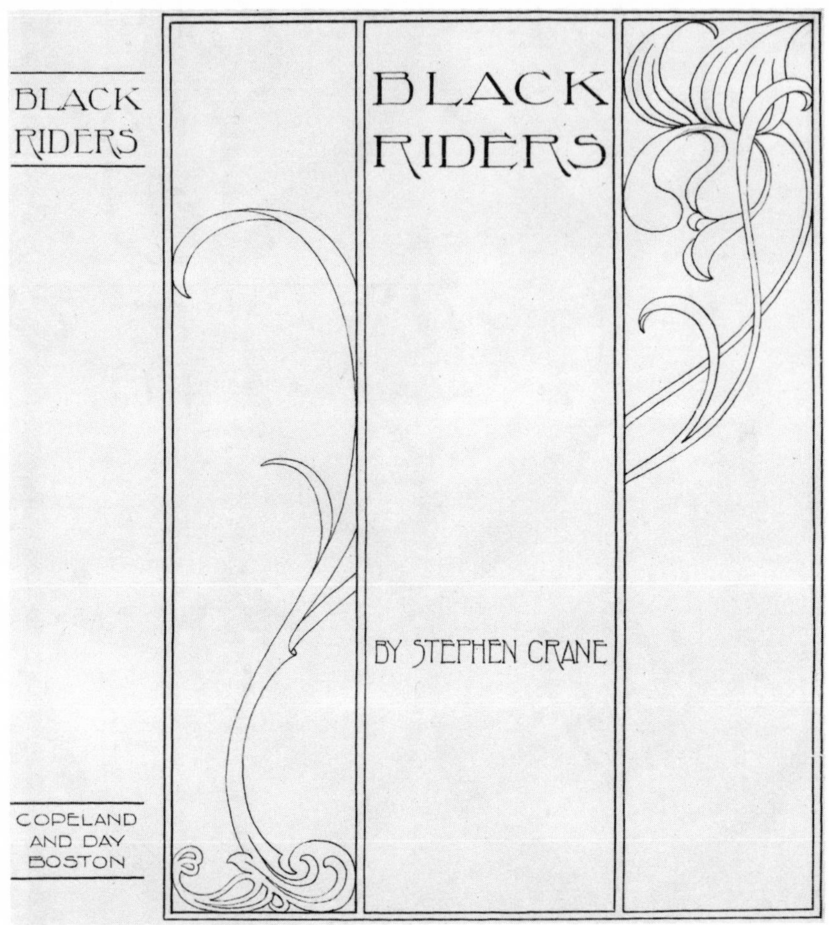

Alternate rejected front cover design by Gordon for the first American edition (University of Virginia—Barrett)

LVI

56 A man feared that he might find an assassin;
Another that he might find a victim.
One was more wise than the other.

LVII

57 With eye and with gesture
You say you are holy.
I say you lie;
For I did see you
Draw away your coats
From the sin upon the hands
Of a little child.
Liar!

LVIII

58 The sage lectured brilliantly.
Before him, two images:
"Now this one is a devil,
"And this one is me."
He turned away.
Then a cunning pupil
Changed the positions.
Turned the sage again:
"Now this one is a devil,
"And this one is me."
The pupils sat, all grinning,
And rejoiced in the game.
But the sage was a sage.

LIX

59 Walking in the sky,
A man in strange black garb
Encountered a radiant form.
Then his steps were eager;
Bowed he devoutly.
"My lord," said he.
But the spirit knew him not.

LX

60 Upon the road of my life,
Passed me many fair creatures,
Clothed all in white, and radiant.
To one, finally, I made speech:
"Who art thou?"
But she, like the others,
Kept cowled her face,
And answered in haste, anxiously,
"I am Good Deed, forsooth;
"You have often seen me."
"Not uncowled," I made reply.
And with rash and strong hand,
Though she resisted,
I drew away the veil
And gazed at the features of Vanity.
She, shamefaced, went on;
And after I had mused a time,
I said of myself,
"Fool!"

LXI

I

61 There was a man and a woman
Who sinned.
Then did the man heap the punishment
All upon the head of her,
And went away gayly.

II

There was a man and a woman
Who sinned.
And the man stood with her.
As upon her head, so upon his,
Fell blow and blow,
And all people screaming, "Fool!"
He was a brave heart.

III

He was a brave heart.
Would you speak with him, friend?
Well, he is dead,
And there went your opportunity.
Let it be your grief
That he is dead
And your opportunity gone;
For, in that, you were a coward.

LXII

62 There was a man who lived a life of fire.
Even upon the fabric of time,
Where purple becomes orange
And orange purple,
This life glowed,
A dire red stain, indelible;
Yet when he was dead,
He saw that he had not lived.

LXIII

63 There was a great cathedral.
To solemn songs,
A white procession
Moved toward the altar.
The chief man there
Was erect, and bore himself proudly.
Yet some could see him cringe,
As in a place of danger,
Throwing frightened glances into the air,
A-start at threatening faces of the past.

LXIV

64 Friend, your white beard sweeps the ground.
Why do you stand, expectant?
Do you hope to see it
In one of your withered days?
With your old eyes
Do you hope to see
The triumphal march of justice?
Do not wait, friend.
Take your white beard
And your old eyes
To more tender lands.

LXV

65 Once, I knew a fine song,
—It is true, believe me,—
It was all of birds,
And I held them in a basket;
When I opened the wicket,
Heavens! They all flew away.
I cried, "Come back, little thoughts!"
But they only laughed.
They flew on
Until they were as sand
Thrown between me and the sky.

LXVI

66 If I should cast off this tattered coat,
And go free into the mighty sky;
If I should find nothing there
But a vast blue,
Echoless, ignorant,—
What then?

LXVII

67 God lay dead in Heaven;
Angels sang the hymn of the end;
Purple winds went moaning,
Their wings drip-dripping
With blood
That fell upon the earth.
It, groaning thing,
Turned black and sank.
Then from the far caverns
Of dead sins
Came monsters, livid with desire.
They fought,
Wrangled over the world,
A morsel.
But of all sadness this was sad,—
A woman's arms tried to shield
The head of a sleeping man
From the jaws of the final beast.

LXVIII

68 A spirit sped
Through spaces of night;
And as he sped, he called,
"God! God!"
He went through valleys
Of black death-slime,
Ever calling,
"God! God!"
Their echoes
From crevice and cavern
Mocked him:
"God! God! God!"
Fleetly into the plains of space
He went, ever calling,
"God! God!"
Eventually, then, he screamed,
Mad in denial,
"Ah, there is no God!"
A swift hand,
A sword from the sky,
Smote him,
And he was dead.

War is Kind

69 Do not weep, maiden, for war is kind.
Because your lover threw wild hands toward the sky
And the affrighted steed ran on alone,
Do not weep.
War is kind.

Hoarse, booming drums of the regiment
Little souls who thirst for fight,
These men were born to drill and die
The unexplained glory flies above them
Great is the battle-god, great, and his kingdom——
A field where a thousand corpses lie.

Do not weep, babe, for war is kind.
Because your father tumbled in the yellow trenches,
Raged at his breast, gulped and died,
Do not weep.
War is kind.

Swift, blazing flag of the regiment
Eagle with crest of red and gold,
These men were born to drill and die
Point for them the virtue of slaughter
Make plain to them the excellence of killing
And a field where a thousand corpses lie.

Mother whose heart hung humble as a button
On the bright splendid shroud of your son,
Do not weep.
War is kind.

"What says the sea, little shell?
"What says the sea?
"Long has our brother been silent to us
"Kept his message for the ships
"Awkward ships, stupid ships."

"The sea bids you mourn, oh, pines
"Sing low in the moonlight.
"He sends tale of the land of doom
"Of place where endless falls
"A rain of women's tears
"And men in grey robes
"—Men in grey robes—
"Chant the unknown pain."

"What says the sea, little shell?
"What says the sea?
"Long has our brother been silent to us
"Kept his message for the ships
"Puny ships, silly ships."

"The sea bids you teach, oh, pines
"Sing low in the moonlight.
"Teach the gold of patience
"Cry gospel of gentle hands
"Cry a brotherhood of hearts
"The sea bids you teach, oh, pines."

"And where is the reward, little shell?
"What says the sea?
"Long has our brother been silent to us
"Kept his message for the ships
"Puny ships, silly ships."

"No word says the sea, oh, pines
"No word says the sea.
"Long will your brother be silent to you
"Keep his message for the ships
"Oh, puny pines, silly pines."

71 To the maiden
The sea was blue meadow
Alive with little froth-people
Singing.

To the sailor, wrecked,
The sea was dead grey walls
Superlative in vacancy
Upon which nevertheless at fateful time,
Was written
The grim hatred of nature.

72 A little ink more or less!
It surely can't matter?
Even the sky and the opulent sea,
The plains and the hills, aloof,
Hear the uproar of all these books.
But it is only a little ink more or less.

What?
You define me God with these trinkets?
Can my misery meal on an ordered walking
Of surpliced numbskulls?
And a fanfare of lights?
Or even upon the measured pulpiting
Of the familiar false and true?
Is this God?
Where, then, is hell?
Show me some bastard mushroom
Sprung from a pollution of blood.
It is better.

Where is God?

73 "Have you ever made a just man?"
"Oh, I have made three," answered God
"But two of them are dead
"And the third——
"Listen! Listen!
"And you will hear the thud of his defeat."

74 I explain the silvered passing of a ship at night
The sweep of each sad lost wave
The dwindling boom of the steel thing's striving
The little cry of a man to a man
A shadow falling across the greyer night
And the sinking of the small star.

Then the waste, the far waste of waters
And the soft lashing of black waves
For long and in loneliness.

Remember, thou, oh ship of love
Thou leavest a far waste of waters
And the soft lashing of black waves
For long and in loneliness.

75 "I have heard the sunset song of the birches
"A white melody in the silence
"I have seen a quarrel of the pines.
"At nightfall
"The little grasses have rushed by me
"With the wind-men.
"These things have I lived," quoth the maniac,
"Possessing only eyes and ears.
"But, you——
"You don green spectacles before you look at roses."

76 Fast rode the knight
With spurs, hot and reeking
Ever waving an eager sword.
"To save my lady!"
Fast rode the knight
And leaped from saddle to war.
Men of steel flickered and gleamed
Like riot of silver lights
And the gold of the knight's good banner
Still waved on a castle wall.

* * * * * *

A horse
Blowing, staggering, bloody thing
Forgotten at foot of castle wall.
A horse
Dead at foot of castle wall.

77 Forth went the candid man
And spoke freely to the wind——
When he looked about him he was in a far strange
country.

Forth went the candid man
And spoke freely to the stars——
Yellow light tore sight from his eyes.

"My good fool," said a learned bystander
"Your operations are mad."

"You are too candid," cried the candid man
And when his stick left the head of the learned
bystander
It was two sticks.

78 You tell me this is God?
I tell you this is a printed list,
A burning candle and an ass.

79 On the desert
A silence from the moon's deepest valley.
Fire-rays fall athwart the robes
Of hooded men, squat and dumb.
Before them, a woman
Moves to the blowing of shrill whistles
And distant-thunder of drums
While slow things, sinuous, dull with terrible color
Sleepily fondle her body
Or move at her will, swishing stealthily over the sand.
The snakes whisper softly;
The whispering, whispering snakes
Dreaming and swaying and staring
But always whispering, softly whispering.
The wind streams from the lone reaches
Of Arabia, solemn with night,
And the wild fire makes shimmer of blood
Over the robes of the hooded men
Squat and dumb.
Bands of moving bronze, emerald, yellow,
Circle the throat and the arms of her
And over the sands serpents move warily
Slow, menacing and submissive,
Swinging to the whistles and drums,
The whispering, whispering snakes,
Dreaming and swaying and staring
But always whispering, softly whispering.
The dignity of the accursèd;
The glory of slavery, despair, death
Is in the dance of the whispering snakes.

80 A newspaper is a collection of half-injustices
Which, bawled by boys from mile to mile,
Spreads its curious opinion
To a million merciful and sneering men,
While families cuddle the joys of the fireside
When spurred by tale of dire lone agony.
A newspaper is a court
Where every one is kindly and unfairly tried
By a squalor of honest men.
A newspaper is a market
Where wisdom sells its freedom
And melons are crowned by the crowd.
A newspaper is a game
Where his error scores the player victory
While another's skill wins death.
A newspaper is a symbol;
It is fetless life's chronicle,
A collection of loud tales
Concentrating eternal stupidities,
That in remote ages lived unhaltered,
Roaming through a fenceless world.

81 The wayfarer
Perceiving the pathway to truth
Was struck with astonishment.
It was thickly grown with weeds.
"Ha," he said,
"I see that none has passed here
"In a long time."
Later he saw that each weed
Was a singular knife.
"Well," he mumbled at last,
"Doubtless there are other roads."

82 A slant of sun on dull brown walls
A forgotten sky of bashful blue.

Toward God a mighty hymn
A song of collisions and cries
Rumbling wheels, hoof-beats, bells,
Welcomes, farewells, love-calls, final moans,
Voices of joy, idiocy, warning, despair,
The unknown appeals of brutes,
The chanting of flowers
The screams of cut trees,
The senseless babble of hens and wise men——
A cluttered incoherency that says at the stars:
"O, God, save us!"

83 Once a man clambering to the house-tops
Appealed to the heavens.
With strong voice he called to the deaf spheres;
A warrior's shout he raised to the suns.
Lo, at last, there was a dot on the clouds,
And—at last and at last—
—God—the sky was filled with armies.

84 There was a man with tongue of wood
Who essayed to sing
And in truth it was lamentable
But there was one who heard
The clip-clapper of this tongue of wood
And knew what the man
Wished to sing
And with that the singer was content.

85 The successful man has thrust himself
Through the water of the years,
Reeking wet with mistakes,
Bloody mistakes,
Slimed with victories over the lesser
A figure thankful on the shore of money.
Then, with the bones of fools
He buys silken banners
Limned with his triumphant face;
With the skins of wise men
He buys the trivial bows of all.
Flesh painted with marrow
Contributes a coverlet
A coverlet for his contented slumber.
In guiltless ignorance, in ignorant guilt
He delivers his secrets to the riven multitude.
"Thus I defended: Thus I wrought."
Complacent, smiling,
He stands heavily on the dead.
Erect on a pillar of skulls
He declaims his trampling of babes;
Smirking, fat, dripping,
He makes speech in guiltless ignorance,
Innocence.

86 In the night
Grey heavy clouds muffled the valleys
And the peaks looked toward God, alone.
"Oh, Master that movest the wind with a finger
"Humble, idle, futile peaks are we.
"Grant that we may run swiftly across the world
"To huddle in worship at Thy feet."

In the morning
A noise of men at work came the clear blue miles
And the little black cities were apparent.
"Oh, Master that knowest the meaning of rain-drops
"Humble, idle, futile peaks are we.
"Give voice to us we pray oh, Lord
"That we may sing Thy goodness to the sun."

In the evening
The far valleys were sprinkled with tiny lights.
"Oh, Master
"Thou that knowest the value of kings and birds
"Thou hast made us humble, idle, futile peaks.
"Thou only, needest eternal patience;
"We bow to Thy wisdom, oh, Lord——
"Humble, idle, futile peaks."

In the night
Grey heavy clouds muffled the valleys
And the peaks looked toward God, alone.

87 The chatter of a death-demon from a tree-top.

Blood—blood and torn grass—
Had marked the rise of his agony——
This lone hunter.
The grey-green woods impassive
Had watched the threshing of his limbs.

A canoe with flashing paddle
A girl with soft searching eyes,
A call: "John!"

* * * * * * * *

Come, arise, hunter!
Can you not hear?

The chatter of a death-demon from a tree-top.

88 The impact of a dollar upon the heart
Smiles warm red light
Sweeping from the hearth rosily upon the white table,
With the hanging cool velvet shadows
Moving softly upon the door.

The impact of a million dollars
Is a crash of flunkeys
And yawning emblems of Persia
Cheeked against oak, France and a sabre,
The outcry of old Beauty
Whored by pimping merchants
To submission before wine and chatter.
Silly rich peasants stamp the carpets of men,
Dead men who dreamed fragrance and light
Into their woof, their lives;
The rug of an honest bear
Under the feet of a cryptic slave
Who speaks always of baubles
Forgetting place, multitude, work and state,
Champing and mouthing of hats
Making ratful squeak of hats,
Hats.

89 A man said to the universe:
"Sir, I exist!"
"However," replied the universe,
"The fact has not created in me
"A sense of obligation."

90 When the prophet, a complacent fat man,
Arrived at the mountain-top
He cried: “Woe to my knowledge!
“I intended to see good white lands
“And bad black lands——
“But the scene is grey.”

91 There was a land where lived no violets.
A traveller at once demanded: “Why?”
The people told him:
“Once the violets of this place spoke thus:
“ ‘Until some woman freely gives her lover
“ ‘To another woman
“ ‘We will fight in bloody scuffle.’ ”
Sadly the people added:
“There are no violets here.”

92 There was one I met upon the road
Who looked at me with kind eyes.
He said: "Show me of your wares."
And I did,
Holding forth one.
He said: "It is a sin."
Then I held forth another.
He said: "It is a sin."
Then I held forth another.
He said: "It is a sin."
And so to the end.
Always he said: "It is a sin."
At last, I cried out:
"But I have none other."
He looked at me
With kinder eyes.
"Poor soul," he said.

93 Aye, workman, make me a dream
A dream for my love.
Cunningly weave sunlight,
Breezes and flowers.
Let it be of the cloth of meadows.
And—good workman—
And let there be a man walking thereon.

94 Each small gleam was a voice
—A lantern voice—
In little songs of carmine, violet, green, gold.
A chorus of colors came over the water;
The wondrous leaf-shadow no longer wavered,
No pines crooned on the hills
The blue night was elsewhere a silence
When the chorus of colors came over the water,
Little songs of carmine, violet, green, gold.

Small glowing pebbles
Thrown on the dark plane of evening
Sing good ballads of God
And eternity, with soul's rest.
Little priests, little holy fathers
None can doubt the truth of your hymning
When the marvelous chorus comes over the water
Songs of carmine, violet, green, gold.

95 The trees in the garden rained flowers.
Children ran there joyously.
They gathered the flowers
Each to himself.
Now there were some
Who gathered great heaps—
—Having opportunity and skill—
Until, behold, only chance blossoms
Remained for the feeble.
Then a little spindling tutor
Ran importantly to the father, crying:
"Pray, come hither!
"See this unjust thing in your garden!"
But when the father had surveyed,
He admonished the tutor:
"Not so, small sage!
"This thing is just.
"For, look you,
"Are not they who possess the flowers
"Stronger, bolder, shrewder
"Than they who have none?
"Why should the strong—
"—The beautiful strong—
"Why should they not have the flowers?"

Upon reflection, the tutor bowed to the ground.
"My Lord," he said,
"The stars are displaced
"By this towering wisdom."

"INTRIGUE"

96 Thou art my love
And thou art the peace of sundown
When the blue shadows soothe
And the grasses and the leaves sleep
To the song of the little brooks
Woe is me.

Thou art my love
And thou art a storm
That breaks black in the sky
And, sweeping headlong,
Drenches and cowers each tree
And at the panting end
There is no sound
Save the melancholy cry of a single owl
Woe is me!

Thou art my love
And thou art a tinsel thing
And I in my play
Broke thee easily
And from the little fragments
Arose my long sorrow
Woe is me.

Thou art my love
And thou art a weary violet
Drooping from sun-caresses.
Answering mine carelessly
Woe is me.

Thou art my love
And thou art the ashes of other men's love
And I bury my face in these ashes
And I love them
Woe is me.

Thou art my love
And thou art the beard
On another man's face
Woe is me.

Thou art my love
And thou art a temple
And in this temple is an altar
And on this altar is my heart
Woe is me.

Thou art my love
And thou art a wretch.
Let these sacred love-lies choke thee
For I am come to where I know your lies as truth
And your truth as lies
Woe is me.

Thou art my love
And thou art a priestess
And in thy hand is a bloody dagger
And my doom comes to me surely
Woe is me.

Thou art my love
And thou art a skull with ruby eyes
And I love thee
Woe is me.

Thou art my love
And I doubt thee
And if peace came with thy murder
Then would I murder.
Woe is me.

Thou art my love
And thou art death
Aye, thou art death
Black and yet black
But I love thee
I love thee
Woe, welcome woe, to me.

97 Love forgive me if I wish you grief
For in your grief
You huddle to my breast
And for it
Would I pay the price of your grief.

You walk among men
And all men do not surrender
And thus I understand
That love reaches his hand
In mercy to me.

He had your picture in his room
A scurvy traitor picture
And he smiled
—Merely a fat complacence
Of men who know fine women—
And thus I divided with him
A part of my love.

Fool, not to know that thy little shoe
Can make men weep!
—Some men weep.
I weep and I gnash
And I love the little shoe
The little, little shoe.

God give me medals
God give me loud honors
That I may strut before you, sweetheart
And be worthy of—
—The love I bear you.

Now let me crunch you
With full weight of affrighted love
I doubted you
—I doubted you—
And in this short doubting
My love grew like a genie
For my further undoing.

Beware of my friends
Be not in speech too civil
For in all courtesy
My weak heart sees spectres,
Mists of desires
Arising from the lips of my chosen
Be not civil.

The flower I gave thee once
Was incident to a stride
A detail of a gesture
But search those pale petals
And see engraven thereon
A record of my intention.

98 Ah, God, the way your little finger moved
As you thrust a bare arm backward
And made play with your hair
And a comb, a silly gilt comb
Ah, God—that I should suffer
Because of the way a little finger moved.

99 Once I saw thee idly rocking
—Idly rocking—
And chattering girlishly to other girls,
Bell-voiced, happy.
Careless with the stout heart of unscarred womanhood
And life to thee was all light melody.
I thought of the great storms of love as I knew it
Torn, miserable and ashamed of my open sorrow,
I thought of the thunders that lived in my head
And I wish to be an ogre
And hale and haul my beloved to a castle
And there use the happy cruel one cruelly
And make her mourn with my mourning.

100 Tell me why, behind thee,
I see always the shadow of another lover?
Is it real
Or is this the thrice-damned memory of a better
happiness?
Plague on him if he be dead
Plague on him if he be alive
A swinish numskull
To intrude his shade
Always between me and my peace.

101 And yet I have seen thee happy with me.
I am no fool
To poll stupidly into iron.
I have heard your quick breaths
And seen your arms writhe toward me;
At those times
—God help us—
I was impelled to be a grand knight,
And swagger and snap my fingers,
And explain my mind finely.
Oh, lost sweetheart,
I would that I had not been a grand knight.
I said: "Sweetheart."
Thou said'st: "Sweetheart."
And we preserved an admirable mimicry
Without heeding the drip of the blood
From my heart.

102 I heard thee laugh,
And in this merriment
I defined the measure of my pain;
I knew that I was alone,
Alone with love,
Poor shivering love,
And he, little sprite,
Came to watch with me,
And at midnight
We were like two creatures by a dead camp-fire.

103 I wonder if sometimes in the dusk,
When the brave lights that gild thy evenings
Have not yet been touched with flame,
I wonder if sometimes in the dusk
Thou rememberest a time,
A time when thou loved me
And our love was to thee thy all?
Is the memory rubbish now?
An old gown
Worn in an age of other fashions?
Woe is me, oh, lost one,
For that love is now to me
A supernal dream,
White, white, white with many suns.

104 Love met me at noonday,
—Reckless imp,
To leave his shaded nights
And brave the glare,—
And I saw him then plainly
For a bungler,
A stupid, simpering, eyeless bungler,
Breaking the hearts of brave people
As the snivelling idiot-boy cracks his bowl,
And I cursed him,
Cursed him to and fro, back and forth,
Into all the silly mazes of his mind,
But in the end
He laughed and pointed to my breast,
Where a heart still beat for thee, beloved.

105 I have seen thy face aflame
For love of me,
Thy fair arms go mad,
Thy lips tremble and mutter and rave.
And—surely—
This should leave a man content?
Thou lovest not me now,
But thou didst love me,
And in loving me once
Thou gavest me an eternal privilege,
For I can think of thee.

Uncollected Poems

"I'D RATHER HAVE——"

106 Last Christmas they gave me a sweater,
And a nice warm suit of wool,
But I'd rather be cold and have a dog,
To watch when I come from school.

Father gave me a bicycle,
But that isn't much of a treat,
Unless you have a dog at your heels
Racing away down the street.

They bought me a camping outfit,
But a bonfire by a log
Is all the outfit I would ask,
If I only had a dog.

They seem to think a little dog
Is a killer of all earth's joys;
But oh, that "pesky little dog"
Means hours of joy to the boys.

107 Ah, haggard purse, why ope thy mouth
Like a greedy urchin
I have nought wherewith to feed thee
Thy wan cheeks have ne'er been puffed
Thou knowest not the fill of pride
Why then gape at me
In fashion of a wronged one
Thou do smile wanly
And reproachest me with thine empty stomach
Thou knowest I'd sell my steps to the grave
If t'were but honestie.
Ha, leer not so,
Name me no names of wrongs committed with thee
No ghost can lay hand on thee and me
We've been too thin to do sin
What, liar? When thou was filled of gold, didst I riot?
And give thee no time to eat?
No, thou brown devil, thou art stuffed now with lies as with wealth,
The one gone to let in the other.

108 Little birds of the night
Aye, they have much to tell
Perching there in rows
Blinking at me with their serious eyes
Recounting of flowers they have seen and loved
Of meadows and groves of the distance
And pale sands at the foot of the sea
And breezes that fly in the leaves.
They are vast in experience
These little birds that come in the night

109 A god came to a man
And said to him thus:
"I have an apple
"It is a glorious apple
"Aye, I swear by my ancestors
"Of the eternities before this eternity
"It is an apple that is from
"The inner thoughts of heaven's greatest.

"And this I will hang here
"And then I will adjust thee here
"Thus—you may reach it.
"And you must stifle your nostrils
"And control your hands
"And your eyes
"And sit for sixty years
"But,—leave be the apple."

The man answered in this wise:
"Oh, most interesting God
"What folly is this?
"Behold, thou hast moulded my desires
"Even as thou hast moulded the apple.

"How, then?
"Can I conquer my life
"Which is thou?
"My desires?
"Look you, foolish god
"If I thrust behind me
"Sixty white years
"I am a greater god than god
"And, then, complacent splendor,
"Thou wilt see that the golden angels
"That sing pink hymns
"Around thy throne-top
"Will be lower than my feet."

110 One came from the skies
—They said—
And with a band he bound them
A man and a woman.
Now to the man
The band was gold
And to another, iron
And to the woman, iron.
But this second man,
He took his opinion and went away
But, by heavens,
He was none too wise.

111 There is a grey thing that lives in the tree-tops
None know the horror of its sight
Save those who meet death in the wilderness
But one is enabled to see
To see branches move at its passing
To hear at times the wail of black laughter
And to come often upon mystic places
Places where the thing has just been.

112 intermingled,
There come in wild revelling strains
Black words, stinging
That murder flowers
The horror of profane speculation.

113 A soldier, young in years, young in ambitions
Alive as no grey-beard is alive
Laid his heart and his hopes before duty
And went staunchly into the tempest of war.
There did the bitter red winds of battle
Swirl 'gainst his youth, beat upon his ambitions,
Drink his cool clear blood of manhood
Until at coming forth time
He was alive merely as the grey-beard is alive.
And for this—
The nation rendered to him a flower
A little thing—a flower
Aye, but yet not so little
For this flower grew in the nation's heart
A wet, soft blossom
From tears of her who loved her son
Even when the black battle rages
Made his face the face of furious urchin,
And this she cherished
And finally laid it upon the breast of him.
A little thing—this flower?
No—it was the flower of duty
That inhales black smoke-clouds
And fastens its roots in bloody sod
And yet comes forth so fair, so fragrant—
Its birth is sunlight in grimest, darkest place.

114 A row of thick pillars
Consciously bracing for the weight
Of a vanished roof
The bronze light of sunset strikes through them,
And over a floor made for slow rites.
There is no sound of singing
But, aloft, a great and terrible bird
Is watching a cur, beaten and cut,
That crawls to the cool shadows of the pillars
To die.

115 Chant you loud of punishments,
Of the twisting of the heart's poor strings
Of the crash of the lightning's fierce revenge.

Then sing I of the supple-souled men
And the strong, strong gods
That shall meet in times hereafter
And the amaze of the gods
At the strength of the men.
—The strong, strong gods—
    —And the supple-souled men—

116 If you would seek a friend among men
Remember: they are crying their wares.
If you would ask of heaven of men
Remember: they are crying their wares.
If you seek the welfare of men
Remember: they are crying their wares.
If you would bestow a curse upon men
Remember: they are crying their wares.
        Crying their wares
        Crying their wares
If you seek the attention of men
Remember:
Help them or hinder them as they cry their wares.

117 A lad and a maid at a curve in the stream
And a shine of soft silken waters
Where the moon-beams fall through a hemlock's boughs
        Oh, night dismal, night glorious.

A lad and a maid at the rail of a bridge
With two shadows adrift on the water
And the wind sings low in the grass on the shore.
        Oh, night dismal, night glorious.

A lad and a maid in a canoe,
And a paddle making silver turmoil.

"LEGENDS"

118 I

A man builded a bugle for the storms to blow.

The focussed winds hurled him afar.
He said that the instrument was a failure.

119 II

When the suicide arrived at the sky,
The people there asked him: "Why?"
He replied: "Because no one admired me."

120 III

A man said: "Thou tree!"
The tree answered with the same scorn: "Thou man!
Thou art greater than I only in thy possibilities."

121 IV

A warrior stood upon a peak and defied the stars.
A little magpie, happening there, desired the soldier's
plume,
And so plucked it.

122 V

The wind that waves the blossoms
Sang, sang, sang from age to age.
The flowers were made curious by this joy.
"Oh, wind," they said, "why sing you at your
labour,
While we, pink beneficiaries, sing not,
But idle, idle, idle from age to age?"

123 Oh, a rare old wine ye brewed for me
Flagons of despair
A deep deep drink of this wine of life
Flagons of despair.

Dream of riot and blood and screams
The rolling white eyes of dying men
The terrible heedless courage of babes

124 Tell me not in joyous numbers
We can make our lives sublime
By—well, at least, not by
Dabbling much in rhyme.

125 When a people reach the top of a hill
Then does God lean toward them,
Shortens tongues, lengthens arms.
A vision of their dead comes to the weak.
The moon shall not be too old
Before the new battalions rise
—Blue battalions—
The moon shall not be too old
When the children of change shall fall
Before the new battalions
—The blue battalions—

Mistakes and virtues will be trampled deep
A church and a thief shall fall together
A sword will come at the bidding of the eyeless,
The God-led, turning only to beckon.
Swinging a creed like a censer
At the head of the new battalions
—Blue battalions—
March the tools of nature's impulse
Men born of wrong, men born of right
Men of the new battalions
—The blue battalions—

The clang of swords is Thy wisdom
The wounded make gestures like Thy Son's
The feet of mad horses is one part,
—Aye, another is the hand of a mother on the brow of a son.
Then swift as they charge through a shadow,
The men of the new battalions
—Blue battalions—
God lead them high. God lead them far
Lead them far, lead them high
These new battalions
—The blue battalions—.

126 A man adrift on a slim spar
A horizon smaller than the rim of a bottle
Tented waves rearing lashy dark points
The near whine of froth in circles.
God is cold.

The incessant raise and swing of the sea
And growl after growl of crest
The sinkings, green, seething, endless
The upheaval half-completed.
God is cold.

The seas are in the hollow of The Hand;
Oceans may be turned to a spray
Raining down through the stars
Because of a gesture of pity toward a babe.
Oceans may become grey ashes,
Die with a long moan and a roar
Amid the tumult of the fishes
And the cries of the ships,
Because The Hand beckons the mice.

A horizon smaller than a doomed assassin's cap,
Inky, surging tumults
A reeling, drunken sky and no sky
A pale hand sliding from a polished spar.
God is cold.

The puff of a coat imprisoning air.
A face kissing the water-death
A weary slow sway of a lost hand
And the sea, the moving sea, the sea.
God is cold.

127 There exists the eternal fact of conflict
And—next—a mere sense of locality.
Afterward we derive sustenance from the winds.
Afterward we grip upon this sense of locality.
Afterward, we become patriots.
The godly vice of patriotism makes us slaves,
And—let us surrender to this falsity
Let us be patriots

Then welcome us the practical men
Thrumming on a thousand drums
The practical men, God help us.
They cry aloud to be led to war
Ah—
They have been poltroons on a thousand fields
And the sacked sad city of New York is their record
Furious to face the Spaniard, these people, and crawling worms before their task
They name serfs and send charity in bulk to better men
They play at being free, these people of New York
Who are too well-dressed to protest against infamy.

128 On the brown trail
We hear the grind of your carts
To our villages,
Laden with food
Laden with food
We know you are come to our help
But—
Why do you impress upon us
Your foreign happiness?
We know it not.
(Hark!
Carts laden with food
Laden with food)
We weep because we don't understand
But your gifts form into a yoke
The food turns into a yoke
(Hark!
Carts laden with food
Laden with food)
It is our mission to vanish
Grateful because of full mouths
Destiny—Darkness
Time understands
And ye—ye bigoted men of a moment—
—Wait—
Await your turn.

129 Rumbling, buzzing, turning, whirling Wheels,
Dizzy Wheels!
Wheels!

"THE BATTLE HYMN"

130 All-feeling God, hear in the war-night
The rolling voices of a nation;
Through dusky billows of darkness
See the flash, the under-light, of bared swords—
—Whirling gleams like wee shells
Deep in the streams of the universe—
Bend and see a people, O, God,
A people rebuked, accursed,
By him of the many lungs
And by him of the bruised weary war-drum
(The chanting disintegrate and the two-faced eagle)
Bend and mark our steps, O, God.
Mark well, mark well, Father of the Never-Ending Circles
And if the path, the new path, lead awry
Then in the forest of the lost standards
Suffer us to grope and bleed apace
For the wisdom is Thine.
Bend and see a people, O, God,
A people applauded, acclaimed,
By him of the raw red shoulders
The manacle-marked, the thin victim
(He lies white amid the smoking cane)
—And if the path, the new path, leads straight—
Then—O, God—then bare the great bronze arm;
Swing high the blaze of the chained stars
And let them look and heed
(The chanting distintegrate and the two-faced eagle)
For we go, we go in a lunge of a long blue corps
And—to Thee we commit our lifeless sons,
The convulsed and furious dead.
(They shall be white amid the smoking cane)
For, the seas shall not bar us;
The capped mountains shall not hold us back
We shall sweep and swarm through jungle and pool,
Then let the savage one bend his high chin
To see on his breast, the sullen glow of the death-medals

For we know and we say our gift.
His prize is death, deep doom.
(He shall be white amid the smoking cane.)

131 Unwind my riddle.
Cruel as hawks the hours fly,
Wounded men seldom come home to die,
The hard waves see an arm flung high,
Scorn hits strong because of a lie,
Yet there exists a mystic tie.
Unwind my riddle.

132 A naked woman and a dead dwarf;
Wealth and indifference.
Poor dwarf!
Reigning with foolish kings
And dying mid bells and wine
Ending with a desperate comic palaver
While before thee and after thee
Endures the eternal clown—
—The eternal clown—
A naked woman.

133 A grey and boiling street
Alive with rickety noise.
Suddenly, a hearse,
Trailed by black carriages
Takes a deliberate way
Through this chasm of commerce;
And children look eagerly
To find the misery behind the shades.
Hired men, impatient, drive with a longing
To reach quickly the grave-side, the end of solemnity.

Yes, let us have it over.
Drive, man, drive.
Flog your sleek-hided beasts,
Gallop—gallop—gallop.
Let us finish it quickly.

134 Bottles and bottles and bottles
In a merry den
And the wan smiles of women
Untruthing license and joy.
Countless lights
Making oblique and confusing multiplication
In mirrors
And the light returns again to the faces.

* * * *

A cellar, and a death-pale child.
A woman
Ministering commonly, degradedly,
Without manners.
A murmur and a silence
Or silence and a murmur
And then a finished silence.
The moon beams practically upon the cheap bed.

An hour, with its million trinkets of joy or pain,
Matters little in cellar or merry den
Since all is death.

135 The patent of a lord
And the bangle of a bandit
Make argument
Which God solves
Only after lighting more candles.

136 My cross!

Your cross?
The real cross
Is made of pounds,
Dollars or francs.
Here I bear my palms for the silly nails
To teach the lack
—The great pain of lack—
Of coin.

LITERARY REMAINS

I. [NOTES ON MADAME ALBERTI]

DELSARTEAN systim and the [n made] inquiries as to [which] methods made <   > philosophy prominen[t] about ten years [ago] In the fall of 18[6]9, Mr Steele Mc[Kaye] fresh from his studies with Mr. Franco[is] <   > Delsarte, came to this country and

II. [TWELFTH CAVALRY AND THE INDIAN WARS]

"THE new colonel was an infernal martinet, sir, as all the boys said before he had taken command a week," said Corporal Smith as he lighted his brier wood again and leaned lazily back against the post in front of his colors. "Any man who would make a famous regiment like the Eleventh Cavalry go through a series of skirmish drills for three days in a broiling sun just as quick as we got back from a three weeks campaign after the Apaches, was a martinet. He was an awful stiff old duffer with a grey mustache. Oh! no! he was transferred to the Fifteenth sometime ago. I will never forget Captain Grey's face when, after the first dress parade, the old man said to him 'Captain, the third man in your second set of fours had gloves on that were not mates, and your first serjeant's fifth button was not properly shined.' I overheard this as I held the captain's horse for I was an orderly then <[an]d> I says to <   > this here regiment is going to get put through an awful course of sprouts. Well, sir, the colonel went for us, the worst way. He was great on reforms. Have you ever got settled into a nice little way of doing things and then have someone sail in with a lot of new wrinkles and then have [to] learn all over again. Well, the Twelfth felt just that way. A good many of us was old Indian fighters and we wore broad felt hats but the colonel settled it that fatigue caps was the proper thing. But you wanted to know how I got corporal. That [was] all along of the old man, too. We were ordered further west to quell an insurrection of the Apaches about six months after the new colonel come in. And one day about two hours after leaving camp as the column was crossing a rolling prairie, the scouts in advance, discovered Indian signs and the colonel ordered my lieutenant to take sixteen men and go support the scouts; and [I] was one of 'em. We rode over the rise of ground and disappeared from the column. The lieutenant rode about three paces in advance of the head trooper. We were no more than out of sight when one of the privates sings out, 'Boys, I'll be blessed if I wear this thing anymore. I am going to put on a decent hat,' and he pulls a felt hat out from under his blouse and hangs the fatigue to his saddle. Well, in a moment more, the whole squad had on sombreros and the fatigue hats hung at the saddle bows. And that lieutenant never turned his head but rode on with out paying any attention to what we might be up to. Well, we rode to the top of the next rise and, bless your soul and [the] place was alive with Indians. We staid no more than to catch [sight] of them before we wheeled our horses and were pulling for the main column. We had about a mile to ride and as we fancied we heard yells of pursuit we rode as if the dickens was after us. A mile shows plainly enough the qualities of a horse and by the time we reached the top of the divide we were strung out in a long line. We galloped up to the head of the column in wild disorder, horses foaming and men panting. We drew up in a sheepish looking line, all privates with the forbidden hats on. If we had only known we were to return in a hurry we would have kept on the fatigue caps, but now we had our lieutenant in hot water, and were in up to our necks, ourselves. We were a sorry crowd indeed as we sat our horses with eyes cast down. The colonel rode toward us with fire in his eye. He drew up his horse in front and cast a scornful glance along the shamed faces. 'Well, this is encouraging to a commander, lieutenant. Sixteen men of the Twelfth United States Cavalry disobey orders and appear before their colonel in the act. Rush back to the column like a crowd of frightened school boys, too. Don't you know sir, a soldier should never lose his head and scamper like a scared rabbit if five thousand Indians were after him.' And so the colonel harangued at a great rate. He finally stopped and we sneaked back into line

III. [MR. RICHARD EDGEMONT SHARP]

MR. RICHARD EDGEMONT SHARP walked slowly down the little narrow street of Newburyton, Eng. His face wore an intensely thoughtful expression. He whistled thoughtfully to himself

IV. "JACK"

[MS[1]]

A PARTY of campers on the Mongaup River in Sullivan County, New York had brought with them a large black mastiff called Jack. Jack was a good dog, he was lazy except when aroused but he never took advantage of the fact that he could [take] a man's arm or lower limb in his mouth without stretching his jaws anymore than an ordinary man would in biting a stick of candy. And he dearly loved everybody connected with the camp. His black tail would wag with the force of an Irishman's shillelah when one spoke kindly to him. He would follow the cook all around the camp in pursuit of a morsel wagging the terrible tail with a disregard for all consequences. When he invaded the sacred precincts near the cooking stove, his tail would generally knock down a few tin pails and pans that were on the rocks and a big black paw would often land in any baskets that might happen to be near when a roar from the cook would startle Jacobus out of his senses and he [would] leave the vicinity with a rapidity and force that would have overturned two or three men if they had happened to be in the way. He would then go off and seek the seclusion of an adjacent thicket where he would undoubtedly mourn over the fact that he was such a bad, bad dog and everybody disliked him so. A minute before his soul had been suffused with joy, his heart had palpitated with rapture in unison with the wag of his tail but, now, he was down in the depths of wrong and degradation. His tail which had wrought part of the mischief lay curled up under his legs. This tail was used by Jacobus as a means of communicating with his friends not unlike the one used by the United States Signal Corps. Every one of us carried a mental signal book in our heads. We would note the signals and interpret them. For instance, the tail moved from right to left, meant joy or gratitude, straight out behind was the sign of danger or the approach of some one, straight up in the air meant important business, that Jack was going some where

[MS[2]]

We were camping in the Adirondacks that summer. It was long ago, before peaked hats and leather gun cases had invaded the grand old hills and fish and game were plentiful. A party of five of us camped along a little mountain river. Two young New York sportsmen and myself and a Mr Northcote with a little son scarcely seven years old. The circumstances that brought the father to take a little lad like his son away on a hunting expedition into the wilds of the Adirondacks were peculiar and have no connection with this tale. But he was there, a little golden-haired boy who ran merrily among the flowers and mosses near the camp or played with pebbles, and miniature boats in the brook. The child was not such a care to us as one might imagine. We always had to leave a man at camp when we went hunting or fishing and the boy amused himself readily. He was seldom out of sight of the guard to the camp and then, a call would bring him back.

He had one companion in all his rambles. A friend whose staunch old heart would stand between him and every danger. Jack, Northcote's mastiff knew his duty and he did it like a grenadier. He was always at little Teddie's heels wagging his tail with due appreciation at the little child's merriment or joy at finding new woodland treasures. Jack's duty kept him very busy. Only at mealtimes and at night was the old guard's duty relaxed. Twice he dragged Teddie gently out of the brook and he had shaken any number of snakes to pieces who had ventured too near the sacred pathway of his charge

[MS[3]]

"Jack"

We were camping in the Adirondacks that summer. It was long ago, before peaked hats and leather gun-cases and other paraphernalia of the modern sporting gentleman, had invaded the grand old hills. A party of five of us were encamped on one of the little brooks that rumble and tumble down the great water shed toward Lake Champlain. The party was composed of two young New York sporting men, as good hunters and as jolly companions as ever sighted a gun. For, you know, I, an old hunter, don't judge a sportsman by the way he pulls on a partridge or sights deer tracks. I take these things into consideration and then I wait and see how he takes it if there are sticks in his coffee and dirt on his hoe-cake. If he takes all these little discomforts with a laugh and a joke, nor grumbles at night if his hemlock boughs are harder than goose feathers, then will he be a good companion. If he comes to camp after a hard day's fishing, wet, soaked to the skin, while the heavens open their flood-gates, and the wild night wind howls through the hemlocks. If he comes home to camp, tired, hungry, and sits down on a wet log, in the rain, and eats a supper of raw bacon and uncooked biscuits, and goes to sleep in a pool of water, thankful and happy that he had found one dry match to light his pipe. Then, the man is a thoroughbred and my heart warms to him. The remainder of the party was composed of a Mr. Northcote, with a little son of seven years, and myself. The circumstances that caused the father to bring a little lad like Teddie away off on a hunting expedition were peculiar but have no reference to my story and I would but weary the reader with an account of them. But, he was there, a little golden haired boy who ran with merry laughter among the flowers and mosses near the camp or sailed his little boats in the brook. The child was not such a care to us as one might imagine. We always left a guard at camp when we made long trips; in fact there was always one of the fellows whose duty it was to stay at the camp. Teddie was seldom out of sight of the guard. Bears were plentiful around us; we never went a quarter of a mile from the camp without seeing sign.

V. [A SMALL BLACK AND WHITE AND TAN HOUND]

[MS[1]]

THE riotous little brook recklessly whirling and tumbling over the boulders and stones of the glen made sounds that broke upon the crisp morning air like mad laughter. The sun peeked cautiously above the east ridge, heavily wooded with pines and threw a pale yellow glance upon the old house as if it meant to gently awaken it.

[MS[2]]

A ragged boy, rubbing his eyes and yawning sleepily, came out of the old, unpainted and rickety house on the mountain side. A riotous little brook, recklessly whirling and tumbling over the boulders of the glen made sounds that broke upon the still morning air like mad laughter. The sun peeked cautiously over the east ridge, heavily wooded with pines, and threw a pale yellow glance at the drowsy boy as if it meant to more surely awaken him.

The boy stretched his arms over his head, and yawned again. Then he shambled awkwardly

[MS[3]]

A small, black and white and tan hound stood wagging his tail enthusiastically and rattling his chain in front of a kennel made from two old boxes, with an irregular hole sawed in the end for the exits and entrances of the canine inhabitant. In his eagerness to watch the path which led toward an old, unpainted and crumbling house, he was continually placing his fore feet in a battered tin pan which was evidently doing duty as a receptacle for his bones at meal times. But he would speedily take them out again and beat an impatient tattoo on the hard earth, never removing his brown eyes from the path to the house.

[MS[4]]

A small black and white and tan hound stood wagging his tail and rattling his chain in front of a kennel made from two old boxes. His eager brown eyes were fixed on a path which led to an unpainted and crumbling house on the mountain side not far away. He was continually placing his fore feet in a battered tin pan which was evidently doing duty as a receptacle for bones, and taking them out again with great speed, never removing his eyes from the pathway, but continuing his impatient tattoo on the hardened ground.

VI. [APACHE CROSSING]

[MS[1]]

THE inhabitants of Apache Crossing were discouraged over their grave-yard. There were only twelve rotting shingles over only twelve irregular and misshapen graves. The thriving town of Blazer, forty miles across the red, uneven plain, had a cemetery with thirty-three graves in it, a number of which contained some of the most noted fighters and desperados of Arizona. It also boasted a small marble shaft which had been transported to be erected over all that remained of old Jim Thompson who had been buried with two revolvers and a wound in front as a good man should.

Old man Miller remarked in the bar-room of the Metropolitan Hotel at Apache Crossing: "Boys, I tell you what it is. We've got to hustle. Simerson Simpkins was in from Blazers yesterday and afore he went, he up an' told me that Blazers' got more good men laid away in her cemet'ry than we've got in our hull blamed town. I hit up there," and he pointed to a small round hole in the door a little higher up than a man's head. Spiteful Johnson, the gambler, then was heard to remark softly as he intently regarded a jack, a nine, a six, and a pair of trays that "ol' Jim Miller couldn't hit a herd uv hosses at two rod."

Miller leaned back against the bar and regarded with cool dignity the man at card-table who had remarked

[MS[2]]

Boys, I tell you what it is—we've got to hustle. Simerson was in from Blazers yesterday and afore he went, he up an' tol' me that Blazers' got more good men laid away in her cemet'ry than we've got in our hull blamed town. I hit up there," and Old Miller, the proprietor of the famous Metropolitan Hotel at Apache Crossing, pointed a lean finger at a round hole in the top of the door.

"Ol' Miller couldn't hit a flock of barn-doors flyin'," murmured Spiteful Johnson to his associates at the card-table, as he gazed with a reflective air at a nine, a six, a jack and a pair of trays.

The group of leathery cow-boys at the bar gazed alternately at Old Miller and Johnson, with glances of men who expect something.

VII. [IN THE COUNTRY OF RHYMERS AND WRITERS]

[MS[1]]

Little Mary Laughter went to sleep upon the grass under the peach-tree in her mother's garden. When she awoke, the world had changed. She lay on paper ground under a paper tree while a brook of ink babbled noisily at her feet.

"Heigho," she exclaimed, as is the habit of lost maidens, "Heigho, where am I?"

"My name ain't Heigho," indignantly cried a voice at her elbow, and a little man appeared, fantastically clothed in the paper leaves of magazines and newspapers.

"My name is Mr Rudolph Alfonso Moaner," he went on wrathfully, "and I am the talented author of that famous poem, 'Winter Wails Without in Wrath.' Didn't you ever read it?"

"No, sir, please, sir. I am very ignorant. Will you kindly tell me where I am, sir?"

"You are in the country of Rhymers and Writers, little girl," said the talented author, scowling at her. "Come along, now. I'll have to take you to the king. I don't want to, though," musingly. "Say," with sudden anger, "what did you come for anyhow? Didn't you know the country is over-inhabited?"

"No, sir, please, sir. I didn't know it. I didn't want to come here either. I just went to sleep and came."

"Humph," said the author, scornfully, "We'll see if the king will take that excuse. Little girl, if you get to your home once more, I'd advise you to never go to sleep again."

By this time, they had come upon a winding white road which led toward the East. Upon this road were numbers of travellers going one way. They all carried huge manuscripts under their arms. Some passed along with shrinking timidity; others held their heads so high that they stumbled at every step. At intervals, certain men would rush from the road-side and beat the travellers unmercifully. Sometime, one would cry aloud under the lusty blows but most of the travellers proceeded on their ways making no sign except a defiant tossing of heads among some and a great timidity upon the part of those who shrunk before.

"Oh, my goodness, who are those cruel men?" cried Mary.

"They, my dear," said the author as his brow darkened, "are the Critical Guards, a band in the service of the king."

Mary and her conductor walked along the road for some distance. Ahead of them there went a bold man. To him, there came a body of the Critical Guards.

"Ho, ho, my fine fellow," cried a big villain in the van, "what have you in that bundle."

With a confident smile, the bold man un-rolled his large manuscript and handed it them to read and even as they read, he smiled at them.

[MS[2]]

Along a winding, white Road which led toward the East, a large Number of Travellers proceeded with huge Manuscripts under their Arms. Some passed along with shrinking Timidity; Others held their Heads so high that They stumbled at every Step. At Intervals, certain Men would rush from the Woods at the Roadside and beat the Travellers unmercifully. Sometimes, One would cry out under the lusty Blows but Most of the Travellers proceeded on their Way, making no Sign excepting defiant Tosses of the Head by Some and a greater Exhibition of Timidity by Others. A young Man who but recently had taken the Road said to an old Plodder by his Side: "O, Father, who are these great Scoundrels?"

"These, O, Son," said the old Man in Wrath, "are the Critical Guards of the great Emperor."

The young Man held his Peace for He knew not whether He would be beaten. And in front of the young Man there marched a bold Man who appeared very Valiant. To Him, there came a Number of the Critical Guards.

"Ho, ho, my fine Fellow," cried a big Villain in the Van. "What have You in that Bundle."

With a confident Smile, the Bold Man un-rolled his large Manuscript and handed It Them. And even as They read, He smiled in Their Faces. But the Guards burst into furious Wrath, when They finished and sprang upon Him and clubbed Him terribly. He roared and turned and ran, while They followed for They were enraged beyond Expression. But the erst-while Man of Valiant Heart did out-strip Them and as He disappeared over the Edge of the Horizon, He roared back to Them His Determination to be for the Rest of His Days, a Lumber Merchant.

More of the Guards accosted the young Man and after investigating the Contents of His Bundle They beat Him but It only caused Him to bestir Himself and get further upon the Road, for He had understood that It was not Virtue that saved One from these Beatings.

And soon the young Man arrived at the City of the great King, Publico. And He went at once to the Court and there He saw, upon the Throne, King Publico who looked rather stupid for a great Ruler. And as He looked, the King began to pound the Table in front of Him with his Fists and cry out: "Bring Me Poetry! Bring Me Rhymes! Bring Me Prose and Everything! I want to have some Fun, and also I want to learn Something."

So the Young Man rushed forward and bending His Knees presented his Poem to the King, and the King handed It to a Scribe and the Scribe read:

"Little Jack Horner
Sat in a Corner
Eating a Christmas Pie
He put in his Thumb
And pulled out a Plum
And said: 'What a good Boy am I.' "

"Good!" roared the King, pounding the Table furiously. "That's fine! Read-It-over-again! Good! Good! I wish We could get more——"

"Your Majesty," shrieked a great Litterateur Who thought He knew a Lot. "That's the most Stupendous Plagiarism of the Age. There is not a single Syllable of Originality in the whole Composition. I have seen every individual Word of that Poem in the Works of Other Authors. The Phrase, 'In a Corner,' was used by Saint Paul in his well-known Epistle to the Calliopeans, Hundreds of Years ago. 'He put in his Thumb' is taken bodily from the Works of Homer. The Immortal Virgil was the Author of the Words, 'Eating a Christmas Pie.' 'Pulled out a Plum' is in the well-known Language of William Tweed. The Words 'Jack' and 'Horner' are copied from a Directory of the City of London. 'Little' was used several Times by Lord Byron and Napoleon once said 'What a good Boy am I.' The whole Poem is a gigantic Robbery which this young Sprig wants to foist off on an amiable and innocent King. As a Lover of pure Literature, I protest. We cannot endure, in the Kingdom, these Imitators, these Copyists. They are the Enemies of Creative Genius, They trample upon the sacred Rights of the——" but the great Litterateur was compelled to sit down for He was frothing at the Mouth.

And the Young Man arose and said: "This great Litterateur is certainly a Liar. For I have not read the Works of Saint Paul, nor of Homer, nor of Virgil, nor of Tweed, nor of the City of London, nor of Byron, nor of Napoleon, neither have I any cognizance of Them nor Their Sayings. How then could I plagiarize."

As It happened, the great King Publico was not so dumb as He looked, for He immediately made Speech and said that It happened sometimes that One Thought came to Two Men and He didn't understand It nor know how It was but It was certain that no Man was guilty in such Cases although His Work was not so valuable. And He spoke kind Words to the Young Man and the Young Man prospered.

And having achieved literary Success, He departed with a gladsome Heart. As He passed through the City, He thought he would look about Him a Little and see the Sights. And He came upon two Men quarreling and giving Each Other the Lie, and Other Men joined the Two and there came a general Row. The Young Man called to Them saying: "Why do You quarrel." And one Man made Answer: "O, Stranger, behold, I wrote a Poem and I wrote as the first line, 'Fain would I sing a Song' and these Dogs, these Swine, did copy it from me, and now we have a dozen Poems here commencing thus." And each Man made Out-cry and said: "It was I, O, Stranger, Who first penned that Line." And then They fell upon Each Other and had a great Go. The Young Man passed on for this Sort of Thing made Him quite tired.

VIII. THE CAMERA IN A COMPROMISING POSITION

The Camera in a Compromising Position.

A MAN with a wild eye and a worn overcoat rushed into the store of Snap, Shot and Co., with a small, square-cornered bundle which he deposited upon the counter with a bang

IX. [LISTEN OH MAN-WITH-A-GIGANTIC-NERVE]

LISTEN oh man-with-a-gigantic-nerve," said the aged and quivering chieftain as he stretched his

[*verso*]

Listen, oh, gre

X. [HEARKEN, HEARKEN, OH, MAN-WITH-A-COPPER-STOMACH]

HEARKEN, hearken, oh, man-with-a-copper-stomach, hearken, for the voice of the old chieftain grows faint as the wind in the trees," and the aged and quivering Zulu throbbed and trembled as he lifted the

XI. A FLURRY OF CONDENSED MILK

A Flurry of Condensed Milk.

THE little man balanced upon one hand a collection of tin plates, cups and spoons, while he gesticulated finely with the other.

"I'm goin' down to the lake to wash these dishes," he said, "and I tell you fellows, now,—that if, when I get back, anyofyer don't like the way I wash'em, you can wash'em yourselves. Hear?"

The other three men bowed meekly for they could not have dishes for lunch until the little man returned with them. Satisfied with their submission, he strode valiantly downward.

[p. 26]

In the morning, they cast veils over their hearts and bade him a friendly adieu, for they considered the effect of the weird gruesome tale they would tell down among the flats and smoke. They departed from the wilderness timidly and with faint livers but when their feet touched cobble-stones once more they immediately became valiant.

XII. A DESERTION

The door clanged behind him.

A Desertion.

In a large hall that blazed with light, there were crowds of women at small polished tables. Large doors ceaselessly slammed letting in and out two interminable processions of men. A stout waiter with a straw-colored moustache was stowing some mopping cloths, soaked with beer, in a handy crevice between the fore-legs of a bronzed, crouching lion. The sounds from without of rattling traffic blended with the clanking melody from a hidden machine.

In a shaded corner a man and a woman were seated at a table. He was a well-dressed and young fellow. A cigarette was held daintily in his gloved hand. His round, well-fed face wore the marks of cheer and good-nature. Her face was painted.

She was chatting blithely, evidently telling him of incidents of preceding days. She spoke with womanish confidence as if sure of interest and sympathy.

He stared steadily at the remains of an amber-colored liquid in a round glass. He fingered his cigarette gently. He was apparently absorbed in thought. The stream of chatter from the woman opposite seemed to go in unheeding ears.

After a time, he seemed to make up his mind to something. He moved his hands nervously and shot uneasy glances at the woman.

XIII. [GUSTAVE AND MARIE]

returned." He followed this rebuff with a hurried question. "And Madame—where is she?"

The man bended his legs in a solemn bow. He spoke impassively. "In her boudoir, I think, monsieur."

Gustave hastened softly up the great curving stairway. He was about to go boisterously to his wife but near the threshold of her apartments he halted and with a finger upon his lips, impressively cautioned himself. He penetrated then on his toes with a laughing slyness to the boudoir.

There, too, for a moment heavy purple shadows frustrated his vision. An open window directly before him filled his eyes with the sparkling yellow dots of the great Paris without, and the objects about him were shrouded in gloom.

As he stood blinking there, the form of his wife was gradually born out of this blackness until she was revealed in plainness to him. She lay asleep on a couch which she had drawn close to the windows. A silver-covered book which had dropped from her fingers, glowed with reflected light on the floor.

Gustave ejaculated under his breath. "Marie!"

XIV. LITERARY NOTES

Literary Notes.

EDITOR JONES has neatly papered his hall bed-room with Brilliant T. Hodgson's story entitled: "Love's Dream."

XV. IN BRIEF

In Brief.

AS PETER PETERSEN, 32, of 963 East 67th St. was viewing a base ball game he was mistaken for the umpire and killed.

The new apartment-house on West 57th Street is so great in height that the cellar is seven stories from the ground.

It is rumored that the people of Brooklyn have petitioned the legislature for forty-two new bridges across the East River. Meanwhile, escape will be facilitated by pneumatic tubes.

The Bartholdi Statue has written to a friend that the twin lights at Navesink are two fine bouncing youngsters, bright as buttons.

XVI. [MATINEE GIRLS]

HERE are some matinee girls. To read of them, you would think they crowded every theatre in New York but really I don't think them a very familiar type. I often wonder too if they are so ridiculous as we are told to believe. My curiosity over-came me so far once that I listened to the conversation of two of them. As a matter of fact, it was much more rational than that of the man at my elbow who was talking of himself. I have wondered if they were an exception. I believe they were not and <⌊fo⌋r> the following <formidable> reason.

After you get a fact firml<y> into the public mind it has ceased to be true in many cases. The public began to be told long ago that it worshipped actors, men of paint and cloth, who were so human that in reality after the play they were likely to sup on welsh rabbits and beer. Just as the public came to believe it, it ceased to be. Today, a man, or a matinee girl too, sees actor and beer and welsh rabbit all together and has not an idea that a man six feet can live on bunches of violets.

XVII. [LITTLE HEAP OF MATCHES]

little heap of matches, a whisk-broom, a little blue cup and saucer, a soiled towel mingled in a heap with manuscript and unfinished sketches. The youth had cleared a little space near the end and he was busily writing there, his figure cramped to an uncomfortable attitude.

He bit the end of his pen and slowly scanned the sentence he had just finished.

"Art, in the splendor of her processional toward the everlasting altars, does not disclose those of her train who hobble in tatters, their mouths filled with goblin-laughter, their hands making ironical gestures toward the fat and complacent public."

He regarded the sentence critically. He tried to mentally shift his point of view, so that he might look at it from here and then from there. His first impression was that it was singularly fine. He stared at it for a few moments, feeling an agreeable thrill of self-appreciation. Later, the prolonged scrutiny caused a decay of his admiration. The sentence began to look flat and intensely stupid. It was meaningless. Yes it was absolutely idiotic.

XVIII. [SIXTH AVENUE]

SIXTH AVENUE is a street that leads a dual existence. It typifies the man who walks very primly in the observing light of the sun but who, when in the shadows, cuts many and strange pranks. The day finds it thronged with shoppers; the doors of the great shops clash to and fro in endless motion. Huge windows disclose wonderful masses of goods that have been dragged from all corners of the earth. Hosts of women crowd the side-walks. The elevated trains and the street-cars unload battalions of them. The huge stores uprear their austere fronts to glance across the street at little saloons that in this white light of respectability remain subdued and silent. It is the time of the marching and counter-marching of the feminine buyers; it is the time when Sixth Avenue is profoundly busy but profoundly decorous.

XIX. [A MOURNFUL OLD BUILDING]

[MS[1]]

A MOURNFUL old building stood ⌊between⌋ two that were tall and straight and proud. It was, in a way, a sad thing, symbolizing a decrepit old man whose lean shoulders are jostled by sturdy youth. The old building wore an air of timidity, as if it glanced upwards at its two companions. It stood there awaiting the inevitable time of downfall, when progress marching to the music of tumbling walls and chimneys would come striding up the avenues. Already one could see from the roof, a host advancing, an army of enormous buildings coming with invincible front that extended across the city, trampling under their feet the bones of the dead, rising tall and supremely proud on the crushed memories, the annihilated hopes of generations gone.

And this mournful old building stood awaiting its turn. It had once been relatively tall and supremely proud with its feet imbedded in ruins. And its

[MS^{2}]

A mournful old building stood between two that were tall and straight and proud. In a way, it was a sad thing, symbolizing a decrepit old man whose lean shoulders are jostled by sturdy youth. The old building seemed to glance timidly upward at its two neighbors, pleaing for comradeship, and at times it assumed an important air derived from its environment, and said to those who viewed from the side-walks: "We three—we three buildings."

It stood there awaiting the inevitable time of downfall, when progress, to the music of tumbling walls and chimneys would come marching up the avenues. Already, from the roof one could see a host advancing, an army of enormous buildings, coming with an invincible front that extended across the city, trampling under their feet the bones of the dead, rising tall and supremely proud on the crushed memories, the annihilated hopes of generations gone. At sunset time, each threw a tremendous shadow, a gesture of menace out over the low plain of the little buildings huddling afar down.

Once this mournful old structure had been proud. It had stood with its feet unconcernedly on the grave of a past ambition and no doubt patronized the little buildings on either side.

XX. [THE TOY SHOP]

As THE last clerk passed out of the toy-shop and locked the great doors behind him, the china dog on the secon[d] shelf relaxed his rigid pose and with an air of relief: "At last!" Some tin soldiers on the counter dropped their tin guns with a little tinkling crash and then swung their arms and puffed in the manner of benumbed teamsters in winter. A small wooden horse harnessed to a cart began to wriggle between the shafts and cry: "I say, you fellows, come and help me out of this, will you?"

XXI. [MEXICAN SKETCH]

THERE were blue mountains in the west whose tops were in regular undulations like sea waves. A plain, baked brown and cracked from the rays of the flaming Mexican sun stretched in a weary level to the hills. The dust which arose in tall coils from the ground, settled at last heavily upon the cactus plants and smudged all green from them.

Four horsemen cantered slowly along the wide and hideously straight trail which led through the cactus. Huge sombreros eclipsed a good part of their heads and on their shoulders flared gorgeous serapes.

"Chicken boiled with rice!" said one horseman bitterly.

"Well, that's better than tortillas, isn't it?" demanded another horseman.

XXII. [FRANKLY I DO NOT CONSIDER]

FRANKLY I do not consider your story to be very good but even if you do me the honor to value my opinion you need not feel discouraged for I can remember when I wrote as badly as you do now. Furthermore there are many men, our superiors, who once wrote as badly as I do now and no doubt as badly as you.

XXIII. [HE TOLD ME ALL HE KNEW]

HE TOLD me all he knew of the people of the island and their ways. He said that the government of the country was monarchial when the church gave it an opportunity but he said the peculiar solemnity of his high office and the fact that he had to make a great stir in order to keep the reverence of the people made it necessary for him to say a great deal about public matters. Moreover he told me that there was considerable political trouble going on and that he was arrayed on the side of the queen against a very considerable number of notables and high men.

"A queen?" said I. "I don't like queens."

"Bedad, that is usually a matter of personal acquaintance," said he. "You wait 'til you see her."

For a number of weeks he kept me shut up quite tight in his palace plying me with the new language and educating me in all the ways of my new estate. I don't remember now why I submitted to all the learning he crowded into me and to his over-bearing ways of doing it. Once indeed I said to him: "How is this? Am I in prison?"

"No," said he, "you are not. I would scorn to keep the news from you. No, you are as free as the air but, by all the four-eyed fish in the sea," said he, banging the table, "you can't go out from here until I can make that tongue of yours walk backwards. In a word," said he, "you must learn the speech of the country before you are free to go among these poor people."

XXIV. DAN EMMONDS

As soon as my father set foot in America he became a very great success, and it was not long before he sent for my mother and me. I was very glad to get to New York and I became a fine man in a very little time, occupying myself in the saloon and in other gentlemanly amusements. But in truth my father never extremely admired me for some reason or another. "You should have been the son of a big brewer, Dan," he often said to me. "A poor little saloon-keeper like me is dazzled by you. However, the business is coming on, and I hope one day to be able to maintain you properly." At last I conducted some affairs for my father in a particularly clever manner and upon learning of it he declared that it was a great pity it was no longer the fashion to send youths out as cabin-boys so that sea-captains might give them instruction and that he much feared he would have to pay my fare on some distant voyage in order that his commercial ventures might have opportunity to get strong again. I told him at once that I regarded a sea-voyage as a fine thing in an educational way and no doubt I would return greatly benefited. I had always a great passion for the sea.

My father looked upon my acquiescence with suspicion, and for a long time I could see him debate in regard to the wisdom of sending me. "By the piper," said he, "there's some opportunity for mischief here. I must examine it further."

At last, however, I conducted some more business for my father, and at its conclusion he said he had no doubt but that a sea-voyage would be a great thing. Accordingly he obtained for me a passage on the ship "Susan L. Terwilleger," which was about to begin a long voyage to Melbourne. The time up to my going on board was without incident save when my father detected two cases of sherry and one of port in my baggage. Having taken them in charge he parted from me with a tender smile.

For two or three hours, I occupied myself in bidding farewell to New York harbor which in the morning light was a broad gold cloth. As I hung upon the rail I occasionally turned to watch the captain and the mates who were motioning and swearing in all directions until no one knew his own business. Up in front, a crowd of ragged sailors were running this way and that way and hauling into view a number of dirty sails.

At last after great labor we got the ship out to the breeze and Sandy Hook was no more than a little strip of sand. It was then the sails began to drag the ship forward and the old thing reeled and swayed. I discovered that I was afloat on what has always been called the deep blue sea.

I need not weary you with any details of the first part of the voyage excepting to say that the captain's rum and tobacco were good, and he was a first-class companion with a bottle between him and me. We became great philosophers and conversed deeply upon many things that were not usually understood, cocking up our legs and puffing and letting the ship go to ruin.

But when we were almost to Australia there came a terrible storm and our ship got the worst beating at the hands of the sea that has happened since Robinson Crusoe's ships used to sail up and down mountains. Salt water surged on the deck here and there and from side to side until it was all I could do to keep my mouth from getting full of it. I hung near the captain's rum and prayed for land. As for the officers and crew, they were greatly frightened. They swathed themselves in oil-clothes, and went about bawling at each other when only six feet apart. They could only console themselves with thinking of what they might tell of it afterward.

The great wind blew the poor helpless vessel for many miles in one direction, and then blew it violently in another. In truth the wind never paused to reflect where to hurl us, but merely hurled us in all directions until the captain did not know whether he was upon his own quarter-deck or in his father's barn-yard or the old farm in Connecticut, of which he had often told me. And as for me, I might have been standing on my head in the middle of the main street of Dublin for all I knew to the contrary. The quantity of rum I consumed makes me ashamed to think of it.

"Captain," said I, "I'm no great hand at courage, and I particularly request you will not allow the ship to founder before I have at least two hours steady work at the bottle."

"Drink fast, my lad," the captain replied. "It is a good thing you have not the head of my old friend Jerry Martin of Portland who required four days of hard lifting at the glass before he could grow indifferent to the death of his second wife whom he disliked exceedingly. Drink fast or you will leave behind you that which will be a hard thing to leave in any such senseless tub as this."

I obeyed the captain's order until it was a matter of indifference to me if the ship turned hand-springs and, as a matter of truth, that is what she did presently. Six sailors were spilled to starboard at one lurch. Their screams were so dreadful to me that I ran for the cabin. I was resolved to do great things, only the captain and all three of the mates were there before me.

When night came it was as if a black cloth had been thrown over a dog and the convulsions of our poor ship was a dreadful thing. We were blind with the spray, and drenched to the skin, and we felt that if we all died presently it would relieve us from a great anxiety. The captain himself said that anyhow we should have been drowned hours before, speaking from the standpoint of a scientific seaman. Some of the men came near us and the second-mate, who was an old officer of the navy, was quite civil to them. It was then I made up my mind that the hour of our destruction was at hand.

Sure enough at that moment our ship gave a great groaning cry and flew into a thousand pieces. I remember that the flashing white waves looked like teeth when they swallowed me. I sank over two hundred feet in the sea, and I reflected upon twenty ways in which I might have conducted my father's business in New York. When I thrust my head out of water there was nothing to be seen of ship nor companions. However, a hen-coop that had been lashed to the galley flew past me on a high wave, and I had sufficient wit left in me to grasp the slats.

I need not describe to you how fearfully the storm raged nor how hard I clung to the hen-coop. Eventually the winds abated, and I saw that I was alone upon the sea with no company but the hen-coop and the dead body of a pig named Bartholomew, who had been a great favorite with the ship's cook.

I propelled the coop with great difficulty over to the floating body of the pig, for I thought that if the coop failed me, I could use the pig, and if the pig disappeared, I would still have the coop. Anything was better than being left out there with nothing.

Presently the sun broke clear and mild from the clouds with a great air of innocence as if he had never been gone when the captain wanted him, and I saw a fair blue streak on the horizon which I knew to be land. "It's just as I expected," I said out loud. "But here's the point—I don't know how to get to you, miserable undiscovered country that you are."

I first tried pushing the coop away from the pig, and then dragging the pig up and so on, but I soon tired of this mode of travelling, for the pig lay like a block of marble in the water, and I despaired of reaching the island in less than nine years. But it was at this moment that I descried a small boat, something like a fishing-smack, skimming over the water quite near to me. It had been previously hidden by the huge waves, for I was so low in the water that I couldn't have perceived a light-house many feet away.

I set up a great howl when I discovered the smack and she went in stays with a shiver and shake as if my cry from the sea had startled half the life out of her. She came toward me then like a bird, and it was not long before I could see a row of heads hanging over the side, staring at me and conversing. The craft was so well-sailed that she pulled up within ten feet of me, and lay with her nose to the wind as quiet as my own hen-coop. The men in her were all copper as a door-plate, and had straight black hair, very peculiar. Some of them that I saw running were dressed in little kilts.

We eyed each other for a minute and then sure as I am alive, they of a sudden burst into cheers and began to hug each other for joy. I was too amazed to speak. You would have thought they had found a diamond floating upon the water. I did not suppose I was truly the reason of their celebration until they dragged me over the side, and fairly went into convulsions over me.

I began to think how to treat these strange people, for I knew that I must pay my respects to everything I could see, and be very circumspect and wise upon all religious matters. So, as soon as I could get enough liberty I bowed politely to them and said: "The height of good living to you all, gentlemen, and may you know that there is nothing I admire so much as I do you. First of all, I pay my respects to your old venerable king if you have one; if not, to your beautiful maiden queen and to the aged high-priest with the long whiskers, if there be such among you. I wish you to know that I am a man of peace and am arrived here against my wishes and with no plan of any kind against you. I beseech you to observe that my only object in coming here, is to get away again as soon as possible. More power be with me. But, above all, gentlemen—and now heed me closely here—I am a man of great liberality in religious matters, and am willing to worship anything from fire and the sun to a large stone kitten if it will be a comfort to the people of the country. Furthermore I am a quiet and modest citizen of the city of New York, and have no desire to hobnob with your king nor your queen, nor your high-priests for that matter, as it breeds trouble in countries of this kind. If you have a small detached house with a bit of a garden, maybe, in the outskirts of your beautiful white city, I would pay what rent I am able, and try to live at peace with those about me until I can regain my own country. May the light of the sun illumine the faces of your clay gods when they look at you—that is to say, if you have clay gods. If you have not, I can only say that what you do have must needs be right in my opinion, since you are enlightened citizens of this great country while I am only a citizen of New York City, and not up to the average when there."

This was a pretty neat speech, and it was not until the conclusion of it that I began to wonder whether a man of them understood me. However, when I looked at them, they were all smiling in clear delight, and I could see that my eloquence had been no less than music to them. They lay back as if they had just been listening to me playing on a harp.

I was a trifle bewildered by such great appreciation. "What's this," said I to myself. "This might do me harm. They will never part with me if I turn out to be a valuable popular amusement."

I reflected for a time and they all sat around like images waiting for me to speak. Finally I saw there was no good in pondering. I must wait until the situation came out more. So I sat there.

Presently they turned the boat and headed for the island. She flew like a duck, with those coppery fellows dancing for joy, and seeming anxious to tell their friends. "Well," said I to myself, as the island in front began to grow large, "here you are, my boy, with nothing to back you, now that you have left Bartholomew and the chickens. Devil knows what kind of a stew you will make for these grinning barbarians." I was greatly frightened. "Good fortune be with you, Bartholomew," said I addressing the distance. "You are better off than I am indeed, if I am going to be killed after taking this long troublesome voyage."

XXV. [DURING A SESSION OF CONGRESS]

DURING a session of congress, Pennsylvania Avenue displays more types of people than any other street in America. One suddenly becomes aware of the diversities of American life. It is a good education for the New Yorker who always considers that Union Square is the centre of the republic.

You discover then the typical American—a thin-faced shrewd-looking fellow walking at a slow pace and with eyes that see everything.

If you stand on a corner and watch people board the cable-cars you can easily learn to distinguish between New Yorkers and Southerners. The southerner signals the car to stop and then approaches it leisurely as if it were his private carriage. If his mind wavers between the choice of two seats, he pauses on the asphalt and debates. The New York man comes out suddenly, waves a quick finger and the moment the car stops, climbs aboard, meanwhile giving the gripman a grateful look and as if it were his duty to be much obliged for being allowed to board the car at all. The police, the Broadway gripman, the elevated railway guards have well-trained the average New Yorker.

Owing to a curious dispensation of Providence, visitors always arrive in the audience galleries when Congress is debating the erection and maintenance of a jetty at the mouth of some unheard-of harbor or a bill for the dredging of some unknown harbor.

Of course everyone understands that the congress does not meet solely for the purpose of surrounding itself with works of art and if it remains deaf to the orations of the artists and the art associations, one cannot altogether blame it. There are two sides to the question. A man may have a very good idea of how to adjust the annual appropriations and yet not know good from bad in statuary and it is to be supposed that he is performing his highest obligation when he knows all he can about taxation and appropriations. Still, it is a great wonder—the quantity of specimens of bad art generation after generation of congressmen have managed to get into the capitol.

XXVI. [THE RIGHT OF ARREST]

EVERYONE who thinks is likely to know that the right of arrest is one of the most dangerous powers which organized society can give to the individual. It is a power so formidable in its reaches that there is rarely a situation confronting the people which calls for more caution. A blackguard as a private citizen is lamentable; a blackguard as a police officer is an abomination. Theoretically the first result of government is to put control into the hands of honest men and nullify as far as may be the ambitions of criminals. When government places power in the hands of a criminal it of course violates this principle and becomes absurd.

XXVII. [NEW YORK BOARDING HOUSE TALE]

[MS^1]

[Fol. 1^r]

I

AT THE foot of the street, the rigging of ships lay black against the steel-colored water and slanting over the roofs of the southside came a stream of copper light from the setting sun, making the higher part of the northward walls resplendent and accentuating the sombre growing shadow of the lower part.

The boarders in No. 936 were coming from their dinner in the basement. The two young clerks from a famous shoe store lit cigarettes and taking seats upon the topmost step in front of the house prepared to gossip in the dark way of their age. Thorpe, the old book-keeper, came with his regular evening cigar and perched on the iron railing. The four old ladies went at once to their rooms panting up the flights. Trixell, clerk in a Broadway flower-store, waited for a time at the head of the gloomy basement stairs. He thought, perhaps, that   the landlady's daughter would ascend and in such case he wished to have the joy of going with her to her throne on the front steps.

One of the shoe clerks pulled wise<⌊ly⌋> at his cigarette and addressed the old | [*pages wanting*]

[Fol. 2^r]

II

Finally Trixell remarked: "They give transfers now almost all over the city on the street-car-lines. It seems funny for them to do that in New York. I can remember when they didn't give transfers at all—not a line in New York that I know of."

It was the opening gun. Thorpe then told his information concerning the matter and one of the shoe-clerks ventured some original theories.

The other shoe-clerk seized this opportunity to lean back and say confidentially to the girl: "You look tired tonight."

She pushed a stray lock from her temples with a gesture of fatigue. "Yes, I am. Very tired." Her foot however was swinging to and fro in the way that youth proclaims its superabundant energy and her cheek had upon it a flush of pink. "Yes, I'm very tired!"

The shoe clerk murmured sympathetically and having thus gone into the social whirl with success, he subsided and devoted himself to his comrade clerk. | [*pages wanting*]

[Fol. 3ʳ]

"Well," she said, "there's a small room on the third floor—are you in business in the city?"

"No, not now. I don't live in the city and I've come here to look for a position with my cousin."

She reflected for a time. At last she said: "Well, there's only the small room on the third floor. You can look at it if you wish."

Under the influence of her preternatural composure or indifference, he was beginning to believe that he resembled a thief but at her permission to look at the room he said gratefully "Oh, thank you very much."

She nodded slightly at the gas-jet.

They ascended two flights and then she exhibited a small hall bed-room, grim and grey, like a cell. "This is six dollars a week," she said.

[Fol. 3ᵛ]

VI

Alone in his grey and grim cell at the top of the house the young man reflected on his state. Life now presented a new aspect to him and he reflected upon these vague figures which peopled his changed world.

His window opened upon the mystic gulf of the evening and

from time to time a murmur of voices arose. He heard often the mellow tones of the young girl.

He was saddened by his change of environment and in his mood he wondered if she would feel sorrow for him if she understood his loneliness. The thought of her sympathy loomed in his mind until in proportion it was great.

[Fol. 4^r]

In the morning the young man awoke with a conviction that he had over-slept. He consulted his old silver watch however and discovered that it was not yet six o'clock. From the streets came the long roar, the thunder of the city's life. Sometimes a wagon passed the house with noise like musketry volleys.

At last a bell was rung and the tomb-like silence of the house itself was broken. Doors slammed.

As the young man entered the dining-room in the basement, he paused in the middle of the floor in a slight embarrassment. Five young men and two old women with their faces turned toward their plates, ate steadfastly.

He felt like retreating but the young girl of his previous experience appeared suddenly having come from the kitchen with dishes. She smiled at him and conducted him to a seat.

[Fol. 4^v]

The five young men

During the meal he covertly watched her. He was glad when a certain one of the five young men finished breakfast and left the table for he ogled the girl as she passed to and fro in what was considered a bold and exasperatingly confident manner as if she would descend a throne to receive one of those smiles which he performed just after taking a mouthful of bread, perhaps.

[Fol. 5^r]

The cousin who was expected to give him employment was said to live at one of the large hotels and so he started soon after breakfast to find him. He enquired until he came to the great structure towering above him in an

[MS[2]]

I

At the foot of the street the tiny riggings of ships grew like grass. They lay black against the water which, faintly seen, appeared as impalpable as a mist. Slanting over the roofs of the southern side came a stream of copper light from the setting sun, making the higher part of the northern walls resplendent, causing each window there to blaze like a topaz, and accentuating at the same time the gentle soft shadows of the lower part and of the street.

The boarders in No. 936 were coming from their dinner in the basement. Two young clerks from a famous shoe-store lit cigarettes and taking seats upon the topmost step in front of the house, prepared to gossip in the dark way of their age. Thorpe, an old book-keeper, took his regular evening cigar from among the lead pencils in a top pocket of his vest. He perched on the iron railing at the side of the landing. Trixell, a clerk in a Broadway flower shop, waited for a time at the head of the gloomy basement stairs. He thought that perhaps the landlady's daughter would ascend and in such case he wished to have the joy and the distinction of appearing to conduct her to her throne on the front steps. Four old ladies toiled heavily past him.

One of the shoe clerks pulled wisely at his cigarette and addressed the old book-keeper. "Say, Thorpe, Trixell seems to be making the pace for all of us, don't you think?"

Thorpe smiled. "Well he certainly does seem to be cutting some ice. Why don't some of you smooth people get a hustle on you?"

Both shoe-clerks were silent for a moment and then one said: "She's a mighty pretty girl."

"Pretty girl!" cried Thorpe. "She's the prettiest girl in town. If I was as young as you boys!"

"Well, old Holmes is older than you," said one shoe-clerk, nudging the other. "And anybody could see that you, Thorpey, me boy, could make a lobster out of Holmes."

"Holmes never had a chance. He is an old idiot. And, anyhow, you two fresh kids, what right have you got to be talking about her?"

"None at all," they responded. "Didn't say we did, did we? We ain't hurting anybody, are we?"

"Shut up," whispered Thorpe suddenly. "Here comes Trixell."

II

Apparently the daughter of the house was perverse or busy for Trixell came out alone. He lit a cigarette and thrusting his hands in his pockets and throwing back his shoulders, surveyed the street with composure and dignity. To an action of this kind some men can impart a majesty which radiates entirely from their minds. His glance lifted high, Trixell gazed at the meek brown houses across the way as an emperor might gaze at his passing squadrons. He said: "Baltimore won again today. That makes two straight out of the series."

But his fellow-boarders on the steps were exchanging sly glances which related apparently to another subject. Finally one of the shoe clerks said: "You look lonesome tonight, Trix?"

"Oh, I don't know," he replied airily.

"What's the matter, Trix," asked Thorpe. "Lost something, haven't you?"

"Have I?" said Trixell with irony. "What have I lost?"

"Why——" said Thorpe. "You seem to have lost—er—What's wrong, Trix? Is she sick?"

"I don't know who you mean," said Trixell cleverly. "Who do you mean?"

The shoe clerks chuckled. "Oh, you old rat! Maybe you don't know who he means!"

But Trixell had turned toward the door. "Ah, good evening," he said. There was a stir among the shoe clerks. They arose and looked at the houses across the street expressing in this way their desire to have the landlady's daughter take what seat she pleased and their perfect willingness to be content with what remained. There was stiffness as well as hauteur in their poses at this time for they were of the age and class which looks upon a movement of courtesy as being almost equivalent to a proposal of marriage or at least a declaration of love. Each being willing to have the landlady's daughter care for him, each wished to appear manfully indifferent and so they pretended they had arisen quite by accident. But no one heeded them so presently they took seat again and puffed stolidly at their cigarettes.

Evidently Trixell had arranged in his mind where the girl was to sit and he offered her the position with a bland wave of his hand. But she said: "No, thanks. I'd rather sit here." She perched side saddle fashion on one of the railings. Trixell dropped gracefully to the top-step. Thorpe coughed to celebrate some joke which he perceived and, catching a sidelong glance from a shoe-clerk, he winked gravely.

The social group being now arranged there fell upon it the singular quiet which ensues when people chase their thoughts from pole to pole and seven times around the equator in search of the effective sentence.

III

Finally Trixell remarked: "They give transfers now on the street car-lines almost all over the city. It seems funny for them to do that in New York. I can remember when they didn't give transfers at all—not a line in New York that I know of."

There was a moment of silence. Then Thorpe told his information concerning the matter and at the end stated some kind of theory. Trixell at once objected to some part of it. He drew a heavy indictment. He talked rather too rapidly and from time to time he looked to find if the girl was heeding his eloquence.

A shoe-clerk seized this opportunity to lean backward and say confidentially to the girl: "You look tired tonight."

She pushed a lock from her temple with a gesture of fatigue. "Yes, I am. Very tired." Her foot was swinging in the way that youth proclaims its superabundant power and her cheek had upon it a flush of pink.

The shoe clerk murmured sympathetically and having thus gone into the social whirl with success he subsided and devoted himself to his comrade.

On the steps of the next house a man in shirt sleeves was reading an evening paper while two babies tumbled on the side-walk. In front of other houses, after-dinner groups had gathered. At one corner of the block, street cars moved past endlessly like links of a chain. At the other corner, a man ground steadily at a hand-organ and the brilliant melodies from the thing were interrupted at intervals by the sudden great roar of an elevated train.

At 936, Trixell talked long. He was engaged in an essay upon the Raines law when Thorpe said: "Somebody coming here."

IV

A young man had halted before the house and was peering up at the dim transom where some gilt numerals shone inadequately. He carried a valise and an umbrella.

The boarders of No. 936 surveyed him keenly, measuring him from his umbrella to his necktie with all the curiosity and suspicion of New Yorkers who know no shame in these matters. He evidently made an effort to have it appear that he was not aware that the steps was a fortress armed with a formidable battery of eyes.

After an ineffectual attempt to solve the riddle on the transom, he addressed a shoe-clerk. "This is 936, isn't it?"

The shoe-clerk answered in the affirmative and the young man asked: "It's a boarding-house, isn't it? Is the lady that keeps it in?" The shoe-clerk turned and glanced at the top of the steps throwing the responsibility upon the landlady's daughter.

She spoke as one having authority. "If you'll come in, please, I'll go find her."

The young man threaded his way among the knees and outlying elbows on the steps while the boarders continued their measurements in the same silence.

In the hallway the girl lit the gas and said: "Wait here please."

"Thanks," said the young man. It entered his head to accept any room in this house which might be offered him for the young girl seemed to him beautiful. He dwelt long in his mind upon her graceful pose as she lit the gas.

V

It is a legend that at one time the mistresses of boarding houses welcomed their arriving prey with cordial words and smiles. It is not known that a prey of this period need expect cordial words and smiles. On the contrary, he might expect to go before a bar of judgment where he is scanned for a resemblance to men whose perfidy is engraven on the mind of the boarding house mistress, men who lied with skill and went away leaving an empty trunk in the house and a stone heart in the breast of the land-lady. These men of sin leave thorns in the path of the virtue that comes afterward. "In God we trust," is a motto often hung on boarding house walls. Here it expresses more than usual. It expresses a limit.

The proprietress of No. 936 came slowly toward the young man. Many wrinkles about her eyes were owing to her intensity of gaze.

"Good evening," he said with a strategic smile.

"Good evening?" she said.

"I've come to see if you have any room for another boarder," he ventured still smiling.

"Well," she answered, "there's a small room on the third floor—are you in business in the city?"

"No, not now. I don't live in the city but I've come here to take a position with a cousin of mine."

She reflected. At last she said: "Well, there's only the small room on the third floor. You can look at it if you wish."

Under the influence of her preternatural composure or indifference he was beginning to believe that he resembled a thief and so at her permission to look at the room he said humbly and gratefully: "Oh, thank you very much." She nodded slightly at the gas-jet in vague acknowledgment of the young man's words.

They ascended two flights and there she exhibited a small hall bed-room grim and grey like a cell. "This is six dollars a week," she observed.

He made a show of deep consideration and at last said: "Well I'll take it if you don't mind."

As he paid her six dollars she smiled, quietly amiable, and he was made to know that he did not yet resemble a thief.

VI

Alone in his grey and grim cell at the top of the house the young man reflected on his state. Life now presented a new aspect to him and he thoug<[ht]> upon the dim figures which people<[d]> his changed world.

His window opened upon t<[he mystic]> gulf of the evening and from time <[to]> time a murmur of voices arose<[.]> He heard often the tones of the young girl.

He was saddened by his chang<[e]> of environment and he was in the mood to wonder if she would feel sorrow for him could she know his loneliness. The thought of her sympathy loomed in his mind until in proportion it was great.

VII

In the morning the young man awoke with the thought at once in his mind that he had overslept. He consulted his old silver watch however and discovered that it was not yet six o'clock. Dusky grey light entered through the unclean panes of the window. The long roar, the thunder of the city's life came from the streets. Sometimes a wagon passed the house, its wheels rattling over the cobbles with a noise like innumerable musketry volleys. Then at last a bell was rung and the tomb-like silence of the house itself was broken. Doors slammed.

As the young man entered the dining-room in the basement he paused in a slight embarrassment seeing none to direct him. Five young men and two old women with their faces turned toward their plates ate steadfastly.

He felt like retreating but the young girl of his previous experience appeared suddenly having come from the kitchen with dishes. She smiled at him and conducted him to a seat. At the sound of the chair being drawn out from the table, the five young men and two old women looked up and seeing the new boarder gazed at him as they gazed at their plates. The young girl poured water into his glass and as she performed this office he did not dare to let his eyes waver in fear that she would discover that the charm of her near presence affected him. Nevertheless he was enabled to watch her hand as she tipped the pitcher and he thought it a perfect hand. She asked him to make a choice between steak and bacon and eggs.

During the meal he covertly watched her. He was glad when a

certain one of the five young clerks finished breakfast and left the table for that particular clerk ogled the girl as she passed to and fro in a way that the new boarder considered exasperatingly bold and confident. It was evident that the clerk believed that the girl would descend a throne to receive one of these smiles which he performed soon after taking a mouthful of bread perhaps. And so the new boarder reflecting upon his own nobility rejoiced at the exit of the trickster.

He dallied with a second cup of coffee until nearly all of the boarders had vanished from the table. He tried to note each move of the young girl. Still, he thought he contrived to do this without the young girl being aware. His instinct taught him that her too sudden knowledge of his interest would somehow shame him for she certainly did not seem to recognize his existence in any way save as a boarder.

XXVIII. [CHURCH PARADE]

DURING the social season London is blessed by a solemn and austere Sunday ceremony which is called Church parade. It consists in a certain portion of the populace driving slowly along a certain prescribed route in Hyde Park and recognizing or ignoring members of another and larger portion of the populace that lines a rail to the left of the drive. Stated simply, it may seem unimportant but in reality it is one of the bits of social masonry whose destruction would totter the British Empire dangerously toward its fall. This is not an expanded remark. A sight of the Church Parade fills one with the truth of it. It is a pageant more solemn than the crowning of kings.

XXIX. [AND HIS NAME SHALL BE CALLED UNDER TRUTH]

AND his name shall be called under truth because he said far less than he was able

XXX. [PLAY SET IN A FRENCH TAVERN]

NOTE:—Interior of a little inn in old France. Door, C. Fireplace, L. <[and]> before it tables and benches. Four soldiers, carousing. Red fire-reflections upon the wall. Above it, and R., a window showing moonlight. Room rather shadowy.

G.— "Well, let us have more wine, eh?"

B.— "Bah, there is not a half-crown in the company and these country landlords, they are the very devil for demanding that good honest soldiers pay for what they get."

A.— "Well, let us see. There is wine, song, women and fighting. Pray you, ——, give us song since we are denied wine."

B.— "Not me. My throat is a chimney. Good singing is in wine even as the winning of woman is in song and even as the cause of fast and fierce brawling is woman. We must have wine. After that, song, intrigue and fighting follow easily."

P.— "No, no, we can fight without wine. What is to hinder our fighting?"

G.— "Surely! Surely! He is right! What is to hinder our fighting?"

A.— "Aye, we can fight. Surely! After all, it is very simple!"

B.— "But—who will we fight?"

P.— " 'Who'? Anyone! It is a question of being entertained. No gentleman who happens here will refuse the earnest prayers of four honest guardsmen rusting here in a wretched country inn and thinking always of great Paris where one has to flip a coin to make choice of a round dozen of brawls."

B.— "Now, look! Perhaps, only one gentleman will appear! Who, then, is to be the selfish villain who will have the pleasure of drawing upon this gentleman, to the great discomfort of his three friends who may only sit and twiddle their thumbs?"

P.— "I, indeed! Since it was I alone who had the heaven-born thought that we could fight, when you three were stupidly bewailing the lack of wine."

G.— "Aye, it is his privilege!"

A.— "Aye, his was the thought! Curses be on my wooden head.

I did not know that I ever neglected to think about fighting. It is this miserable country air."

B.— "Well, look you, ——, I give you up the first gentleman, since I must, but if you are to reap all the pleasure, I think you should belabor more wine out of the landlord so that we may abide the coming of the second, third, and fourth gentleman with some patience."

P.— "Generous comrades! For your unselfishness you shall witness the prettiest fight to be seen out of Paris. Egad, these provincials should come from miles about us, for it will be a sword-play with metropolitan actors. Or one, at least."

G.— "Wine! Wine! Do you begrudge us a cudgel on a landlord's shoulders when we grant you a sword at a gentleman's breast?"

P.— "No! No, comrades! You shall have wine if I am obliged to flog a cask for it! Ho, landlord! (bawling) Landlord! Landlord! Landlord! Egad, the rascal smells my empty pocket! (bawling again) Landlord! Landlord! Snail! Tortoise! Old ox of a landlord, come hither! No, no, comrades, I'll not begrudge you cudgels! I will go——"

(Enter gentleman, in travel stained green and black suit. Riding-whip. Boots.)

Gentleman: (bawling) "Landlord! Landlord! (pauses to listen) Landlord! Landlord! What, have you no more ears than your casks, villain? Landlord! Landlord!" (Strides about impatiently.)

B.— "Ten thousand devils, P—, there is your first gentleman. Ah, you lucky dog! And a fine strong fellow he is too and with a long sword!"

P.— "Aye, surely, there he is, heaven bless his forethought. Now, comrades, sit silent and don't interrupt the play, like a good audience. (Arising and addressing the stranger.) Sir, do you mistake this inn for a trumpet that you bawl through it so loudly?"

Stranger: (facing about) "Sir!!"

P.— "I said that it was distasteful to me that you shatter all the bottles in this very good inn by that thunderous voice of yours."

Stranger: "You seek a quarrel, I think!"

P.— "Not at all! Not at all! Thank heaven, my sword has been proven too often in the service of the king to need to seek glory in a tavern quarrel. I am merely protesting against the destruction of glass and the consequent spilling of wine by that hail-storm which comes from your lungs. I am a man of quiet and peace and your tempestuous uproar disturbs my meditations."

Stranger: "And may I not call the landlord, sir?"

P.— "Egad, I thought you were cannonading him. No, you may not call the landlord, sir."

Stranger: (bawling) "Landlord! Landlord! Landlord!"

(P. takes his glass from the table and throws it violently to the floor where it shatters.)

P.— "There, a hundred thousand demons and furies, his wretched yelling has broken my glass. Ah, this is too much for my stomach, man of repose though I be. (Draws) Turn, sir, turn! Turn while I pin that monstrous voice of yours fast to the wall and paint the arms of the house of hell upon it with your blood. Draw!"

Stranger: "What, have the king's guards gone mad? You 'a man of quiet and peace', son of a storm-king."

P.— "Fury! Sir, will you not draw?"

Stranger: " 'Draw'? And why? I was a gentleman and a knight of France and served my king when you knew not swords nor gentlemen nor France. Must I draw my honest blade now because a scabbard has knocked against the legs of a child long enough to fill his veins with poisonous courage?"

P.— (in despair) "Name of heaven, hear the words come from him! What, sir, would you reason with me? Do I look like a man who can be reasoned with?"

Stranger: "No, in truth, there is no resemblance between you and any manner of reason."

P.— "A new insult! A new insult! Comrades, is not that a new insult?"

B.— "Aye, a new insult."

A.— "Aye!"

G.—"He must now fight or you may cudgel him!"

P.—"There, sir, you see! These gentlemen attest that you have again insulted me!"

Stranger: "But I merely admitted what you seemed to wish me to admit."

P.— "Ah, words, words, words. You churnfull of language, have you no sword? Do you carry that jewelled hilt to blandish scullery maids? Coward!"

Stranger: " 'Coward'! (Then slowly) So you are serious? I did not know but that it was a child who had learned some part of the plays. (Enter landlord) Ha, adder, do you come at last after having involved me in a strange quarrel with this young babe-eater?" (Beats the landlord.)

P.— (interfering) "Sir, it is a good landlord and I will not have him beaten. All my life I have devoted to protecting honest landlords from over-bearing blades of your kind!"

Landlord: "Noble P—!"

Stranger: "Sir, you need go no further! I am at your service at daylight. You have too much of the hangdog about you to be shaken off."

G., B. and A.— (disappointed) " 'At daylight'!"

P.— (pleading) "And why, sir, at daybreak? Here is plenty of room and enough light."

Stranger: "Well, I am weary with hard riding and in my present condition, I wouldn't afford you much entertainment. I am come here on earnest business and I rode at a great expenditure in horses. I am greatly in need of rest."

P.— (after reflection) "And what assurance have I that before daylight you will not do some more hard riding?"

Stranger: "What?"

P.— "And what assurance have I that, before daylight you will not do some more hard riding?"

Stranger: "A plague chase these intemperate swordsmen! Sir, J— E— has rode toward his enemies on many battlefields but he never rode away without glory or without wounds!"

All: " 'J— E—'!! Lord E—!!"

P.— (bowing) "My lord will pardon me for supposing for an instant that such a great gentleman would not keep an appointment at daybreak."

Stranger: (bowing) "Sir, I have kept many such appointments and shall doubtless live to keep many more."

P.— (bowing) "It would certainly be presumption on my part to hinder you in any way, my lord."

Stranger: "Not at all, sir, if your sword is honest and you are able."

P.— "We shall see, my lord! And, now, as there will be one palate among us that may not hereafter thrill at the flow of good wine, your lordship will surely consent to join our little carouse?"

Stranger: "It will afford me pleasure, sir!"

P.— "Come, then, scoundrel, fetch us wine before I beat that skin of yours into leather belts and ladies' purses!"

Landlord: "What, noble P—? Beat me? I, one of the good landlords to whom you have——"

P.— (interrupting) "What, do you stand there and gape at me? When I cry wine, landlords fly! Go, run, fly, before I cudgel a pair of wings upon your shoulders!"

Landlord: "Cudgel me!!"

P.— "Rascal, do you not understand the word cudgel? Here's a strange landlord! Now, look you, it is usually written with a walking-stick upon the backs——"

Landlord: "Say no more, sir! (Going) I have had twenty years of education in the language of gentlemen and, in faith, if my inn don't burn down I shall doubtless have twenty years more——" (Exit mumbling)

P.— (seating himself where in the meantime the stranger has been seated with G., B. and A.) "My lord will have trouble in making friends with the wine here! When we first come from Paris, we quarreled day after day with the inn-keeper until we discovered that no eloquence can change bad wine to good. And, really, we wasted much valuable time for my comrade G— here found that after the eighth bottle it was an indifferent matter and so we grow into the fashion of drinking eight bottles in the afternoons that we might spend our nights in comfort."

G.— "And I was slow in thought too, for I ever followed this rule of eight. I remember well the first girl I loved, but after I had come to the eighth——"

All: "Ha, ha, G—! Old shrivelled heart! Ha, ha! The eighth, eh? Eight is the number of indifference, eh, wisdom?"

G.— "Truly! The ancients were wise in stopping everything at beautiful seven! If they had gone on to eight, they would have sold their seven for a fig."

(Enter landlord with wine.)

P.— "Well, G—, here's a start, with all sails set, toward your eight of indifference! My lord! (Drinks to stranger. Exit landlord.)

Stranger: "Gentlemen, your health!" (All drink.)

(Enter Landlord conducting cloaked figure in red.)

Landlord: "This way, sir! A table right here." (Conducts figure to table, R. and sets wine before it.)

B.— (at other table, to his friends) "I remember once when I was in Flanders——" (continues to tell tale in pantomime to great amusement of his friends.)

Landlord: (to the figure, lagging near it) "Eh, yes sir, inn-keeping in these times is a hard labor! A man needs a head of granite and shoulders of hammered steel! What I get for my pains is principally blows! Now, if I had choice of a business in life I would be the maker of all kinds of stout sticks! It is certainly the most thriving trade in the whole kingdom of France! If I had a crown for every time—but, ah, why do I waste language over it! It must be apparent to everyone that an innkeeper's lot is the most miserable of all! Look there, now! There is that young Mon. P—, he who ordered wine at the top of his lungs when I was only two paces from him. Will he pay me? Not he! If I demand it tonight he will flog me once for every drop in every bottle and as soon as it gets light enough, he goes out to get killed by the lord in green and black. And if afterward I ask it of his friends—— (kicks in the air and imitates G. in a rage) 'What, sirrah, would you try to beat your dirty crowns out of the white soul of poor dead P—?' And there, you see, my coin goes to have the king's face melted from it, along with 'the white soul of poor dead P—.' I tell you, sir, the world is made of cudgelers and sorcerers! Of course, I prefer cudgels to witchcraft! Truly! Eh, sir? Would not you? (Looks at silent figure—draws back a pace—then rather quaveringly) Of course, sorcerers are all honorable gentlemen and—er—er—they can have the best that my house affords— (backing away) —and I have a very great respect for them and—er—er——"

A.— (leaning back in his chair) "Who is your other guest, landlord? He seems a silent fellow. Is he a gentleman?"

Landlord: "No, sir, he is a doctor. He is an old sorcerer I think sir and says little. I think he conversed more freely with me tonight than he has in months. He comes here for his wine and drinks alone."

A.— "Well, well, he is surely a very wicked man!"

Landlord: "Aye, tonight he was very bitter against gentlemen of the sword and as I upheld them, the discussion was furious indeed. I was frightened."

A.— "Is he a young man?"

Landlord: "Young? He is as old as the moon! He was born when the earth was a little child clinging to its mother's skirts! He, young!!" (Exit.)

(B. has continued to tell his tale of Flanders. For a moment, A., inattentive, continues to stare across the room at the figure in red.)

All: (at conclusion of story) "Ha, ha, good, B—, good! And did you fight him?"

B.— "Of a surety! Yes, we fought! He said as he died that he must have been mistaken."

(All drink.)

Stranger: "And may I ask what brought four such gallant gentlemen away from the shine of Paris? I think it must have been some great thing to make you abide the darkness of the country."

B.— (looking at A.) "Well——"

A.— (looking at G.) "Well, in truth——"

G.— (looking at P.) "My lord, it seems——"

P.— "What, G—, would you stammer until you make my lord think he is to fight at daybreak with one of a band of cutthroats? Out with it, man! Tell it, at once, since you three have already surrounded it with the mystery of a crime! Out with it?"

Stranger: "Gentlemen, it was a careless remark! I would not pry!"

P.— "No, my lord, no! It must be told! Come, G—!"

G.— "Well, my lord, my young friend there, he is a man of peace and repose and can seldom be aroused but one day he walked abroad in Paris and by chance met a gentleman who remarked to a companion that my comrade's feather curled too much. Now, this companion of the gentleman told it to a friend who laughingly repeated it in a certain salon where there chanced to be a lady who knew my comrade. Now, we others were obliged to accompany our comrade in order that the companion of the gentleman, the friend of the companion, and a certain accommodating acquaintance of the friend, might feel that proper attention was being paid to them. Afterward, it was our misfortune to find that the gentleman had been very well known at court and that the friend of the companion or the acquaintance of the friend—I forget—had been a great lord somewhere or other. The king, God bless him, became very wroth against duelling directly after breakfast that morning and we felt obliged to leave Paris for a week or so until the great wound made in the heart of society should have been healed."

P.— "It is my misfortune that the wound in the heart of the gentleman would not heal so readily for his sister is a very fair and virtuous lady. I went to pay my respects some time afterward and she positively refused to admit me."

Stranger: "Well, well, swords do unkind things occasionally. I remember once my cousin and I——"

B.— "But, pardon me, my lord, you have not yet told us what has carried so great a gentleman of the court down into this somber country."

Stranger: "Sir, you are right! I think you are four honorable gentlemen and having granted me your story like frank soldiers, I would do ill not to trust you. Gentlemen, this is an earnest business and lies close to the welfare of my family. I am engaged in an attempt to find my child. I am looking for a man with a cross-shaped scar upon his wrist!"

(At this sentence, a peculiarly wild and inhuman laugh breaks from the figure in red. All start up and look about them.)

G.— "What demon's cackle was that?"

P.— "Egad, that was a screech!"

Stranger: "From whence came it? By my faith, that was not a human throat!"

(All look about them)

A.— (suddenly remembering figure in red) "Ha, ha, why it is nothing but that villainous old doctor babbling over his wine! Come, sit down again, comrades, it is no more than a laugh winding in a toothless mouth. He is old as the moon, in faith!"

P.— "Aye, come, sit again! An old woman of a doctor dreaming of the good men he has bled. Come, sit, again."

(All seat themselves)

Stranger: (Shrugging his shoulders) "I confess to no love for the company of such serpents!"

B.— "Nor I!"

P.— "Well, then, let us cudgel him forth. (Rising to his feet and calling to the figure) Sir——"

G.— (interrupting P. and dragging him again to a seated position) "Oh, come, come, P—, now, why fret the old rat with your blowing of cudgels! Come, sit down, man! Do you ever bother of doctors before you have wounds! Come, the wine is not all gone!"

P.— (reluctantly) "Well——"

G.— "Nonsense! Nonsense! Pay court to the wine, man! Would you be in the presence of the goddess without a bow or a scrape? And, ha, there, B—, sing! Sing, lad, and let us have no more of mummery."

B.— "There is not a song in my throat since that wild howl! I—I——"

P.— "Bah, nonsense, B—, do you turn trembler? Why a song, gay heart, a song!"

B.— "There is no voice left to me."

P.— "Well, then, since I cannot sing I am even obliged to offer a toast and a mighty toast it will be, lads, and drink to it like whales! Here, boys, (rises enthusiastically) I drink to a face seen at a window, I drink to a name overheard from a servingm'n, I drink to the fairest face and the fairest name in France, I drink to the beautiful J—!"

(As P. holds aloft his glass in a great gesture and as the name rings out, the red cloak flashes from the figure and a grey ghastly head is discovered staring at P. A moment of silent staring.)

P.— (calmly) "Here's the devil's head!"

Stranger: (with a shiver) "An omen, sir, an omen! We fight in the morning! Pray heaven——"

P.— (steadily) "It is as chance may have it, my lord! In the meantime, I will see what ghoul dare start and stare at toast that I offer."

(All restrain him)

B.— "No, no, P—! It is some damnable child of witches and devils!"

A.— "It is death, P—! No, no, come back!"

P.— (shaking them off) "Nonsense! If he is death, he shall explain why he is here to take men's hearts from them on the eve of fighting or I'll—cudgel him. (Draws and advances toward the imperturbable figure and in mid-stage halts) Sir, are you a man or a corpse? Speak quickly or a sword will make you."

(The figure rises and goes slowly toward P. who does not flinch)

The figure: "A threat of wind! If I am a corpse why need I fear thrust of thine?" (Exit through door C.)

(All remaining transfixed staring at the closed door)

(Curtain)

XXXI. THINGS STEPHEN SAYS

Things Stephen Says

STORY of Leuitenant of Cavelry asking for, and insisting upon having a bottle—finally saying he wanted to write the name of his dead pal, on a piece of paper and put it in the bottle—to bury bottle with the body of his friend.

Capt. Green & Leuiten—Exton of 20 infantry—gave Stephen and Marshall luncheon—Then as they were going away they saw these officers wash their—his dishes—having to walk some way to do it—made Stephen feel ashamed.

When I ran back from the end of the rough-rider fight, to get help for Marshall I met on a narrow wood path the whole 71st N.Y. Regiment, and every one seemed to know me, princepaly because I had been on their transport the night before. I had already passed three troops of the 9th Cavelry (collored.) and they had had absolutely no questions to ask but every body in the 71st Reg. set up a yell for information as I floundered through the bushes past their incrediblely long line. (single file.) Afterward I passed in much the same way the 6th & the 16th Regular infantry reg's. And they preserved an absolute silence almost an indifference as to what had transpired when they had heard the heavy firing. It seemed as if they were solly occupied with their own business, and had no nerotic intrest in matters which gave them no casualty report.

A Marine picked up a shell in the smouldering ruins of a village —Guantanimo—I asked if it was loaded and he said he did not know but that it was hot. He took & put it in the sea to cool. It was loaded—gave it to me—I buried it under Palm tree. Looked for it later but it was gone.

Reddie Johnston in Church Porto Rico—crossed himself in front of the Christ & I said "For God sake don't do that." He answered "Why, I was in earnest you damn fool!"

Cavelery men fine types—guns looks like toy guns in their hands.

Marshall lied about statement having money belt on when shot with $700—all he had was gun—Artist "Point" got that. I gave him my blanket in the morning & he told me where he left that.

Printed in cabin of The Three friends

"English they be and Japanis that hang on the Brown Bear's flank. And some be Scot, but the worst, God wot, and the boldest thieves, be Yank!"

McCrady spouted "The Three Sealers" all the time

Arriving at N.Y. from Havana, they made us all & each put thermometer's in our mouths. I tried to think of something to say to break up crowd—but could not talk with it in my mouth. Finally one old major in an [ ]regiment said "What Damn rot."

Make an Open Boat story of Cusico (?) Start where Marine went crazy and jumped over cliff killing himself, when the outpost was cut off— —Trumperts called "Music" Next day the "music" went to edge of cliff & leeres over, Capt. Short called & said whats that damn red headed music gloating over then he called to him sharply——

XXXII. [SPANISH-AMERICAN WAR PLAY]

Characters

Mr. John Stilwell: an English sugar-planter in Cuba.
Marjorie Stilwell: his daughter.

Lucy Stilwell: his daughter.
Don Patricio de Mavida y Aguilar:
colonel of the Tequila Battalion,
No. 206, of the Spanish army.
Henry Patten: a first lieutenant commanding D Troop,
20th. United States Cavalry.
Sylvester Thorpe: for the New York Eclipse.
Serjeant Brown: of D Troop.

(*ACT I*)

SCENE: The dining-room of John Stilwell's house on his plantation in the province of Santiago de Cuba.
TIME: The evening of a day in late July, 1898.

John Stilwell, his two daughters, and Colonel Mavida discovered at dinner.

(SCENE I)

Mavida: (gesturing) "Well, you see, if the Americans come here, they will have some troubles. I have my mens—over 300—in the blockhouse and in the town. And if the Americans come here they will not find that I am like General Linares."

John Stilwell: "Well, you know, I don't like it. Directly, you know we'll have you chaps potting at each other here under our very noses."

Marjorie: (shuddering) "It will be dreadful——"

Lucy: "And, O, perhaps somebody will be killed!"

Mavida: (puzzled and gentle) "Killed? I think many mens will be killed, senorita. (He plumes himself a trifle.) If they come here, you will see—you will see. I myself will kill the first American—(impressively)—the first one."

Marjorie: "Oh, Don Patricio, please don't say it. It is too horrible——"

Mavida: (solemnly) "The first one!"

Marjorie: "And you really mean that you are going to kill the first American who comes here without particular discrimination?

Oh, Don Patricio! It might be an awfully nice chap, you know."

Lucy: "And he may have a wife and babies and all that kind of thing."

Stilwell: (soothingly) "O, don't mind him. He don't mean it."

Lucy: "But Papa, he says he means it."

Mavida: (earnestly) "My friends, I cannot help myself. I am a soldier of Spain. I must meet the enemies of my country."

Lucy: "But, Don Patricio, don't you think the matter would be made so much more simple and agreeable if you just sort of casually surrendered, you know."

Stilwell and Marjorie: (together, scandalized) "Lucy!"

Mavida: (with gloomy dignity) "The senorita is so good as to have been misinformed as to the honor of Spanish soldiers."

Lucy: (sorry that she has hurt him) "Oh, well, I didn't really mean surrender, you know. I meant giving in, really, and of course——"

Marjorie: (hastily interrupting) "Yes, Don Patricio, but your honor does not require you to kill the first American, you see. He may have, as Lucy so well has said, a wife and a number of babies at home."

Stilwell: "That is his own affair—his own affair. Hang it all, you can't hold Don Patricio responsible for every wife and baby in the American army."

Marjorie: (coldly) "I did not understand there were wives and babies in the American army."

Mavida: "The senoritas do not understand too much of the character of our nation. We have an enemy and we kill him. We are insult' and we kill him, when first we see him!"

Lucy: "But don't you ever think, Don Patricio, of all the mothers sitting up at night and waiting for the return of their sons?"

Mavida: "If a man has a mother it is his own fault."

Marjorie: "How do you mean? I don't understand."

Stilwell: "He is quite right. He doesn't mean exactly, my dear, that if a man has a mother it is his own fault. He means that when a man goes gratuitously into danger, he's got to pay the piper."

Marjorie: "Oh.—I thought he must mean something like that. Of course at first, Don Patricio's sentiments sounded rather revolutionary."

Mavida: (growing excited) "I am convince'. I am firm. The senoritas should understand the character of my nation. Our enemies—we kills them."

Lucy: (to Marjorie, tearfully) "Isn't it horrible to think of all the new widows and orphans that will be in the United States within the next few weeks."

Mavida: (haughtily) "The senoritas misunderstands. I intend to make no move against the widows and orphans of the Americans."

Stilwell: "No! no! You misunderstand, Don Patricio. My daughter means merely to pity the new American widows and orphans."

Mavida: (shrugging his shoulders) "Well if they insist upon fight' with Spain."

Stilwell: "No! no! you misunderstand again. There are no widows and orphans in the American army. My daughter means——"

Mavida: (interrupting Stilwell with an impressive outstretched hand) "I am sorry. The time is much serious. I am a Spaniard. I have been insult' and I will kill the first American which I see."

(a knock on the door, C, the dinner party start.)

(—business—)

Stilwell: (arising and moving toward the door) "Who's there?"

Patten: (without) "An officer of the United States Army. Open the door." (a scene of agitation and consternation. Mavida arises and draws his revolver. He fiercely indicates his resolution to kill Patten upon his entrance. While the two girls, terrified, pantomime wildly at him. Stilwell stands near the door facing Mavida and making comic signs. Mavida is partly led and partly thrust through the doorway L, meantime protesting in dumb show that he will kill Patten.)

Patten: (without, sternly) "Open the door."

(Lucy and Marjorie resume their seats
and hastily compose themselves.
Stilwell opens the door. Enter Patten.)

Patten: "You may stay outside, Serjeant."

(Serjeant Brown is seen in the darkness
directly back of threshold.)

Serjt. B.: "Yes sir."

Patten: (he swiftly takes in scene before him) "Extremely sorry, I'm sure, to give you any trouble. Fact is we find so many of these sugar-plantations deserted that I didn't expect to find so much—(hesitates)—civilization."

Stilwell: "Oh, of course, it's all right you know but then you did give us a bit of a start. I've got nothing to do with this business at all, you know, I'm an Englishman, you see."

Patten: "Oh, an Englishman? Well——that's all right."

Lucy: (advances timidly toward Patten) "But you are not going to fight anywhere about here, are you?"

Patten: "Fight? no! Not the slightest intention. You see, I'm merely running around with stores for the reconcentrados and —(looking at Marjorie)—I wouldn't fight for worlds. That is—if it would annoy you in any way."

Stilwell: "Won't you sit down?"

Patten: "Oh, thank you." (takes rocking-chair the back of which is within two feet of the door L which leads into the room where Mavida is. A period of silence during which the Stilwells become gradually more and more agitated, while Patten watches them blandly.)

Patten: "Of course,—I—I—it is rude to break in upon you in this manner and of course—(suddenly and covering them all with a cold and contemptuous glance)—I'm sorry that I disturbed you in the matter that some danger menaces me at my back."

(—business—)

"I don't know—whether I should interfere in a thing which seems so purely domestic, but if you will allow me—(suddenly) —Serjeant!"

(enter Serjeant Brown.)

Serjt. B.: "Sir?"

Patten: (waves a hand carelessly behind him indicating the door.) "Go in and see what that is."

Serjt. B.: "Yes—sir." (exit Serjt. B.—door L.)

(Patten speaks icily.)

Patten: "I see that you have some machinery here for assaulting people who turn their backs to strange doors." (a muffled sound of disturbance begins off stage L) (business)

Stilwell: "Look here, this won't do at all. It is strictly his own affair."

Patten: (inflexibly) "Whose affair?"

Stilwell: "I mean—look here you know—I'm not going to have you hurt in my house, and I am not going to give him away."

Patten: "I rather imagine the Serjeant is giving him away all well enough."

Stilwell: "He was dining here—and he said that he was going to kill the first American who came and we didn't want to have it done. That's all there is to it."

Patten: "Oh, I see. I don't think we—you note that I say we—I mean the race—I don't think we lend ourselves readily to theories of assassination."

Stilwell: (stiffly) "Thank you very much."

Patten: (calmly) "It would have surprised me greatly to have been murdered in the house of an English gentleman."

Stilwell: "Quite so." (after a pause) "I hope—you are not alone?"

Patten: "Oh, no, the troop is outside—thank you. I came to enquire for good camping ground with water and forage close by. (Twisting his head with swift impatience toward the door, L) Why don't you bring him out, Serjeant?"

Serjt. B.: (from without in muffled voice) "All right, sir, in a minute."

Patten: "I suppose you wouldn't mind if we took a little sugar-cane for the horses?"

Stilwell: "Not at all—if you can find any. What between the Insurgents and the Spanish troops, I'm in doubt whether this is a sugar plantation or a stone quarry."

(Private soldier opens the door C and steps aside for the entrance of Thorpe.)

Thorpe: (over his shoulder to private) "Thank you." (looks about him in some bewilderment and bows hurriedly at sight of the girls.) "I beg your pardon. I was told—oh, there you are, Patten."

Patten: (immovable in chair) "Hullo, Thorpe."

Thorpe: (staring at Patten) "What's the matter?"

Patten: "Nothing."

Thorpe: (mystified) "What's the row in the next room?"

Patten: "That is my first Serjeant engaging the enemy."

Thorpe: "Why don't you go and help him?"

Patten: "I don't think he needs it."

(commotion inside door L.)

Marjorie: (unable to contain herself; moves toward Patten; her hands are clasped) "Will you please move away from that door —or—or—or—turn about so that you will face it in some way."

Patten: (with alacrity) "Why of course." (he moves R down stage)

(enter Serjt. B. and Mavida; Brown has Mavida by the scruff of the neck; Mavida is furious but disarmed)

Serjt. B.: (bursting out excitedly) "I had an awful time with him, sir. He fought like a cat and he bit my finger—see? If it hadn't been that I was on duty, I would have taken and everlastingly broken——"

Patten: (swiftly, in a hard voice) "Be quiet, Serjeant." (sudden rigidity of Serjt.; Patten looks at Mavida) "Who is he, Serjeant?"

Serjt. B.: "Well he's a Spanish officer, sir. That's all I know. And he bit me on the fing——"

Patten: "Be quiet, I tell you." (he turns deferentially to Stilwell.) "I'm sorry but I'm afraid that I will have to ask you who is this remarkable man?"

Stilwell: "Well, you know—your man here says he bit his finger—and of course when people begin to bite other people's fingers —by Gad you know! But—he was dining here you know and—of course—you—you will have to make your own investigations you know."

Patten: (promptly) "Of course; I see." (he turns to the Serjt.) "Does he speak English, Serjeant?"

Serjt. B.: "I don't know, sir. I've only heard him swear and it has been all in Spanish."

Patten: (addressing Mavida) "Do you speak English?"

Mavida: "None of your beesness."

Patten: "Thank you, I thought you did. Well then, I have a few serious words to speak to you. Your force has been surrendered by your superior in the city of Santiago who has surrendered the entire Spanish force in the Province of Santiago de Cuba. It is thus clear that he has surrendered you——. A colonel inclusive so to speak. Now I'm here with a force of American cavalry guarding and bringing some stores for the people in the town and—really you ought to behave yourself you know."

Stilwell: (interpolating) "I have always found Don Mavida a gentleman and I'm sure you can trust—but still if it's true that he bit the Serjeant's finger you know, by Gad——"

Lucy: "Oh, it can't be possible that Don Patricio really bit the poor man's finger?"

Marjorie: "No! no! the idea is outrageous."

Serjt. B.: "But—he did!"

Patten: (formally to Marjorie) "I am sorry but the Serjeant's communications are always reliable. I do not think he would have the genius to invent such a mishap for himself."

Stilwell: "Well, you know, it is incredible that I should have a guest who would bite another man's finger.—Now if he had punched him——"

Serjt. B.: (heatedly) "If he had—why——"

Patten: "Stop it, Serjeant."

Thorpe: (laughing) "What a strange way to conduct military operations."

Lucy: (to Thorpe) "Oh, what are they going to do to him, please?"

Thorpe: (deferentially) "Why, I wouldn't worry if I were you. I suppose Patten will just take and sort of naturally run him off the face of the earth."

Lucy: "Oh, that's in the American language. I want to know whether it will hurt."

Thorpe: (gently) "What? To be run off the face of the earth? Why no, I don't suppose so. Don't you be worried. I'll keep an eye out."

Patten: (addressing Mavida) "I know perfectly well that it would be impossible for you to disobey the orders of your superiors."

Mavida: (quietly) "What are you going to do with me?"

Patten: (slowly) "Technically you are a prisoner of war and I expect that you will march your battalion into Santiago and take ship for Spain with the others."

Mavida: "Yes officially I am given to my enemies but actually I and my battalion can still fight for our honor."

Patten: "I thought that was what you were doing in the next room."

Mavida: "I will tell you with much clear, that I will not march my men to Santiago and deliver my honor into the hands of your accursed nation."

Patten: "You will sooner or later. We don't want your honor, particularly but we are somewhat serious about having you."

Mavida: "Sir, you talk as if you had many mens at your command."

Patten: "Well, I've got—a few. I'm not here to fight you. I'm here to distribute stores to the reconcentrados. As I said, I tell you plainly I have some men and—mark you—I'm going to let you run off home, but don't you come shooting in this particular locality because if you do—many things might happen and most irregular proceedings would occur."

Mavida: "Sir, I shall bring my battalion against you as soon as I can reach my subordinates."

Serjt. B.: (suavely) "Of course, sir, as far as reaching his subordinates is concerned——"

Patten: "Of course." (he addresses Mavida) "But to me you are simply a man who has been officially surrendered and you do not appeal to me as an addition to the baggage. So you trot along and behave yourself."

Mavida: (furiously) "I shall attack——"

Patten: (interrupting) "Oh, no you won't. Run along."

(exit Mavida.)

Marjorie: "Oh, but he will."

Patten: "Well if he does, I suppose he will be able to manage it somehow."

(CURTAIN)

ACT II

SCENE: same.
TIME: daybreak, next morning.
(Patten discovered having breakfast alone.
After an interval—enter Marjorie. Patten arises
hurriedly with his napkin in his hand)

Patten: "Oh, it seems I'm taking a tremendous advantage of you in accepting your invitation to breakfast at day-light. I didn't expect to see anybody down——"

Marjorie: (simply) "I couldn't sleep."

Patten: "I'm very sorry. Was it the—was it the—the—possibility?"

Marjorie: "Yes. I feel sure that he will fight with you. He is a very determined man."

Patten: "Is he?"

Marjorie: "Yes. Of course a lot of these stories of cruelty are exaggerated, but then there is something in them, you know—more or less."

Patten: (insidiously) "You mean that perhaps it is possible that you may have some small cursory interest in my welfare?"

Marjorie: (hastily) "Not at all."

Patten: "Oh,—(impudently)—I thought that I might have been honored by some part of your consideration."

Marjorie: "You were entirely mistaken. You are impudent."

Patten: "You don't mean to say that you warned me about that Spanish colonel on—on simply human ground? I thought you did it because we were—cousins you know, or something like that."

Marjorie: (she sees that he is teasing her; she speaks sharply) "I'm very sorry to admit that I thought of you merely as a human being—I understand on good authority that there are many millions of human beings."

Patten: (he makes a sudden submissive bow in which there is no derision) "I am glad to be considered among those whom you recognise in existence."

Marjorie: "But I do not know—I do not know whether it is proper to admit you quite that far."

Patten: (submissively) "It would of course be a great concession on such short acquaintance." (again insidious and impudent) "Of course if you mean that it would please you that this Colonel Mavida should come to no harm through D Troop of the 20th. Cavalry——"

Marjorie: "I can't understand you."

Patten: "Well it would be hard to keep from shooting him if he tries to rush the sugar mill. But then (insinuatingly) I might prevail on my men to miss him somehow. You don't want him killed, I judge?"

Marjorie: (indignantly) "It is nothing to me whether he is killed or no."

Patten: (serenely) "Oh, then we shall kill him."

Marjorie: (aghast) "Oh, no! no! no! I didn't mean that. You mustn't kill him."

Patten: "Well then I understand that you make a personal request for the life of this Spanish colonel."

Marjorie: (ingenuously) "Do I?"

Patten: "Why of course you did. You request that I should take particular pains to preserve Colonel Mavida. I look at the matter in a broad way and I say that if the preservation of this invaluable Colonel Mavida is of special importance to you, I shall try my best to do as you wish."

Marjorie: (after deliberation; strainedly) "Well—it is of importance."

Patten: (after a pause) "Of special importance?"

Marjorie: (abruptly) "Yes."

Patten: "Oh, * * * I daresay I can manage it somehow."

Marjorie: "Of course you know this Colonel Mavida will do even as he announces."

Patten: (suavely) "I have no doubt but what he is the most excellent of men. For my part I shall not be surprised if he does about twice as much as he announces."

Marjorie: "He is extremely dangerous—really."

Patten: (abruptly) "I understand what you mean but if he gets within my line of fire at fair range, I don't see what I'm going to do about it."

Marjorie: "You don't understand at all. I mean—(hesitates; and then rapidly) I mean—here you are sitting down quietly at breakfast and at any moment he might be down upon you like rain."

Patten: "Well, previous to the rain there will be heard some picket-shooting from the north, east, south and west and from any other cardinal point of the compass which I may happen to have forgotten."

Marjorie: (stiffly) "I understand your type, now. You're one of those young officers who have just left school."

Patten: "Oh, no; I've just come apparently."

Marjorie: "Well, I hope the time is not approaching when I shall be compelled to be sorry for you."

Patten: "I don't think it is and then again it might be."

(enter Sylvester Thorpe)

Thorpe: "Good morning, Miss Stilwell. Hullo Patten."

Marjorie: "Good morning, Mr. Thorpe. Where's your note-book?"

Thorpe: (looks in a puzzled way about the room) "Note book! Note book!"

Marjorie: "Yes. I always thought that war-correspondents appeared with note books and wrote in them at inconsequent times."

Thorpe: "Oh,—yes, I guess they do—only, you see, I'm new to the business."

Marjorie: "But look here, seriously, Mr. Thorpe—I do not at all know how to interfere in the affairs of men—but cannot you explain to Mr. Patten the great danger he is in?"

Thorpe: (in great amazement) "Who! Patten?"

Marjorie: (she begins as if it were her duty to explain all that she apprehends) "Yes, I've been saying to him that he is in great danger and he insists that it is a foolish—foolish—foolish——"

Thorpe: (to Patten, agitatedly) "Patten, have you no pickets out?"

Patten: (angrily) "Don't be a fool."

Marjorie: (relieved) "Oh, then you mean that you have everything arranged so nobody will be hurt at all?" (small business by Patten and Thorpe)

Thorpe: "Well—no—not exactly that."

Marjorie: (she turns in an appealing manner to Patten) "But really Mr.—Mr. Patten, I beg you to understand that Colonel Mavida is a dangerous man."

(noise without, enter Serjt. Brown)

Serjt. B.: (saluting) "Sir, a man has come in from the out-post down the road with the report that the Spaniards are advancing."

Patten: "Were they able to make out the number of the enemy, Serjeant?"

Serjt. B.: "He says, sir, that they thought it was the whole battalion of Spaniards advancing from the blockhouses and the town."

Patten: "Send word to the outpost to fall back on us, firing as they come. That is, if they need the word. The troop will occupy the sugar-mill." (a few far-away shots are heard) "Drive the wagons into the Sugar house. The door is wide enough."

(In meantime Patten and Serjeant are headlong off stage simultaneous with entrance of John Stilwell; a small volley is heard which sounds nearer than previous fire.)

Stilwell: "Oh, I say! What is this you know? Damn it, I'm not going to have a battle fought on my own place you know."

Marjorie: (panic-stricken) "Father, father you'll be killed! Don't you hear them, father! They're fighting!"

Stilwell: "Fighting, are they? I thought I heard a funny sound."

Marjorie: "Oh, it's going to be dreadful, and perhaps somebody will be killed."

(enter Lucy—precipitately)

Lucy: "Oh!—Oh!—Oh! I was looking out of my window and I heard them fighting and then seven or eight Americans came running as fast as they could and—(ingenuously)—I was awfully frightened."

Stilwell: "I hope to Heaven I've not made a serious mistake in keeping you two little people here during this war."

(the door C flies open and Patten enters)

Patten: "I'm awfully sorry but I'm about to be attacked and I thought that I would rather invite you—inasmuch as your house is of thin wood and the sugar-mill is of stone—I rather thought I would invite you—oblige you—compel you to take refuge in the sugar-mill."

(the door flies open, a corporal appears)

Corporal Mulligan: "Lieutenant, they're on us."

(*CLOSE OF SCENE*)

SCENE II

Scene: Interior of sugar-mill. Open windows L and back stage. These windows are long and wide. Each window is occupied by four or five American soldiers. The floor is cluttered with haversacks. From time to time can be heard the sing of bullets entering the deep windows. A man is hit in the arm. He sits down quietly on the floor of the sugar-mill and binds up his arm as best he can. The Americans have not yet opened fire. Enter, R, Patten.

Patten: (sternly) "Use the cut-off. Don't let me hear any magazines."

(enter John Stilwell)

Stilwell: "Well, look here, you know, this is a devil of a funny business. I don't quite understand. I've got a plantation here you know which is worth £23,000. Of course if you want to fight on it, I suppose you will but——"

Patten: "Where are your daughters?"

Stilwell: "They are right behind me."

(enter Marjorie and Lucy.)

Patten: (advancing upon Marjorie and Lucy) "Oh, please—will you lie down? I can't bear to see you stand up. One can't tell what might happen. Please lie down." (the last words were addressed particularly to Marjorie)

Marjorie: "Lie down?"

Patten: "Oh, of course, I didn't mean exactly to lie down—but—if you could manage in some way to sort of—get your head below the line of fire—of course that's what I mean."

(Marjorie, Lucy and John Stilwell seat themselves upon the floor of the sugar-mill; the firing has continued steadily but in skirmishing shots; Patten walks along the line of his men; he exits R but returns immediately.—Finally there is a lull in the firing; he returns to the group of three seated on the floor of the sugar-house)

Patten: "I am afraid that it is our friend of last evening who is making us this little trouble."

Marjorie: "Oh, but nobody is hurt?"

Patten: "I don't know whether they are hurt or not but two of my men have been hit. They failed to say whether or not they were hurt."

Lucy: "But don't you think we are all going to be killed?"

Patten: "Well, I don't know. Of course it's possible.—But I'm sure they wouldn't kill you anyhow. Of course they might kill me you know——"

Marjorie: "No, but why would they kill you?"

Patten: "Oh, I don't suppose there would be any particular reason —they might do it simply as a matter of course—but then you know when I have D Troop playing away in a sugar-mill, I don't anticipate death to any great extent."

Marjorie: "D Troop? What do you mean by D Troop? Do you mean those men there?"

Patten: "Yes, I mean those men there. They are all I've got in the world. I own them as you might own a diamond necklace. They may be no good but—I hope they may be able to protect you from any slight inconvenience."

Stilwell: "Look here, when's this thing going to stop, you know?"

Patten: "Well the firing up to the present has merely indicated that an attack is beginning. I apprehend that after the attack begins I may be able to get an idea of when it's going to stop."

Stilwell: "But I thought this was the attack."

Patten: "You have been misinformed. This is the introduction. Else, much as I would like it, I could not be here. The enemies' advance are firing from three hills which I have already noted and then of course as a detail your house is on fire."

Stilwell: (uprising in great rage; thunderously) "Sir, my house on fire?"

Patten: "Pardon me; your house is on fire through the inability of your friend to understand that he has been surrendered. I would order out my men to save what were possible if it were not for the fact that they would probably be killed in doing so."

Stilwell: "You are quite right. Really you know I—I—I wouldn't like to play the goat and if the house is burning down by Gad let it burn down."

Patten: "Thank you very much."

Stilwell: "I don't mean you know that I won't make a big claim against the American government—of course it is a very rich government—but by Gad when you come to think that he bit the Serjeant's finger—it's different all round you see."

Patten: "Well of course I would understand what you mean by that but I want you to understand a matter far more important than your attitude towards me or my attitude toward you. The simple strange fact is that I and my 36 men have to fight for our lives."

Stilwell: (politely) "And of course I and my daughters are unavoidably involved in this."

Patten: "I think *I* may say unavoidably. Colonel Mavida might prove unable to use the word."

Stilwell: "Well, we're in it. And we'll have to play the game. And —I don't know—but I suppose the best way to play a game is to play it the best way you can."

Patten: (with feeling) "Of course you understand that it is far from my wish that you are caused the slightest annoyance."

Lucy: "Not in the least, Mr. Patten. I think Colonel Mavida is a regular wretch to come here and fight you without any warning."

Patten: "Oh, no, not at all."

Lucy: "And when he knows that he might hurt somebody."

Patten: "Oh, well, it's all right."

Stilwell: "But look here, he is shooting at you. Why don't you shoot at him?"

Patten: "Oh, this shooting is of no matter. I'd rather wait."

Marjorie: "It isn't? Why I thought this was a battle."

Patten: "Oh, no."

Lucy: "Mr. Patten, when it is a really-truly battle, will you let me know? I don't want to be frightened over a little—er—popular amusement, you know, but of course if a really-truly battle comes, I'd like to be told about it."

Patten: (bowing) "I'll make a point of it."

(enter Serjeant Brown)

Serjt. B.: "Lieutenant, they're coming down through those trees at the other end." (exit Patten and Brown R. Stilwell, Marjorie and Lucy are seated on some low things C.)

Lucy: "I wish that nice Mr. Thorpe would come and tell us when it is a really-truly battle."

(a voice is heard without R)

Voice: "Eight hundred yards! Use the cut-off! Fire at will—Fire!!" (a noise of shooting, agitation of the girls. Enter Serjt. Brown.

He prowls along the line of men. Some of the men have turned their heads to look back of them at that part of the sugar house that is now supposed to be more severely attacked.)

Serjt. B.: "What are you looking at? You want to see it do you? Your own affairs are not enough for you, eh?—You've got to get busy with other people's? Don't let me catch a man of you turning his head again." (He scolds vigorously in pantomime. The pop of Mausers—the long mellow thudding of Krag-Jorgensens —business by the Stilwells. Enter Thorpe R)

Thorpe: "Oh, here you are. Patten told me to come and tell you that it was really nothing—so far."

Lucy: "Why! Isn't it a battle yet?"

Thorpe: (frankly) "Well, I think it is, but Patten is a man of peculiar ideas."

Marjorie: "Have they hurt any of the Spaniards, Mr. Thorpe?"

Thorpe: (gently) "Er—I don't know, Miss Stilwell. Er—some of them acted as if they were rather hurt."

(enter Patten hurriedly. He is dirty and a trifle disheveled. Pays no heed to Stilwells.)

Patten: (loudly, resolutely) "Now men, here's where they are going to make their main attack. Sight for 300 yards. But don't use the magazine until I tell you. Now!—hold it on them—Fire!!"

(The rattle of fire. The men buckle up to the six window sills and fire carefully. Big business. Men shot here and there. The roar increases, indicating the close approach of the Spaniards.)

Patten: (yelling) "Magazines. Point blank."

Serjt. B.: (yelling) "Magazines. Point blank."

Thorpe: (coolly drawing revolver and holding it on his knee) "Well here they come." (The Stilwells look at him in horror. Fight continues; suddenly Patten jerks his whistle from his pocket and blows. The firing ceases entirely after a few scattered shots indicative of men who have been too excited to pay heed to the whistle.)

Patten: (calling out loudly) "Steady now men. They are going to palaver." (he mounts a window-sill and calls out L) "Come on, you won't be hurt." (a pause) "What can I do for you?"

Voice: (from without) "I have the honaire to present the compliments of Colonel Mavida of the 206 Battalion of the Spanish Army. He would like to know if you are ready to surrender."

Patten: "Why no! I hadn't thought of it."

Voice: (from without) "Then Colonel Mavida of the 206 Battalion of the Spanish Army is very sorry, but he will have to continue the battle."

Patten: "Why of course."

Voice: "Then you will not yet surrender? You will continue ze battle?"

Patten: "Yes, I—I think so. You tell the colonel I will let him know when I'm through."

Voice: "Colonel Mavida wishes to say that because you have taken prisoner three of his English friends he will spare no American at the end of the battle."

Stilwell: (moves to window beside Patten) "No! no! That is a mistake. We're all right here. We're not prisoners. You tell the Colonel not to worry."

Patten: "If Colonel Mavida guarantees the safe conduct of the three non-combatants, I will of course agree not to fire until they have passed his lines."

Thorpe: (hurriedly to Marjorie and Lucy) "Look here, you had much better be in here having the Spaniards shoot at you than to be out there having *these* men shooting at you."

Lucy: "And anyhow after all the trouble that dear Lieutenant has taken and all those men bleeding and—everything."

Marjorie: "Oh, I hope Father won't consent."

Stilwell: (calling out the window) "Thank you very much but we'll just stay here and sit tight." (Patten bows to Stilwell)

Patten: (calling through the window) "I shall withhold my fire until the flag of truce has disappeared, when I shall conclude that hostilities have been resumed."

Lucy: (to Thorpe) "Oh, now you are all going to be killed because we are here with you."

Thorpe: "But it doesn't matter, really."

Lucy: "What, that you will all be killed?"

Thorpe: "Oh, no. I mean—we would like to do anything you know to oblige you."

Marjorie: "Well I will tell you how. (strenuously) *Beat them!*"

Thorpe: (calling out to Patten who is busy looking from the window) "Patten!"

Patten: (impatiently) "What?"

Thorpe: "Miss Stilwell requests that you beat them."

Patten: "Oh, thank you. I daresay I will be able to manage it somehow. It is very kind of Miss Stilwell to trouble herself on our account."

Stilwell: (turning from window) "Since I found out that he bit that soldier's finger, my opinions have been changing."

Patten: (suddenly) "Look out, now! Use the magazine! Fire at will—Fire!"

(The fighting is resumed. From time to time men fall. Light smoke. Chatter of Krag-Jorgensens. Pop-pop-pop of Mausers. Song of bullets. * * * Suddenly Patten winces. He looks at his left arm.)

Lucy: "Oh, he's hit."

Marjorie: "Oh——" (She advances upon Patten who continues to attend his business)

Patten: (to his men) "Now take it coolly. They'll never get that charge home."

Marjorie: (to Patten) "Let me bind it, will you?"

Patten: (waving her away without looking) "Pardon me. You are in danger. Please get down. (to his men) Look at that squad sneaking in the tall grass there, Mulligan."

(He walks along his men followed by Marjorie with a handkerchief)

Marjorie: (finding a temporary pause) "Please, let me tie it up."

Patten: (seeing her) "Oh,—pardon me. Yes—if you care to. (she begins) You may find it amusing."

(Brief exchange between Marjorie and Patten. Enter Serjt. B. on a run R)

Serjt. B.: (breathless) "Lieutenant, we can see four mounted men on a hill that way (pointing R) and they look——"

Troopers on stage: (yelling) "Ammunition. Ammunition. Good God, can't you give us ammunition."

Patten: (yelling toward R) "Ammunition there."

Serjt. B.: (yelling toward R) "Ammunition. Ammunition."

(Enter two men with regulation box 1000 cartridges. They drop box on stage and it breaks open. Men from firing line grab feverish handfuls. Close pop of Mausers)

Stilwell: "God help us, this *is* a fight."
Lucy: (wailing) "I don't want to die. Oh, I don't want to die."
Marjorie: "Lucy—Lucy—poor little sister."

(A distant bugle is heard calling the charge for United States cavalry)

Serjt. B.: (leaping in air) "I can name the man that blew that bugle."
Patten: (turning hastily to Marjorie) "It's all right now. Here come some friends of mine."

(A crescendo roar and thud of many hoofs sweeping past the sugar mill. One or two hoarse orders. Shots. Grand excitement in sugar house.)

Patten: (*shouting*) "All ready to double out now. Magazines full —Charge."

(Troopers led by Patten leap through windows. Stilwell, Marjorie and Lucy crowd up to a window-ledge)

Lucy: "Oh—oh—look at those men on horses."

XXXIII. PLANS FOR NEW NOVEL

Plans for New Novel.

WRITE Stokes full description of project. Ask Will and Stokes to get books on subject Rev. War. Ask Will look in Father's library and send any books devoted to the period of Rev. War. Write sec. N.J. Historical society. Make point joining N.J. historical society. Ask Will about any of Father's papers, recalling to his mind an essay which Father must have written in 1874 called, I think, "The history of an old house." Ask him to borrow the essay for me explaining that it can be typewritten and the original sent home again. Recall to Will's mind a certain book in father's library called, I think, "The N.J. historical collection." Also remind him of the life of Washington, which I believe was the property of our sister Agnes. Write letters to all the men whom I think could help me. This list to include Henry Cabot Lodge, the librarian of Princeton Col., the president of the N.J. branch of the sons of the American rev. etc. Here in England collect the best histories of that time and also learn what British regiments served in America also what officers who served published memoirs; get books if possible. This will be difficult and it will become necessary to write to various people who might know.

XXXIV. PLANS FOR STORY

Plans for Story

POSSIBLE opening chapter, Time 1775—scene an Inn at Elizabeth N.J. People talking over the situation. Their attitude. Strong Tory element. Patriots bitter. Loud words. Their denunciation by old Stephen Crane. For theme see Geo. Bernard Shaw's Napoleon, as quoted in N.Y. *World*. As American infantry use the sixth N.J. regiment of the line, Col. Wm Crane. Use him as chief character, making young Jonathan Crane a minor string. Emphasise Hessians strongly. Look up dates, appearance and conduct of French troops. Make picture of marching British army as it passed Stephen Crane's house when he lay dying. Battle of Monmouth probably central dramatic scene. Find out if Lord Chatham's speeches were known in colonies soon after deliverance. Read Fenimore Cooper's "Spy." Pay no great heed to the dress of the people or to their manner of speech. Ask Will about the vegetation in the northern part of N.J., the names of the familiar trees and shrubs. Might have young Howard Crane off to sea with John Paul Jones and let him turn up in last few chapters as a sort of a benign influence. Study carefully the mood of the N.J. people with the idea that they were not very keen upon rebellion, showing great influence of Crane family in carrying the revolution through. Make some people wag their heads, declaring what a desperate business it will be and make some others treat it lightly saying it will be over in a few weeks. Make no distinction of diction save a use of what might be called biblical phraseology. Stephen Crane rather old, venerable, grey haired, imposing, calm. (Find out age at this time.) Make William Crane handsome, alert, slight but strong, a bit of a dandy, anxious for the conflict, in love with a girl in the neighborhood, natural leader, admired and respected by the farmers. Mention incident in which some Englishman—a magistrate or a magnate of some kind—offended him. Make Jonathan simple-minded, honest lad who gains his devotion to truth and honor mainly through his father's influence. Read D[r]. Weir Mitchell's last book. In describing battle of Monmouth discard the Mollie Pitcher story as being absurd and trivial. Point out in some way that Americans were excessively willing to meet the British in pitch battles whereas that was not their best policy at all. Their policy was to make guerilla warfare; vide the Cubans against Spain and the Philo's against Americans. On second thoughts this was because of the stability of the American home. It was a house; not a hut and if the inhabitants fled from it to the hills or wood they left behind them considerable material property. Introduce Henry Fleming's grand-father as first farmer.

XXXV. THE FIRE-TRIBE AND THE PALE-FACE: PLAY

"The Fire-Tribe and the Pale-Face."

SCENE: The Council-hut of the Fire tribe. A fire burns smokily in centre. Thirteen chieftains and old men are squatting in a circle. A long silence.

First chieftain:— "We wait!"
Others:— "We wait!"

(a long silence.)

First chieftain:— "We wait thee, O, Catorce."
Others:— "We wait thee, O, Catorce."

(a long silence. Enter Catorce C)

Catorce:— "I come."
Others:— "We see."
Catorce:— "And would ye hear my words of the new pale-face?"
Others:— "We listen, O, Catorce."
Catorce:— "May the god give me speech."
Others:— "May the god give thee speech, O, Catorce."
Catorce:— "Behold! chieftains, I journeyed into the land of white-faces to see what had been wrought upon our masters of Rostina by these new white warriors—and Rostina was as a man flattened to the earth by a blow of the war-club and my heart leaped at the sight. The olden enemies of my people were flatwise to the ground. Then I looked upon the new whitefaces. I had thought them to be as tall as our pines and mightier than the sword-flame in the sky for they had conquered the warriors of Rostina and we know the warriors of Rostina. Lo! the white-faces of Rostina have made our hearths bloody because we have gone there to warm our wounds. They have been myriad and we have been a handful but we know that they are men because sometimes they have fought us in equal numbers, well and decently. But I did not find that the new whitefaces shone with power. You sent me to learn of the new comers because you knew of the blood-friend which I have in the big city of the whitefaces. I speak now of what mine eyes have seen."
Others:— "Speak on, O, Catorce."
Catorce:— "The new whitefaces are not grand but they are most strange. Mine eyes saw their warriors standing in line lifting crystal things filled with a mysterious coloured water to their lips and this coloured water after they had taken much, made them joyful but always it seemed that their legs became more and more useless and then I saw one warrior who brought his hands heavily down upon the white part of a certain instrument and this instrument gave forth curious sounds which filled me with terror for the like of which had never been heard before and thereupon other warriors gathered there all cried out in a chant. To my blood friend, I said: "Of what do they

sing?" My bloodfriend answered: "They sing of a woman" and I was ready to run away but I remembered the Council of the chieftains and what ye bid me do. And so I stayed and I bid my bloodfriend tell me the words of this song of the new palefaces. And he answered that it told their longing for a certain woman who was called "Annie", and to the hut of this woman they desired to return. I asked my bloodfriend why it came to pass that all these warriors cared for this woman and why they could sing their love song all in company without the shine of a knife being seen? And he answered me that some of the ways of the whitefaces were like the dreams which are dreamed by a sick-man. And we passed from this place because I had the wisdom of my people which says that woman is but a trinket and thus I knew that the new palefaces were fools for they had not the wisdom of my tribe which knows that the wolf-teeth in a warrior's ears are more than foolish eyes turned toward him in the dusk."

(name)

Name:—"We will roll these woman lovers down the cheeks of our mountains like widows' tears."

Catorce:—"Not so, O, name. Down from our mountains we rolled our olden enemies once—twice—thrice—and then—we rolled them no more. And they sat upon our shoulders and they bid us fetch & carry and they set above us a white chieftain who gave the law."

Others:—"Aye, they set above us a white chieftain who gave the law."

Name:—"My knife has eyes and it will be able to see the throat of the first whiteface."

Catorce:—"Aye, O, Name. Your knife has eyes as my heart might know but you little understand the whitepeople. The white-woman bears no children. She sows seed in the field and they spring up, eager to rob. Our women suffer the travail and in pain bring forth a little warrior. Listen! My bloodfriend took me to a man and this man had a curious picture and on a certain part of this picture was a writing which they told me was the name of our village and inclosing this village was a square patch of green which they said was the country of our tribe.

And on this patch of green was written a name in red pigment. I thought that this must be the sign of a river for I had been told how to understand these curious pictures but they told me that it was the name of our new white chieftain."

Others:— "Our new white chieftain?" (moan)

Catorce:— "Aye, our new white chieftain—and he brings with him his small band and they have with them the flame-lances which speak from far."

(uneasiness in circle)

Somebody:— "And is this chieftain like unto our old masters? They gave us blankets and curious things with wheels which were of no service to us. And when the snow-devil came they gave us more blankets, and food."

Catorce:— "He is a young man and he may not have blankets & food to give to us."

Name:— "Does he bear himself like a warrior?"

Catorce:— "No, he is a young man with hair like an autumn sunset and upon his face are small spots which I can liken to nothing unless they be like autumn leaves sprinkled on white ground. I asked my bloodfriend to explain these curious marks and he answered that the white man called them: "freckles". And they were charms against being killed in battle."

Name:— "And did he smile?"

Catorce:— "He was a grave young chieftain and never smiled."

Others:— "Good!"

Name:— "He comes soon?"

Catorce:— "He comes."

Name:— (jumping up) "O, Catorce I speak."

Catorce:— "O, Name you speak." (Catorce takes seat in circle)

Name:—"O chieftains, we know the whiteface. We know that he has power because we have felt his engines and put our hands against his bayonets. We have seen. We have seen again—and once more again him come to us and at first there is bloodshed (our bitter bloodshed where we have lost our sons—and our sons are our drops of blood) and then we find a white man who sits above us and overturns the laws of the councils. Are our laws bad? You can look at the stones that rot at the side of the village street and see that we have been a tribe for 2,000 years.

Is it then possible that this paleface who hardly has a mother, can come to us and deal new laws which are better than the laws of our tribe? A tribe may not exist, for long, without good laws. But here we stand with a history written on the stones. These whitefaces have made some machines and for this, they tell us, that we should be governed in the hills by a whiteface. I cry out to the Fire God! (commotion) I speak to the Fire God. I ask him: 'O Father of life, of war, of love, behold there comes against us a heathen people, hung with mechanical devices, and we turn ourselves toward thee. We plough with the root of a tree; we grind our corn with a

XXXVI. THE FIRE-TRIBE AND THE WHITE-FACE: SPITZBERGEN TALE

The Fire-Tribe and the White-Face.

Stephen Crane.

THE victorious Spitzbergen army lay at the capital of Rostina. The beaten king remained, grieving, in a tightly-closed palace while his ministers strove to wring better terms from the cold inexorable Spitzbergen generals. The police of the capital had vanished into civilian attire and parties of the foreign infantry patrolled the streets. The seats of the magistrates had been taken by curt young officers. But it was plain that the hotel-keepers and cab-drivers were reaping a revenge. They put up the prices of everything so high that the air seemed filled with little balloons.

A party of officers of His Spitzbergen Majesty's 12th Regiment of the Line were seated in a great cafe in the city, drinking cognac while the waiters slowly robbed them.

"This is no good for me," said Timothy Lean, a new captain. "I was never meant to be a policeman. I have been padding these streets and brow-beating the people until I am sick of it. I had fun, though, this morning. A fight started on the edge of my district and I was going toward it, wondering which man would win, when I saw Travers of the 88th, whose district adjoins mine, charging down toward the men. I called out to him that the fight was in my district and he said no-it-wasn't. We disputed this point and the fight proceeded. Finally he offered to bet me five dollars that the man in the red sash would win. I took the bet and my man won. The beaten man tried to run away through Travers' district but Travers nabbed him and swore he would keep him in jail until his hair turned white. I gave my man a dollar and told him not to fight anymore. It was against the law, I pointed out."

"You're a good policeman, Tim," said the mid-major lazily. "I advise you to ask for an appointment as chief of police. This city would then become gay."

An orderly clanked in, saluted, and stood at attention, waiting to be asked what ailed him. It turned out that his disease was a peremptory invitation for Captain Lean to call on Colonel Sponge commander of the 12th. As Lean arose, the adjutant of the regiment chuckled loudly. "I know your fate, my boy."

"What is it?" asked Lean, opening his eyes wide.

"Oh, nothing, nothing, nothing," replied the airy adjutant. "Only, take my advice and don't burn your fingers. Mark that! Don't burn your fingers!"

"Don't burn my fingers?" said Lean, opening his eyes wider.

"Don't burn your fingers," said the adjutant, full of meaning but sententious.

Lean pedalled away on a hired bicycle, sturdily climbing the hill upon which lay the camp of the Twelfth. Passing along headquarters' row he saw the half of a cot and a pair of fat legs sticking out of a tent. Colonel Sponge was taking his afternoon rest but he aroused at sight of Lean. He wasted little time in preliminaries.

"You know, of course, we are going to annex the whole Eskelopo Province to pay us for having thrashed these people. Well, one part of the province is all great grand mountains and—up there is your home."

"Yes, sir," said Lean.

"They have made me governor of a district up there, about two hundred miles long and forty miles wide. It contains tremendous peaks and about twenty warring tribes of copper-coloured people. It will be the business of the Twelfth to police them and to that end two battalions will be split into details. Now, there is a certain tribe away off in the most God-forgotten corner of these hills whom I have been especially warned to watch. They are fire-worshippers and it is believed that after a successful raid upon their enemies, they celebrate the fact by feasting on boiled prisoners. It will be your duty to take your company and go up there and preside over the destinies of this interesting tribe."

"It sounds very enticing, sir," said Lean.

"Yes, I know. But I trust you, Lean, and I thought you were the best man in the regiment for the thing."

"Oh, I didn't mean it that way, sir. I think I would like it greatly. Do they muster many fighting men?"

"Not more than one hundred. But from what I can learn, they are a very * * peculiar one hundred. The strength of your company is about fifty, isn't it?"

"Forty-seven, sir, with two on the sick-list."

"Well, you have enough men. These people largely fight with spears and knives. You can easily control with your force if you manage it correctly."

"Yes, sir."

"Don't let your men run after the tribe's women."

"I know about that, sir."

"It will be fatal if you do."

"Yes, sir."

"I depend upon you to go with your company and dominate a tribe of embittered and war-like savages and you must be to them the white chieftain, the paramount chieftain."

"Yes, sir."

"It requires management."

"Yes, sir."

"They may kill you in some subtle fashion and then you will be boiled prisoner. I want you to understand——"

"Yes, sir, I understand."

"Take a good position over-looking the town, if there is one, and keep your men close."

"Yes, sir."

"Such people always wait until you are bored and yawn—they always wait until you yawn; then they strike."

"Yes, sir."

"And don't let your men run after the tribe's women."

"No, sir."

The anxious colonel fore-told a hundred things which might not happen and disclosed how he would guard against them. "And," said he at last, "don't let your men run after the tribe's women."

"No, sir."

Chapter II

Lean had been warned early because his little column, bound to a remote point, needed much time for preparation. When the news came to the men, the two privates on the sick-list arose wrathfully in the hospital and declared that they were well and sound and further declared that they would not remain in the doctor's care for one more minute. At first, the doctor asserted his authority but they announced damnation to the authority of all doctors. Their captain needed them, they said, and they would arise and go to him if the devil blocked the way. They would take their little fevers with them, they said; they could carry their little fevers. But they could not carry the distinction of remaining in the rear when warm times loomed in the front. The doctor abused them violently. He abused them violently because he admired their point of view. He told Lean and Lean sent to them by a serjeant a brief sharp direction to lie quiet on their cots and attend to their own sickness. Afterward, there was a spell of silence. But Lean relented in two days. He went to the hospital and promised the men that they would be sent to rejoin as soon as they were officially able. Both men cried. Lean felt himself an impostor—thus to have men cry.

The Twelfth Regiment marched off into the mountains of Eskelopo and in the course of events, Lean and his company separated from the main body and took the lonely trail to the land of the fire-tribe. It was a billowy thirty miles to a place behind the heart of the unknown. Lean reflected much as he continually cast his glance here there and everywhere. Four of his men formed a little advance guard and a hundred yards in rear of them marched a body of twenty-five rifles, heading a train of twenty mules attended by hillsmen who shrilly shouted and these latter were attended by three soldiers whose duty it was to swear in a manner impartial and continuous. The column was closed by the remaining fifteen men. Lean marched at the head of the column with two native interpreters telling him lies about the surrounding country.

The shoulders of the great hills were thick with pines and streams brawled loudly in the deep valleys. The crags were grey and bold; often they hung over the trail and looked down upon the crawling expedition. A mile high in the clear blue air two eagles slowly circled.

On the evening of the third day they encamped within five miles of the village of the fire-tribe. Behind them was a history of climbing and sliding and dropping. The sense of isolation, the sense of distance from home was something startling. The men felt both like exiles and like romantic adventurers. Lean re-called to mind the deeds of the great De Soto.

He was deeply stirred by the news that he was only five miles from the place where he was to be tried in a new and strenuous way. His nerves were absolutely tranquil by this time before the prospect of a fight but they quivered at this prospect of a matching of wits, a game of intelligence. It was easy to go up against this tribe and smash them. It was another matter to rule them without asking their leave. But he was young and the blankets were warm and he fell asleep.

At the break of day, a sentry above the camp discerned a figure motionless upon an over-looking crag. The sentry worked upon himself somewhat because the figure was so appallingly still. He called the corporal of the guard and the corporal watched until he too was affected by the figure's statue-like quality. Lean was just rubbing his eyes when the corporal came to him. And the whole camp, following the glance of Lean and the corporal, turned its eyes up to the top of the crag.

The figure was that of a tall straight warrior leaning upon his spear and looking steadfastly downward at the camp. The camp trembled, trembled because this thing was like some kind of terrific emblem and it wouldn't move—it wouldn't move.

The corporal eagerly fingered the sights of his rifle. "May I take a crack at it, sir?" he asked. "I can knock it off that rock." Even then Lean noted that the corporal said, "it."

"No, no," said Lean throwing out a hand, "don't shoot him."

Then he raised his voice. "Where are those interpreters? Send an interpreter here." There was a cry for interpreters and directly one appeared from under his blankets. "Who is that fellow," said Lean pointing.

The interpreter took one look and his face went blank. Lean waited until the man could collect himself. The interpreter was not a coward but he was a serious person.

"Who is he?" said Lean.

"Sir," replied the interpreter, "it is the god of the fire-tribe!"

" 'The god of the fire-tribe!' " repeated the soldiers with wonder and with nervous laughter but the muleteers one and all fell flat on their faces and howled.

"Rubbish!" shouted Lean angrily and he seemed to be about to strike the alarmist. The man bent his neck; if he was afraid of the thing on top of the crag, he was also afraid of Timothy Lean, but one fear was greater than the other. "Sir," he said humbly, "I must say it! It is the god of the fire-tribe." The muleteers stampeded. Lean saw his whole expedition failing because of the glance of this still thing on top of the cliff. "Serjeant Harding!" he cried. A young serjeant sprang toward him. "Yes, sir?" "Shoot that damned thing!" roared Lean furiously. There was an absolute silence. The serjeant looked at the thing for a moment. Then he adjusted his sights. Slowly he raised his rifle; it came to point upward as when a man shoots at a bird in a tree. The silence grew as painful as a weight on the chest. The faces stiffened.

Crrk!

The figure on top of the cliff winced, toppled, sank to its knees, fell. A thunder burst from the men. "Got him!" A long spear came clattering and clinking down the face of the rocks. The men were elate and looked at their captain to see the gladness upon his face but evidently he failed to appreciate the business. He was suddenly as glum as an old woman at kirk. "Chase those muleteers and bring them back—some of you," he muttered.

He knew what had happened. He was coming with peace-offerings to the fire-tribe and his first step had been to order the killing of one of its warriors. Here was a truculent initial blunder which was immeasurable in its power of destruction. It was almost certain to over-turn his plans for the peaceful meeting of lions.

"It's a fine olive branch," said he to himself.

Meanwhile Serjeant Harding was speaking to appreciative comrades. "Why, when I heard the captain call for me, I knew what was wanted and I thought then that I would certainly hit it and if it was a big stone it would stand and if it was a man it would fall and I said, 'You thing up there, you had better be a stone.' Then I fired and down he went. It was easy."

Chapter III

For more than an hour, thirteen chieftains and warriors of the fire-tribe had squatted in a silent circle in their council-hut. Some pine logs burned slowly in the centre of the earthen floor and each man's gloomy and thoughtful glance was directed at the flames wrapping greasily about the wood while the smoke coiled toward a hole in the roof. The night was cold and the warriors kept their robes tight on their chests, concealing the furtive shine of dull brass ornaments. It might have been that the flame was speaking, with many gestures, so attentive were the glances and the silence.

A warrior began to rock his body to and fro. Suddenly, he wailed out, "We wait!"

The chieftains stirred; they lifted their heads. Their wild voices called out the words. " 'We wait!' "

"We wait thee, O, Catorce!"

" 'We wait thee, O, Catorce!' "

The swaying and the chanting ceased and silence came upon the council-hut. Afar off in the mountains an owl hooted a death-note.

The door of bear-skin was swept aside and a tall warrior entered the zone of faint flickering light. "I come," he said.

"We see," said the warriors.

"And would ye hear my words of the new white-face?"

The warrior who had first broken the stillness of the circle again wailed out. "We listen, O, Catorce." He was the tribe's Singer.

"May the god give me tongues."

The circle rocked and wailed. "May the god give thee tongues, O, Catorce!"

The chieftain, Catorce, roved his eye about the circle in a stern and melancholy glance. "O, chieftains," he began in a deep voice, "as ye bade me, I journeyed into the land of the white-faces to see what had been wrought upon our masters of Rostina by these new white warriors and I found that Rostina was as a man flattened to earth by a blow of the war-club. My heart sprang at the sight. The olden enemies of my people were flat-wise with the ground and there were not even dogs to heed them in council. Then I looked upon the new white-faces. I had thought them to be as tall as our king-pines for they had conquered the warriors of Rostina and we know the warriors of Rostina. The white-faces of Rostina have made our hearths bloody because we have gone to our huts to warm our wounds. They have been like leaves and we have been like the bear-claws in a warrior's necklace but we know that they are men because sometimes they fought us in equal numbers, well and decently. Wherefore, I looked upon the new white faces not in any way despising them. But I could not see their strength. It was hidden from me. They were like the warriors of Rostina to my eyes unless it be in one thing. When a Rostina warrior speaks his arms assist him, resembling two tree-branches in a wind. These new white-faces speak with lips of hide, stiffly. Do I tell of what mine eyes have seen?"

"Speak on, O, Catorce!"

"Ye who have been to the pale lands, remember that the warriors of Rostina loved the shining huts at the places where trails crossed and in these shining huts they gathered at little round stones, like altars, and at these they drank a black water. Not so, the new white-faces. Mine eyes saw their warriors erect in line in these shining huts lifting crystal vessels filled with water brown, of the color of dead pine needles. And lifting these crystal vessels, they shouted. And once again they shouted. And for the third time they shouted. And this brown water, after they had taken much, made them joyful but always it seemed that their legs became more and more like pieces of vine, strengthless, unable to hold the weight of a warrior. And I saw one who brought his hands heavily down upon the white part of a certain instrument and this instrument then gave forth loud curious sounds which filled me with dismay for the like has been heard never before. Thereupon other warriors gathered there all cried out in a chant. Now, you sent me to learn of the new warriors because you knew of the blood-friend which I have in the great pale village and to this blood-friend I said: 'Of what do they sing?' My blood-friend answered: 'They sing of a woman named "Annie".' And these sounds were such that I was ready to run away but I remembered the council of the chieftains and brave men and what ye bid me do. And so I stayed and bid my blood-friend tell me the words of the new pale-faces and he answered that it told their longing for the woman named "Annie" and to the hut of this woman they desired to return. And I asked my blood-friend how it came to pass that all these warriors cared for this one woman and why these rivals could sing their love-songs all in company without there being seen the shine of a single knife and he answered me that some of the ways of the white-faces are like the dreams of sick children. And I knew he spake truth."

A stocky warrior, upon his face a deep blue scar, suddenly arose and sprang to a point near the fire. "We will roll these people down the cheeks of our mountains like widows' tears," he hoarsely cried, half choking with rage.

Catorce had courteously given back a step for the new speaker but now he spoke, gravely. "Not so, O, Rudin. Down from our hills we rolled our ancient enemies—once—twice—thrice. And then—we rolled them no more. And they set over us a white chieftain who directed us even in the burial of our warriors who had fallen before them. This white chieftain gave us the law."

The Singer took up the sentence and chanted it. "This white chieftain gave us the law."

The others moaned. "This white chieftain gave us the law."

The warrior named Rudin, he of the blue scar, gestured sweepingly in the fire-glow. "My knife has eyes and it will be able to see the throat of the first white-face."

Again Catorce spoke in a sad and grave voice. "O, Rudin, that your knife has eyes my heart may learn but ye little understand the white faces. Their women bear no children. They sow seeds in the field and babes spring up, eager to rob. Our women suffer the pain and bring forth a little warrior but the children of the white faces are sown like grass."

Rudin again interrupted furiously. "Yes, grass, like grass! But nought can keep Rudin, a chieftain of the fire-tribe, from his grave amid slain enemies." A muttering of assent arose like the roll of drums. The eyes of the men glittered.

The Singer chanted: "Hear, O, hear! Rudin, a chieftain of the fire-tribe, goes to a grave amid slain enemies."

The warriors groaned as they swung their bodies.

"O, Rudin," answered the mournful Catorce, "listen! My blood-friend took me to a seer and this seer had a curious picture and on a certain part of this picture was a writing which they told me was the name of our village and inclosing this village was a patch of green which they said signified the country of our tribe and on this patch of green was written a name in red pigment. It was in my mind that the red pigment must be the sign of a river for my friend had taught me much of the strange pictures but they said that the red writing was the sign of our new white chieftain."

Catorce paused as a gust of anger swept around the hut, warriors leaping to their feet in fiery passion. Through the tumult shrilled the scream of the Singer. "Our new white chieftain."

"Aye, our new white chieftain," said Catorce coldly. "He brings with him his band armed as ye know."

A venerable warrior who had swayed less and sung lower than the others now waved his hand in grave disdain for so much feeling and they subsided to the circle amid a die-away rumble of growling. "O, Catorce," said the old man, "is this new white chieftain like unto our old master? He gave us blankets and food and the curious things with wheels which were of no service to us. When the snow-devils came, he gave us more blankets and food. He was a very rich man."

"Our new white chieftain is young, O, Haryid old and wise," answered Catorce, thoughtfully, "and he may not have much food to give us nor many blankets."

"Does he bear himself like a warrior," asked the aged Haryid.

"He is a young man," repeated Catorce, "and he resembles his people, they being in youth all alike since they are sown in the fields like grass. But his hair marks him. It is the colour of red wintry sun. And upon his face are small spots which I can liken to nothing. I asked my blood-friend to explain these marks and he answered that the white men called them 'freckles' and they were charms against being killed in battle."

Haryid mused and in deference to his musing the circle was silent. "And did he smile?" he asked at last.

"He was a grave young chieftain. I did not see him smile."

"Good," said Haryid in a deep voice and all the warriors seemed to marvel that the veteran chief drew some deep satisfaction from Catorce's answer. They thought it was of the old man's magic. "He comes soon?" he said.

"He comes soon, O, Haryid," answered Catorce.

Here the blue-scarred Rudin with the chest of a bullock and the temper of a leopard, sprang to his feet, frothing. "O, Catorce, I speak," he cried and at these words Catorce quietly squatted down in the circle. "O, Rudin, you speak," cried the Singer.

Rudin for a moment paced in silence about the fire. His form was crouched with ferocious emotion and his scars shone purple. He spoke, finally, in a throaty gasp. "O, chieftains, we know the white-face. We have felt the spirits, little spirits, which he sends through the air to kill us. Our hands have pushed against his spears. We have seen him come up against us once and again and again. And once and again and again we have gone like men to meet them and in battle we have shed blood that was bitter, bitter because it mattered little whether we shed it or kept it in our bodies. And then they send a white-face who sits above the chieftains, mocking even at the wisdom of Haryid, and over-turns the laws of the council so that the meetings of the council have the meaning of crows' chatter."

He paused for a time and breathed. His fierce glance roamed from face to face.

"Are our laws bad?" he demanded suddenly. "You may look at the stones that stand at the side of the village street and see that we have been a tribe as long as the sun has been a sun. Is it true that this pale-face who has even no mother can come to us and deal new laws which are better than the laws of our tribe?"

The Singer, frantic, yelled: "The pale-face has no mother."

Rudin cried on. "A tribe may not exist, for long, without good laws. But we stand with a history written on the stones. These white faces have made some death-machines and for this, they tell us, we in the hills should be ruled by a far-coming white-face. What do they desire? Wealth? We have little. Our lands? The white-faces do not live among such hills. What then do they desire? - - - - - - Our women!"

Only Catorce and old Haryid stayed immovable. The other

listeners leaped and drew their knives, howling. Rudin faced Catorce fixing him with piercing, angry eyes. "O, Catorce, you have a daughter!"

And then Catorce arose in wrath but his words still were deliberate and steady. "My daughter comes not to the councils of the chieftains," he said.

Rudin lifted his face toward the roof and stretched forth both arms straight and rigid to the finger-tips. "I speak to the god," he said in a lowered voice and solemnly.

"O, Rudin speaks to the god!"

"O, love-of-women, O, love-of-war, O, love-of-life, O, master of death, there cometh up against us a heathen people, using magic devices, and we turn to thee. We plough with the root of a tree; we grind our corn with a stone in our hands; we live under the bark of the pine; we dress in skins; we are thy simple people and—" Here Rudin's tone became a wrathful shout. "—And art thou to punish us because we have not been able to invent machines? And art thou to punish us because we have not been able to invent machines?"

After the roaring groan of the warriors had subsided, Catorce said: "O, Rudin, thy wisdom would light a wet log!" And for the remainder of that council, he said no more.

IV

Runners from the fire-tribe saw from the hills Lean's little force detach itself from the main body of the Twelfth and begin its march toward their country. They kept just in advance of it, watching everything. From time to time a runner was sent speeding to the village to make fantastic report to the council of chieftains.

A storm with thunder and lightning dwelt in the council-hut. Rudin, passionate savage, led his blood-thirsty radicals against the calm arguments of old Haryid and Catorce. The discussions of Rudin and his following were a-flame with cries that the tribe should fight to the death and always Haryid and Catorce answered icily. Day and night, the maidens sang prayers before the sacred fire on the hill-top that the tribe's blood might not be shed and Mitredes, the fire-priest, buried his head in his robes and spoke no word for three days.

Catorce's speech often quieted the turbulent ones and so his tongue was often loose in the council. The warriors could not but give him their respect as one fierce in battle, wily in diplomacy and fair in bargaining. No more could be said for any man. "Ye cry out that we should go to our death," he said in the council. "I fear no death save the death of a fool. I will not die the death of a fool. We know little of these strange new people. Let us wait to see. Let us wait to see," he repeated, looking at the Singer but the Singer lowered his chin to his breast and was silent. Catorce paused, confused. If the Singer did not chant the main phrases of an orator it meant that the orator's words were odious to a great part of the tribe. Catorce faltered back and squatted again upon the ground, but his eyes were still bold and cool.

A cry was heard from without. "O, chieftains, a warrior comes, running, and wishes to enter."

The circle cried: "O, runner, enter."

The deer-skin door was dashed to the side and a runner almost fell as he came into the hut.

The circle cried: "O, runner, speak."

"O, chieftains," said the man, puffing, "I bring bad speech in my mouth. At the breaking of day, the coming white-faces used their magic against the warrior Sinrival as he stood on the hill and the great Sinrival has gone to the happy heart of the everlasting fires."

And amid the yelling, old Haryid arose and tightened his girdle. It was the sign of preparation for war. The chieftains rushed from the council-hut, giving the news to the eager crowd of men, women and children waiting near the door.

Preparation was simple. Most of the men were ready as they stood. In five minutes nearly a hundred stalwart warriors gathered near the spot where Haryid, Catorce and Rudin were in conference. The news of the killing of Sinrival had ended all disputes. The tribe must go forth and avenge him. They had no tradition which could enable them to endure this deed. Sinrival, the great leader of the runners, the bounding deer, had been slaughtered by the foul magic of the white faces and his people would strike in answer. As the warriors filed silently and swiftly away, they heard a loud keening of women in the hut of Sinrival who had led the runners. There the crones had gathered about the widow and were keening the ancient words of despair.

Timothy Lean led his column with extraordinary caution on the march of the last five miles. His mules and his muleteers worried him exceedingly. His force was not mobile so long as these two kinds of awkward and stupid creatures were in the column. He exhorted the three men detailed for impartial and continuous swearing to re-double their violence. The column slowly wended down a mountain-side and began to cross a plain.

Suddenly, Lean saw his little advance guard flinch. From out of a thicket ahead, a savage warrior had launched himself at the four men, whirling a great knife and shrieking. The startled guard threw up their rifles and all yelled: "Halt—halt—halt——" But the man came on.

A soldier fired and the shattering bullet made the charging warrior tumble and sprawl so swiftly that he appeared to have been smitten on the head with a huge club. But on the ground he twisted and turned in his great pain and impotence while his face glared hatred and his mouth spat froth. Lean ran forward and found the corporal of the guard drawing himself up deliberately, preparatory to shooting the fallen warrior through the head and thus closing the incident. "No, don't do it," cried Lean. "We've had enough of that."

"Very good, sir," said the corporal in virtuous resignation. "It's what he deserves, sir."

"Yes, I know," said Lean. "But I want to keep him. Where is he hit?"

"In the leg, sir," answered the soldier who fired the shot.

Rudin lay gazing at them wolfishly. His leg was folded beneath him and his radius of action was defined by the sweep of his knife. He was husbanding his strength waiting for the moment when an enemy should venture within reach.

Lean looked at him, puzzled. Finally, he said: "Shoot the knife out of his hand." The pleased corporal moved with alacrity to a proper point, raised his rifle and fired. Rudin dropped the knife and looked at his hand, torn by the bullet. He had been bereft of his weapon by a further issue of the cowardly pale-face magic. He could lie there and hope that one would come within reach. He resolved to bite him.

Meantime, the corporal was walking about the prostrate warrior and addressing him in a lowered voice but considerable emphasis. "You are a nice specimen, you are, running out at people with a knife like that! So, you want to bite, eh? By god - - - - - - - - - you'd bite if I was running this game. Don't snarl! Aw!"

Lean finally thought that he had solved the problem of the wounded Rudin. He called forward some muleteers with ropes and told them to bind the warrior securely. The muleteers looked at Rudin and then began to back away from the scene, saying that they were simple honest muleteers and had no stomach for such business. The man was certainly most dangerous; he opened his mouth like a wounded panther and they did not see how it could be said that it was part of the work of simple honest muleteers to bind and make fast a terrible creature who was plainly certain to seize and kill the first man that approached him. Of course, their lives were at the disposal of the young white chieftain but they must make it clear that there was no part of the contract which had been read to them before they had engaged in this service and adventured upon this journey, which could be construed to mean that they on occasions like the present should——

"Oh," said Lean. "Shut them up. Take their ropes from them and we shall see if we cannot tie this animal." Some of the soldiers laid down their rifles and taking ropes began to walk around Rudin, making all kinds of hitches. They were prodigal in the use of line so that in time Rudin looked like a spool. As an extra precaution the corporal of the advance guard took some half-hitches around the chieftain's head and through his mouth. They bundled him upon a mule's pack saddle along with two tents and a heliograph out-fit, and the little column resumed its march.

V

The advance guard of Lean's force, moving out of some dry grass and scrub pines came suddenly upon a curious sight. They halted abruptly and as usual looked back at Lean. Lean hastened forward at the head of twenty-five men. On a small rise of ground about three hundred yards from the advance guard stood the fire-tribe drawn up for battle. It was a sombre little frieze of men outlined against the sky. Their spears stood straight.

The effect was so pathetically primitive to Lean that he groaned when he saw it. His men could clear that knoll of up-right figures with a few volleys. The warriors awaited a charge, a shock, whereas Lean had simply to order his men to sight for three hundred yards and shoot. But the destruction of the fire-tribe did not form his mission. Besides, his wretched muleteers and mules were forever on his mind. If anything happened, he invariably grew nervous with visions of all manner of stampedes. In any action, he was sure to feel that he was on the defensive. The enemy might be protecting a village of huts but he was protecting a hideously active and unreasonable village of mules.

He became excited. "Harding, tell the rear-guard to bunch the mules and close in around them. If a mule bolts, shoot him. If a muleteer bolts, let him bolt. We've only two miles more." His two interpreters stood near him. They were both trembling. The might of the Kingdom of Spitzbergen was known to them but it mattered little when men came face to face in the mountains. It was then purely a question of who won for the moment. Subsequent punitive expeditions were unlikely to interest a man who had been slain by the fire-tribe.

"We will speak with them," said Lean.

The interpreters cowered. "Sir," said one, "they are arrayed for battle."

"Oh, that don't matter," said Lean. "Come on with me. We will speak with them." He addressed a few succinct words to his serjeants. Then he moved out slowly with the two frightened interpreters. Before they had moved far, Lean saw three warriors detach themselves from the ranks of the fire-tribe and stride with dignity toward him.

The two parties halted when twenty yards separated them. "Tell them," said Lean hurriedly, "that I come in peace."

The interpreter cried out cleverly in the tribe's tongue. "O, little people, the mighty white chieftain speaks that he comes in peace, with his hands white."

It was Catorce who answered. "O, renegade to the hills and servant, your little white chieftain comes with his hands red."

"He say your hands are red," said the interpreter to Lean.

"Tell him," said Lean grimly, "that my hands are red only with the blood of those who attacked me and the hands of an officer of the great Spitzbergen chieftain are ever red with the blood of his enemies."

The interpreter puzzled for a moment as to how he should translate and then conscientiously rendered Lean's words thus: "The great white chieftain says that he is always glad when his hands are red with the blood of his enemies."

Catorce answered slowly. "Your little white chieftain had no word of us that we were his enemies and yet he has killed two of our warriors."

"He calls you always a little white chieftain," said the interpreter to Lean.

"Tell him that I am a big chieftain," said Lean.

"O, little people, the great white chieftain comes and he asks why do ye array yourselves against him since he comes in peace."

Haryid spoke. "O, little wet twig on a dead fire, tell your slave-lord that we are embattled against him because he comes with a cry of peace and yet slays two of our tribe."

"He say you kill two of their men," said the interpreter.

"Tell him," said Lean rapidly, "that I am very sorry that any such thing occurred—really, I am. Tell him I regret it very much. And, besides, we've only killed one man."

"The great white chieftain says," proclaimed the interpreter to Catorce, "that he has only killed one man."

The three listening chieftains became rigid. "And," said Haryid, "your little white chieftain thinks there is a big difference between one murder and two murders."

"He says," announced the interpreter, "you think much about two murders when you only need to think of one."

"Tell them there has been no murder," said Lean. "I came up against them with my hands stretched out."

When Catorce had heard the translation he answered: "Red hands stretched out."

" 'Red hands stretched out'," repeated the interpreter to Lean.

"No," said Lean. "Tell them I come in peace. I do not want to fight. I bring the peace of the great white master of Spitzbergen."

This was fully translated.

"O, little servant of the white face," replied Catorce, "tell your master that we are a free people of the hills. We do not understand these words which you speak as one blowing a tiny horn. Hear now the words of men! We fight here!"

"He say they fight here—now," cried the interpreter aghast.

"No," cried Lean. "Tell them they mustn't. I don't want to fight."

"The great white chieftain says that he does not wish to fight."

"Tell him, tree-toad," said Catorce, "that we asked no question concerning his wishes."

"They say," translated the man, "that they will fight now."

Lean removed his helmet and ran his handkerchief rapidly across his fore-head. These stately idiots seemed determined to ruin everything at the very beginning. He looked at them for a moment in blank despair. How to get the central idea of his position into those alien heads by means of an alien interpreter whom Lean already suspected of being an impostor and a fool—this puzzled the young man. "Tell them—tell them—I come with many presents—many presents, tell them——"

"The great white chieftain comes with many presents, some of them consisting of the large shining dollars which the men of the hills love," cried the interpreter almost tearfully.

To Lean's astonishment, the words of the interpreter seemed this time to have an effect. The chieftains looked at each other; then they were silent; then they held conference. Presently old Haryid cautiously addressed the interpreter in a sort of an aside. "And these dollars—are they of the true size and weight?" said he.

"Larger and heavier, O, chieftain," replied the interpreter unflinchingly. Then he spoke swiftly to Lean. "You have many Mexican silver dollars. I think they light the peace-fire if you give them some dollars."

But Lean would not believe the thing. "No, no, these people wouldn't sell their honor for a few tin dollars. They are warriors and gentlemen. You have misunderstood. Ask again."

Again the interpreter raised his voice. "O, little chieftains, the great white chieftain comes in peace and to prove to you that he wishes to be your friend he will give to every warrior three dollars."

The chieftains grunted; without other expression they turned their backs and walked away to the line of warriors.

"Oh, you've got it all wrong somehow," cried Lean to the interpreter. "They surely won't take money in this way."

The interpreter pled with the young Captain. "Just one minute! Just one little little little minute!"

Presently Haryid and Catorce stalked solemnly back. Catorce addressed the interpreter. "O, little outcast and tree-toad, we have held in our hands the words of your pale master. Wherefore it seems to us that they weigh too lightly. And that there may be peace between us we will speak of our desires. The white chieftain asks that we do not destroy him and his band. We make answer in regard to the shining dollars. It befits our tribe, we think, that each warrior should receive four dollars instead of three dollars and moreover it is the custom of our tribe when exacting tribute from an inferior people to demand that each mother in our tribe's huts should be paid one dollar for every man-child which she has brought into the light. In regard to these matters, the custom of our tribe cannot change. Moreover we esteem that the chieftain, Rudin, whom we now see tied amongst you, should because of this indignity be paid nine dollars. And moreover the wise and aged Haryid has raised his voice in the councils of the tribe speaking that the white-faces should not be killed. And so loud were his words that we think his mercy should be answered with seven dollars. And furthermore, I, Catorce, a chieftain of the fire-tribe have lifted my voice often to preserve these white-faces from destruction and thus it is polite that I should receive five dollars."

The interpreter did not take time to translate to Lean. "It is good," he cried hurriedly to Catorce. "The white chieftain will give from his richness and the shining dollars shall flow out."

"What are you people talking about?" demanded Lean.

"They say—" rejoined the interpreter, pathetically anxious that

Lean should not interfere. "—They say they will take about five six hundred dollars and, afterward—peace."

"No—surely not," cried Lean, his mouth open. "They won't——"

"Yes—yes—yes——" cried the interpreter frantically. "Please—please——"

"All right," said Lean suddenly. "I see." He had discovered that there was not only in the world a code of conduct but that there were codes of conduct.

Catorce spoke. "And," said he, "the new white chieftain is to us a stranger and no doubt he is a man whose tongue darts straight but our warriors are impatient and it would be better if we should receive now our shining dollars."

"Yes," said the interpreter dropping back one pace to Lean. To the latter, he explained. "They say you will give the money and there will be no fight." He told the stipulations.

"All right," said Lean. "I will give the money on one condition—I can't have them think I'm afraid."

"The great white chieftain says he is not afraid," yelled the interpreter.

Haryid and Catorce grinned broadly. "Even so," they answered.

Lean called to the rear. "Bring up that damned specie-mule." He had been given six thousand coined dollars for the payment of labor and food. Several men ran. Soon a respectable-looking mule was brought forward. Boxes were unloaded from his pack-saddle. One box was opened and bags of dollars appeared. The attending soldiers looked upon them with the scorn of men who were on active service. Dollars were of no consequence to them.

Lean poured many coins into a blanket. "Now," said he, "we will arrange for these people to come up and get their wretched money."

The news of the distribution seemed to have spread already back to the tribe's village for women were seen running. They came laughing and leaping. The stolid Spitzbergen soldiers looked upon them in silence.

At the last moment, Lean had a spasm of precautionary impulses. He did not know; he could not see; for some time he had not even thought. Then of a sudden, it struck him with great force that the whole thing was too unutterably quaint to be real, truthful, sincere. "Stop!" he cried to the interpreter who was making the dollars into small stacks. "Stop! How do I know they mean a word they say?"

The interpreter looked up in gentle surprise. "Sir, I know little of the ways of your people but here now you have this fierce tribe willing to lay aside their spears at the rate of four dollars each."

The other interpreter, who had been fuming, now broke in passionately. "Yes—yes. It is very fine. Ve-e-ry fine. But I could have made peace for two dollars to each warrior. It is very fine. This other man, this Mr Cajoles, he calls himself an interpreter but every single speech of Captain Lean's he so turned and twisted that he came near having us all murdered. He——"

"Shut your mouth, confound you," cried Lean. He turned to the first interpreter. "Here, Cajoles—I know your name now—call up this galaxy of imperishable heroes and we will pay them their wages."

The majestic warriors stalked forward to receive their bribes. Lean was the one who felt degraded. They bore themselves like monarchs. Lean handed each man four silver dollars. Each man then waited before Lean for a moment while he carefully bit each dollar. Then he grunted and moved away.

At the end of the file of warriors moved the released Rudin, borne in a litter, Catorce and old Haryid. Lean looked curiously at Rudin and he was rewarded. Rudin sullenly took his nine dollars, bit them, and as he was being carried away he shot one quick hateful glance into Lean's face which informed the young officer that this wounded chieftain would not readily forget the past.

After Rudin came Catorce and Haryid. They took their dollars and thrust them into their shirts but they did not bite them.

Lean was then besieged by a great crowd of laughing scornful noisy women and girls. The interpreter said that they were all crying out they were the mothers of many men children. A slim little thing, not more than eleven years of age, brazenly faced Lean, holding up three fingers.

"What does she mean?" asked Lean nervously.

Both interpreters grinned. "She says," they replied in chorus, "that she is the mother of three men children."

Lean arose hastily from where he had been squatting on a blanket. His face was very red. "Here, serjeant," he growled. "You take charge of this business." And he retreated to the neighborhood of the pack-mules until the fire-tribe, dancing and shouting with joy and pride, had begun their return journey.

He now despised the fire-tribe. For him, there was but one standard of conduct in the world. All its laws were very clear to him. And they named many unpardonable crimes. These unpardonable crimes could forever damn a man or a class in every conceivable direction. The fire-tribe's virtue was a failure. They were men of no character. He settled that point clearly in his mind and his young white face took on an expression of contempt. He decided to treat them as children. They were without doubt rather brave men but surely they could always be controlled either through their superstitions or their immense vanity. No man could be entitled to respect who would sell his honor for four Mexican dollars.

When the column resumed its march, he spoke some of his mind to the interpreters. "I cannot imagine a people so low as to take money for a thing like that. It seems incredible."

The interpreters opened their eyes wide. "Why, sir?" they asked.

"Because they sold their honor," said Lean stiffly.

"But they didn't!" cried one.

"Yes they did," snapped Lean.

The interpreters looked at each other in some pain. "The white chieftain does not understand," said one hesitatingly after a time. "These people are different. They are not the same as white men. They do not think in the same way. They have a way for themselves. It is a way of their own. It is different."

"I should think it was," scoffed Lean. "Very different indeed."

The second interpreter said: "Yes it is very different."

And the two interpreters allowed their feelings of alarm to subside because they judged from Lean's last remark that the truth had come to him. As it happened their own tribe was one whose rhetoric knew no such thing as irony.

Chapter 11

The village of the fire-tribe was under the eyes of Lean and his men. He had taken his company to the top of a small hill over-looking the village of the fire-tribe. Rifle-fire could sweep the single street. Forty feet down a steep bank was a brook of tumbling water. The one avenue of approach to the hill was so precipitous that it would remind the traveller of climbing a tree. However, the loaded mules scaled it with an ease which put the men to shame.

Arriving at the top of this hill, Lean's company dropped to the ground with the great definitive sigh of relieved labor. Prostrate men reached slowly in their tunics after pipes and tobacco. Serjeant Harding, slightly garrulous, re-told how he had shot Sinrival. There was, afterward, a time when there was no speaking and in which only the grateful breathing of the men could be heard. Lean sat alone, gazing down into the straight brown streak of the fire-tribe's village street.

There was two hours of rest and long hours of work

Appendixes

THE TEXT: HISTORY AND ANALYSIS

THE BLACK RIDERS AND OTHER LINES

The earliest piece of Crane's verse that has been preserved is the youthful *I'd Rather Have——* (106) published for the first time in the present edition from a holograph owned by Commander Melvin H. Schoberlin USN (Ret.) and dating probably from late 1879 or 1880.[1] The next appears to be *Ah, haggard purse, why ope thy mouth* (107), from December, 1892.[2] The matter is uncertain but the probabilities are that the two Notebook poems among prose drafts dating from 1893–94 were written after *The Black Riders* group. The earlier of the two as inscribed in the Notebook is *Little birds of the night* (108) in a complete draft form;[3] the opening words of the first line of *Once a man clambering to the house-tops* (83) follow in the Notebook a draft of "In a Park Row Restaurant" printed in the *New York Press* in considerably revised form on October 28, 1894, and precede

[1] Crane's father died on February 16, 1880. The poem, if occasional, could have been anticipatory of Christmas 1879, or after the event. Commander Schoberlin privately communicates that his notes read 1880(?) since it seems established that Crane had a dog until the family left Port Jervis: "If we could date the death of Solomon, a sad-eyed retriever, it might help." If the poem is original, as it presumably is, the question is whether Crane could have dissociated himself so completely in it from his father's death if written for Christmas of 1880.

[2] Corwin Linson writes, referring to the winter of 1892: "Some things we knew because they were so, one of which was that we had to eat. Other things we knew by common report, one of which was that food was to be had at certain resorts of varying cheapness. A wrinkled and yellowed page, dating from that period, whose smoothed creases betray its rescue from an intended oblivion, has survived to witness a state of mind to which Steve was daily subjected for weeks at a time. I think its salvage is justified now; it was but a safety valve to ease the pressure of a mood, and his reputation will not suffer from its printing, while the truth of a certain phase of the Stephen Crane 'legend' is amply verified. Near the top is penciled 'I'd sell my steps to the grave at ten cents per foot, if 'twere but honestie.' Then: . . ." and Linson quotes the poem, obviously from the manuscript he had preserved, which is now at Syracuse University (*My Stephen Crane*, ed. Edwin H. Cady [Syracuse University Press, 1958], pp. 13–14). And he adds, "Early 'lines' which the world never saw, a bit of penny pad wearing the leer of an ironical humor in a lean time." The possibility must be considered that Linson dated the manuscript in his possession by its subject matter instead of by his recollection of Crane writing it. Still, it is the only evidence we have.

[3] The preserved parts of the Notebook contain sketches printed in 1894, their date of origin being obscure. Thus *Little birds of the night* might as readily date from early 1894 as from late 1893 and need not precede in composition the poems mentioned by Linson in February, 1894.

a draft of "Heard on the Street Election Night" that concerns the elections in November, 1894.

The publication of *The Black Riders and Other Lines* in May, 1895, introduced sixty-eight poems, only a few of which have left other record. The majority, if not practically all, of the poems in this volume seem to have been written in a period of intense activity, very likely between January and March, 1894. Corwin Linson saw Crane's "lines" for the first time, he records, in mid-February, 1894. The topmost script was *There was a man who lived a life of fire* (62); others that he read on the occasion were *The ocean said to me once* (38), *There was crimson clash of war* (14), and *In Heaven, | Some little blades of grass* (18).[4]

Hamlin Garland was shown a number of poems before the middle of March, 1894. This date is a firm one, for he states that he gave Crane a letter to take to W. D. Howells the next day, and on March 18, 1894, Howells wrote Crane that he had been unable to interest *Harper's Magazine* in the poems: "I could not persuade Mr. Alden to be of my thinking about your poems. I wish you had given them more form, for then things so striking would have found a public ready made for them; as it is they will have to make one." [5] In his first account of the episode Garland records:

[4] Linson, pp. 48–51: "There by the flaring gaslight of an evening of mid-February [1894], I was at work on a drawing when a rap on the door was followed by the entrance of Steve. Between his snow-flecked derby and his tightly buttoned ulster there hovered a sphinx-like smile. He shook the clinging snow from his hat and from the depths of his coat drew some sheets of foolscap and held them hesitatingly.

" 'What do you think I have been doing, CK?'

"When a question is unanswerable one merely waits. Responding to my inquiring gaze, he laid the sheets on my drawing as if to say, 'That, just now, is of minor importance.' I read the topmost script. . . .

"I became conscious of an uneasy waiting—then a swift challenge. 'What do you think?'

" 'I haven't had time to think! I'm seeing pictures.'

" 'What do you mean?'

" 'Just what I said. They make me see pictures. How did you think of them?'

"A finger passed across his forehead, 'They came, and I wrote them, that's all.' . . . I confessed that their newness of form, their disregard of the usual puzzled me—'but that's their value, after all, Steve. I'm glad they're not Whitman. I thought at first they might be.' He laughed.

" 'That's all right, CK. If you can see them like that it's all I want.' And he broke into a little chant."

[5] *Stephen Crane: Letters*, ed. R. W. Stallman and L. Gilkes (New York University Press, 1960), p. 31. In "The Garland-Crane Relationship," *Huntington Library Quarterly*, XXIV (1960), 80–81, Donald Pizer takes it that Crane brought Garland the poems before Garland left New York on a lecture tour on February 6 or 7. But since Linson puts the date of his seeing the poems in mid-February, and it is likely that Crane would show them to a close friend before a less familiar critic, the probable date can be placed shortly after March 10 when Garland returned to New York. It may have been that Crane was waiting for Garland's return and appeared immediately. By March 18 Howells had seen the poems and failed to interest *Harper's*.

One day he appeared in my study with his outside pockets bulging with two rolls of manuscript. As he entered he turned ostentatiously to put down his hat, and so managed to convey to my mind an impression that he was concealing something. His manner was embarrassed, as if he had come to do a thing and was sorry about it.

"Come now, out with it," I said. "What is the roll I see in your pocket?"

With a sheepish look he took out a fat roll of legal cap paper and handed it to me with a careless, boyish gesture.

"There's another," I insisted, and he still more abruptly delivered himself of another but smaller parcel.

I unrolled the first package, and found it to be a sheaf of poems. I can see the initial poem now, exactly as it was then written, without a blot or erasure—almost without punctuation—in blue ink. It was beautifully legible and clean of outline.

It was the poem which begins thus:

"God fashioned the ship of the world carefully." [6]

I read this with delight and amazement. I rushed through the others, some thirty in all, with growing wonder. I could not believe they were the work of the pale, reticent boy moving restlessly about the room.

"Have you any more?" I asked.

"I've got five or six all in a little row up here," he quaintly replied, pointing to his temple. "That's the way they come—in little rows, all made up, ready to be put down on paper."

"When did you write these?"

"Oh! I've been writing five or six every day. I wrote nine yesterday. . . ."

Garland gave him a letter to W. D. Howells and urged Crane to take the poems to him the next day.

"Come to-morrow to luncheon," I said, as he went away visibly happier. "Perhaps I'll have something to report."

I must confess I took the lines seriously. If they were the direct output of this unaccountable boy, then America had produced another genius, singular as Poe. I went with them at once to Mr. Howells, whose wide reading I knew and relied upon. He read them with great interest, and immediately said:

"They do not seem to relate directly to the work of any other writer. They seem to be the work of a singularly creative mind. Of course they reflect the author's reading and sympathies, but they are not imitations."

Garland's memory here fails him, for he writes that when Crane came the next day he brought the first part of *The Red Badge of Courage* manuscript which he did not see, in fact, until April 21 or 22, 1894.[6] He continues:

"Did you have any more 'lines'?"

He looked away bashfully.

"Only six."

"Let me see them."

[6] For the establishment of this much-discussed date, see F. Bowers, *The Red Badge of Courage: A Facsimile Edition of the Manuscript* (Washington, D.C.: Bruccoli Clark Book, NCR/Microcard Editions, 1973), Introduction, pp. 6–8.

As he handed them to me he said: "Got three more waiting in line. I could do one now."

"Sit down and try," I said, glad of his offer, for I could not relate the man to his work.

He took a seat and began to write steadily, composedly, without hesitation or blot or interlineation, and so produced in my presence one of his most powerful verses. It flowed from his pen as smooth as oil.[7]

In a later account Garland has Crane compose the poem on the spot during the first meeting and believes that it was *God fashioned the ship of the world carefully* (6). He adds: "He continued for some weeks to 'precipitate' others but in diminishing flow. I recall that he came into [the playwright] Herne's dressing room at the theater one night to tell me that he had drawn off the very last one. 'That place in my brain is empty,' he said, but the poem he showed me was not a cull—it was tremendous in its effect on Herne as well as on me."[8] Since Garland left for Chicago on April 25, 1894, the episode would have taken place before that date, probably in early April. This date is the more likely because Garland quotes from a letter Crane sent him about the Uncut Leaves reading (April 14, 1894): "I hope you have heard about the 'Uncut Leaves Affair.' I tried to get tickets up to you, but I couldn't succeed." This follows Garland's recollection that "shortly before I left for the West he called to tell me that he had shown his verses to Mr. John D. Barry and that Mr. Barry had 'fired them off to Copeland & Day.'" The poem that was read in the theater, Crane wrote Garland on May 9, 1894, was called *The Reformer* but he had lost it. He enclosed what must have been *A soldier, young in years, young in ambitions* (113) and remarked complacently, "I have got the poetic spout so that I can turn it on or off."[9]

The sequence of events as it can be reconstructed is something like this. In mid-February, Crane showed to Corwin Linson a number of poems, including *There was a man who lived a life of fire* (62), *The ocean said to me once* (38), *There was crimson clash of war* (14), and *In Heaven, | Some little blades of grass* (18). A short time later he brought a sheaf of lines on legal-cap paper (Linson called it foolscap) to Hamlin Garland, probably in the second week of March since Garland had returned to New York only on March 10. Either *God fashioned the ship of the world carefully* (6) was written down at that time (or the next day), or Garland read it as the first of the poems. Crane's remark about the poems he had in his head—" 'I have five or six all in a little row up here. . . . That's the way they come—in

[7] Hamlin Garland, "Stephen Crane," *The Book-Lover*, II (Autumn, 1900), 7, reprinting "Stephen Crane: A Soldier of Fortune," *Saturday Evening Post*, CLXXIII (July 28, 1900), 16–17.

[8] Hamlin Garland, *Roadside Meetings* (New York: Macmillan, 1930), pp. 194–195.

[9] *Letters*, pp. 36–37.

little rows, all made up, ready to be put down on paper' "—is so close in language to *Three little birds in a row* (2) as to suggest the possibility that it had been written also by this time. Howells was shown the poems within the next day or two and on March 18 confessed that he had failed to interest *Harper's Magazine.* Crane continued to write his lines until at some point in the first two weeks of April he felt drained and showed his last one, *The Reformer* (now lost), to Garland. However, by May 9 he had produced *A soldier young in years* (113) and reported that he was writing verse again.[10]

John Barry, editor of the *Forum,* read one or more of Crane's poems before the Uncut Leaves Society on April 14, 1894, and, if Garland's memory is to be trusted in this matter, put Copeland and Day, of Boston, in touch with Crane.[11] The exact date is uncertain; the earliest

[10] Hamlin Garland's intermediate account of his first acquaintance with the poems in "Stephen Crane As I Knew Him," *Yale Review,* n.s. III (1914), 494–506, seems to be the least trustworthy of his three sets of recollections. In it he recalls that on Crane's first appearance he brought the manuscript of *The Red Badge of Courage.* Although Garland reports that he said to Crane, " 'What have you there? . . . It looks like poetry,' " poems are not mentioned until what seems to be a time after the publication of the *Red Badge.* Crane appeared at his door with a smaller roll of manuscript which contained about a dozen poems written on legal-cap paper. Among the first Garland read *God fashioned the ship* (6) and Crane sat down and wrote out for him *There was, before me, | Mile upon mile* (21), to which he added *Once there came a man* (5). "For several days he came regularly bringing these curious fragments, and then gradually the number of poems dwindled until he had but one or two. At last one night, while I was sitting in Herne's dressing room at Daly's Theatre, the poet (who had also been given the run of the house) came in abruptly and in some excitement said, 'I've got another,' and thereupon handed me the longest and best of his rhymeless rhythmic compositions." This Garland quotes as *I stood musing in a black world* (49). " 'Any more up there?' I inquired, pointing at his head. [¶] 'No,' he replied with a touch of melancholy, 'they're all gone now—the place is empty.' " Much of this account seems to be a fabrication, especially since it is later altered in *Roadside Meetings* (1930) to something closer to his original narrative in 1900. Certainly the poem he quotes as read at the theater was not *I stood musing,* for Crane in his letter called it "The Reformer," a title that scarcely fits *I stood musing.* Garland's initial reminiscences in 1900 can be checked by other evidence in various of their details and shown to be accurate, except for the major error of placing the events in the year 1893, not 1894. The real mystery is what was in the second roll of manuscript mentioned in the earliest account, which Garland does not say he opened—unless it was more poems, or even an early form of the *Red Badge.* Pizer is mistaken in recording that Howells reported that the 'magazine editors' were uninterested, a piece of evidence he brings forward in arguing for a February date for Garland's seeing the poems. In fact, Howells' letter of March 18 says only that he had failed to interest *Harper's Magazine.* If Garland showed Howells the poems immediately, as he says he did (or sent Crane to Howells with them), there was time between, say, March 11 and March 18 for Howells to make an effort with *Harper's* in Crane's behalf and to be rebuffed.

[11] Linson, *My Stephen Crane,* pp. 54–56. In "A Note on Stephen Crane," *Bookman,* XIII (April, 1901), 148, Barry states that he saw about thirty poems in manuscript shortly after Crane had heard Howells read from Emily Dickinson, and that Crane stated they had been written in three days. The date at which Crane heard

record that is preserved of Crane's dealings with Copeland and Day is a letter conjecturally dated in August, 1894, from Interlaken Camp in Parker's Glen, Pike's County, Pennsylvania: 'I would like to hear from you concerning my poetry. I wish to have my out-bring all under way by early fall and I have not heard from you in some time. I am in the dark in regard to your intentions' (*Letters*, p. 39). The references in this letter are ambiguous but may be taken to indicate that Copeland and Day had expressed an interest but little more. The firm must have answered with some promptness, raising objections to the subject matter of some of the poems, for on September 9 Crane returned:

> We disagree on a multitude of points. In the first place I should absolutely refuse to have my poems printed without many of those which you just as absolutely mark "No." It seems to me that you cut all of the ethical sense out of the book. All the anarchy, perhaps. It is the anarchy which I particularly insist upon. From the poems which you keep you could produce what might be termed a "nice little volume of verse by Stephen Crane," but for me there would be no satisfaction. The ones which refer to God, I believe you condemn altogether. I am obliged to have them in when my book is printed. There are some which I believe unworthy of print. These I herewith enclose. As for the others, I cannot give them up—in the book.
>
> In the second matter, you wish I would write a few score more. It is utterly impossible to me. We would be obliged to come to an agreement upon those that are written.
>
> If my position is impossible to you, I would not be offended at the sending of all the retained lines to the enclosed address. [*Letters*, pp. 39–40]

From this letter one may conjecture that Copeland and Day had returned a list, or possibly the manuscripts, of those poems to which they objected, that in this reply Crane enclosed a list of other poems he wanted withdrawn, and that he was not prepared to add to the volume either from stubbornness or from an inability to write poetry at this time.[12]

One result of the dispute was to call Crane's attention to lines that —though innocent from the publisher's point of view—did not measure up on further scrutiny to his standards for publication. How many of these poems that he listed by title in the lost enclosure to the letter of September 9 were finally withdrawn cannot be known. It may be

---

Dickinson read is much disputed, but as Olav Fryckstedt remarks, it cannot be pinned down any more closely than between the end of March, 1893, when Howells encountered *Maggie* and the middle of April, 1894, when Barry appeared before the Uncut Leaves Society ("Crane's *Black Riders*: A Discussion of Dates," *Studia Neophilologica*, XXXIV [1962], 283, 289–290).

12 Despite his boast to Garland, the evidence seems to indicate that Crane had temporarily run dry. The next publication in periodicals was *The chatter of a death-demon* (87) a year later in the *Philistine* for August, 1895, after his return from Mexico. This poem has links with the unpublished *There is a grey thing that lives in the tree-tops* (111) that appears to have been among those withdrawn from *The Black Riders*, but it is a development of no. 111, not to be classed as a revision.

conjectured that the legal-cap manuscript of unpublished *There is a grey thing that lives in the tree-tops* (111) was one of these, and a few guesses may be made about others, but no solid evidence exists. The available evidence, and some speculations, are detailed under the section on "The Dates of the Poems" in connection with the rejected manuscripts for *War is Kind.*

Copeland and Day's lost reply to the September 9 letter appears to have been a temporizing one, for Crane's tone is very different in an undated letter from 33 East 22nd Street which from its envelope can be established as mailed on September 27:

> I have just returned to the city and recieved your letter this morning. I send herewith the other sheets.
>
> Ten per cent is satisfactory to me. As for the title I am inclined toward: "The Black Riders and other lines," referring to that [p *deleted*] one beginning "Black Riders [R *over* r] rode forth," etc. I don't like an index [an *interlined; final* es *deleted from* index], personally, and I think if you agree, we could omit that part. If there is any other matter, my address will be as above until November 20th or about then, when I go west for one of the syndicates. In the meantime, I may come to Boston shortly. I am indebted to you for your tolerance of my literary prejudices. [University of Virginia]

The reference to the sending of "other sheets" is puzzling but may refer to a typographical sample that Copeland and Day had mailed him for approval. In the University of Virginia–Barrett Collection is preserved the printer's-copy manuscript of *Three little birds in a row* with the printer's or publisher's marking in pencil of a roman number I above the first line and, at the head, a circled '2¼ in.' This agrees with a proof-sheet for the poem in the Columbia University Library Special Collections, which is also headed with a roman I and in the text follows the manuscript in its lack of punctuation as against the final printed form—numbered II—and especially in the use of a colon in line 5 to introduce quoted speech instead of the untypical comma found in the book in this poem and elsewhere as part of the publisher's styling. The measure, or width of the full line of type, is 2¼ inches. In fact, this is not an ordinary proof but instead a sample of the proposed typography, and it is significant that it was set from a manuscript numbered I for the purpose, and presumably the first according to Copeland and Day's information. It is also significant that in his letter Crane does not refer to the title poem but instead to 'that one beginning "Black Riders rode forth,"' an indication that it had not been arranged at first as the initial poem and had only recently been selected for the position. In their lost letter Copeland and Day may have indicated some sympathy with Crane's point of view about "anarchy," at least enough to elicit his gratitude in the final sentence, and they seem to have proceeded to business arrangements.

That they had not capitulated, however, or perhaps gone so far as to accept the book formally, is indicated by what is probably their next letter, a bombshell, dated October 19:

We hope you will pardon this delay regarding your verses now with us, and beg to say that we will be glad to publish them if you will agree to omitting those beginning as follows.

1. A god it is said
   Marked a sparrow's fall
2d. To the maiden
   The sea was a laughing meadow
3d. A god came to a man
   And spoke in this wise.
4th. There was a man with a tongue of wood.
5th. The traveller paused in kindness
6th. Should you stuff me with flowers
7th. One came from the skies.

Should you still object to omitting so many we will rest content to print all but the first three in the above list, though all of them appear to us as *far* better left unprinted.

We are sending by post a couple of drawings either of which might please you to be used by way of fronticepiece for the book; one would be something illustrative, while the other would be symbolic in a wide sense.

As to a title for the book, the one you suggest is acceptable if nothing better occur to you. The omission of titles for separate poems is an idea we most heartily agree with.

We are also sending a blank form to recieve your signature should you decide to entrust the book to our hands: a duplicate will be sent to you upon the return of this copy.

Kindly let us hear from you at as early a date as possible. [University of Virginia] [13]

It is a reasonable conjecture that the list made up by Copeland and Day in this letter of October 19 was shorter than that in their original objection that had provoked Crane's protest of September 9, and certainly their offer to print all but three if he insisted was conciliatory. It is odd that Crane did not, in fact, accept this compromise but instead followed their advice, for no one of the last four (which they were prepared to accept) appears in *The Black Riders*. The first, fifth, and sixth have been lost or else are unrecognizable if they are preserved in revised form. The second and fourth Crane printed in *War is Kind* (the second [no. 71] reprinted there from *A Souvenir* and the *Philistine*); the third and seventh remained unpublished.[14]

[13] On the final verso this letter is inscribed in large letters with the autograph 'Stephen Crane | Port Jervis'. Below, in Corwin Linson's hand, is the notation, 'Crane's autograph— | CK Linson'.

[14] In late September, Crane had apparently shown more lines to Howells (no doubt copies of those prepared for *The Black Riders*), who responded on October 2: "These things are too orphic for me. It is a pity for you to do them, for you can do things solid and real, so superbly. However, there is room for all kinds,—need if you like! [¶] I do not think a merciful Providence meant the 'prose poem' to last" (*Letters*, p. 40). This opinion may have had a discouraging effect on Crane's ambitions.

Although Copeland and Day preserved Crane's letters and their envelopes with care and might have been expected especially to have kept a letter of agreement with their October 19 conditions, Crane's answer remains unknown although it presumably existed, for he would have needed to return the signed contract. That he did agree is obvious from the withdrawal of all seven of the specified poems without further reference. Indeed, the next recorded communication is a brief undated note (postmarked October 30, from 143 East 23rd St.): "I enclose copy of the title poem. Please note change of address" (*Letters*, p. 40). The reference to his enclosure of the title poem cannot be to a new composition, for *Black riders came from the sea* had been mentioned a month before on September 27 as his choice for the title. Since on that occasion he quoted the first line as '"Black riders rode forth" etc.', it seems probable that the reference on October 30 is to a revision of the poem that he was sending.

The evidence seems clear that in the original arrangement *Black riders* had not been first; on the other hand, it was almost certainly among the first five of the poems. Not many of the manuscripts are preserved for poems printed in *The Black Riders* (nos. 1, 2, 8, 10, 18, and 33), and of these only nos. 2, 8, 10, and 18 were probably the printer's-copy manuscripts. None of these has a word count or other calculation on its verso. Interestingly, however, the manuscript of *There was a man with tongue of wood* (84), which seems to be the original manuscript of 47 words that was withdrawn at Copeland and Day's specific request, has cumulative calculations on its verso written in pencil. First, 170 is added to 167 for a total of 337, and then 257 is added to this for a total of 594. There seems to be no way of associating these word counts with the poem's later appearance in *War is Kind*, but it is curious and perhaps significant that the first twelve poems of *The Black Riders* total exactly 594 words, the figure found on the verso of no. 84. Unfortunately, at least in their present order these twelve poems do not break down readily into the two figures of 167 and 170 that were added to give 337, and thus were in sequence, followed by another sequence totaling 257. It is not clear, moreover, whether the sequences worked forward from no. 1 to no. 12, or backward from no. 12 to no. 1. In fact, nos. 1–5 total 258 words if 'ninety-nine' in the second line of no. 4 and 'world-wide' in line 7 of no. 5 are each counted as two words, or the correct 257 words of the third total if one or other is counted as a single word. But in their present arrangement nos. 6–8 add up to 183 words, and nos. 9–12 to 152. It is possible to play with figures by radically rearranging the first twelve poems into four or five different groups that would cluster to compose the word counts of 170 and 167, but of all possible reorderings the simplest would consist of placing the present no. 7 *Mystic shadow, bending near me* (41 words) after present no. 9 *I stood upon a high place* (25 words). If this had been hypothetically the earliest sequence, then a grouping of nos. 6, 8, and 9 would total 167 words, and nos. 7, 10, 11, and 12 would total 169 words, perhaps near enough to the 170 figure. It may be, then, that no. 84 came thirteenth in the original arrangement and on its back Crane calculated the word count up to that point. (Number 84 in the Copeland and Day letter quoted above is the first of the four poems which they objected to but were prepared to print if Crane insisted.) But the lack of any evidence that Crane rearranged the early sequence—except for placing *Black Riders* first at some time after submission by moving it from an unknown position among the poems—and the possibility for still other even though considerably jumbled reorderings in the first twelve prevent any certainty of conjecture. It may not even be said with confidence that none of the first three objectionable poems which Copeland and Day utterly declined were among the initial twelve. Thus although there may be some reason to speculate that no. 84 was originally no. 13 in *The Black Riders*, the case is extremely uncertain.

To Crane's letter of October 30 Copeland and Day responded by return, in an unpublished letter of October 31:

> Your letter of yesterday inclosing copy of title lines for your book is recieved, but as yet the drawings have not come to hand: neither new ones or those we forwarded you. Kindly advise us whether others are being made up.
>
> The form in which we intend to print *The Black Riders* is more severely classic than any book ever yet issued in America, and owing to the scarcity of types it will be quite impossible to set up more than a dozen pages at a time. Of course you wish to see proof for correction, but we would ask whether you wish the punctuation of copy followed implicitly or the recognized authorities on pointing of America or England? All those are at variance more or less [*illegible word*]. [Syracuse University]

The drawings that Crane had not returned were very likely the samples for the covers sent him on October 19. (Less likely they were the Melanie Elisabeth Norton trials. For a discussion of these trial illustrations, see p. 242.) The publishers' question whether others were being made up suggests the possibility that even this early in the proceedings Crane had queried whether one or other of his artist friends might not be commissioned for the book.

Crane evidently failed to respond to this letter and thus Copeland and Day did not start to set up the book. On December 10 Crane wrote to them complaining: "I would like to hear something from you in regard to the poems. [¶] Also, I have grown somewhat frightened at the idea of old English type since some of my recent encounters with it have made me think I was working out a puzzle. Please reassure me on this point and tell me what you can of the day of publication" (*Letters*, p. 42). The reference to Old English type is odd since no mention of it as a possibility has been preserved. It would appear that from the beginning Copeland and Day had had in mind the typography of the book as it is known; thus Crane's foreboding appears to have been imaginary and caused by some curious lapse in memory. He responded shortly, on December 16, to Copeland and Day's lost answer: "There has been no necessity for you to wait impatiently to hear from me for I have answered each of the letters sent to me and at any rate, you have had opportunities to inform me of it since the 31st Oct. The type, the page, the classic form of the sample suits me. It is however paragraphed wrong. There should be none. As to punctuation, any uniform method will suit me. I am anxious to know the possible date of publication" (*Letters*, p. 42). Since no paragraphing or indention of any sort is found in the Columbia sample sheet of *Two little birds*, the possibility is present that this represents a revise sent Crane after receipt of his letter.

Crane continued to worry about the slowness of the book's production and the delays in the proof of which he had been warned in the October 31 letter that he had never answered. In a letter conjecturally dated about December 22, 1894, he stated it was unlikely he could come to Boston before his Western trip but would like to hear how the poems were coming on (*Letters*, p. 46); shortly, on January 2, 1895, he returned a proof-sheet and declined to see a revise. He warned that proof would need to be hurried along before he went West, "or I can get to see but few of them." Could an announcement card be printed that he could send to his friends? (*Letters*, pp. 46–47). In a note dated January 6, 1895, from its postmark, he sent a copy of a review of *The Red Badge of Courage* from the *Philadelphia Press* of December 4, 1894, and suggested that a Garland review printed in the *Arena* might be useful also for an extract (*Letters*, p. 47). Conjecturally dated January 10, 1895, another letter gives the reference to the *Arena* review and requests a one-line dedication to Hamlin Garland (*Letters*, p. 47). More proofs are requested in a letter of January 14 before his Mexican trip, and he encloses a list of friends to whom "that notice" should be sent (*Letters*, p. 47). From St. Louis, Missouri, on January 30 he relays his Nebraska address and an enquiry about the notices (*Letters*, p. 49). *The Black Riders* was published on May 11, 1895, in his absence. On June 8 he reports his return (*Letters*, p. 58), and after an undated letter (June, 1895?) responding to Copeland and Day's enquiry about the possibility of printing some of his early prose work (*Letters*, p. 59), on May 29, 1896, he closes the correspondence by requesting an accounting (*Letters*, p. 56, misdated 1895).

In the University of Virginia–Barrett Collection are preserved three stages of proof (Barrett 570413) and the final version of what is very likely the notice (Barrett 57294) that Crane wanted to send to his friends. In its ultimate printed form, on the left appears an announcement by Copeland and Day and on the right the text of no. 28 from *The Black Riders*, beginning *"Truth," said a traveller.* The announcement reads as follows:

Messrs. Copeland and Day announce for early publication THE BLACK RIDERS, AND OTHER LINES, by STEPHEN CRANE. Five hundred copies, small octavo, printed in capitals throughout, on the same paper as this announcement, $1.00. With fifty copies additional, printed in green ink on Japan paper, $3.00.
While reviewing Mr. Crane's *Maggie*, in the Arena, Mr. Hamlin Garland says of his style: "It is a work of astonishingly good style, . . . pictorial, graphic, terrible in its directness. The dictum is amazingly simple and fine for so young a writer. Some of the words illuminate like flashes of light. . . . With such a technique already in command, with life mainly before him, Stephen Crane is to be henceforth reckoned with . . . a man who impresses the reader with a sense of almost unlimited resource." Of the same volume a critic in the Philadelphia Press says: "It contains the evidences of great power, of real imagination, and a sort of poetic quality which will be sure to take its author out of the list of perfunctory realists."

In what is probably the earliest trial, this text is set throughout in capitals (two copies on wove paper); in the next it is set in lower case with sentence caps but italicizing 'Copeland and Day', the book's title, and Crane's name (laid paper, vertical chains); in the probable third stage the title is changed to roman caps and small caps and the publishers' and Crane's names to full capitals (same paper); in the fourth stage on the same paper Crane's name is reduced to small caps with heading capitals. A copy of the final form of the prospectus with this typography is found on a fold of the book paper, one side containing the titlepage and imprint page and the verso the announcement and page 29 of the text, poem no. XXVIII.

From the start Copeland and Day appear to have settled on the typography by which the poems, not ineffectively, are set all in capitals. The decoration of the volume provoked more discussion. The drawings sent Crane as possible "fronticepieces" are probably the designs with tulips (see below); in their letter to Crane of October 31 the publishers requested the return of these samples, but except for this nothing more is heard of them. It is possible that Crane had introduced his artist friend Frederic C. Gordon earlier, but the first actual preserved reference to him is in a letter from Crane on January 10, 1895: "My friend, the artist, is very busy but if you will send him here an exact rendering of the words of the cover, he may submit something shortly" (*Letters*, p. 47). Then in a letter of January 14 Crane wrote as a postscript: "Will you please send, as I requested, the size of the cover, the exact lettering upon it, and, if possible, the probable thickness of the book. The artist needs it" (*Letters*, p. 48), and a few days later, conjecturally still in January, he wrote, "The artist wishes to know what you mean by the phrase: 'Both sides the same' in relation to the book cover" (*Letters*, p. 48). Perhaps still in January (but more likely in early February) Gordon wrote to Copeland and Day: 'In another package I mail you a design for the cover of Mr. Crane's poems. It is drawn twice the dimensions of the book. The same design, with title and author's name omitted is intended for the back of the book. [¶] The orchid, with its strange habits, extraordinary forms and curious properties, seemed to me the most appropriate floral motive, an idea in which Mr. Crane concurred before he left New York. I have just mailed him a tracing of the design. [¶] Will you kindly let me know whether it suits your requirements" (*Letters*, pp. 48–49). Later, on February 25, 1895, Gordon wrote again to Copeland and Day, urging them to have their artist adapt a portion of his drawing to their requirements since he was especially busy. He concluded that he would accept whatever price they decided since his design had not proved satisfactory, and "A little later, if I can find the time, I shall be pleased to submit a design for your lines" (*Letters*, p. 53). The meaning of this last sentence is obscure unless 'for your lines' may be taken to mean 'along your lines', i.e., according to your wishes. That it could refer to an independent design for a dust jacket would seem to be stretching the language in an improbable manner; but the possibility may exist that some decorative framing of the text pages, on the order of Melanie Norton's for the *Bookman,* had been contemplated.

In the University of Virginia–Barrett Collection is preserved an unused design for the front cover measuring 203 × 120 mm., in black ink on tracing paper. The title is drawn in three lines at the head, 'THE BLACK RIDERS | & OTHER LINES BY | STEPHEN CRANE' and below this, filling the rest of the design, are two large tulips with leaves. Another design for the back cover (or, less likely, an alternative for the front) consists of a frame containing five stylized unopened tulips drawn in black ink on heavy cardboard, the frame measuring 196.5 × 133 mm. At the foot is what appears to be a monogram featuring a basic 'G' with what looks like a spear rising through it vertically, the letter filled by a large 'X'. Whether these two trials were by Gordon or (perhaps more likely) made for Copeland and Day in Boston is not known. The design without lettering has a pencil marking above it of 4″ between arrows, apparently the size of reduction planned. These drawings may perhaps represent the "illustrative" and "symbolic" copy for a "fronticepiece" sent Crane by Copeland and Day on October 19. Indeed, it may have been these that suggested to Gordon the use of an orchid.

The rejected design by Gordon is drawn on heavy paper in black india ink. The front cover measuring 276 × 203 mm. is divided into three vertical panels. In the center panel is drawn 'BLACK | RIDERS' and, near the foot, 'BY STEPHEN CRANE'. The left panel contains a formal leaf design, but in the right panel is a stylized orchid. To the left of the cover is drawn the spine, without decoration, '|| BLACK | RIDERS || || COPELAND | AND DAY | BOSTON ||'.

The Copeland and Day artist adapted Gordon's drawing of the orchid plant. His drawing is in india ink on white cardboard with pencil frames surrounding it. The orchid design measures 131 × 95 mm., and is the exact size later found on the book cover. At the head of the drawing is written in pencil, probably in the same hand as that in which the Copeland and Day letters to Crane were inscribed, 'Same size—two plants one like this reversed', and to the left of the design, with pencil lines to the place in the flower referred to, 'use a graver on plate | to open white line | where ink filled up.' Following these instructions the artist made up the plate. Six trial cover proofs of this design are preserved on laid paper of different shades of gray, 196 × 272 mm., vertical chainlines 28 mm. apart, this paper being of the same stock (but with some variation in thickness) as that later used to cover the boards of the first edition. These proofs have the orchid design and the lettered title on the front cover, 'THE BLACK RIDERS | AND OTHER | LINES | BY | STEPHEN | CRANE', but the 'THE' is indented about 1 en. The orchid design alone is on the back cover. The spine is lettered 'THE | BLACK RIDERS | STEPHEN | CRANE | COPELAND | AND | DAY | 1895'. What is probably a later trial is found on four different colored papers of the same stock—three of various shades of gray and one of blue-gray—but with the front cover lettering (the 'THE' indented) also on the back, reversed so that the short lines are to the right of the flower instead of to the left and the final 'S' of 'RIDERS' is indented at right. The slightly yellowish gray of one of these papers subsequently was chosen as the paper for the boards of the first edition. In addition, the trial for a dust jacket, never used so far as is known, is also found in this collection. This consists of a sheet of black paper 162 × 252 mm. lettered in pale gray 'The | Black Riders | and | Other Lines | By Stephen Crane.' on the front. The space for the spine and back is blank.

Two proofs of the titlepage have been preserved. The earlier is on laid paper 214 × 136 mm. with horizontal chainlines 30 mm. apart and reads 'THE BLACK RIDERS | AND OTHER LINES | BY STEPHEN CRANE | PUBLISHED BY COPELAND AND | DAY BOSTON MDCCCXCV'. The title is set as a block to an even measure. The second and later proof is on a slightly thinner laid paper of the same size but with vertical chainlines. Its lettering reads 'THE BLACK RIDERS AND | OTHER LINES BY STE-|PHEN CRANE | BOSTON COPELAND AND DAY MDCCCXCV'. This was the final form. In both the type is set full to the left margin with no indention of the first line.

Copeland and Day applied for copyright on January 14, 1895. On the titlepage of the prospectus in the University of Virginia–Barrett Collection is written in green crayon, 'ordered 500 12 Mar '95'; below the 500 is the figure 50, representing the Japan paper copies. This was presumably the official print order. Deposit was made on May 3, 1895.

THE BLACK RIDERS AND | OTHER LINES BY STE-|PHEN CRANE | BOSTON COPELAND AND DAY MDCCCXCV

Collation: $[1]^2$ $[2\text{–}6]^8$, pp. [i–iv] 1–76 [77–80]; leaf measures 153 × 108 mm., all edges untrimmed; coated wove paper, endpapers front and back 4 quired leaves of text paper, first and last leaves pasted down.

Contents: p. i: title; p. ii: 'ENTERED ACCORDING TO THE ACT OF CONGRESS | IN THE YEAR MDCCCXCV BY COPELAND AND DAY | IN THE OFFICE OF THE LIBRARIAN OF CONGRESS | AT WASHINGTON'; p. iii: 'TO HAMLIN GARLAND'; p. iv: blank; p. 1: text ending on p. 76; p. 77: 'PRINTED BY JOHN WILSON AND SON CAMBRIDGE'; pp. 78–80: blank.

Binding: Yellowish gray laid paper, vertical chainlines 30 mm. apart, over boards. All lettering in black. *Front*: [above and to the left of large orchid drawn rising from left to right] [even left margin] 'THE BLACK RIDERS | AND OTHER | LINES | BY | STEPHEN | CRANE'. *Spine*: 'THE | BLACK | RIDERS | STEPHEN | CRANE | COPELAND | AND | DAY | 1895'. *Back*: same as front but reversed, lettering above and to the right of the orchid rising from right to left; right margin even. Binder's stamp 'DUDLEY & HODGE' at foot of front pasted-down endpaper.

Price: $1. Announced in the *Publishers' Weekly* of May 11, 1895.

Copies: University of Virginia–Barrett (551360) unbound unopened sheets less front and back endpaper quires; UVa-Barrett (551366), unopened, with publisher's tinted glassine jacket; UVa-Barrett (551362), on second free flyleaf presentation 'To Gordon Pike | with the friendship of | Stephen Crane | New York City, June 28, 1895'.

Variant: University of Virginia–Barrett (551364), binding blue-gray laid paper with vertical chainlines over boards; first line on front cover indented 1 en as in trial proofs; reversed orchid but no lettering on back as in earlier trial proofs; no binder's stamp.

Fifty copies printed in green ink on Japan paper and specially bound were published at the same time as the regular edition but were apparently considered by Copeland and Day to constitute the 'second edition.' These collate the same as the wove-paper copies and were printed from the same typesetting without any alteration. On the basis of an advertisement for these copies inserted in the *Bookman*, III (April, 1896), ix, Williams and Starrett (*Stephen Crane: A Bibliography* [1948], p. 17) believed that the Japan printing did not appear until a year later, but this 1896 attempt to dispose of the remaining stock cannot be the announcement of publication. Both copies were announced for future publication in the *Publishers' Weekly*, XLVII (February 9, 1895) and both were listed in the prospectus for the book. The Copeland and Day printer's order jotted on the University of Virginia–Barrett prospectus in March gives 500 copies and then 50. Finally, shortly after publication in an undated letter Crane wrote to Copeland and Day requesting copies to be sent him at the Lantern Club for reviewers and added: "I am particularly anxious to see the green ones. [¶] I see they have been pounding the wide margins, the capitals and all that but I think it great" (*Letters*, p. 59).

The University of Virginia–Barrett Collection has a set of unbound and unopened sheets (551361) wanting the front and back endpaper quires, which were also on Japan paper. Two binding styles have been observed:

University of Virginia–Barrett (551365), cream laid paper over boards, plain without design or lettering; on the spine a white label (21 × 12 mm.) printed in black, '||| THE | BLACK | RIDERS | [short rule] | CRANE | [short rule] | 1895 |||'. No binder's stamp; first and last of quired endpapers pasted down; leaves unopened.

University of Virginia–Barrett (551363) white vellum covers stamped in gold both front and back with the orchid design and the short title above it 'THE BLACK RIDERS', both reversed on the back cover. Three slots are cut near the spine on front and back through which are exposed small sections of flat vellum straps inserted under the vellum cover to strengthen the spine, no binder's stamp. The spine is blank. In this copy the first two and last two of the endpapers are pasted down, leaving two free leaves.

At some unknown date in 1896 Copeland and Day reprinted *The Black Riders*. The collation is the same as the first printing, including the use of a four-leaf quire of endpapers front and back, with the outer leaf of each pasted down. The imprint on the titlepage was reset to read 'BOSTON COPELAND AND DAY MDCCCXCVI | LONDON WILLIAM HEINEMANN', and above the deposit notice on the verso was inserted 'THIRD EDITION'. In the standing type of the text a misprint of a question mark after *friend* in line 8 of *Friend, your white beard sweeps the ground* (64) was altered to an exclamation point, and in *There was a man and a woman* (61) the spelling *gayly* was normalized to *gaily*. Sporadic attempts were made to alter the spelling of *-or* words to *-our* in view of the expected sale in England; otherwise, the text stood as in the first printing. None of these alterations can be taken to have Crane's authority. The binding is identical with that of the first printing except for the substitution of '1896' for the date on the spine, and the lettering of the first line of the cover, on the front and the back, which is not flush, and the lack of a binder's stamp. On May 29, 1896, Crane wrote to Copeland and Day requesting a settlement (*Letters*, p. 56, misdated 1895), and it is possible that the second printing was made about this time. Heinemann did not deposit a copy in the British Museum for copyright; hence no date stamp is available to indicate when he received his share of the books. But he must have received and been selling his allotment for some time prior to November, for in that month he published his own edition.

Copies observed of this printing are British Museum (11688.de.29); University of Virginia–Barrett (551367).

Heinemann's own edition was deposited in the British Museum on November 13, 1896, and advertised in the *Publishers' Circular* on November 14, priced at three shillings. The sheets and the cancellans half-title and title-fold appear to have been printed in the United States but bound in England and in every respect are identical with the sheets of the jointly published second printing.

THE BLACK RIDERS AND | OTHER LINES BY STE-|PHEN CRANE [three horizontal leaf type-orn.] | [vertical acorn type-orn.] | LONDON: | WILLIAM HEINEMANN | MDCCCXVI

Collation: $[1]^2(-1_1+\chi^2)$ $[2\text{–}5]^8$ $[6]^8(-6_{7,8})$, pp. [i–vi] 1–76; leaf measures 152 × 107 mm., top edge gilt, other edges untrimmed; wove endpapers with single conjugate free leaf.

Contents: p. i: half-title, 'THE BLACK RIDERS | AND OTHER LINES'; p. ii: '*By the same Author* | THE RED BADGE OF COURAGE | [short rule] | MAGGIE | A Child of the Streets | [short rule] | THE LITTLE REGIMENT | [short rule] [*Shortly* | *This Edition is limited to Five Hundred copies*'; p. iii: title; p. iv: 'PRINTED BY JOHN WILSON AND SON CAMBRIDGE U.S.A. | *All rights reserved*'; p. v: dedication; p. vi: blank; p. 1: text, ending on p. 76.

Note: The cancellans fold $1(\chi)^2$ is of the same paper as the text; the imprint leaf 6_7 and its following blank 6_8 have been cancelled without substitution. The endpaper folds, the first leaf pasted down, are of uncoated wove stock differing from the text paper.

Binding: Black leather, lettering in gold. *Front*: 'THE BLACK RIDERS | AND OTHER | LINES | BY STEPHEN CRANE' above and to the left of a redrawn orchid in blind. *Spine*: 'THE | BLACK | RIDERS | STEPHEN CRANE | HEINEMANN'. *Back*: reversed orchid in blind.

Copies: British Museum (011653.i.129), datestamped 13 November 1896; London Library (rebound), acquired 20 February 1897; University of Virginia–Barrett (551373), presentation on front flyleaf, 'To M. Henry D. Davray | From the author | Stephen Crane | London | England, Nov. 11, 1897' (A.L.S. enclosed to Davray); University of Virginia–Barrett (551372), A.L.S. to Elbert Hubbard dated February 13 [1896] from Hartwood laid in.

The letter to Davray has a significance in Crane's attempts to secure recognition for his verse. Written on stationery from Ravensbrook, it reads (*Letters*, p. 150):

Nov. 11.

M. Henry D. Davray

Dear sir: I am today taking the liberty of sending you a copy of a little book of mine—The Black Riders—in hopes that some happy accident will perswade you [you *interlined with a caret*] to read it. My importunity is not without it's darker side. My dearest wish is to see these simples [*final* s *added*] translated into French. Some of my other books have recieved German and Russian translations but, let alone translations, the British public nor even my own American public will not [not *interlined above deleted* not] look at The Black Riders. Thus my letter to you [you *interlined with a caret*] is in the nature of an appeal. I wish the distinction of appearing just for a moment to the minds of a few of your great and wise artistic public. I do not know if this will appear absurd to you. At any rate, I send you the book. You will tell me? Perchance, there would be a publisher who would print it. What I wish is the distinction. My American publishers, who own the copyrights, would readily agree. I hope I do not bore you too much? If you reply to this letter I shall be delighted.

Faithfully yours
Stephen Crane

Henri Davray had evidently been called to Crane's attention because of his interest in translating literature in English and his periodical contributions on English subjects (see his obituary in the *New York Times*, January 26, 1944). So far as is known nothing came of the proposal about *The Black Riders* and if any further correspondence developed it has not been preserved. However, after establishing in 1898 the Collections of Foreign Authors published by the Mercure de France, Davray in 1911 translated Crane's *Red Badge of Courage*, with Francis Viele-Griffin, as *La Conquête de Courage*.

On August 16, 1896, the composer William Schuyler wrote as follows to Crane, from St. Louis, Missouri:

Ever since last February when Mr Hamlin Garland, then visiting at my house, quoted some of your verses, & especially since I have read your "Black Riders" over & over—I have wished to write to you.

However a dislike of forcing myself upon another's attention has prevented me from writing until now I have at last a good excuse.— I have set to music three of your poems, & expect at a near date to publish them. To do this, I need your permission to use the words. Will you kindly grant it? I have so far set "Then came whisperings in the winds," "On the horizon the peaks assembled," & "I was in the darkness."

In conclusion permit me to express the great admiration I feel for your work. You are a true poet of the soul. You have dared to express the thoughts & feelings that so many of us entertain but have not the power or the courage to utter. Besides, you have chosen a form singularly suited to the ideas & you have an infallible scent for the right words—the words needed for the full & clear expression of your great thoughts

Yours sincerely
Wm Schuyler
5858 Clemens Ave
St Louis

If you so desire I should send you a copy of the songs— [Columbia University]

On September 6, 1896, in response to a lost letter from Crane, Schuyler wrote again:

Your kind letter was received day before yesterday. I have written to Copeland & Day, & hope I shall receive a favorable answer. Since writing to you, I have set another one no. XXI, & now have my inner ear listening for themes for one or two more nos X & XXIII, and now my idea is to publish a little book of six songs— Those of your poems whose subjects are suited to musical treatment give such a superb opportunity to the composer that I only wish you would write more—

And now I wish to make another request—believe me I shall not feel hurt at your refusal—for I know your time is precious— I have consented to deliver a lecture before the Eliot Society of this city on "Stephen Crane & his Verse"—I have the "Black Riders" and have read two other poems—one in the Chap Book— If you could tell me where others (if they are published) are to be found—or if you could tell me how you came to choose the form you have used— It would be a great favor. Mr. Garland told me about your bringing the verses to him before they were published—which was a most interesting item.

I intend to have the songs published here in St Louis by Thiebes & Stierlin, & will send you them as soon as they come out. If I hold to my present idea of a set of six, I must wait for the other two to come to me—which may be a little while. If however you would like to see what sort of stuff my work in them is—I would gladly send you MS. copies of those already finished. Hoping that you will not abandon writing such poems—& and thanking you for your kindness

I remain yours sincerely,
Wm Schuyler
[Columbia University]

Between February 20 and May 1, 1897, Schuyler published the five songs he eventually composed in *The Criterion*, a weekly in St. Louis, entitled "Songs from Stephen Crane's 'Black Riders' " (nos. 10, 43, 21, 44, and 37). Subsequently, the five were issued by the St. Louis firm of Thiebes-Stierlin Music Co. The Library of Congress deposit copy was received on September 16, 1901. It consists of a folding of four leaves, or eight pages, page 1 being the undated titlepage in which the price is given as fifty cents and the songs are entitled "Consecration", "Good Bye", "Longing", "Darkness", and "The March of the Mountains", the whole being called *A Song Cycle from Stephen Crane's Black Riders Set to Music by William Schuyler* and *As sung by the Famous Baritone David Bispham*. The same plates as in *The Criterion* appear to be used, set for voice and piano, but with different headings, the Thiebes-Stierlin copyright notice, and marks added for pedaling.

WAR IS KIND

Before *The Black Riders* had appeared, and indeed while negotiations for its publication were in progress, Crane wrote *A soldier, young in years* (113) to preface a Memorial Day article for the *New York Press*, but when the article was rejected the poem remained unpublished. The writing of this poem in late April or early May, 1894, after a period in which his ideas had stopped led Crane to boast to Garland on May 9, 1894, that he could now turn the poetic spout on or off at will. The evidence suggests, however, that he had been overoptimistic. Thus his refusal to amplify *The Black Riders* collection as requested by Copeland and Day seems to have been prompted by a drying up in the latter half of 1894. About a year later he started to write poems once more so that sixteen had been printed between the publication of *The Black Riders* in May, 1895, and that of *War is Kind* in May, 1899. Only four were published in 1895—nos. 87, 94, 82, 75—the first three of these in the *Philistine* in August, September, and December respectively, and the fourth in the menu for the Philistine dinner tendered Crane on December 19. However, several others were probably written in 1895, among these no. 70 dated December 28 in a fair copy now in The Lilly Library and published in 1896 and no. 69 (printed in early February, 1896). Other poems must have been among the things that Crane had left in Corwin Linson's studio and which he requested on January 4, 1896, be bundled up and shipped C.O.D. to him at Hartwood. He particularly specified, "There is some 'lines' among them which I will be very glad to get; and also my contract with Copeland and Day, and with Appleton & Co." (*Letters*, p. 96). Never again did Crane have the spurt of intense energy that had produced his first volume, and it is with some resignation that he wrote to Heinemann on February 17, 1896: "I am sending you today a copy of *The Black Riders*. I imagine that when you see the volume you wont care to publish it anywhere. If however I am wrong in this opinion, I will be only too happy to have you say so. [¶] I have written very little of that sort of thing during the past year and they are all now out of my hands but if you wish [ed *deleted*] to be protected by additional copy, I can perhaps contrive it in time" (Indiana University).[15] Heinemann participated with Copeland and Day in a joint second printing and later in the year reissued the American sheets (probably in another impression) under his own imprint in November, 1896, but he did not accept Crane's offer to add new poems to the collection, no doubt because he relied exclusively on American sheets for both occasions.

Crane's publication in 1896 was only slightly larger. Of the eleven poems published in this year, nos. 69 (probably) and 70 had been written the previous December. A third, no. 71, was printed in April but was a reject from *The Black Riders*. For the rest, no. 86 came out in March, no. 76 and the set of five brief "Legends" (118–122) in May, and no. 74 (another *Black Riders* reject) in October.

The evidence of no. 88 *The impact of a dollar upon the heart* is of importance in dating about a dozen poems. We know that on March 1, 1898, Crane for the first time broached the subject of another collection of his lines in a letter to his American agent Paul Reynolds, quoted below, and promised to mail him copy 'this week'. We know that twenty-five poems are found typed by the same typewriter on the same paper, chiefly carbons of the typescripts that were the printer's copy for *War is Kind*, and had therefore been sent to Reynolds in March. (These poems are nos. 70–79, 81–82, 85–88, 90, 93–100.)

[15] The complete letter was printed for the first time in *An Exhibition of American Literature* (Bloomington, Ind.: Lilly Library, 1973), pp. 47–48.

Two pieces of evidence suggest that the typescripts were made up in December of 1897 or early January of 1898. The manuscript of no. 85 *The successful man has thrust himself* is dated December 5, 1897, below Crane's signature. If this is the date of completion of the final version, then the copy for this poem, which is in the series, must have been typed after that date. Number 88 *The impact of a dollar upon the heart* is also in this series, and perhaps among the very last to be typed since it begins the final sequence of ten poems (nos. 88, 90, 93–95, plus 96–100) which in contrast to the blue carbons of most of the others were typed with black carbons. This poem was written early enough to be printed in the *Philistine* for February, 1898. For various reasons given in the Note to the apparatus of this poem, it is possible that the *Philistine* was set up from the manuscript; no. 72 *A little ink more or less!* is among these typescripts and was also sent to Hubbard in manuscript. One may conjecture that Crane was willing to release the manuscripts of these two poems and probably those of nos. 78 and 79 printed in the *Philistine* respectively in April and May, 1896, because he already had their texts in typescript with a carbon file copy that has been preserved. Indeed, no. 78 was credited to the *Philistine* in the *War is Kind* typescript and therefore had been sent (although not necessarily accepted) before this TMs was made up.

If the typescripts were begun after December 5, 1897, they must have been completed in time for Crane to send the manuscript of no. 88 to Hubbard so that it could be printed in the February *Philistine.* We know that Crane received and marked proof for no. 79 before he sailed on April 14 for the Spanish-American War, and that it appeared in the May issue, without the proof having been returned. If Hubbard had rushed no. 88 into print without sending a proof to Crane, he might have received the manuscript in January, 1898, but if we must allow for the time to mail a proof to England and back, the odds favor a December, 1897, date. On the whole, then, although early January, 1898, is not altogether impossible as a date for the typescripts, mid-December is perhaps better. If so, then the nine poems nos. 72, 73, 78, 79, 81, 88, 90, 93, and 95 must have been written before mid-December of 1897. The date of no. 92, a revision of no. 33, cannot be known except that it would have been added to the copy sent to Reynolds and must therefore have been ready by early March, 1898, even though no typescript for it has been preserved. Nor are typescripts preserved for the early nos. 83 and 84, or for nos. 80, 89, 91, probably of early date as well, nor for nos. 101–105 of "Intrigue."

Among the poems first to appear in *War is Kind,* "Intrigue" (96–105) has customarily been taken as dating from early October, 1898, on the basis of Crane's letter of October 20, 1898, to Reynolds enclosing a piece—'a "personal anecdote" thing for McClure'—which is probably to be identified as "Marines Signaling under Fire at Guantanamo." After urging Reynolds to send him money by cable, Crane concludes with the brief paragraph, 'The "Intrigue" lot goes to Heinemann' (*Letters,* p. 189). The usual inference has been that Crane enclosed "Intrigue" with "Marines Signaling," although what Reynolds would be doing sending the sequence to Heinemann when he had sold (or was selling) the whole collection to Stokes is obscure. Physical evidence, moreover, establishes that at least nos. 96–100 of "Intrigue" had been typed up as printer's copy for *War is Kind* along with the poems whose typescripts have been identified. The evidence is of two kinds. First, the unwatermarked wove paper of the regular batch of typewritten copies measures 268 × 202.5 mm. The leaves of the typescripts for "Intrigue" are on the same unwatermarked wove paper but the sheets have been cut into small leaves 142 × 202.5 mm., their top margins formed from the original vertical edges of the sheets. More important than this use of the same paper is the fact that the typewriter can be positively identified as the same machine used to produce the regular printer's-copy typescripts for *War is Kind.* Letter for letter the two are identical, and the case is confirmed by the appearance in both sets of typescripts of the letter 'm' with a marked defect in its middle minim so that it scarcely inks. Typescripts have not been preserved for "Intrigue" nos. 101–105, but there can be no question that even though "Intrigue" nos. 96–100 were typed separately on precut leaves made from the wove-paper sheets and not on the full sheets in fixed order like the preceding poems, they would have been typed at approximately the same time and with very little if any interval between them and the poems ending with no. 95; that is, probably in December, 1897. The manner in which the torn-apart sections of the regular typescripts preceding "Intrigue" can be fitted together shows that they were in general typed in the exact order in which they were printed in *War is Kind.* Moreover, the early carbons made for Crane's file were exclusively blue, but the blue carbons stop and black carbons begin with no. 88 and continue with nos. 90, 93, 94, and 95 (all the poems preceding "Intrigue" for which typescript carbons have been preserved). Thus it is significant that "Intrigue" nos. 96–100 with black carbons were typed in their correct order following no. 95 to end the copy being prepared for the volume. Finally, the evidence of the word counts on the versos of the typescripts of "Intrigue" and the shuffling of their order even after typing, with notes for still another order on their backs, all indicate a serious intention to publish. This copy could not have been prepared in Cuba but is demonstrably a part of the preparation of the collection before Crane sailed on April 14, 1898. The unusual treatment of the paper in contrast to the other typescripts seems to have resulted from the typing of one stanza per leaf so that they could be exchanged and tried in different orders in a manner impossible if they had been typed in sequence on full sheets of the paper, as were the earlier poems.

Very little record is preserved of the publishing history of Crane's second book of verse, *War is Kind.* The most important document is a transcript of a letter dated March 1, 1898, addressed from Ravensbrook to his American agent Paul Reynolds.

> I will forward you this week copies of about thirty "Lines" which are to be issued with about twenty more in a small volumn the size of the Black Riders. In fact, I can turn in half the copy. I think we ought to be able to raise a little wind, say £30.0.0 on a contract at once. The stipulations are as follows:—A payment of £30.0.0 upon the delivery of stuff amounting to half a book the size of the Black Riders. The rest of the copy to be ready in time to have the book on the market for the Xmas sales. The £30.0.0 to be considered as an advance on the 15/-percent royalty.
>
> I have written to my friend Elbert Hubbard of East Aurora Erie Co. N.Y. that you will give him the first chance. I think he is quite sure to accept this offer. . . .
>
> P.S. Please see MacArthur and get from him a copy of an old number of the Bookman which contains some "Lines" of mine entitled War is Kind. Make a copy of these lines yourself to include in the stuff which I shall send you and send another copy to me. [Syracuse University, typed transcript]

As usual, Crane was optimistic, but the advent of the Spanish-American War and his departure for Cuba somewhat over a month after this letter interrupted his plans to write the proposed number of new lines. *War is Kind* includes only thirty-seven poems, of which the last five in the "Intrigue" sequence may have been written later in Havana. Crane proposed to send 'about thirty "Lines" ' to Reynolds in the first week of March and he may have sent, in fact, thirty-two. Of these, ten (nos. 69–71, 74–76, 82, 86, 87, and 94) had previously appeared in periodicals; these are included in the typescripts prepared for *War is Kind* and now preserved. In addition to these ten, sixteen other typescripts have been preserved (72, 73, 77–79, 81, 85, 88, 90, 93, 95–100) that must have been sent. Among these no. 77 (an early manuscript of which is at Columbia) was written in the United States. The manuscript of no. 85 is on English paper and therefore later. Numbers 72, 78, 79, and 88 were sent in manuscript to the *Philistine* after being typed and all but no. 72 were printed there during 1898. At least six and possibly eleven poems that appeared in *War is Kind* have had no typescripts preserved. Two of these are demonstrably early work: no. 83 probably dates from 1894, and no. 84 was rejected by Copeland and Day from *The Black Riders.* (The manuscripts of both Crane had kept in England.) Another older poem is no. 92, a revision of *The Black Riders* no. 33. No information can be recovered about the remaining three which lack both typescripts and manuscripts—nos. 80, 89, and 91—to which for the moment may be added the nos. 101–105 of "Intrigue." Typescripts must have existed at one time for nos. 83, 84, and 92 (although it is odd to find them missing for three early poems). Whatever it was that affected the preservation of typescripts for these three may also have operated for nos. 80, 89, and 91. One may only speculate. If these last three may be included among the lot sent to Reynolds in early March, then Crane had brought together the copy for thirty-two poems. In his letter to Reynolds he recognized that these were only about a half of what would be necessary for the volume, and he cheerfully promised to write twenty more. So far as can be told, he did nothing to add other poems before he sailed for Cuba on April 14, 1898, although one cannot be sure, of course, that the six poems without typescripts had not been mailed to supplement only twenty-six posted in the first week of March. If so, by the inclusion of nos. 83, 84, and 92 he was scraping the bottom of the barrel, and his failure to include any from rejected 109–111, 113, 115–117, and 126 —all of which are known to have been written before he made up *War is Kind*—is difficult to account for since these eight poems (and possibly others of less certain date) would have brought him closer to his target. Such as the evidence is, it suggests that he deliberately excluded these eight from his collection although their manuscripts were available to him in England.[16]

However, some poems were indeed written later. After the war had ended and he was living in Havana, Crane wrote Reynolds on September 14, 1898, "I enclose you the rest of the poems for Stokes co." (Syracuse University, typed transcript). Since the typescripts at Columbia University represent the printer's copy for *War is Kind,* and since it can be demonstrated that this copy had been typed before early March, 1898, and probably in December, 1897, the twenty-six poems preserved in these uniform typescripts (including nos. 96–100 of "Intrigue") must be excluded from consideration, and to these may certainly be added the early nos. 83, 84, and 92 without typescripts. Thus the only possibilities remaining for the lines Crane sent from Havana on September 14 are nos. 80, 89, and 91, and nos. 101–105 of "Intrigue," none of which are preserved in typescript. Critics have over-

[16] The preservation at Columbia of the carbon on American-made paper of the typescript that Reynolds ordered indicates that he followed the instructions in Crane's letter of March 1. Unless Crane took the manuscripts of various poems to the war (a most unlikely conjecture) we must believe that between his letter of March 1 to Reynolds and the dispatch of printer's copy he wrote no new poems that are not represented among the typescripts preserved at Columbia, except perhaps for no. 129. Crane sailed from England on April 14, 1898. It is not likely that in the final few weeks he would write more verse, if indeed there had been time after the mailing of copy to Reynolds. Evidently he had occupied himself in the main with assembling published poems and bringing together and looking over (and occasionally revising) earlier poems still in manuscript; only a dozen or so could represent new current compositions in late 1897 to early 1898. After he had assembled and mailed the copy—although lacking the twenty new poems promised—the pressure was wanting that seems to have stimulated him to write more poetry in Havana. Thus it is unlikely that any of the unpublished manuscripts preserved at Columbia that were not typed up on the single lot of paper used as printer's copy represent poems written in late March and early April after the copy had been dispatched.

looked this September 14 letter and thus have misconstrued Crane's mention on October 20 of 'The "Intrigue" lot [that] goes to Heinemann' as signifying that "Intrigue" in its entirety had been composed in Cuba and had been sent to Reynolds, as a lot, on October 20. At the most, only nos. 101–105 could qualify. As for nos. 80 *A newspaper is a collection of half-injustices,* no. 89 *A man said to the universe,* and no. 91 *There was a land where lived no violets,* internal evidence, as well as external, is wanting that would associate them with poems written in Cuba. Number 80 does not mention the war, in a poem whose point might invite the subject, no. 89 is much in the style of *The Black Riders,* and no. 91 still clings to the violet symbol which, for example, had been present in line 9 of no. 82 *A slant of sun on dull brown walls* in its December, 1895, *Philistine* appearance but in the typescript for *War is Kind* had been replaced by 'flowers'. The odds, then, would seem to favor the hypothesis that 'the rest of the poems for Stokes' sent on September 14 was limited to "Intrigue" nos. 101–105, and that in his October 20 letter Crane was not, in fact, sending the poems but instead was answering a query from Reynolds. This query is not difficult to reconstruct. Crane had enclosed to Reynolds on September 14 "Marines Signaling under Fire" and, say, "Intrigue" nos. 101–105, which in his view would complete the collection of *War is Kind.* "Marines Signaling" in his letter was to be sent to McClure and the poems to Stokes. Reynolds was aware that Crane was angling for English publication of his poems but apparently did not know for certain what firm was interested. Presumably he asked Crane in a lost letter where to send copies of the supplementary poems in England, and Crane answered, to Heinemann. It would follow that Crane had left copies of the typescripts with Heinemann before he sailed from England, and thus would want the last batch of poems to be added so that the collection would be complete in England as well as in the United States. The absence of typescripts for nos. 101–105 fits with the reference to "Intrigue" in the letter of October 20 to make this reconstruction plausible enough to form a working hypothesis.

Since the printer's-copy manuscripts were in existence before March, 1898, although their black carbons suggest that nos. 96–100 were perhaps the last of the typescripts to be made up, an earlier date for the composition of the first part of "Intrigue" than the conventional one is indicated. The absence of all manuscripts with paper that might have been identified means that internal evidence alone can bear on the problem. The terms of sexual intimacy that are present in some of the poems in the first group suggest strongly that they were written to Cora Stewart, and a date corresponding to Crane's first violent infatuation between late November and the end of December 1896 may be proposed. His one preserved love-letter to her (undated but assignable perhaps to January, 1897) is much in the mood and makes "poetic" use of the theme of his no. 74 *I explain the silvered passing of a ship at night* (*Letters*, p. 138). That Crane was a literary man seems to have appealed to Cora from the start, and Crane played up the role, even to inscribing a copy of *George's Mother* to her as 'an unnamed sweetheart' perhaps within a few days of their first meeting (*Letters*, p. 132). A sequence of poems to her would have proved most acceptable. Placing the date of the first part of the sequence back into late 1896, or perhaps early 1897, helps a little to explain the old-fashioned romantic style and language of this series, but it is attractive to speculate—for one can do no more—that in an earlier form they may have derived from Crane's infatuation with Lily Brandon and were originally written as early as 1894. Whatever the date of their original (or transferred) inspiration, however, it is another of the mysteries surrounding Crane that of all subjects for poetry in Havana in the autumn of 1898 he would revert to this series and add five more (though briefer) sections, still in the same perfervid vein. Even so, some clarification of his biography may result from emphasis upon the hard—and new—fact that nos. 96–100 of "Intrigue" were not written in Cuba and must have been composed at some unknown time before they were typed up in December, 1897.

Records are not preserved of the acceptance of the book by Stokes, the terms, or anything about the negotiations, such as whether Reynolds first offered the volume to Hubbard according to Crane's original instructions. (Reynolds could scarcely have been enthusiastic about this suggestion.) It would seem that Reynolds was discouraging about the prospects of publication in the United States, for in a letter dated May 30, 1898, off Havana, enclosing the first of the Whilomville stories, Crane added: "Dont take the poems to Lane. Try an American house" (Syracuse University, typed transcript). However, by September 14 Stokes must have expressed some definite interest, for not only did Crane send Reynolds more poems (perhaps at Stokes's insistence) but he also urged, "Collect the 30 and hold it subject to my cable." The reference to closing the deal by collecting the advance of £30 sounds definite enough and it may be taken that at that time Reynolds signed the contract with Stokes. After Crane had returned to England he continued his attempts to interest Heinemann. In a letter to his English agent Pinker on February 4, 1899, Crane remarked that he had told Pawling, of Heinemann's, "that if 'disposing of the lines (poems) is giving him any trouble' I would like to have them handed over to you" (*Letters*, p. 207).

Stokes applied for copyright on March 10, 1899—perhaps at the end of typesetting—and made deposit in the Library of Congress on April 17. The book was announced in the *Publishers' Weekly* for May 20.

Between Crane's return to the United States from Cuba on November 21, 1898, and his sailing for England in early January, he was busy, in poor health, and unlikely to have concerned himself with his poems. Moreover, it is also unlikely that proofs were available this early. The brief interval between his return to England and the production of the book in finished form on April 17, 1899, would have been sufficient for proofs to have been sent and returned, providing that typesetting had been started before the date of copyright on March 10 but not otherwise. However, no evidence is preserved to indicate that Crane saw proofs and corrected the copy for *War is Kind.* When carbons are available of the typescript that was the printer's copy, the wording is identical except for a few book errors, and the relatively few instances of variation that seem to have some authority can be attributed as readily to changes made in the lost typescript printer's copy but not transferred to the carbons as to alterations in proof.[17]

The English rights hung fire. It was expected that Heinemann would publish the book since he had issued *The Black Riders*, but evidently he was unwilling to make up his mind from whatever copies Crane had submitted to Pawling and preferred to wait for the sheets. On April 17, 1899, the same day that Stokes deposited his copyright volume, Reynolds wrote Crane:

> Stokes is publishing shortly your book of verses "WAR IS KIND" which has been made up by him in a very attractive shape by Bradley. He is sending some copies to Heinemann to have him copyright it. I would advise your seeing Heinemann and seeing if you can make an arrangement with him to publish the book. Stokes will quote him terms for sheets when he sends him the copies. You will remember I wrote to Heinemann about the book a number of months back and he replied that he would not pay any advance but that he would publish the book on a royalty basis. Of course if you can do better with some one else, why I suppose you will do it. [Columbia University]

Stokes sent Heinemann advance copies, and Heinemann went so far as to secure his copyright by depositing in the British Museum on April 29, 1899, a copy of the Stokes edition with a black handstamp '*LONDON.* | *WILLIAM HEINEMANN*' above the New York imprint. In the end, however, Heinemann seems to have declined the venture and the book was not published in England.

The description is as follows:

[17] Examples would be *War is Kind* 'thud' for TMs 'third' in *"Have you ever made a just man?"* (73), line 6; WK 'displaced' for TMs 'misplaced' in *The trees in the garden rained flowers* (95), line 27; WK 'desire' for TMs 'desires' in *Love forgive me if I wish you grief* (97), line 40. In WK 'There' for TMs 'The' in *Thou art my love* (96), line 13, the TMs mistake was obvious and could have been corrected in the print-shop. These are slim pickings for the substantives; the rest are accidentals but do include the probably authoritative change in the lineation of line 14 in no. 96.

[within a rule-frame divided into panels; to the right a single vertical panel containing two candles on tall candlesticks, with bunches of grapes and a bird; to the left, below a top blank panel of double rules, five horizontal panels with decorations of a bird and a lyre] [bird] WAR iS | KiND *by* | STEPHEN CRANE || [lyre] | DRAWiNGS | *by* WiLL | BRADLEY || [blank panel] || NEW YORK | FREDERiCK A | STOKES *Company* | MDCCCXCIX

Collation: [1]^2 [2–8]^4 [9]^8 [10–11]^4; pp. [5–8] 9–96; leaf measures 212 × 130 mm., all edges deckle untrimmed; thick gray laid paper, vertical chain-lines 30 mm. apart; endpapers of four quired leaves of text paper front and back, the outer leaves pasted down.

Contents: p. 5: title; p. 6: 'Copyright, 1899, by | Frederick A. Stokes Company | *Arranged and Printed by Will Bradley at the* | *University Press, Cambridge and New York*'; p. 7: spear decoration; p. 8: drawing of woman with sword and decorations of arrows, birds, and sprays of flowers; p. 9: text with head-title '[horizontal leaf] WAR IS KIND', ending on p. 96.

Note: In order to space out the relatively few poems, the text fills only the upper half of the pages, two-line heading caps marking the start of poems, which are untitled and unnumbered. Full-page art nouveau illustrations appear on pp. 13, 29, 37, 61, and 75; on their versos, pp. 14, 30, 38, 62, and 76 a flower or plant design substitutes for text. Tailpieces of birds, flowers, candles, lyres, swords, masks follow text on pp. 15, 19, 35, 49, 53, 66, 70, 79, 85, and 88. The pagination beginning the text on sig. 2_1 with page 9 was planned for an initial quire of four leaves, not of two as was printed. The latter two of the free flyleaves cannot be counted as inferential pages 1–4.

Binding: Heavy gray laid paper, horizontal chains of the same stock as the text, over boards, all lettering in black. *Front*: '[symbolic design in panels, including trees, a woman with a sword, a harp, and an urn, signed in upper left panel 'BRADLEY'] | WAR iS | KiND *by* | STEPHEN | CRANE'. *Spine*: gray paper label (42 × 19 mm.) [within two panels within a rule-frame] [panel 1] WAR | IS | KIND | [panel 2] STEPHEN | CRANE'. *Back*: blank.

Publication: Price, $2.50. Copyright applied for on March 20, 1899, and deposit made on April 17; announced in *Publishers' Weekly* on May 20.

Copies: University of Virginia–Barrett (551465), endpapers front and back consist of a single fold, the outer leaf pasted down; Harvard University; British Museum (11687.ee.15), datestamped 29 April 1897, above imprint is black handstamp '*LONDON.* | *WILLIAM HEINEMANN*'.

UNCOLLECTED POEMS

During Crane's lifetime the only other interest shown in publishing his poems was that of Edward Clarence Stedman, editor of the influential *An American Anthology 1787–1900: Selections Illustrating the Editor's Critical Review of American Poetry in the Nineteenth Century*, published by Houghton, Mifflin in 1900. Stedman's letter to Crane has not been preserved, but on September 4, 1899, Crane wrote him from Brede Place: 'The two little books—"The Black Riders" and "War is Kind" contain every line which I've written outside of prose form. I hope you are now entirely recovered from your illness and I hope that the new book will be the success which its distinguished author has the right to exact. Pray give my regards to your son Mr. Arthur Stedman, and believe me to be with the most pleasant remembrance. Yours faithfully *Stephen Crane*' (*Letters*, p. 229). Stedman chose nos. 1, 22, 25, 27, 65 from *The Black Riders* and nos. 74, 81, 91 from *War is Kind.* Since these are reprints without independent authority, variants have not been recorded in the present edition.

After Crane's death Cora typed almost all of the poetic manuscripts she found among his papers and attempted to sell various of them, although she had only a hazy idea of what had and had not appeared and was inclined to think that any poem found in manuscript had not been printed. One of her attempts was the collection of five typed poems offered for sale as "Lines" with a titlepage that gave her address as 6 Milborne Grove, The Boltons, S.W., an address to which she had moved in September, 1900. This set consists of three leaves of Indian & Colonial wove paper plus a titlepage of the same, containing nos. 88, 136, 85, 109, and 110, of which the first and third had already appeared in *War is Kind.*[18] Another collection, but one that Cora broke up, typed on Excelsior Fine laid paper, consisted of seven poems on eight sheets now in the Special Collections of the Columbia University Library: no. 115 was paged 1 and noted by Cora in ink as not used in the United States; no. 74 was paged 2 and noted in ink as in *War is Kind*; no. 116 paged 3 was noted as not used in *War is Kind*; no. 117 was paged 4; no. 111 paged 5; no. 109 paged 6–7 but the numbers deleted and replaced in pencil by 1–2; and no. 110 was paged 8 (deleted) and on its verso noted as sent to the magazine *Truth* on April 3, 1901.[19]

None of the typed versions of poems left unpublished at Crane's death is on paper resembling that of the carbons of the printer's copy

[18] The original typescript is preserved in the Syracuse University Library. A carbon on Excelsior Fine paper of a similar titlepage but in a different typing is at Columbia University (see below). If this group had been for sale only in England, Cora would have been justified in including the poems from *War is Kind*, but the odds are that she had not checked their previous publication.

[19] Whether this notation refers only to no. 110, which has had its original pagination deleted (as is probable), or to the set before the file copies were broken up is not to be determined, although Cora would have been foolish to try to reprint no. 74 in the United States. It is also uncertain whether a titlepage at Columbia University similar to that in the five-poem collection but of another typing was originally attached to this seven-poem collection. Since the five-poem sequence at Syracuse University is typed on Indian & Colonial wove paper, and the Columbia titlepage on laid Excelsior Fine, like the original seven poems, the odds favor its identification with the set of seven, although it is a blue carbon whereas the poems are black ribbon copies.

for *War is Kind*; so far as the evidence is preserved, therefore, it would seem that none of these poems can be identified as originally typed for that volume but subsequently rejected, although a few poems that should have been available remained in manuscript either through oversight or by choice. The manuscripts that Crane left were a miscellaneous lot. For some reason Cora apparently did not type the manuscripts of nos. 113 and 128, nor of course the slight no. 124 or the fragment no. 112. When no. 130 was given to her by Michelson of the *New York Journal* as found in Crane's saddle bags (Lillian Gilkes, *Cora Crane* [1960], p. 228), she typed it with a carbon on wove paper watermarked Indian & Colonial but it found no sale. A report that it was offered to and rejected by the *Pall Mall* is substantiated by the appearance of this poem as "Battle Hymn" on page 2 of an inventory of Crane's short pieces, with their place of publication, that Cora made up after his death. There it is assigned to the "Pall Mall Magazine" but with the notation followed by a question mark. (See the illustration in *Works*, Volume VIII, TALES, SKETCHES, AND REPORTS.) About the same time nos. 132–136 were typed on an unwatermarked laid paper, the carbon of no. 136 being found on Indian & Colonial. Numbers 133, 134, and 136 were typed on full sheets of this laid paper, but the other two on part sheets that do not fit together: no. 132 is on a mid-section torn across at top and bottom, and no. 135 on the top half of a sheet. It is a reasonable conjecture that other poems were typed on the remaining parts of these sheets but the copies have been lost. For the rest of the unpublished poems, Cora typed no. 117 on laid paper watermarked Excelsior Fine and no. 114 on the top half of what is probably a sheet of this same paper. She copied by hand no. 123 (paged 3) and 126 (paged 4), both on Excelsior Fine, and no. 128 (paged 2) on a cheap wove copy paper. Typed copies of these three poems (which she signed in Stephen's name) are not preserved. The other poems now known were not available to her at Brede. Number 108, it is true, was buried in Crane's early Notebook, which was in her possession and which she quarried after his death, but perhaps the poem was overlooked or thought to be a duplicate. The manuscript of no. 107 had been kept by Corwin Linson, and no. 131 had been the epigraph for the short story "The Clan of No-Name." Cora seems not to have been acquainted with "Legends" (118–122) printed in the *Bookman* in May, 1896, or with "Wheels" (129), printed in the *Philistine* in December, 1898. The manuscript of no. 125 was at Brede, but she may have known of its publication in the *Philistine* in June, 1898, for she typed no copy even for English sale so far as is known.

At some unknown time after Crane's death Cora made up a three-page inventory of his short pieces, with note of the place of publication when the information was available to her. (For reproductions, see the illustrations in *Works*, VIII.) This inventory was headed 'For book'. Its first two items were 'Lines–"War is Kind." published U.S.'

and 'Lines–never yet published' assigned the figure of 1,210 words. On the versos of various of the unpublished poems are Cora's cumulative word counts which on the back of no. 127, after a series of errors, reaches the total of 1,210 repeated in the inventory.

For a time Pinker had these unpublished poems, but in a letter of August 28, 1900, from 47 Gower Street, London, she lost patience at his inability to sell them: "I explained my position to you yesterday. And so I must ask you to return me all the MS. & the verses to see what I can do with them personally" (Dartmouth). But she was no more successful than Pinker, and in case she placed them subsequently in the hands of her new agent, Perris, he in turn must have failed to find any acceptances. In the meantime, Reynolds in New York had a set, received in late August, 1900. He was not optimistic about sales. On September 4, 1900, he wrote to Cora, "With regard to the verses of poetry which you send me, I doubt if I can sell them, but I will look them over and see" (Columbia University). Two days later, on September 6, he wrote again: "I have also offered to Harper the story you sent me called 'A Self-Made Man' and the verses you sent me. Am I to understand that these verses have never been published? I assume so from your letter, but as I wrote you by the last mail, I am quite sure that the lines ending with the refrain 'God is cold' have already appeared in the volume of verses published by Mr. Stokes. I arranged that book with Mr. Stokes, and I am strongly of the opinion that I remember reading these lines. The book was entitled 'War is Kind' " (Columbia University). The poem to which Reynolds refers is *A man adrift on a slim spar* (126), which had not been published. It is odd that Reynolds should have recalled the poem—or thought he did—but the evidence is too uncertain on which to hinge any speculation that no. 126 had passed through his hands in manuscript but had been withdrawn from the volume. It is also most uncertain whether Reynolds could have read it in a lost typescript Crane had sent him to sell. No evidence exists for Reynolds having acted as agent for Crane's poems to be sold to periodicals except on this occasion for Cora. As he had feared, Reynolds also was unable to place any poem. Magazines both in England and in the United States had lost all interest.

In 1905 a second edition of *The Black Riders* appeared, copyrighted by Copeland and Day and privately reprinted by courtesy of Small, Maynard & Co., to whom the copyright had passed. The entrepreneur is not known. This was the last edition of the poems before Follett's in 1930.

THE DATES OF THE POEMS

Crane made two lists of his poems, both of which are preserved in the Special Collections of the Columbia University Libraries. The order of the two is not demonstrable but can be conjecturally established.

The first list was written in what is now a brown-black ink on the recto of a sheet of legal-cap paper 294 × 200 mm., 28 rules spaced about 9.8 mm., extending full across. The vertical pink-blue-pink rules are 37 mm. from the left margin. The headspace is 27 mm. deep and the tailpiece 1 mm. In the following transcription the poem numbers according to the present edition are added in brackets as well as the place and date of first publication.

[70] The Shell and the Pines [*Philistine*, February, 1896]
[69] War is kind [newspapers, February 9, 1896]
[86] The Prayer of the Peaks [*Chapbook*, March, 1896]
[77] The Candid Man [*War is Kind*, 1899]
[76] The Knight rode fast— [*Souvenir*, May, 1896]
[87] Chatter of a Death-Demon in a tree top [*Philistine*, August, 1895]
[82] The Noise of the City [*Philistine*, December, 1895]
[short double rule]
[115] Chant you loud of punishments [unpublished]
[74] I explain the path of a ship [*Bookman*, October, 1896]
[116] If you would seek a friend [unpublished]
[117] Oh night dismal, night glorious [unpublished]

The date of inscription can be assigned within fairly narrow limits. With the exception of no. 77 (which appears in both lists among the poems printed in periodicals as if Crane expected its imminent publication), the poems above the rule had been published. The earliest date is August, 1895, for no. 87, and the latest is May, 1896, for no. 76, although Crane may have been thinking here, as he did in the second list, of its appearance in the *Philistine* a month later, in June. It is clear that the purpose of the rule between the sections was to distinguish published from unpublished poems, at the time of inscription; hence when one finds no. 74 in the second group although published in October, 1896, the inference is obvious that it was placed among the unpublished poems because Crane had not sold it at the time he wrote the list. The list can be dated, therefore, between the outer limits of May and October, 1896, but more narrowly, in all likelihood, in July–August.

The second list is written on a cheap wove lined pad paper 251 ×171 mm., in a black ink now turned brown. This list numbers the items and gives the place of publication. The original list was confined to poems printed in periodicals, with the exception of no. 77, which was given last.

[94] 1 The Lantern Song Philistine [September, 1895]
[75] 2 The White Birches Philistine [January, 1896]
[87] 3 The Death-demon Philistine [August, 1895]
[71] 4 The Sea—Point of View Philistine [April, 1896]
[76] 5 The Knight and his Horse Philistine [June, 1896]
[70] 6 The Sea to the Pines Philistine [February, 1896]
[69] 7 The Drums of the Regiment. Bookman [February, 1896]

[82] 8 The City. Philistine [December, 1895]
[86] 9 The Prayer of the Mountains— Chap-book [March, 1896]
[77] 10 The Candid Man ———
[125] 11 [The Call *deleted*] Blue Battalions [Philistine, June, 1898]
[126] 12 [The *deleted*] "A man afloat on a slim spar. [unpublished]
13
14
15

The date of this list is less easy to assign. All of the fifteen numbers were written out in the original ink, which also was used for the inscription of the titles of the first ten poems. The titles of the eleventh and twelfth poems (125, 126) with the false starts were written both at the same time, apparently, with a finer pen and in an ink that has not faded from its blackness. One may conjecture that these last two titles were added before June, 1898, the date of publication of no. 11 (125) (actually before Crane left England on April 14), that they recorded newly written poems, and thus that the June, 1898, date has no bearing on the inscription of the original list. It is no doubt significant that all of the published section in the first list is represented in the second list, but with the addition of nos. 94, 75, and 71 in the second. These three additions have no bearing on the dates of the two lists, however, since their publication came within the spreads of the records of other titles. In both lists June, 1896, remains the last date for a published entry. However, the greater comprehensiveness of the second list and its specification of the periodicals, plus its extra numbers left vacant for future use, may suggest that it was later than the first. The variant titles indicate that the second was made up from memory without reference to the first list, however; thus its added titles may have little importance in dating, except that it would be unusual, perhaps, for a second list to be deficient when the first had been full. In fact, the second list is complete for the periodical publication of new poems up to June, 1896 (save for "Legends" in May, missing from both lists), and since it attempts to record only published items, a significance can be found in its omission of no. 74, not printed until October, 1896. It would seem probable, then, to conjecture that this second list was inscribed shortly after the first—possibly when the first had been mislaid, but possibly to start an orderly record of publication—and with greater care. The same months of July–August, 1896, appear to be the best dates for the second list as well, in its original form. The added eleventh and twelfth titles would have been written-in in England, on the evidence of the English laid paper of their manuscripts. No. 126 could not have been written in the last days of 1896, before the sinking of the *Commodore,* nor could the present manuscript have been inscribed before Crane's return to England from Greece in June, 1897. Late 1897 for the composition of these two poems, the first resumption of Crane's poetry writing after

1896, seems to be an acceptable date for the addition of the two titles. A third poem is evidently represented by the deleted title "The Call" (perhaps incomplete) before no. 11, and partly repeated before no. 12. Footnote 25 below, discussing the conjectural dating of no. 72, makes a speculative identification of that poem with the deleted title.

Evidence about the dating of poems other than the sparse information of the two lists is dependent upon their publication in periodicals or in *War is Kind*, but bibliographical analysis of paper and of authorial markings, together with some references in letters and memoirs, on occasion enable a critic to assign relatively exact dates within a few months.

Save for the accounts of Corwin Linson and Hamlin Garland, the only titles mentioned for *The Black Riders* poems come in Crane's correspondence with Copeland and Day. On September 27, 1894, he decided to title the book after *Black riders* (a decision that moved it up to no. 1, displacing *Three little birds in a row*), and on October 30 he sent in a revised text for the poem. Earlier, on October 19, Copeland and Day had positively refused to print three poems, including nos. 71 and 109). They advised against four more, including Nos. 84 and 110. Crane withdrew all seven. Number 71 came out in the *Philistine* in April, 1896, and then in *War is Kind*, whereas no. 84 in a revised text was printed only in the later collection. Copeland and Day's first, fifth, and sixth discards have been lost, at least in any recognizable form.

Nothing in the preserved (though incomplete) correspondence suggests that Crane ever added to the collection once he had submitted it, probably in late April, 1894. If Garland's memory is accurate that before April 25 and his own departure from New York Crane told him that Barry had fired them off to Copeland and Day, then the dispatch of the collection coincided roughly with the drying up of his output with the lost "Reformer" that he showed to Garland and Herne probably in April. We know that before May 9, however, Crane had written *A soldier young in years* (113). Possibly his remark to Garland that he could now turn on and off the poetic spout indicates that other poems had also been written; possibly Crane took the writing of this poem as evidence that he could still compose lines. The case is obscure, and it is not materially clarified by the false start of no. 83 on the verso of the last leaf of the essay to which no. 113 is prefixed, even supposing that this trial preceded no. 113—a most uncertain matter. However, the appearance of a trial of the first few words of no. 83 in Crane's Notebook in a position that suggests either late summer or early autumn of 1894 may conjecturally place the trial on the leaf of no. 113 as after, not before, the composition of that poem in late April or early May. The preserved full manuscript of no. 83 as it was finally composed is on unidentifiable paper and appears to be a fair copy which could have been made at any time after the writing-out of the original draft form; however, that the text of no. 83 was further revised for *War is Kind* may suggest that the fair copy manuscript was early. Thus it is quite possible to speculate that by September Crane had not reached a satisfactory version of no. 83 that he was prepared to see printed, and it is very likely that he was still struggling to get some complete form down on paper. At any rate, no. 113 when declined by the *New York Press* before May 9 remained unpublished. It would have been out of place in *The Black Riders*; thus from its example no inference can be made that poems Crane wrote about the same time or shortly afterwards (if indeed he wrote any that he regarded as satisfactory for publication) were excluded from the collection. We know that on September 9 he told Copeland and Day firmly: "You wish I would write a few score more. It is utterly impossible to me. We would be obliged to come to an agreement upon those that are written." If appropriate poems had indeed been composed between May and September, this would have been an odd answer. Wanting any indication to the contrary, we may be justified in leaning on the conjecture that no. 113 was a single swallow only (joined later by a rejected draft of no. 83) and that we have no evidence that Crane wrote more poems than these two between "The Reformer" and the letter of September 9. It is possible, of course, that he had and that his refusal to write more (meaning to send some already written) was actuated by pique at Copeland and Day's first attempt at censorship and that he refused to give them any poems that might be considered to substitute for those they wished to remove. But the whole matter is subject only to speculation. What evidence there is suggests that no poems were available that Crane felt were suitable to print, and that when he withdrew the seven at Copeland and Day's request on October 19, he made no attempt to replace them, perhaps for the obvious reason that he had none in shape. Thereafter Crane seems to have thought that the volume was closed and about to go to the printer once he had sent in the revised no. 1 on October 30.

With the exception of the three preserved manuscripts from the four poems withdrawn at Copeland and Day's request, no concrete evidence associates any of the unpublished manuscripts found after his death with *The Black Riders* or its immediate period. A temptation exists to make such an association, for in the letter of September 9 Crane had voluntarily withdrawn an unknown number, listed in an enclosure, which he believed 'unworthy to print.' Hence the possibility must be surveyed that some of the unpublished manuscripts that we have, or even some of the poems first printed in *War is Kind*, represent these withdrawn lines. The example of no. 83 (without a typescript) shows that early poems may exist. Indeed, the paper of its manuscript providing no evidence, the early date of no. 83 (probably in the autumn of 1894) would never have been known had it not been for the trials appearing in Crane's Notebook and on the verso of a leaf of no. 113. On the other hand, the only typescript that was made (or at least has been preserved) for a rejected early poem is that of no. 71 *To the maiden,* which Copeland and Day had declined to print. However, this may represent a special case, for it is the only one of the withdrawn poems that was ever published in a periodical before *War is Kind* and the typescript was a copy not of a manuscript but of the *Philistine* text of April, 1896. So far as is known, then, Crane acquiesced in his publishers' judgment that the seven poems should not be published, save for no. 71 and no. 84 *There was a man with tongue of wood,* which was also included in *War is Kind* but without a preserved typescript.

That from the start no. 71 was accepted as a poem for *War is Kind* is indicated by the fact that it is typed on the same page as no. 70, indeed the first page of the typescripts to be made up (no. 69 having been typed for Reynolds in the United States at Crane's request). Its publication in the *Philistine* in April, 1896, shows that Crane disagreed with Copeland and Day about its subject and its merits. Nevertheless, the manuscript not being preserved we have no means of knowing whether he had revised the text before its periodical publication. The inference is that he had, since its second line differs in the *Philistine* from Copeland and Day's quotation in their letter of October 19, 1894. Although *War is Kind* also gave refuge to no. 84, nos. 109 and 110 were not included despite the fact that Crane had their manuscripts in England. It is interesting that no. 84, like the early no. 83, was revised for *War is Kind.* Thus some document stood between these two early manuscripts and the printer's copy. Number 92, a revision of no. 33 of *The Black Riders,* also joins this group. No typescript for it is preserved, and its manuscript has been altered in the final text. Of the six poems (barring "Intrigue" nos. 101–105) which appear in *War is Kind* without known typescripts, three are demonstrably early and date from 1894. Two of them are rejects from *The Black Riders,* but no. 83 was probably not completed in time for *The Black Riders.* The manuscript of no. 83, as remarked, was thoroughly revised for *War is Kind* even though it had itself been a fair copy. If three of the six date from 1894, perhaps the other three may lack typescripts for the same cause, whatever it was.[20] These would be no. 80 *A newspaper is a collection of half-injustices,* no. 89 *A man*

[20] There is not much point in trying to guess why these typescripts are wanting. It will be shown below that the strong possibility exists they were inserted in the collection as substitutes for withdrawn poems. If so, the decision was made after the typing of the collection was completed, and perhaps in a hurry. It is possible that by some error only one carbon (which would have gone to Heinemann) was made instead of the two that allowed Crane to keep a file copy for the original typescripts.

said to the universe, and no. 91 *There was a land where lived no violets.*

These three poems were remarked above as candidates for writing in Havana in September, 1898, along with the composition or revision of "Intrigue" nos. 101–105, but the hypothesis was rejected, first on the ground that there was nothing in them that suggested a Cuban subject or background, and second because it was most improbable that Crane would have requested Reynolds to see that Heinemann was sent the supplementary poems of "Intrigue" but not these as well to complete the file. More important, physical evidence seems to associate these three poems with the early nos. 83, 84, and 92. The order of the poems in *War is Kind* corresponds exactly to the order of the typing from no. 70 to 79, which concludes a leaf below no. 78. Next comes no. 80 with no TMs. After this are nos. 81 and 82 on one leaf. The evidence here is ambiguous. Some leaves contain as many as 44 typed lines in one or two poems, whereas others have as few as the 24 of combined nos. 81–82, the 25 lines of no. 86 on a single leaf, and—uniquely—the 12 lines of no. 87 on a full leaf. Thus the 21 lines of no. 80 could have occupied a full leaf which, if lost, would have left no physical trace. The case is altered for nos. 83–84, however. Together these total only 15 lines. It is not impossible, of course, to speculate that these two short poems took up a full sheet (although one could compare the three poems nos. 72–74 totaling 38 lines typed on one sheet and the three nos. 75–77 of 37 lines on the next). But a manifest disruption has occurred with no. 85, the very next poem. Here only the upper part of the leaf is preserved on which are typed its 24 lines, and the lower part measuring 100 mm. and capable of holding 15–20 lines is missing. Since no. 86 on a full leaf then follows, it seems evident that some typed poem has been withdrawn after no. 85. This missing portion could not have held nos. 83–84 since they would then have been out of sequence, the only known case in *War is Kind.* Number 89 is the next poem without a typescript. It is preceded by no. 88, of 22 lines, which is preserved on the upper part of a leaf, the lower portion measuring 101 mm. being lost. The five lines of no. 89 could readily have fitted here; but the case is by no means certain, for still another disruption occurs when no. 90, of 6 lines, is found on the lower part of a leaf, the upper measuring 111 mm. not preserved. Whereas a hypothetical typescript of no. 89 could have fitted onto either of these part-leaves—below no. 88 or above no. 90—it could not have been in two places at once, and clearly another disruption has taken place. The last two poems without typescripts, nos. 91 and 92 totaling 26 lines, come between no. 90, which is on the lower half of a leaf, and no. 93, which occupies a full leaf with no. 94.

This evidence for disruption is ambivalent for no. 80 between two full leaves, for nos. 83–84 between a full leaf and the upper part of the next, and nos. 91–92 between the lower part of a leaf and the full leaf of no. 93. But it is clear that something is missing when no. 89 comes between the upper part of the typescript of no. 88 and the lower part of the typescript of no. 90. (The two halves, moreover, do not form a single leaf.) It is significant, also, that except for no. 80, sandwiched between two full leaves of typescripts, the other poems appear always in connection with some disruption as evidenced by the only incomplete leaves in the sequence. The conclusion is inevitable that these six poems never did exist in the original typed series but that they were inserted as substitutes for withdrawn poems that had been typed. If so, the association of nos. 80, 89, and 91 with the demonstrably early poems nos. 83, 84, and 92 suggests strongly that they represent poems of approximately the same date and are part of a set that is being utilized to replace now lost rejections.

What was removed from *War is Kind* as evidenced by the half leaves of poems below nos. 86 and 88 and above no. 90 (and probably on one or more full leaves between nos. 79 and 81) cannot be known. If one must guess, perhaps they were the five poems nos. 132–136 preserved only in posthumous typescripts made by Cora. Such a guess is at least as good as the conjecture that they represent poems Crane wrote after his return from Cuba but too late to include in *War is Kind.* The guess may perhaps be supported by the odd fact that in the posthumous inventory Cora made of the 1,210 words of unpublished poems, placed just below the notation that *War is Kind* had been published only in the United States, these poems between nos. 132–136 are not counted. On the other hand, their typescripts are on different paper from that utilized for *War is Kind* and are clearly produced after Crane's death. Unfortunately, in connection with this matter the offset of no. 136 on the verso of no. 88, the upper part of a sected leaf, is meaningless, for the offsetting typescript of no. 136 can be identified as posthumous typing by Cora; hence the offset was produced, presumably, when Cora abstracted the typescript carbon of no. 88 for sale and wrote *By Stephen Crane* across its head when it had been laid on the fresh TMs of no. 136. All one can say is that it is evident that material was removed from the typed printer's copy, but the identification from preserved documents of what was removed is purely speculative. That the six poems without typescripts were substitutes for this excised material is strongly suggested by the evidence for their connection with the disruptions. Thus if two of these six are rejects from *The Black Riders* and the third is datable in 1894 although not demonstrably associated with *The Black Riders,* it is a reasonable inference that the remaining three poems in this set came from the same period. On these grounds it is possible to place nos. 80, 89, and 91 in 1894.

The question then arises whether one may go further and identify these three as among the poems that Crane withdrew for lack of literary merit on September 9, 1894. Such a hypothesis would by no means be impossible. Crane's first list of July–August, 1896, gives no. 77, in manuscript, among the published items as if he were momentarily expecting to sell it; he also gives four—nos. 115, 74, 116, and 117—below a rule as then unsold. Among these only no. 74 was printed, in the *Bookman* for October, 1896. If this list of unpublished items (especially with no. 74 among them) means that they were poems Crane approved of and hoped to sell, the omissions from this list are as significant as those named. Omitted are Copeland and Day's rejected nos. 109 and 110, never published, and omitted also are the three lost poems known only from the titles given in the letter of rejection; omitted also is unpublished 111. This last seems to be not a draft of no. 87 *The chatter of a death-demon from a tree-top* (named in the list and published in the *Philistine* in August, 1895) but instead an earlier seminal poem giving a less focused treatment to the same idea. The two could not be expected to exist side by side; the writing of no. 87 automatically ended the usefulness of no. 111. If no. 87 was composed after Crane's return from Mexico in June, 1895, and published immediately, its prototype no. 111 must go back to 1894, and it could readily have been among the poems Crane himself withdrew from *The Black Riders*.

These two lists give as published or unpublished all of Crane's periodical appearances, save for "Legends," up to the summer of 1896. That these listed poems looking forward to periodical publication were brought together makes it very difficult to believe that they were survivors from the group of Crane's own withdrawn poems from *The Black Riders*. Instead, on the evidence of nos. 109 and 110 and possibly of no. 111, as well as nos. 83–84 perhaps, the unmentioned United States manuscripts appear to be the early ones. If indeed there is a general unity in this group comprising nos. 80, 83, 84, 91, and 92, it lies in the fact that they do not appear in the first list and that three of the six were missing for what seem to be good reasons. Number 92 is a clear-cut case since it had been printed in *The Black Riders* and was perhaps an inadvertency in *War is Kind*. Number 84 was a reject from *The Black Riders*, and no. 83 just possibly a similar reject which had to be thoroughly revised in *War is Kind* to make it publishable. In fact, in each case the text of nos. 83, 84, and 92 is revised in *War is Kind*. As for nos. 80, 89, and 91, they did not appear in the first list either because they were as yet unwritten or else because, like the others that were omitted, they were in existence but their texts were in unsatisfactory shape at the time. Of the two choices, the first with its logical association of all six of these substitutes with early work seems to be the more probable, and the poems themselves agree sufficiently with this estimate of their date if we grant that they had also been revised for publication in *War is Kind*. The odds favor these poems as written in 1894, therefore, before Crane left for Mexico in

January, 1895. If so, there is a good chance that they had been intended for *The Black Riders* but removed.

On the contrary, nos. 74, 115, 116, and conjecturally no. 117, all written on legal-cap paper and thus at least relatively associated,[21] can be argued for as written in 1895 after Crane's return from Mexico in June. We know from no. 82 *A slant of sun on dull brown walls* (published in the *Philistine* in December, 1895) and unpublished no. 114 *A row of thick pillars* that Crane had begun to write lines on his return, and indeed the evidence of the publication of no. 87 in August suggests an almost immediate resumption. It seems reasonable to associate the poems in the first list awaiting sale with those already published, in which case nos. 74, 77, 115, 116, and 117 should date from some indeterminate period in the second half of 1895 to the first half of 1896. That various poems published in 1896 date from 1895 is indicated by a letter of January 6, 1896, addressed to Nellie Crouse: 'I am sorry that you did not find the "two poems"—mind you, I never call them poems myself—in the *Philistine.* No more did I. But as a matter of truth, the *Philistine* will have something of mine in every number in 1896 so if you ever see that little book again this year, you will in search discover the last one' (*Letters,* p. 96). This may be a reference to *I have heard the sunset song of the birches* (75) printed in the *Philistine* in January, 1896. Actually, Crane was being optimistic, for the *Philistine* in 1896 printed only, in addition, *What says the sea, little shell?* (70) in February, *To the maiden* (71) in April (a BR reject), and *Fast rode the knight* (76) in June. The *Chapbook* printed *In the night* (86) in March (possibly a Mexican poem); the *Bookman* published "Legends" (118–122) in May and *I explain the silvered passing of a ship* (74) in October. These could also be poems from 1895 to be included in his boast to Miss Crouse. It seems most probable, therefore, that the latter half of 1895 was another period of activity for Crane, and that in 1896 comparatively little was written although publication continued of the 1895 output. Number 123 *Oh, a rare old wine ye brewed for me* is quoted in a letter of March 1, 1896, to Nellie Crouse: "If there is a joy of living I cant find it. The future? The future is blue with obligations—new trials—conflicts. It was a rare old wine the gods brewed *for mortals.* Flagons

21 Identification of this legal-cap paper is almost impossible when it does not come from the very same pad and thus shares with other leaves the same cutting that produced the pad. The total evidence shows that 29 horizontal lines were standard and that leaves with 27 or 28 have had the extra lines trimmed off in the manufacture of the pad. The closest one can come to associate paper of different pads is by its horizontal width of 203, 200, or 197 mm., and also by the rare variety in which the rules stopped with the vertical colored lines and left the margin up to the vertical lines unruled. Both the draft and the final manuscripts of *The Red Badge of Courage* in 1894 are written on various kinds of legal-cap paper. It was a favorite with Crane throughout 1895, however, and—on the evidence of the first list particularly—into 1896. It was never used in England.

of despair——" (*Letters*, p. 120). The terms of this reference make it perfectly clear that no. 123 is not a love poem addressed to Nellie Crouse, or a warmed-over relict of Lily Brandon, but instead a poem addressing the gods as 'ye' which he must have sent to her just before. Only thus would she have understood and appreciated the allusion. On January 6, 1896, continuing his remark to her that he would be represented in every issue of the *Philistine* that year, he wrote: "I never encourage friends to read my work—they sometimes advise one—but somehow I will be glad to send you things of mine. Not because I think you will refrain from advising one either. But simply because I would enjoy it—sending them. I think your advice would have a charm to it that I do not find in some others" (*Letters*, pp. 96–97). Although we know from a letter of January 12 that she had read and remarked upon the short story "A Grey Sleeve" (*Letters*, p. 99), one would expect Crane to have sent her poems that he had written; in fact, two poems of his were under discussion in the preceding sentence of the January 6 letter. Thus it seems natural enough to suppose that she had received no. 123 shortly before Crane's letter of March 1. That it had been freshly written is probable, and thus a date, probably in February, 1896, can be assigned it.

The following complete listing attempts to arrange Crane's poems in a rough order of composition by year. Various of the dates, such as those of publication, are obviously only *termini ad quem* and not the actual dates of composition; nevertheless, something of an order of composition within the years can occasionally be achieved. (Poems that can be given specific dates are listed ahead of those with indeterminate dates within the year.) Since no poem can be identified as written in 1893, the general assumption is that *The Black Riders* poems date from January–March, 1894, for the mentioned poems, with a possible extension into April for the others, although what evidence we have suggests that the bulk must date before April. The poems (5, 21, 49) named in Garland's later accounts are not specified in this list since the references to them are contradictory and appear to be manufactured. In this listing a brief note on the evidence is appended in parentheses when the item has already been discussed above. Footnotes elaborate the evidence for certain dates when a more extensive account is required.

c. 1879–80

(106) "I'd Rather Have——" (early hand and subject)

1892

(107) Ah, haggard purse, why ope thy mouth (December, *teste* Linson)

1894

(14) There was crimson clash of war (by mid-February, *teste* Linson)

(18) In Heaven, | Some little blades of grass (by mid-February, *teste* Linson)
(38) The ocean said to me once (by mid-February, *teste* Linson)
(62) There was a man who lived a life of fire (by mid-February, *teste* Linson)
(6) God fashioned the ship of the world carefully (by 11 March, *teste* Garland)
(2) Three little birds in a row (by 11 March, phraseology in remarks to Garland)
(1) Black riders came from the sea (revised by October 30)
(3) In the desert (BR)
(4) Yes, I have a thousand tongues (BR)
(5) Once there came a man (BR)
(7) Mystic shadow, bending near me (BR)
(8) I looked here (same paper as nos. 109–110)
(71) To the maiden (letter, BR reject)
(84) There was a man with tongue of wood (letter, BR reject)
(109) A god came to a man (letter, BR reject)
(110) One came from the skies (letter, BR reject)
(9) I stood upon a high place (BR)
(10) Should the wide world roll away (BR)
(11) In a lonely place (BR)
(12) Well, then, I hate Thee, unrighteous picture (BR)
(13) If there is a witness to my little life (BR)
(15) "Tell brave deeds of war." (BR)
(16) Charity, thou art a lie (BR)
(17) There were many who went in huddled procession (BR)
(19) A god in wrath (BR)
(20) A learned man came to me once (BR)
(21) There was, before me (BR)
(22) Once I saw the mountains angry (BR)
(23) Places among the stars (BR)
(24) I saw a man pursuing the horizon (BR)
(25) Behold, the grave of a wicked man (BR)
(26) There was set before me a mighty hill (BR)
(27) A youth in apparel that glittered (BR)
(28) "Truth," said a traveller (BR)
(29) Behold, from the land of the farther suns (BR)
(30) Supposing that I should have the courage (BR)
(31) Many workmen (BR)
(32) Two or three angels (BR)
(33) There was One I met upon the road (BR)
(34) I stood upon a highway (BR)
(35) A man saw a ball of gold in the sky (BR)
(36) I met a seer (BR)
(37) On the horizon the peaks assembled (BR)
(39) The livid lightnings flashed in the clouds (BR)
(40) And you love me? (BR)
(41) Love walked alone (BR)
(42) I walked in a desert (BR)
(43) There came whisperings in the winds (BR)

(44) I was in the darkness (BR)
(45) Tradition, thou art for suckling children (BR)
(46) Many red devils ran from my heart (BR)
(47) "Think as I think," said a man (BR)
(48) Once there was a man (BR)
(49) I stood musing in a black world (BR)
(50) You say you are holy (BR)
(51) A man went before a strange god (BR)
(52) Why do you strive for greatness, fool? (BR)
(53) Blustering god (BR)
(54) "It was wrong to do this," said the angel (BR)
(55) A man toiled on a burning road (BR)
(56) A man feared that he might find an assassin (BR)
(57) With eye and with gesture (BR)
(58) The sage lectured brilliantly (BR)
(59) Walking in the sky (BR)
(60) Upon the road of my life (BR)
(61) There was a man and a woman (BR)
(63) There was a great cathedral (BR)
(64) Friend, your white beard sweeps the ground (BR)
(65) Once, I knew a fine song (BR)
(66) If I should cast off this tattered coat (BR)
(67) God lay dead in Heaven (BR)
(68) A spirit sped (BR)
(108) Little birds of the night (Notebook, related to no. 2)[22]
(111) There is a grey thing that lives in the tree-tops
(112) intermingled (fragment, early paper?)
(113) A soldier, young in years, young in ambitions (by May 9)
(83) Once a man clambering to the house-tops (trial on no. 113 and in Notebook)
(80) A newspaper is a collection of half-injustices (WK no TMs)
(89) A man said to the universe (WK no TMs)
(91) There was a land where lived no violets (WK no TMs)

1895

(87) The chatter of a death-demon from a tree-top (*Philistine*, August)
(94) Each small gleam was a voice (*Philistine*, September)
(114) A row of thick pillars (after June, like no. 82)
(82) A slant of sun on dull brown walls (*Philistine*, December)
(75) "I have heard the sunset song of the birches (Philistine dinner menu, December 19)
(69) Do not weep, maiden, for war is kind (autograph date 1895; published February 9, 1896)
(70) "What says the sea, little shell? (MS dated December 28)

[22] The date of inscription in the Notebook is uncertain. Perhaps it was later than March–April, 1894, and so the poem escaped inclusion in *The Black Riders*. But since no other manuscript is preserved, it is as possible that Crane did not believe it had passed from the draft stage and so did not include it or rework it later.

1895–1896

(74) I explain the silvered passing of a ship at night (*Bookman*, October, 1896)
(76) Fast rode the knight (*Souvenir*, May, 1896)
(77) Forth went the candid man (lists 1,2)
(86) In the night (*Chapbook*, March, 1896; lists 1,2; legal-cap paper)
(115) Chant you loud of punishments (list 1)
(116) If you would seek a friend among men
(117) A lad and a maid at a curve in the stream

1896

(118–122) "Legends" (*Bookman*, May)
(123) Oh, a rare old wine ye brewed for me (quoted in letter March 18)
(96–100) "Intrigue" (late November–December or early 1897)

1897

(124) Tell me not in joyous numbers (associated with *Westminster Gazette*) [23]
(125) When a people reach the top of a hill (English paper, added to list 2)
(126) A man adrift on a slim spar (English paper, added to list 2) [24]
(127) There exists the eternal fact of conflict (English paper)
(85) The successful man has thrust himself (MS dated Dec. 5; WK TMs)
(72) A little ink more or less! (WK TMs; perhaps "The Call" in list 2) [25]

[23] The association of this little *jeu* with the beginning of a letter to the editor of the *Westminster Gazette* may place these lines doubtfully in 1897 when, after his return to England in June, Crane was contributing his "Irish Sketches" to the *Gazette.*

[24] The Britannia-watermarked laid paper of nos. 125 and 126 demonstrates that the manuscripts were written in England. The association of the subject of no. 126 with Crane's experience in the sinking of the *Commodore* suggests that the poem came after January, 1897. Since no. 85 on the same paper is subscribed December 5, 1897, it is possible that all these poems were written at approximately the same time. However, when at some time after his return to England from Greece in June, 1897, Crane picked up his List 2, written in America, and added the unpublished 125 and 126 to it, without note of magazine, the natural inference is that these were the first two poems he had written in England. If so, they may be taken to precede unmentioned no. 85, but probably by no very great interval. That no. 125 was not published until the *Philistine* for June, 1898, does not necessarily place it in 1898 against the evidence suggested above. The 1898 *Philistine* printings of Crane's poems appear to come from verses already written and collected for *War is Kind* by early March 1898.

[25] All that is certain of no. 72 is that it was written before the printer's copy for *War is Kind* was made up in early March, 1898. Hubbard alleged that he had received it a few weeks before Crane died, but this statement is false since the poem had appeared in *War is Kind* and it is clear from his comment that he had held it because he did not like it. It is quite possible to conjecture that in his statement in the July, 1900, *The Fra* Hubbard was deliberately disguising the length of time he had retained the manuscript in order to free himself from the allegation that in printing it then he was cashing in on Crane's death. Instead, it was sup-

(88) The impact of a dollar upon the heart (WK TMs; *Philistine*, Feb., 1898)[26]
(78) You tell me this is God? (WK TMs; *Philistine*, April, 1898)
(79) On the desert (WK TMs; *Philistine*, March, 1898)
(73) "Have you ever made a just man?" (WK TMs)
(81) The wayfarer (WK TMs)
(90) When the prophet, a complacent fat man (WK TMs)
(92) There was one I met upon the road (revision for WK of no. 33)
(93) Aye, workman, make me a dream (WK TMs)
(95) The trees in the garden rained flowers (WK TMs)
(128) On the brown trail (English paper)

1898

(129) Wheels (*Philistine*, Dec., 1898)
(130) All-feeling God, hear in the war-night (June–August campaign)
(101–105) "Intrigue" (composed or revised by Sept. 14)
(131) Unwind my riddle (late October)

Uncertain Dates[27]

(132) A naked woman and a dead dwarf (posthumous TMs)
(133) A grey and boiling street (posthumous TMs)

posed to have been a recent arrival, put away for the moment but then reread and approved. The paper of the manuscript is not demonstrably American but it is the sort of cheap lined writing pad paper Crane often used in the United States, whereas his English manuscripts are ordinarily on laid foolscap. Moreover, it is tempting to put the poem in the period of considerable activity in 1895–96 when Crane was most closely associated with Hubbard. Whether the comment to Hubbard at the foot of the poem, 'oh, Hubbard, mark this well. Mark it well! If it is over-balancing your discretion inform me. S. C.' sounds appropriately youthful for 1895–96 but less so for late 1897–98 may be a matter of opinion, nor is it evidence that the informality does not give the impression that an ocean stretched between the two. Nevertheless, several considerations argue more forcibly for a date in late 1897, although early 1898 is not impossible. This is also a period of active contribution to the *Philistine* as Crane endeavored to get into print a number of poems before publication in *War is Kind.* It is also a question whether Crane would not have secured the return of a manuscript sent as early as 1895–96 but unpublished, whereas he might have let it slip as late as 1897 once *War is Kind* was scheduled and little chance held of placing it elsewhere before the book appeared. Of course, the Spanish-American War also intervened not very long after he would have sent off the manuscript to Hubbard. Finally, although it can scarcely be admitted as evidence, there is the curious start of a title 'The Call' (whether or not complete) which was deleted before Crane wrote 'Blue Battalions' as the eleventh title in his second list, the first poem recorded as written in England. 'The Call' is a possible title for no. 72, especially its latter part. One may amuse oneself by guessing that Crane started to write in the titles for composed poems but then deleted 'The Call' since there was no news of publication and substituted 'Blue Battalions,' when he was more confident that it would be accepted, or, indeed, on news that it had been accepted. He must have been confident also (as well he might) of 'A man afloat on a slim spar,' which follows, again after a false start for 'The Call,' although the omission of this excellent poem from *War is Kind* is not to be understood.

[26] The early date of publication across the Atlantic in 1898 suggests that the poem had been composed in late 1897.

[27] Unfortunately, these poems are preserved only in typescripts made up by Cora for sale. Thus evidence about date that might have been secured from the

(134) Bottles and bottles and bottles (posthumous TMs)
(135) The patent of a lord (posthumous TMs)
(136) My cross! (posthumous TMs)

THE EDITORIAL PROBLEM

Since only a few manuscripts of poems in *The Black Riders* have been preserved by chance, the copy-text and sole authority for most of this volume is the printed first edition. That Crane read proof is known; and indeed only one observable misprint escaped the care that Copeland and Day expended on the production. In his correspondence with the firm Crane gave permission for them to punctuate his manuscripts as they chose. The almost stylized lack of punctuation in the manuscripts was given conventional pointing in Boston, the difference being observable especially in the early trial for no. 2, set from manuscript with only slight alteration, but then reset in final edited form. The Copeland and Day pointing cannot be called unduly heavy, but it does set off line-ending and internal pauses and also syntactical units. The one alteration that produced punctuation markedly uncharacteristic of Crane was the publisher's use of commas to introduce quoted speech instead of Crane's almost invariable colons. Although one can understand from the evidence of the manuscripts that much of the styling is Copeland and Day's—especially in the matter of commas introducing dialogue—when the printed edition for any poem is the copy-text and sole authority an editor has no choice but to reproduce what was printed. In McKerrow's strict interpretation of physical evidence, this is the only authority we have. Tempting as it could be to alter certain features here and there to conform to what one may be conjecturally persuaded were the characteristics of the lost underlying copy, interference of this kind with authority cannot be consistent nor logically restricted only to a few specific matters, and hence the temptation has been resisted by the present editor.

Of course, when a manuscript is preserved for a *Black Riders* poem, it becomes the copy-text and the printed edition is only of secondary authority. Inevitably, the result of editing a book collection like *The Black Riders* not from a single copy-text like the printed edition but when possible from the greater authority of manuscripts, creates an occasional break with the book styling in order to take advantage of the superior authority of a manuscript. This selectivity makes for a

paper of their manuscripts is wanting. They need not necessarily represent lines written after publication of *War is Kind*, between the time of Crane's return to England from Cuba and his death. It is possible that some could have been early work overlooked when Crane was putting together the collection. If no. 126 could be omitted in this manner, others need not have been immune. But since all external evidence is missing, only critical judgment can attempt to place these five poems in their relative positions in the canon.

lack of uniformity in the presentation of the collection, but the price is small for the privilege of reading Crane as he wrote, whenever possible, and not in the conventional manner the publisher believed he should have written.[28]

The most marked characteristic of Crane's poetic manuscripts is the relatively consistent omission of normal line-ending punctuation save for periods, and even these full stops are not always present. From early to late this practice continues; thus it must be taken as a distinctive peculiarity of Crane's style, not as an inadvertency.[29] The problem faced by an editor is whether this eccentricity is worth preserving when manuscripts (and occasionally typescripts) are the copy-texts or whether—for reading purposes in a critical text—the standard punctuation publishers gave Crane's lines should be substituted. The present editor has opted for maintaining the integrity of the copy-texts with minimum interference, not as a pedantic device but because experience indicates that in few cases does the lack of punctuation lead to ambiguity or difficulty in following the syntax once the reader has grown accustomed to Crane's ordinary usage. Moreover, uniformity of publishers' styling throughout the present edition would be impossible: the unpublished poems preserved only in manuscript or typescript would still be anomalous, for no editor of an unmodernized scholarly text could dream of repunctuating them to suit himself. Actually, the effect produced—presumably why Crane continued his personal idiosyncracy without interruption—is one of syntactical leveling and from that effect derives an increase in the objectiveness of the lines. Whatever expressiveness one may insert on reading is the reader's affair: the poems themselves eschew the normal signposts in favor of a peculiar and undoubtedly effective starkness. If as Crane wrote to Copeland and Day there is anarchy in *The Black Riders*, it is an oddly controlled anarchy, a cool and objective expression materially aided by the styling. Since the manuscripts represent the way in which Crane saw and heard these lines, it would be an act of supererogation to alter his style to accord with conventional reading habits. Enough present-day poets adopt idiosyncratic ways of presenting their

[28] Problems may arise when as with no. 18 *In Heaven, Some little blades of grass* the manuscript is very much of an early draft. However, in this case the accidentals are similar to those one finds in Crane's fair copies; thus it is possible to take over the more authoritative substantive variants from the book for the text of this poem but to clothe them in the accidental texture of the draft.

[29] Not that Crane was always consistent, of course. The fortunate reproduction in facsimile of the manuscript used for the first appearance in print, earlier in the *Bookman*, of no. 69 *Do not weep, maiden, for war is kind* shows that the punctuation in the original was heavier than in the fair copy Crane made for Howells on the flyleaf of *The Red Badge of Courage*, a copy now in the Berg Collection of the New York Public Library. The facsimile, an important document to establish the text, has not been previously noticed. It is found in the *Bookman*, IX (July, 1899), 400.

verse, which one would not dream of normalizing, to permit the pioneer Crane to retain his own system. Much less important than the matter of syntactical pointing, the old-fashioned use of hanging quotation marks before each line of dialogue has been preserved as in the manuscripts and in *The Black Riders.*

The printed forms of the poems, particularly in *The Black Riders,* are not without their special problems. There seemed to be no point in faithfully transcribing the Copeland and Day setting of full capitals, particularly since this typography bears no relation to the manuscripts and was decided on without prior consultation with Crane although with his later approval. Thus in *The Black Riders* and occasionally in periodicals that imitated *The Black Riders* typography (as if Crane's poems were always intended to be set in full caps), the full capitals are transcribed normally in lower case with the usual capitalization of words at the start of lines and beginning a new sentence after a period. This capitalization follows manuscript practice and is unrecorded. On the other hand, in some texts the present editor has chosen to capitalize such words as 'God', 'He', 'One', 'Heaven', according to what can be determined was Crane's usual practice—admittedly not always consistent—in his manuscripts and the typescripts that seem to have copied his manuscripts with some faithfulness. Such capitalizations must be regarded as technical emendations, for Crane's intentions in the several texts are concealed by the typography and can be conjectured only by analogy. As emendations, then, the adoption of such capitals is recorded in the apparatus.

In the second collection *War is Kind* copy-text problems vary from those in *The Black Riders.* Fortunately, in this later volume the number of preserved manuscripts increases, and typescripts are usually available in the form of the carbons of the printer's copy, made up under Crane's supervision in late 1897. The typist is unknown but could not have been Crane himself, who did not type, nor Cora, the Cranes not yet having purchased a typewriter. When comparisons are possible between manuscripts and typescripts, the evidence suggests in general a rather remarkable fidelity in detail, including the reproduction of Crane's light punctuation, although the typescripts also exhibit a small amount of British styling like 'O' for 'oh', 'towards' for 'toward', and the different positioning of punctuation in relation to quotation marks. Since the originals of these carbons were used by Stokes to set *War is Kind,* it follows that when manuscripts are not preserved these typescripts become the copy-texts, being closer to the lost manuscripts than is the book. Crane does not seem to have read proof on *War is Kind;* thus although a variant or two in the book may be authoritative as conjecturally marked in the printer's copy but not in the carbon, the printed texts in *War is Kind* are selected as copy-texts only as a last resort when earlier documents are wanting.

Typescripts for *War is Kind* were ordinarily made up from Crane's manuscripts even when the poems had previously appeared in periodicals. The case of no. 69 *Do not weep, maiden, for war is kind* is exceptional in that Crane had to write Reynolds to order a typescript from the *Bookman* printing. However, no. 69 is not unique, for the textual evidence indicates that the typescript of no. 70 *"What says the sea, little shell?* was copied from the *Philistine* text, as was no. 71 *To the maiden* and no. 76 *Fast rode the knight.* On the other hand, the evidence is clear that no. 75 *"I have heard the sunset song of the birches* was typed from a manuscript, not from the 1896 *Philistine* text, as were, also, no. 78 *You tell me this is God?*, no. 79 *On the desert*[30] (both from *Philistine*, 1898), no. 82 *A slant of sun on dull brown walls* (*Philistine*, 1895), no. 87 *The chatter of a death-demon from a tree-top* (*Philistine*, 1895), and no. 94 *Each small gleam was a voice* (*Philistine*, 1895).[31] When a typescript is derived from a periodical as is no. 71, it can have no independent authority, at least for the accidentals. (Substantive authority would require Crane to have revised the periodical copy.) On the other hand, when a manuscript is wanting and the typescript derives from this lost manuscript, it and the periodical text stand in a radiating relationship to each other and at substantially the same remove. Under these circumstances of divided authority, the demonstrably greater faithfulness of the typescripts to the accidentals of the manuscripts in comparison with the customary house-styling of the periodicals promotes the typescripts to the position of copy-text, as in nos. 75, 78, 82, 87, and 94.

Other examples may be more complex. For instance, the evidence for no. 86 *In the night* suggests that Crane himself transcribed a now lost manuscript version from the 1896 *Chapbook* printing after revising the printed form and that this manuscript was given to the typist of the copy for *War is Kind.* Although in this case the preserved holograph draft manuscript has a sufficiently parallel text to be accepted as a practicable copy-text, the typescript accidentals need consideration since they have more authority than the *Chapbook* version, having passed through the inscription of the author once again. On the other hand, if the marked-up clipping of the *Chapbook* had not been preserved, the typescript of course would have been the document providing the prime substantive authority of a revised text, although less authoritative for the accidentals than the draft manuscript in this case. Other problems arise when the extant manuscripts are early drafts that are considerably removed in their readings from

[30] In this case the typist had no option since the typescript was prepared before the date of the *Philistine* publication.

[31] Most of the typescripts made up as printer's copy for *War is Kind* subscribe the name of the periodical in which the poem had appeared. On evidence such as found in this poem, however, it is clear that these ascriptions have nothing to do with the source of the text since the ascriptions occur even when the typescripts were copied from manuscripts.

the revised texts. Number 74 *I explain the silvered passing of a ship at night* is partly such a case in that the lost manuscript sent to the *Bookman* for October, 1896, publication was a later version than that preserved; yet either the *Bookman* manuscript had a duplicate or (less likely) was returned, for the typescript of the poem from which *War is Kind* was printed derives not from the *Bookman* printed text but from this other manuscript still further revised. Here an editor is fortunate to find that the original manuscript's text is not so distant from the revised forms as to prevent its selection as copy-text, thus incorporating automatically its superior accidental authority. On the other hand, the manuscript of no. 77 *Forth went the candid man* is so very much a draft that the typescript becomes the most practicable copy-text except where its readings can be compared with those of the draft. This is also the situation with no. 83 *Once a man clambering to the housetops,* except that the typescript copy is missing and one must revert to *War is Kind* for a text, even though styled by the printer, that was set from the lost typescript of superior general authority to the distant draft.

Only five poems, nos. 132–136, must be printed from typescripts made posthumously by Cora Crane from her husband's lost manuscripts, these typescripts being the only preserved documents for the texts. The faithfulness of Cora to her copy is less than that of the unknown typist of the copy for *War is Kind.* That on the whole she did not seriously corrupt the texts has been suggested by Professor Joseph Katz as a result of an analysis of other typescripts of poems she made from known copy in which her variants can be isolated.[32]

The editorial principles of this edition may be summarized as follows.[33]

1. In all but a few exceptional cases, preserved manuscripts are chosen as copy-texts; into the texture of their accidentals are placed variant readings from later typescripts or from later periodical or book printings when these readings are assessed as authoritative revisions by Crane. In a very few poems the early-draft manuscripts are too remote from the final version to be utilized as copy-texts. In such cases the documentary source nearest to the lost revised manuscript is selected as copy-text, but reference is made whenever possible to the known authority of the accidentals of the draft.

2. When manuscripts are not available, typescripts may be selected

[32] "Cora Crane and the Poetry of Stephen Crane," *PBSA*, LVIII (1964), 469–476.

[33] The principles for copy-text were originally laid down by W. W. Greg, "The Rationale of Copy-Text," *Studies in Bibliography*, III (1950–51), 19–36, reprinted in W. W. Greg, *Collected Papers*, ed. J. C. Maxwell (Oxford: Clarendon Press, 1966), pp. 374–391. This may be supplemented by the additional discussion found in Bowers, "Multiple Authority: New Problems and Concepts of Copy-Text," *The Library*, 5th ser., XXVII (1972), 81–115.

as copy-texts if they derive immediately from lost holograph manuscripts. Most of the preserved typescripts are the carbons of the printer's copy for *War is Kind,* but five poems are known only in typescripts made by Cora Crane.

3. Periodical appearances of poems may be taken as copy-texts when no other version has been preserved or when other versions are copied from the periodical texts and are therefore without accidental authority.

4. Book appearances become copy-texts when they represent the only known versions or when antecedent versions are drafts that in their accidentals are less generally authoritative than the accidentals accompanying the revised substantives of the book.

In the apparatus the documents preserved for each poem within the range of possible authority are listed in their chronological order. An asterisk precedes the selected copy-text. Any complication in the textual history of the poem is analyzed in the notes to its apparatus. Full collations of variants from the established text in each of the listed documents are provided, both substantive and accidental. The second printing of *The Black Riders,* in 1896, is noted as BR(ii), and the Heinemann issue as E1 when variants occur.

APPARATUS

[NOTE: In this poetry section all the apparatus for each poem is presented together. Every editorial change from the copy-texts (indicated by a preceding asterisk in the list of texts for each poem)—whether manuscript, typescript, newspaper, magazine, or book versions, as chosen—is recorded both for substantives and accidentals. Only the direct source of the emendation with its antecedents is noted. In the case of only one text, or where there are no symbols immediately following the bracket, that alteration is understood to be a Virginia emendation and is made for the first time in the present edition, if by the *first time* is understood the *first time in respect to the texts chosen for collation*. The variants list records every difference in the listed documents from the selected copy-text and corresponds to the Historical Collations of previous volumes. The inclusion of accidentals as well as substantive variants allows the reader to reconstruct every text considered in the editorial decision. The wavy dash (~) represents the same word that appears before the bracket and is used exclusively in recording punctuation or other accidentals variants. An inferior caret (‸) indicates the absence of a punctuation mark. A plus sign (+) following a text symbol indicates that the cited text and all texts listed after it in the list heading the apparatus to each poem agree in the reading, i.e., No. 86, emendation on line 4: 4 movest] Ch+; moveth MS, this could also be written: 4 movest] Ch,Ch(r),TMs,WK; moveth MS. A complete list of the alterations to the manuscript(s) is given after the emendations and a list of typescript alterations only if the typescript is the copy-text. After the emendations, alterations, and variants, each manuscript or typescript is described physically. In some cases where there is a particularly intricate editorial problem involved in the selection of copy-text, a note outlining the evidence ends the apparatus.]

THE BLACK RIDERS AND OTHER LINES

1. BLACK RIDERS CAME FROM THE SEA

*MS (CLU), holograph
BR(caps)

No variants

MS: University of California at Los Angeles. Black ink, unwatermarked laid paper (176 × 221 mm.), horizontal chainlines 26 mm. apart, written on one-half of a fold as a presentation copy, signed and dated March 19, 1896. Described by R. M. Weatherford, "A Manuscript of

'Black Riders Came from the Sea,'" *Stephen Crane Newsletter*, IV (Summer, 1970), 3–4, with facsimile.

Note: In his letter of September 27, 1894, to Copeland and Day, Crane quoted the first line as '"Black Riders rode forth" etc.' He seems to have sent the present form of the text on October 30, 1894, as a revision of the original. In the fair copy of March 19, 1896, Crane did not capitalize 'sin' in line 6, a point obscured by the full caps of *The Black Riders* typography. This presentation manuscript is on paper identical with that of no. 69, which is subscribed Washington, D.C., March 18, 1896, and was thus written in Washington, as R. M. Weatherford had conjectured.

2. THREE LITTLE BIRDS IN A ROW

*MS (ViU), holograph
BR (trial proof, caps)
BR (caps)

Variants: 3 place‸] ∼ . BR
5 said:] ∼ , BR
6 laugh.] ∼ ‸ BR(p)
9 curious‸] ∼ , BR

MS: University of Virginia–Barrett. Black ink on laid paper (188.5 × 127 mm.), vertical chains 23.5 mm. apart. At head is the publisher's circled '2¼ in.,' and his numbering 'I'; slightly above, in Crane's hand, is an erased title, partly illegible, 'A <   > Passing.' The word after 'A' may just possibly be 'Curious'. Cora seems to have owned this manuscript at one time since in the lower left corner she wrote the code letters 'V V' and beneath these an 'o' or 'd'.

BR Trial: Columbia University. A trial proof for Crane's approval of the typography (86 × 90 mm.) set from the ViU MS. On the sheet of paper to which the proof is pasted Crane wrote in black ink 'Copeland and Day.' The proof numbers the poem 'I'.

3. IN THE DESERT | I SAW A CREATURE

*BR (caps)

4. YES, I HAVE A THOUSAND TONGUES

*BR (caps)

5. ONCE THERE CAME A MAN | WHO SAID

*BR (caps)

Variant: 5 clamor] clamour BR(ii), E1

6. GOD FASHIONED THE SHIP OF THE WORLD CAREFULLY

*BR (caps)

Emendations: 3, 4, 6 He] HE BR
6 His] HIS BR
8 God] GOD BR

7. Mystic shadow, bending near me

*BR (caps)

8. I looked here | I looked there

*MS (NSyU), holograph
BR (caps)
N[1] (*Kansas City Star*, Feb. 19, 1899, p. 5, entitled *The Image in the Heart*; subscribed '*—Stephen Crane, "The Black Riders."*')

Emendation: 8–9 fair as she | In] BR,N[1]; fair | As herself in MS

MS Alteration: 2 I] *follows deleted* 'And', *the final* 'd' *not quite completed*

Variants: 1 here∧] ~ ; BR,N[1]
2 there∧] ~ ; BR,N[1]
3 No where] Nowhere BR,N[1]
6 Truly∧ then∧] ~, ~, BR,N[1]
6 complaint∧] ~ , BR,N[1]
7 'though] ∧ ~ BR,N[1]
7 fairer∧] ~ , BR,N[1]

MS: Syracuse University. Black ink on wove paper (181 × 116 mm.) watermarked *Dexter Mills.*

Note: Crane read proof for BR and therefore could have made the change from *herself* to *she*. (Some possibility exists that the NSyU manuscript was the printer's copy.) A grammatical alteration like this could always come from the publisher, of course, but the coincidence of verbal change with relineation may perhaps point to the author. Although the authority of the BR reading can never be wholly certain, the change would almost certainly not have been made without Crane's approval, given the general scrupulousness with which Copeland and Day seem to have dealt with the text. For general parallels, see *The Red Badge of Courage*, Virginia edition, 18.10 and 49.31, and *The Third Violet*, Virginia edition, 45.8, in which the *-self* form is substituted for the simple pronoun.

9. I stood upon a high place

*BR (caps)
Bk(p) (*Bookman* proof, caps)
Bk (*Bookman*, III [May, 1896], 196, caps)
Ph (*Philistine*, VIII [March, 1899], back wrapper)

Variants: 1 high place] High Place Ph
2 devils] Devils Ph
4 sin.] ~∧ Bk(p); Sin. Ph
6 said,] ~ . Bk(p),Bk

Note: The *Bookman* reprinted this poem from BR, including its number IX, with X *Should the wide world roll away* on the facing page. The occasion was to advertise the work of the artist who drew the illustration for the *Bookman's* publication of Crane's "Legends" (nos. 118–122) in the same number. Each of the two poems is enclosed by an illustration. On p. 196 a note reads: 'We feel a proper editorial pride in giving our readers in this number a chance to see a specimen of the work of Miss Mélanie Elisabeth Norton, a young artist of this city, who has made the marginal illustrations to Mr. Stephen Crane's "Legends" on page 206. Miss Norton has caught to perfection the spirit of Mr. Crane's unique imaginings, and the truth of this is even better seen in the reproduction given above of her designs for two of his poems from *The Black Riders*. As grotesque as anything of Aubrey Beardsley, they have a thought and a meaning that his work often lacks, and are fairly startling in their weirdly imaginative power. We predict for Miss Norton an immediate vogue and a brilliant future.' The University of Virigina–Barrett Collection has a proof of the text and illustrations for the two pages of nos. 9–10 but without the surrounding letterpress in the magazine. In no. 9 the proof wants the period after "sin" in line 4, present in the *Bookman* text. The reprint in the *Philistine* was placed below a cartoonlike illustration, signed 'DEN' by the artist W. W. Denslow.

10. Should the wide world roll away

*MS (NSyU), holograph
BR (caps)
Bk(p) (*Bookman* proof, caps)
Bk (*Bookman*, III [May, 1896], 197, caps)

MS Alteration: 3 Limitless] *second* 'i' *formed from start of* 't'

Variants: 1 away$_\wedge$] ~ , BR,Bk(p),Bk
2 terror$_\wedge$] ~, BR,Bk(p),Bk
5 essential$_\wedge$] ~ , BR,Bk(p),Bk
6 there$_\wedge$] ~ , BR,Bk(p),Bk

MS: Syracuse University. Black ink on a cut-off piece of legal-cap paper (240 × 195 mm.), 43.5 mm. headspace, 38 mm. from left margin to pink, blue, pink vertical rules. Another hand has written the number 11 in pencil at the head.

Note: For the *Bookman* illustration to this poem and the circumstances of its printing, see the Note to no. 9.

11. In a lonely place

*BR (caps)

12. Well, then, I hate Thee, unrighteous picture

*BR (caps)

Emendations: 1,2 Thee] THEE BR
3 Thy] THY BR

Note: The epigraph is based on *Exodus* 20:5.

13. If there is a witness to my little life

*BR (caps)

14. There was crimson clash of war

*BR (caps)

Variant: 8 clamor] clamour BR(ii), E1

15. "Tell brave deeds of war."

*BR (caps)

16. Charity, thou art a lie

*BR (caps)

17. There were many who went in huddled procession

*BR (caps)

18. In Heaven, | Some little blades of grass

*MS (NSyU) holograph
BR (caps)

Emendations: 5 Then . . . blades] BR; all save one | Of the little blades MS
12 little] BR; *omit* MS
12 Oh,] BR; *omit* MS
13 "Memory] BR; ‸ ~ MS
14 "For] BR; ‸ ~ MS
15 "I] BR; ‸ ~ MS

MS Alterations: 4 "What] ' "W' *over* 'w'; *preceding* ' "And' *deleted*
5 Then . . . blades] MS 'All save one' *written below deleted line* 'All the little blades'
8 small] *interlined above deleted* 'little'
11 "And] *inserted before* ' "What', *the final* 'd' *deleting the original quotes;* 'What' *was not reduced to* 'w' *since the initial* 'w' *resembled a minuscule, anyway*
11 you do] *double underlining deleted*
16–18 Then . . . said.] *written vertically in upper right margin*

Variants: 8 behind‸] ~ , BR
10 Presently‸] ~ , BR
10 said:] ~ , BR
12 answered:] ~ , BR
12 lord] LORD BR
13 me‸] ~ , BR
14 For‸] ~ , BR
14 deeds‸] ~ , BR
16 God‸ . . . splendor‸] ~ , . . . ~ , BR
18 grass,] ~! BR

MS: Syracuse University. Black ink on wove paper (181 × 116 mm.) watermarked *Dexter Mills*. In pencil is written in another hand at the head 61, the figures spaced. As of mid-1973 this manuscript has not been available.

19. A god in wrath | Was beating a man

*BR (caps)

20. A learned man came to me once

*BR (caps)

21. There was, before me, | Mile upon mile

*BR (caps)

22. ONCE I SAW MOUNTAINS ANGRY

*BR (caps)

23. PLACES AMONG THE STARS

*BR (caps)

24. I SAW A MAN PURSUING THE HORIZON

*BR (caps)
Ph (*Philistine*, I [June, 1895], 27), quoted in commentary
S (*Roycroft Quarterly: A Souvenir and a Medley*, May, 1896, p. 2), credited to *The Black Riders*

Emendation: 6 never——"] ~"— BR; ~"—— Ph; ~—" S

Variants: 5 futile,"] ~ ‸" S
6+ [*space*]] *no space* Ph
7 cried,] ~ . Ph

25. BEHOLD, THE GRAVE OF A WICKED MAN

*BR (caps)
Emendation: 10 it——] ~— BR

26. THERE WAS SET BEFORE ME A MIGHTY HILL

*BR (caps)
Variant: 5 labor] labour BR(ii), E1

27. A YOUTH IN APPAREL THAT GLITTERED

*BR (caps)

28. "TRUTH," SAID A TRAVELLER

*BR (caps)

29. BEHOLD, FROM THE LAND OF THE FARTHER SUNS

*BR (caps)

30. SUPPOSING THAT I SHOULD HAVE THE COURAGE

*BR (caps)

31. MANY WORKMEN | BUILT A HUGE BALL OF MASONRY

*BR (caps)

32. TWO OR THREE ANGELS | CAME NEAR TO THE EARTH

*BR (caps)

33. There was One I met upon the road

*MS (NNC), holograph
BR (caps)
WK (*War is Kind*, 1899)

Emendations: 9 another.] WK; ~ ‸ MS; ~ ; BR
12 He] WK; he MS; HE BR
13 And, finally,] BR; At the end‸ MS; At last, WK

MS Alterations: 12 sin."] *a stroke above the period just possibly may be intended to form an exclamation mark*
15 He] 'H' *over* 'h'

Variants: 1 One] ONE BR; one WK
3,6,8,10,12 said:] ~ , BR
4 this] *omit* WK
4 did‸] ~ , BR,WK
7,9 held I] I held WK
7 another.] ~ ; BR
11 end‸] ~ ; BR; ~ . WK
13 out:] ~ , BR
15 Then did He look] He looked WK
17 soul,"] ~ !" BR
17 He] HE BR; he WK

MS: Columbia University. Blue-black ink with thick pen on wove paper (254 × 203.5 mm.), alterations in same ink.

Note: The version in *War is Kind* is independent and derives from a lost revised manuscript, not from BR. For its text, see no. 92. The present manuscript is probably not the printer's copy for BR.

34. I stood upon a highway

*BR (caps)

Emendation: 6,7,11 God] GOD BR

35. A man saw a ball of gold in the sky

*BR (caps)

Emendation: 3 it——] ~— BR

36. I met a seer

*BR (caps)

Emendation: 6 "Child——"] "~—" BR

37. On the horizon the peaks assembled

*BR (caps)

Emendation: 5(*twice*) We] WE BR

38. The ocean said to me once

*BR (caps)

39. The livid lightnings flashed in the clouds

*BR (caps)

Emendations: 4 [2]Hearken] HEARKEN BR
4,6 God] GOD BR

40. AND YOU LOVE ME?

*BR (caps)

Emendations: 1 me?] ~ ^ BR
24 beloved——] ~— BR

41. LOVE WALKED ALONE

*BR (caps)

Emendation: 6 Heart's Pain] HEART'S PAIN BR

42. I WALKED IN A DESERT

*BR (caps)

N[1] (*Kansas City Star*, Feb. 16, 1899, p. 4, entitled 'The Desert'; subscribed '—Stephen Crane, "The Black Riders." ')

Emendations: 3 God] N[1]; GOD BR
5 but——] ~— BR,N[1]

Variants: 1 desert.] ~ , N[1]
6 "The] ^~ N[1]

43. THERE CAME WHISPERINGS IN THE WINDS

*BR (caps)

N[1] (*Kansas City Star*, Feb. 12, 1899, p. 4; entitled 'Good-bye'; subscribed '—Stephen Crane, "The Black Riders." ')

Emendation: 6 [2]No——] ~— BR,N[1]

44. I WAS IN THE DARKNESS

*BR (caps)

Emendation: 4 light——] ~— BR

45. TRADITION, THOU ART FOR SUCKLING CHILDREN

*BR (caps)

Emendation: 4 Then——] ~— BR

46. MANY RED DEVILS RAN FROM MY HEART

*BR (caps)

Emendation: 2 page.] ~ , BR

47. "THINK AS I THINK," SAID A MAN

*BR (caps)

48. ONCE THERE WAS A MAN,— | OH, SO WISE!

*BR (caps)

49. I STOOD MUSING IN A BLACK WORLD

*BR (caps)

50. You say you are holy

*BR (caps)

51. A man went before a strange god

*BR (caps)

52. Why do you strive for greatness, fool?

*BR (caps)
Emendations: 4 lord] LORD BR (see MS, no. 18, line 12)
7 shoe-buckles] ~-|~ BR

53. Blustering god

*BR (caps)
Emendation: 22 I——] ~— BR

54. "It was wrong to do this," said the angel

*BR (caps)

55. A man toiled on a burning road

*BR (caps)
Emendation: 7 you——] ~— BR

56. A man feared that he might find an assassin

*BR (caps)

57. With eye and with gesture

*BR (caps)

58. The sage lectured brilliantly

*BR (caps)

59. Walking in the sky

*BR (caps)
Emendation: 6 lord] LORD BR (see MS, no. 18, line 12)

60. Upon the road of my life

*BR (caps)
Emendations: 9 Good Deed] GOOD DEED BR
15 Vanity] VANITY BR
19 Fool] FOOL BR

61. There was a man and a woman

*BR (caps)
Variant: 5 gayly] gaily BR(ii),E1

62. THERE WAS A MAN WHO LIVED A LIFE OF FIRE

*BR (caps)

63. THERE WAS A GREAT CATHEDRAL

*BR (caps)

64. FRIEND, YOUR WHITE BEARD SWEEPS THE GROUND

*BR (caps)
Emendation: 8 friend.] ~ ? BR(i); ~ ! BR(ii),E1

65. ONCE, I KNEW A FINE SONG

*BR (caps)
Emendation: 6 They] THEY BR

66. IF I SHOULD CAST OFF THIS TATTERED COAT

*BR (caps)
N[1] (*Kansas City Star,* Feb. 11, 1899, p. 4; entitled *After;* subscribed '—Stephen Crane, "The Black Riders." ')
Variant: 5 ignorant,—] ~‸— N[1]

67. GOD LAY DEAD IN HEAVEN

*BR (caps)
Emendation: 1 Heaven] HEAVEN BR

68. A SPIRIT SPED

*BR (caps)

WAR IS KIND

69. DO NOT WEEP, MAIDEN, FOR WAR IS KIND

*MS[1] (facsimile of signed holograph, *Bookman,* IX [July, 1899], 400)
MS[2] (NN), holograph
MS[3] (ViU), holograph, signed, lines 6–11 only
Bk (*Bookman,* II [Feb., 1896], 476, signed, titled, caps)
N[1] (*San Francisco Chronicle,* Feb. 9, 1896, p. 4, titled, caps)
PO (*Public Opinion,* XX [Feb. 27, 1896], 277 titled)
LD (*Literary Digest,* XII [Feb. 29, 1896], 520 titled)
TMs (NNC)
WK
Emendations: 5 kind.] MS[2],Bk+; ~‸ MS[1]
25 weep.] Bk+; ~‸ MS[1-2]
MS[1] Alterations: 3 steed] *interlined above deleted* 'horse'

20 virtue] *interlined above deleted* 'glory'

MS^3 Alteration: 11 field] *interlined above deleted* 'place'

Variants: 1,4 Do] "Do MS^2
1 kind.] ~∧ MS^2
2 Because] "Because MS^2
2 toward] towards TMs
3 And] "And MS^2
3 alone,] ~ ∧ MS^2
6 Hoarse,] ~ ∧ MS$^{2-3}$
6 regiment∧] ~ , BK+
7 who] that MS^3
7 fight,] ~ ∧ MS$^{2-3}$
8 die∧] ~ . Bk+
9 them∧] ~ , Bk+
10 battle-god] Battle-God TMs
10 kingdom] Kingdom TMs
11 A] —A MS^2
12 kind.] ~ ∧ MS^2,TMs
13 trenches,] ~ ∧| MS^2
14 died,] ~ ∧ MS^2
15,25 weep.] ~∧ MS^2
16 kind.] ~∧ MS^2
17 Swift,] ~ ∧ MS^2,Bk+
17 regiment∧] ~ , Bk+(−PO); ~ . PO
18 gold,] ~ ∧ MS^2
19 die∧] ~ . Bk+(−TMs); ~ , TMs
20 slaughter∧] ~ , Bk+
22 And] and TMs
22 lie.] ~ ∧ MS^2
24 son,] ~ ∧ MS^2

MS^1: Known only from a signed facsimile reproduction in the *Bookman*, IX [July, 1899], 400, where it is identified as the original from which the *Bookman* text of February, 1896, was set. The title 'LINES.' triple underlined has been added by another hand; the *Bookman* title was 'War is Kind'. Some uncharacteristic punctuation appears in MS^1, particularly in lines 6 and 17, and in general the fair copy MS^2 is closer to Crane's usual lack of punctuation. However, so far as can be told from the facsimile, the punctuation was not editorially inserted and thus it must be accepted. In the *Bookman* and in the newspapers the poem was printed in full caps in the manner of *The Black Riders*. Since no variants appear, the relation of the newspapers to the *Bookman* text is undemonstrable; however, the use of the capital letters suggests that the newspapers were set from *Bookman* proofs.

MS^2: New York Public Library (Berg Collection). Holograph fair copy subscribed 1895 on the flyleaf of *The Red Badge of Courage* (1896) presented to William Dean Howells.

MS^3: University of Virginia–Barrett. Lines 6–11 written on one-half of a fold of laid paper 221 × 176.5 mm., vertical chainlines 24 mm. apart, unwatermarked, signed, and dated 'Washington, D.C. | March 18, 1896'. In the text, in line 11 'field' is interlined with a caret above deleted 'place'. For a similar presentation copy written in Washington on March 18, 1896, see no. 1.

TMs: Blue carbon on laid paper (265 × 202 mm.), vertical chainlines 24 mm. apart, watermarked 'REGENT LINEN ☆ W. S. & B. | MADE IN USA'. Signed (typewritten) Stephen Crane. This must be the printer's copy Crane asked Reynolds on March 1, 1898, to have typed up from the *Bookman*.

Notes: The poem was second in Crane's first list, titled 'War is Kind', and seventh in the second list, titled 'The Drums of the Regiment'. The appearance of the title 'War is Kind' before the poem in the collection *War is Kind* may represent the head-title to the collection but more likely is a simple copy of the titled typescript which had itself copied the *Bookman* title. It is the only titled poem in the collection, and the only poem for which Crane did not provide the typescript or manuscript.

70. "WHAT SAYS THE SEA, LITTLE SHELL?

*MS^1 (NN), holograph, signed
MS^2 (InU), holograph, signed
Ph (*Philistine*, II [Feb., 1896], 94–95, signed)
S (*Roycroft Quarterly: A Souvenir and a Medley*, May, 1896, p. 31, caps)
TMs (NNC)
WK

Emendations: 5 Awkward] MS^2+; Awkard MS^1
11–12 robes | "—Men] ~ | —"~ MS$^{1-2}$; ~— | "~ Ph+
20 moonlight.] ~‸ MS$^{1-2}$; ~, Ph,S,TMs; ~; WK
31 sea.] Ph+; ~‸ MS$^{1-2}$

MS^1 Alterations: 0.1 *deleted underlined title* 'The Shell and the Pines'
30 No] *in another hand over illegible letters*

MS^2 Alterations: 6,24 sea] *final 's' deleted*
10 women's] *apostrophe deleted in error in* MS^2

Variants: 3,16,27 us‸] ~, Ph+
4,17,28,33 ships‸] ~, Ph+
5,18,29 ships."] ~". TMs
6,19,24,30 oh,] O, TMs; O‸ WK
6,19,24,30 pines] Pines TMs,WK
6,19,30 pines‸] ~, Ph+ (*except* TMs '~‸' *at* 19)
8 doom‸] ~, Ph+
10 tears‸] ~. Ph,S; ~, TMs,WK
13 pain."] ~". TMs
21 patience‸] ~, Ph+
22 hands‸] ~, Ph+
23 hearts‸] ~, Ph,S; ~. TMs,WK
24,34 pines."] ~". TMs
32 you‸] ~, Ph+
34 Oh,] O‸ TMs,WK

MS^1: New York Public Library (Berg Collection). Black ink on three leaves of cheap wove paper (221 × 143 mm.) numbered 1–3 (third page cut to 195 × 143 mm.). Title 'The Shell and the Pines', underlined, deleted. (This is the title given it in Crane's first list.) Signed at the end. In ink a curving line is drawn on fol. 2 in the left margin against lines 19–24 and the ink initials 'SC.' are placed at the foot of the line below the stanza. The meaning of the marking is obscure and though it may be in another hand it can scarcely represent a direction for a printer.

MS^2: Lilly Library at Indiana University. Black ink on two leaves of unwatermarked laid paper (with a wove effect) 334 × 202 mm., faint blue rules, leaf embossed *Columbia*, page 2 numbered above a semicircle. Poem signed at the end and subscribed 'To my friend, Dr. A. L. Mitchell. | Hartwood, N. Y. Dec 28, 1895.' Since Dr. Mitchell's office was next door to the *Philistine*, it is just possible that this manuscript served as printer's copy. On January 29, 1896, Crane sent his photograph inscribed to Dr. Mitchell from Hartwood.

TMs: Columbia University. Black typewritten carbon copy on a leaf of unwatermarked wove paper (268 × 202.5 mm.). Below it is typed no.

71 *To the maiden*, separated by a double line of hyphens. The poem is credited to the *Philistine* in parentheses.

Note: Since the texts of MS[1] and MS[2] are identical in all respects, except for the matter of an apostrophe in line 10, and the misspelling in line 5, it is probable that one was copied from the other. So far as can be determined, the *Philistine* was set up from MS[2] or some similar copy; the *Souvenir* derives from the *Philistine*. The Columbia TMs carbon, the original of which served as printer's copy for *War is Kind*, seems to have been typed from the *Philistine* and so has no independent authority. The poem was given in Crane's first list in the sixth position as 'The Sea to the Pines'; it heads the second list as 'The Shell and the Pines'.

71. To THE MAIDEN

*Ph (*Philistine*, II [April, 1896], 152, caps, signed)
S (*Souvenir and a Medley*, May, 1896, p. 32, caps)
TMs (NNC)
WK

Variants: 2 meadow‸] ~, WK
7 vacancy‸] ~ , WK
8 time,] ~ ‸ TMs,WK

TMs: Columbia University. Black typewritten carbon at foot of a sheet of unwatermarked wove paper (268 × 202.5 mm.) separated from no. 70 by a double row of hyphens, with another row at its foot. Credited to the *Philistine*.

Note: The identical text (except for one punctuation variant) of TMs and *Philistine* suggests that TMs was typed from the printed text, like no. 70 above it, for it does have the credit to the *Philistine*. This is probably the poem given as fourth in Crane's first list under the title 'The Sea—Point of View'. The text may have been revised after its withdrawal from *The Black Riders* at Copeland and Day's insistence, for in their letter of October 19, 1894, they quote the first two lines as 'To the maiden | The sea was a laughing meadow'.

72. A LITTLE INK MORE OR LESS!

*MS (NSyU), holograph, signed, lines 7–19 only
TMs (NNC), copy-text for lines 1–6
WK

Emendations: 2 can't] WK; cant TMs
13 familiar] WK; familar MS, TMs

MS Alterations: 8 trinkets] *preceded by deleted* 't [*and the beginning of an* 'h']'
12 upon] *interlined with a caret*

Variants: 10 numbskulls] numskullsWK
12 pulpiting] pulpitings TMs,WK

MS: Syracuse University. Lines 7–19 written in black ink on a leaf of wove paper (330 × 205 mm., blue-green rules, signed, with the note at the foot, 'oh, Hubbard, mark this well. Mark it well! If | it is overbalancing your discretion, inform me. | S. C.'

TMs: Columbia University. Dark blue typewritten carbon on upper section of a part sheet of unwatermarked wove paper (135–139 irregular × 202.5 mm.), credited to the *Philistine*. At foot is typed in black a double line of hyphens. No. 73 was originally typed below.

Note: The TMs ascription to the *Philistine* was apparently based on Crane's intention to send it to Hubbard after typing and his expectation that it would be accepted. In fact, Hubbard did not publish the poem until July, 1900, and then in *The Fra*, p. xxv, where instead of the text he reproduced the leaf in facsimile with the headnote: 'A few weeks before his passing, Stevie Crane sent me this manuscript. I thought it tipped a bit too much to t' other side, when I first read it. But I got it out the other day and read it again. I liked it better. THE FRA readers shall judge.' Hubbard's date for its receipt is less than candid, for the poem had appeared in *War is Kind* in early 1899 and was almost certainly sent to him in December, 1897, after its printer's copy TMs had been typed, or at the latest in early 1898. Very likely Hubbard did not like to admit that he was cashing in posthumously on a reject. A problem is raised in that the MS which Hubbard reproduced and which is now at Syracuse University consists of the second (unnumbered) leaf, although it is odd that the first leaf should have contained no more than six lines. However, the second stanza, starting this second leaf, is written closer to the head than Crane usually started a poem, and it would seem that Hubbard had lost the first leaf during the two and a half years he had kept the poem, or else that he disliked the first stanza and suppressed it, the more particularly because it would have interfered with the facsimile reproduction on a single page. Given the conjectural history of this manuscript, it is unlikely that Crane would have written the first stanza and had it typed after having sent off to Hubbard a poem consisting of the present second stanza. It is true that superficially the connection between the two stanzas does not seem to be intimate; but the association is closer than might appear on the surface if Daniel Hoffman is right (*The Poetry of Stephen Crane* [1957], p. 78) that lines 1–6 refer to "the voluminous clerical writings of Crane's family" or even if the allusion is not so specific as that but refers to religious controversy in general and is not simple literary satire. At any rate, the typist of the Columbia TMs, working from authoritative copy, spaced a clearly marked stanzaic division between the two sections.

If the hypothesis is correct that TMs was made up from MS before it was mailed to Hubbard, the TMs, WK variant 'pulpitings' in line 12 must be an error, for Crane did not alter the MS copy. If, instead, TMs was copied from a duplicate manuscript (less likely), then it could have read the plural. However, the plural is more likely to represent a typist's error by contamination with the plurals 'numbskulls' and 'lights' ending the two preceding lines. Syntactically, 'pulpiting' in the singular should agree with the collective singular 'walking' of line 9, and with the singular 'fanfare' of line 11. Of course, the plural could be defended as agreeing with the different sermons, both true and false, which were preached, but the reference is not so exact as to require alteration of the manuscript's authoritative collective singular, especially given the conjectured textual transmission.

73. "Have you ever made a just man?"

*TMs (NNC)
WK

Emendations: 6 thud] WK; third TMs
6 defeat."] WK; ~ ". TMs

Variants: 1 "Have] ‸~ WK
2 God‸] ~ , WK
3 dead‸] ~ , WK

TMs: Columbia University. Dark blue typewritten carbon on a slip of unwatermarked wove paper (28–40 irregular × 202.5 mm.), torn across at head and foot. Originally typed below no. 72 and above no. 74.

Note: In line 6 the WK variant *thud* appears to represent the correct reading for the misreading or memorial error of the typist *third*. Since proof was very likely not read by Crane for this volume, we must suppose that he corrected the ribbon printer's copy but neglected to alter the carbon.

74. I explain the silvered passing of a ship at night

*MS (NNC)
Bk (*Bookman*, IV [Oct., 1896], 149, signed, entitled 'Lines', caps)
TMs^{1} (NNC)
WK
TMs^{2} (NNC)

Emendations: 1 explain] Bk+; Explain MS
1 passing] TMs^{1},WK; path MS,Bk,TMs^{2}
5 A] Bk,TMs^{1},WK; The MS,TMs^{2}
7 of] Bk,TMs^{1},WK; *omit* MS,TMs^{2}
8 waves‸] Bk,TMs^{1},WK; ~. MS,TMs^{2}
9,13 loneliness] Bk,TMs^{2},WK; lonliness MS,TMs^{1}
10 Remember . . . love] Bk,TMs^{1},WK; Oh, thou, my ship | Remember, thou, in thy stern straight journey MS,TMs^{2}
11 Thou . . . waters] Bk,TMs^{1},WK; Thou leavest a waste, a waste of far waters MS,TMs^{2}

MS Alterations: 1 I] *added in left margin without reducing capital of* 'Explain'
5 The] 'T' *over* 't'; *follows deleted* 'Then' (*emended to* 'A' *in* Bk)
7 Then the waste] *on line above is deleted false start* 'Then the silence'
9 For . . . lonliness.] *added below line* 8 *without deleting period after* 'waves' (*emended to* 'loneliness' *in* Bk)
10 Oh, thou] *on line above is deleted false start* 'Explain' ('Oh, thou . . .' *emended to* 'Remember, thou . . .' *in* Bk)
12 waves] *interlined above deleted* 'waters'

Variants: 1 night‸] ~, Bk,Tms^{1}, WK
2 sad‸] ~, Bk
2 wave‸] ~, Bk,WK
3 striving‸] ~, Bk,WK
4 ^{2}man‸] ~, Bk,WK
5 night‸] ~, Bk,WK
6 star.] ~; WK
7,11 waters‸] ~, WK
9+ [*space*]] *no space* TMs^{2}
10 oh] O Bk,TMs^{1},WK
10 love‸] ~! Bk; ~, WK

MS: Columbia University. Black ink, revisions in the same ink, on legal-cap paper (308 × 200 mm.), 29 rules 9.8 mm. apart, vertical pink-dark blue-pink line 38 mm. from left margin, 32 mm. head space, 7 mm. tail space. On verso, in pencil, circled 100, and 100 added to 60 for a total of 160, in Cora's hand.

TMs[1]: Columbia University. Dark blue typewritten carbon on tail section of a leaf of unwatermarked wove paper (92–102 irregular × 202.5) torn across at top. Credited to the *Bookman*. The ribbon mate would have been used as printer's copy for WK. This poem was originally typed below no. 73 on a leaf starting with no. 72.

TMs[2]: Columbia University. Black ribbon typewritten on laid paper (260 × 203 mm.), vertical chains 26 mm. apart, watermarked EXCELSIOR FINE. Paged '–2–'. In black ink at a slant in upper left corner Cora Crane wrote 'War is Kind'. This is a copy made up posthumously from MS by Cora for sale.

Note: For a paraphrase utilized as a love letter to Cora in January, 1897, see *Letters*, ed. Stallman and Gilkes, p. 138. It is among the four added to Crane's first list, where it is given as 'I explain the path of a ship', the reading of MS, Bk and TMs[2]. The lost manuscript sent to Bk contained revisions from the draft MS version in lines 5, 7, 10, and 11. The further revision of line 1 from 'path' to 'passing' was made in the lost copy of the Bk manuscript from which TMs[1] derived, or else from the ribbon copy sent to the WK printer, but the change not transferred to the carbon. Evidently this manuscript was not available to Cora after Crane's death so that she utilized the draft manuscript to make up her typescript.

75. "I HAVE HEARD THE SUNSET SONG OF THE BIRCHES

M (Menu for Philistine Dinner, ' "The Time Has Come," the Walrus Said, "To Talk of Many Things." ' [East Aurora, N.Y.: The Roycroft Printing Shop, 1895], p. 8, caps, signed)
Ph (*Philistine*, 11 [Jan., 1896], 62, caps, signed)
S (*Souvenir and a Medley*, May, 1896, p. 30, caps)
*TMs (NNC)
WK

Emendations: 6 With] M,Ph,S,WK; with TMs
6 wind-men] M,Ph,S; ~ ^ ~ TMs,WK
7 lived,"] M,Ph,S,WK; ~", TMs
10 roses."] M,Ph,S,WK; ~". TMs

Variants: 1 birches^] ~, WK
2 silence^] ~. M,Ph,S; ~, WK
4 nightfall^] ~, M,Ph,S
7 maniac,] ~^ M,Ph,S
9 But,] ~^ WK

M: Below the poem Crane inscribed in pencil: 'Dear Willis: I am com-|ing to New York on Tues-|day morning. | Stephen Crane | [at lower right] East Aurora; | Saturday – 1895.' Elbert Hubbard added the note: 'I wish I could too | Elbert Hubbard'.

TMs: Columbia University. Blue typewritten carbon on top section of unwatermarked wove paper (82–85 irregular × 202.5 mm.) credited to the *Philistine*. Given in Crane's second list as no. 2 'The White Birches'. The Philistine dinner was tendered Crane on December 19, 1895. TMs seems to have been made up from a now lost manuscript; hence it and the Menu radiate from some lost originals and both are of authority. This section of TMs was originally typed above no. 76.

76. FAST RODE THE KNIGHT

*MS (NSyU), holograph, signed
S (*Souvenir and a Medley,* May, 1896, p. 33, caps)
Ph (*Philistine,* III [June, 1896], 20, caps, signed)
TMs (NNC)
WK

Emendations: 7 flickered] S+; flicked MS
13,15 of] S+; of a MS

Variants: 2 reeking$_{\wedge}$] ~, WK
3 sword.] ~, WK
4 "To (*no indention*)] *indention* TMs
5 knight$_{\wedge}$] ~, WK
8 lights$_{\wedge}$] ~, WK
9 knight's] knights S,Ph
9 knight's good banner] good knights banner Ph
11 horse$_{\wedge}$] ~, WK
12 thing$_{\wedge}$] ~, WK

MS Alterations: 8 Like] 'L' *over possible* 'I'
9 knight's] *apostrophe inserted*

MS: Syracuse University. Fair copy written in black ink on blue-ruled pad paper (240 × 200 mm.), signed.

TMs: Columbia University. Dark blue typewritten carbon on piece of unwatermarked wove paper (95 irregular × 202.5 mm.), torn across at head and foot, credited to the *Philistine*, line of hyphens visible at head. Above this poem was originally typed no. 75, and below it no. 77.

Note: In Crane's first list the poem is given fifth as 'The Knight rode fast—'; in his second list it is fifth, 'The Knight and His Horse'. It would appear that TMs was typed from a copy of Ph, corrected in line 9.

77. FORTH WENT THE CANDID MAN

MS (NNC), holograph draft
*TMs (NNC)
WK

Emendations: 7 fool,"] MS,WK; ~", TMs
8 mad."] MS,WK; ~". TMs
9 candid,"] MS,WK; ~", TMs

Variants: 3 him$_{\wedge}$] ~, MS
3 a far strange] far unknown MS
6 Yellow] Flashing yellow MS
7 bystander$_{\wedge}$] ~, WK
8+ [*space*]] *uncertain in* MS *because of deleted false start above*
9 man$_{\wedge}$] man in a passion$_{\wedge}$ MS; man. WK
10 stick] cane MS
11 It was] It had become MS
11 sticks] canes MS

MS Alteration: 9 "You are] *on line above is deleted false start* 'And when his'

MS: Columbia University. Black ink on cheap wove buff paper (252–254 irregular × 195–200 mm. irregular).

TMs: Columbia University. Dark blue typewritten carbon on tail section of wove paper (89–90 irregular × 202.5 mm.), double line of hyphens at foot. Nos. 75 and 76 were originally typed above this piece.

Note: The MS is an early draft, replaced by a lost version from which TMs derives and is given in fourth place as 'The Candid Man' in Crane's first list, and as no. 10 under the same title in the second list. A long dash in this latter substitutes for the place of publication.

78. You tell me this is God?

*TMs (NNC)
Ph (*Philistine*, vi [April, 1898], back wrapper, caps, signed, entitled 'Lines.')
WK

Variant: 2 this] IT Ph

TMs: Columbia University. Black typewritten ribbon copy heading a leaf of unwatermarked wove paper (268 × 202.5 mm.), credited to the *Philistine*. Below is no. 79.

Note: Ph was probably printed from the manuscript after it had served as copy for TMs; thus both Ph and TMs radiate from this lost document and are authoritative. Under these circumstances the 'this' in line 2 of TMs (and automatically in WK) could be a contamination from 'this' in line 1, and the Ph version, from a manuscript, could be authoritative. But since Hubbard might as readily have altered the repetition 'this' on his own responsibility, the case is far too uncertain to justify emendation of TMs.

79. On the desert

*MS (ViU), holograph, signed
Ph(p) (*Philistine* proof sheet, holograph revision, signed, entitled 'Lines.')
Ph (*Philistine*, vi [May, 1898], 166–167, signed, entitled 'Lines.')
TMs (NNC)
WK

Emendations: 7 distant-thunder] WK; ~—~ MS,Ph(p),TMs; ~‸~ Ph
8 slow] Ph(p) *holograph revision*; mystic MS,Ph(p[u]),Ph,TMs,WK
28 accursèd] Ph(p),Ph; accurséd MS,WK; accursed TMs

MS Alterations: 7 distant-thunder] *intended hyphen inserted as dash*
15 reaches] *followed by deleted dash*
18 Over] *interlined for clarity above deleted mended* 'Over' *which had been formed from original* 'On' *by inscribing* 'v' *over* 'n' *and adding* 'er'
20 bronze,] 'e' *inserted over original comma and comma inserted*

Variants: (Ph[p] disagrees with Ph in every case)

3 Fire-rays] ~‸~ TMs,WK
7 drums‸] ~, Ph,WK
8 color‸] ~, WK
9 body‸] ~, Ph
12 snakes‸] ~, WK
13 staring‸] ~, Ph,WK
18 men‸] ~, Ph
20 moving] the moving TMs
20 yellow,] ~‸TMs
21 her‸] ~, Ph,WK
26 staring‸] ~, WK
27 softly‸] ~. TMs
29 death‸] ~, Ph,WK

MS: University of Virginia. Black ink on unwatermarked laid paper (308.5 × 202.5 mm.), chainlines 29 mm. apart, 34 blue rules 8 mm. apart, head space 22 mm., tail space 2.5 mm. Signed. At foot, to left '(The Philistine)'; to right 'Please send proof'. In pencil in strange hand entitled 'Lines'. Black ink thumbprints indicate this MS was the Ph printer's copy.

Ph(p): Columbia University. Proofsheet with holograph deletion of 'mystic' in line 8 and marginal substitution of 'slow'. In lower left corner in strange hand, 'Proof for | Correction for | May Philistine'.

TMs: Columbia University. Black typewritten ribbon on leaf of unwatermarked wove paper (268 × 202.5 mm.) placed below no. 78 and without credit for publication. No lines of hyphens separate the two.

Note to "One Dash—Horses" 18.35 in Tales of Adventure, *Works*, v the fact that its revision never entered the textual tradition indicates that it was not returned. The revision is nonetheless valid: for Crane's alteration elsewhere of his overused adjective *mystic*, see the Textual Note to "One Dash—Horses" 18.35 in Tales of Adventure, *Works*, v (1970), 199–200. The difficulty in line 7 over 'distant-thunder' stems from the original inscription in MS of 'distant thunder' widely spaced without a hyphen; then when Crane inserted the hyphen it stretched so far as to resemble a dash and was mistaken for one both by the typist of TMs and the compositor of Ph. This error, plus the markings on MS, indicates that TMs was typed from the MS before it was sent to Hubbard for publication. The lack of an acute accent in 'accursed' in TMs but its presence in WK suggests that the accent was added in the copy sent to the printer but not in the preserved duplicate.

80. A newspaper is a collection of half-injustices

*WK

81. The wayfarer

*TMs (NNC)
WK

Emendations: 5 Ha,"] WK; ~ ", TMs
7 time."] WK; ~ ". TMs
10 Well,"] WK; ~ ", TMs
11 roads."] WK; ~ ". TMs

Variants: 1 wayfarer‸] ~ , WK
2 truth‸] ~ , WK

TMs: Columbia University. Blue typewritten ribbon heading leaf of unwatermarked wove paper (268 × 202.5 mm.) with no. 82 below it, separated by double line of hyphens.

82. A SLANT OF SUN ON DULL BROWN WALLS

Ph (*Philistine,* 11 [Dec., 1895], front wrapper verso, caps, signed)
S (*Souvenir and a Medley,* [May, 1896], p. 29, caps)
*TMs (NNC)
WK

Emendation: 2+ [*space*]] Ph,S,WK; *no space* TMs

Variants: 1 walls$_\wedge$] ∼ , WK
3 hymn$_\wedge$] ∼ , WK
4 collisions] clashes Ph,S
4 cries$_\wedge$] ∼ , Ph,S,WK
9 flowers$_\wedge$] violets, Ph,S; flowers, WK
13 O,] ∼ $_\wedge$ WK
13 God,] ∼$_\wedge$ Ph,S

TMs: Columbia University. Blue typewritten ribbon below no. 81 on sheet of unwatermarked wove paper (268 × 202.5 mm.), credited to the *Philistine.*

Note: In Crane's first list the poem is seventh as 'The Noise of the City'; in the second list it is no. 8 as 'The City'. The evidence suggests that TMs was typed from an independent and slightly revised manuscript, not from an altered copy of the *Philistine.* Hence both radiate from a holograph, but TMs should have superior authority.

83. ONCE A MAN CLAMBERING TO THE HOUSE-TOPS

MS^1 (NNC), holograph trial start
MS^2 (NNC), holograph draft
*WK

Emendation: 1 house-tops] MS^2; housetops WK; house tops MS^1

Variants: 1 Once$_\wedge$ a man$_\wedge$] ∼ , ∼ ∼ , MS^2
1 house-tops$_\wedge$] ∼-∼, MS^2
2 Appealed] Cried there MS^1
2 heavens.] imperturbab (*last of text*) MS^1; empty heavens$_\wedge$ MS^2
3 deaf spheres;] imperturbable stars$_\wedge$ | MS^2
4 suns.] higher suns: MS^2
5 a dot on the clouds,] an indication, a dot. MS^2
6–7 And . . . armies.] Then, finally—God—the sky was filled with armies$_\wedge$ MS^2

MS^2 Alteration: 3 he] *altered from* 'is'

MS^1: Columbia University. Black ink on reversed verso of fol. 6 of no. 113, *A soldier, young in years,* followed by essay [*Gratitude of a Nation*]. The full text reads, 'Once a man clambering to the house tops | Cried there to the imperturbab | [space] | [in pencil] Once | Stephen Crane | Hartwood Club | Port Jervis N.Y. | [at foot] The name of this club | shall be the'.

MS^2: Columbia University. Blue-black ink on thick wove paper (192 × 117 mm.).

Note: MS^1 being a mere fragment and MS^2 an elementary draft, the *War is Kind* text is chosen as the most trustworthy copy-text since it derives (through a lost typescript) from a revised manuscript. The unpublished essay given the courtesy title of "Gratitude of a Nation" was written for Decoration Day, 1894, and can be dated before May 9, when Crane wrote from 111 West 33rd St., New York, to Hamlin Garland that it had been rejected by the *New York Press* (*Letters*, pp. 36–37). It is possible that for the sixth leaf of the combined Decoration Day poem and article Crane utilized the original blank verso of a discarded sheet of paper containing the trial beginning of no. 83. On the other hand, some physical evidence is probably to be interpreted to the contrary, that Crane scribbled notes on the back of a manuscript already written out. The six leaves are legal-cap paper, but whereas fols. 1–4 are of one variety from a pad measuring 317 × 197 mm. with the ruled lines wanting in the left margin before the vertical colored rules, fols. 5–6 are from a different pad measuring 317 × 197 mm., the lines extending through the vertical rules to the left margin. The identity of the paper of fols. 5–6 suggests that they were inscribed in order from the same pad, and indeed it would be difficult to account for Crane picking up a new pad for the fifth leaf and then making use of a discarded leaf from the same pad for the sixth. Thus the first week of May, 1894, provides us only with the anterior date for the composition of no. 83; that it did not appear in *The Black Riders*, however, need not indicate that it was later than September 9, 1894, when Crane informed Copeland and Day that he would write no further poems to piece out the collection (*Letters*, pp. 39–40). On the other hand, the appearance of another trial of the first line on fol. 49ᵛ of Crane's Notebook may suggest that he had not yet worked out the poem by the autumn of 1894, for the first few words occur on a page that concludes "In a Park Row Restaurant" published in the *New York Press* on October 28, 1894, and just before another sketch "Heard on the Street Election Night" that dates from November. That Crane did not add to *The Black Riders* no. 113 *A soldier, young in years* (the Decoration Day poem written before May 9, 1894) has no bearing on the availability of no. 83 for the collection, since Crane may well have considered that no. 113 was not suitable for the volume—and indeed he never printed it. No. 83 appears to have remained in draft state until it was revived for *War is Kind.*

84. There was a man with tongue of wood

*MS (NNC), holograph
WK

Emendations: 5 The . . . wood‸] WK; And in the clip-clapper | Of this tongue of wood MS

6–7 And . . . sing] WK; He understood | What the man wished to sing MS

8 And . . . content.] WK; And with this | The singer was well satisfied. MS

Variants: 2,7 sing‸] ~ , WK

3 lamentable‸] ~ . WK

MS: Columbia University. Blue-black ink on unwatermarked wove paper (230 × 197 mm.). On the verso are word counts in ink: 170 added to 167 for a total of 337 and then 257 added to this for a total of 594.

Note: This is the fourth of the seven poems that Copeland and Day declined to print. Their title 'There was a man with a tongue of wood'

contains what is probably an inadvertent slip in 'a tongue', for the manuscript is an early version but the reading does not change from 'with tongue' between this draft and the revised WK text. MS is, probably, the copy submitted to Copeland and Day for *The Black Riders* and then withdrawn. The calculations on its verso appear to refer to *The Black Riders.*

85. THE SUCCESSFUL MAN HAS THRUST HIMSELF

MS (NNC), holograph, signed
*TMs[1] (NNC)
WK
TMs[2] (NSyU)

Emendations: 3 mistakes,] MS; ~ ; TMs[1-2]; ~ ,— WK
4 mistakes,] MS; ~ ; TMs[1-2],WK
9 Limned]WK; Limmed TMs[1-2]; limmed MS
17 wrought."] MS,WK; ~ . ‸ TMs[1] (*added by hand* TMs[2])
18 smiling,] MS,WK; ~ ‸ TMs[1-2]
22 dripping,] MS,WK; ~ ‸ TMs[1-2]

Variants: 1–2 The . . . years] *one line in* MS
2 years,] ~ ‸ MS
3–4 Reeking . . . mistakes] *one line in* MS
5 lesser‸] ~ , WK
7 Then,] *omit* MS
8–9 He . . . face] *one line in* MS
9 face;] ~ ‸ MS
11 all.] ~ ‸ MS
12–13 Flesh . . . Contributes] Flesh and marrow contribute MS
13 coverlet‸] ~ , WK
14 slumber.] ~ ‸ MS
15 ignorance,] ~ ; MS
15 guilt‸] ~ , WK
16 delivers] delivered WK
17 ²Thus] thus MS
21 babes;] babes‸ | Protests his murder of widows. MS

MS Alterations: 2 water] *interlined above deleted* 'paper'
9 Limned with] 'limmed with' *interlined above deleted* 'bearing'; *upstroke of* 'l' *intentionally deletes comma following* 'banners'

MS: Columbia University. Black ink on laid paper (327 × 203 mm.) watermarked CARISBROOK SUPERFINE, vertical chainlines 26 mm. apart. Below the signature and to the left is the autograph date 'Dec. 5th, 1897', the 9 written over an 8. TMs[1] was made up from a revision of MS, however.

TMs[1]: Columbia University. Dull blue typewritten ribbon copy on unwatermarked wove paper (167 irregular × 202.5 mm.), the upper part of a leaf. The lower part has not been identified.

TMs[2]: Syracuse University. The third of five poems typed posthumously by Cora on Indian & Colonial watermarked wove foolscap for sale as a sequence. The copy seems to have been TMs[1]. The separate titlepage reads 'LINES. || BY Stephen Crane. || [lower left] From– Mrs Stephen Crane. | 6 Milborne Grove. | The Boltons S.W.' The poem occupies the second leaf of the text (the third of the typescript), is numbered 3 within parentheses in the upper left corner, and has a typewritten line below it. In the left margin Cora wrote in black ink, 'War is | Kind'. Columbia University owns a detached blue carbon of a similar titlepage although of a different typing, on laid paper watermarked EXCELSIOR FINE: 'LINES. | BY | Stephen Crane. | [lower left] From–Mrs Stephen Crane. | 6 Milborne Grove. | The Boltons S.W.' This title-page does not seem to be associated with the 5-poem sequence Cora typed out, now preserved as TMs² at Syracuse, but instead with a 7-poem sequence, broken up, at Columbia.

Note: MS being a draft, the more convenient copy-text is TMs¹ made from a revised manuscript. Ordinarily, TMs¹, the copy for WK, reproduces its manuscripts with considerable fidelity, but reference has been made in this particular case to MS for some of the accidentals.

86. IN THE NIGHT

*MS (NcU), holograph, signed
Ch (*Chapbook*, IV [March, 1896], 372, signed, entitled *Verses*)
Ch(r) holograph alterations revised clipping
TMs (NNC)
WK

Emendations: 4,17 Master] Ch,TMs,WK; master MS
4 Master‸] TMs,WK; ~, MS,Ch
4 movest] Ch+; moveth MS
7 Thy] Ch,WK; thy MS,TMs
7+,14+,22+ [*space*]] Ch+; *no space* MS
11 meaning] Ch(r),TMs,WK; wherefore MS,Ch
13 oh,] ~‸ MS; O‸ Ch+
14 sing] Ch(r),TMs,WK; chant MS,Ch
14,21 Thy] Ch,TMs,WK; thy MS
16+ [*no space*]] Ch+; *space* MS
18 that] TMs,WK; who MS,Ch
18 birds‸] Ch(r); swallows‸ MS; swallows, Ch; birds, TMs,WK
20 patience;] Ch,TMs,WK; ~‸ MS
22 peaks."] Ch,WK; ~.‸ MS; ~". TMs

MS Alterations: 11 knowest] *altered from* 'knoweth'
13 Give] *interlined above deleted* 'Grant'
20 only, neediest] *interlined above deleted* 'alone needeth'

Variants: 2,24 Grey‸] ~, Ch
2,24 valleys‸] ~, Ch,WK
3,25 God,] ~‸ TMs,WK
4–7 [*indention*]] *no indention* TMs
4,11 Oh,] O‸ Ch,WK; O, TMs
4 finger‸] ~, Ch,WK
5 Humble, idle,]~‸~‸ TMs
6 world‸] ~, Ch
7 feet."] ~.‸ TMs
9 miles‸] ~, Ch,Wk
11 Master‸] ~, Ch
11 rain-drops‸] ~-|~, Ch; ~-~, TMs; raindrops, WK
13 us‸ we pray‸] ~, ~ ~, Ch+
13 Lord‸] ~, Ch+
14 sun."] ~". TMs
16 were] *omit* TMs
17 Oh,] O‸ Ch,WK; O, TMs
17 Master‸] ~ , Ch,TMs,WK
19 hast] has TMs
20 only,] ~ ‸ Ch,TMs,WK
21 oh,] O‸ Ch,TMs,WK
22 peaks."] ~ ". TMs

MS: University of North Carolina at Chapel Hill. As of mid-1973 the manuscript was not available and thus full details cannot be provided. Maurice Bassan, "A Bibliographical Study of Stephen Crane's Poem, 'In the Night'," *PBSA*, LVIII (1964), 173–179, does not describe the paper nor mention whether there were markings on its verso. From a xerox, one can state that it is legal-cap paper, approximately 307 × 203 mm., considerably rumpled and dog-eared. In the upper left corner Crane wrote at an angle, 'Stephen Crane | Hartwood | Sullivan Co. | N.Y.' and he also signed the poem at the foot.

Ch(r): Columbia University. A page from the *Chapbook* pasted to a sheet of laid paper (226 × 203 mm.) watermarked CARISBROOK SUPERFINE, vertical chains 26 mm. apart. The headline as well as the title and signature have been deleted in black ink. In the same ink three substantive alterations (recorded in *Emendations*) were made in Crane's hand.

TMs: Columbia University. Dark blue typewritten ribbon on unwatermarked wove paper (268 × 202.5 mm.), credited to the *Chapbook*. On the verso, in black ink, are financial calculations and the word 'Lines' in another hand.

Note: The evidence of the accidentals suggests that the revised page of the *Chapbook* was not the physical copy for TMs (itself the copy for WK) but that Ch(r) was instead transcribed by Crane to form a new manuscript which was given to the typist. In this copying process Crane seems to have followed the capitalizations of 'Master' and 'Thy', although slipping with 'thy' in line 7. (The TMs typist normally changed Crane's 'oh' to 'O'.) In his study of this poem Professor Bassan (*PBSA*, LVIII [1964], 173–179) chose the revised *Chapbook* page as the most authoritative version, but his conclusions are unacceptable owing to his failure to work out accurately the relationship of Ch(r) to TMs and of TMs to *War is Kind*. In turn, Professor Katz in his edition took TMs as his authoritative copy-text, but this choice ignores the editorial distinction between authoritative accidentals and substantives. Moreover, Katz like Bassan did not recognize TMs as the printer's copy for WK and therefore dates the typescript about a year too late (*The Poems of Stephen Crane* [1966, rev. 1971], p. 206). The poem was not typed on the Crane typewriter, as Katz assumes, but instead on the typewriter that was used to make up all the rest of the WK printer's copy. TMs is certainly the most authoritative document for the substantives, but it would appear that some of its accidentals derive from the typist; thus there is no reason not to select the holograph MS as the copy-text and to insert into this texture Crane's authoritative substantive revisions. In Crane's first list this poem is given third as 'The Prayer of the Peaks'; in the second list it is no. 9 as 'The Prayer of the Mountains'.

87. THE CHATTER OF A DEATH-DEMON FROM A TREE-TOP

Ph (*Philistine*, I [Aug., 1895], 93, caps, signed)
S (*Souvenir and a Medley*, [May, 1896], p. 27, caps)
*TMs (NNC)
WK

Variants: 4 hunter.] ~ , S
7 paddle‸] ~ , Ph,S,WK
8 soft‸] ~ , Ph,S
10 hunter!] hunter! | Lift your grey face! Ph,S
12 tree-top] ~ ‸ | ~ Ph

TMs: Columbia University. Dark blue typewritten carbon on unwatermarked wove paper (267 × 202 mm.), credited to the *Philistine*.

Note: The well-advised deletion of the line in Ph,S following line 10 appears to have been a revision in the lost manuscript behind TMs. (Of course, it could have been a proof-revision in Ph which was not transferred to the manuscript, but this hypothesis is less likely than deletion as revision.) In Crane's first list the poem is sixth under the title 'Chatter of a Death-Demon in a tree top'; in his second list it is no. 3, 'The Death-demon'.

88. THE IMPACT OF A DOLLAR UPON THE HEART

*TMs[1] (NNC)
Ph[1] (*Philistine*, VI [Feb., 1898], back wrapper, caps, signed, entitled *Some Things*)
Ph[2] (*Philistine*, IX [Oct., 1899], 149–150, reprinted from Ph[1] by Hubbard as part of a story about the Roycroft shop's odd-jobs man "Ali Baba")
WK
TMs[2]

Emendation: 19 place] Ph[1-2]; state TMs[1-2], WK

Variants: 2 red] and Ph[1-2]
2 light‸] Light, Ph[2]; light, WK
3 table,] ~‸ Ph[1]
4 shadows‸] ~, Ph[2]
5+ [*space*]] *omit space* Ph[1-2]
7 flunkeys‸] flunkys, WK
9 sabre,] ~ . Ph[1-2]
10 Beauty] BEAUTY Ph[1]; beauty Ph[2],WK,TMs[2]
11 Whored by pimping] Simpered at by pimpled Ph[1-2]
13 stamp . . . carpets] stamps . . . carpet TMs[2]
15 lives;] ~ . Ph[1-2]
16 rug] pelt Ph[1-2]
18 baubles‸] ~ , WK
19 work‸] ~, WK
19 state,] ~; Ph[2]
20 hats‸] ~ , Ph[1-2],WK
21 Making . . . hats,] *omit* Ph[2]
22 Hats.] ~ ! TMs[2]

TMs[1]: Columbia University. Black typewritten carbon on unwatermarked wove paper (166 irregular × 202.5 mm.), the top section of a leaf torn across below the poem. At the head, in Cora's hand, in black ink, 'By | Stephen Crane.' (underlined). On the verso in blue typewriter offset is the mirror image of no. 136 *My cross!*, for which see the Note to that poem.

TMs[2]: Syracuse University. The first, numbered between parentheses, of the series of five poems posthumously typed for sale as "Lines" by Cora. For details, see no. 85.

Note: As worked out in "The Text: History and Analysis," the odds favor the hypothesis that the manuscript of this poem was first used as the copy for TMs (being prepared in December, 1897, as printer's copy) and was then mailed to Hubbard for the *Philistine*. If this is true, both TMs and Ph[1] radiate from the same manuscript and have technical equal authority. The marked divergences between the two texts cannot be imputed to late and early states, therefore. The best evidence that some of the differences resulted from *Philistine* censorship comes in line 11, 'Simpered at by pimpled merchants' in Ph for TMs 'Whored by pimping merchants', the more especially since in context Ph makes no sense when followed by line 12 'To submission before wine and chatter', which relates to the TMs version. Other changes are less easy to evaluate. Whether Ph 'The pelt of an honest bear' or TMs 'The rug of an honest bear' is superior may be a matter of opinion. Whether Ph line 2 'Smiles warm and light' is a sophistication of TMs 'Smiles warm red light' is not wholly certain, perhaps, although one would expect Crane's favorite color word 'red' to have been in the original. On the other hand, it would seem that Ph preserves the correct reading in line 19, 'Forgetting place, multitude, work and state', and that TMs 'Forgetting state' is a memorial error by contamination from 'work and state'. (The alternative would be to take it that TMs represented an incomplete state of revision in which the two words were to be switched; but this hypothesis would require two different manuscripts as copy for TMs and for Ph.) In other poems whenever an earlier manuscript has been present, or a similar typescript, the *Philistine* texts have not shown editing of substantives so far as one can determine, with the possible exception of line 9 of no. 76 *Fast rode the knight*, in which the prior *Souvenir* version 'the knights good banner' wrongly appeared in Ph as 'the good knights banner'. On the other hand, language as strong for the time as TMs 'Whored by pimping merchants' had not previously been encountered by Hubbard in Crane's poems, and censorship seems to be the only explanation, especially given the clumsiness of the change in context. The real questions center on 'warm and light' and 'pelt' in Ph. We do not know whether proof was sent to Crane or, if it were, whether he returned it. We do know, however, that the manuscript of no. 79 *On the desert* sent to Hubbard from England and printed in the *Philistine* in May, 1898, only three months later, requested proof and the unreturned proofsheet was preserved among Crane's effects. It is not wholly impossible, therefore, for the Ph variants to represent Hubbard's queries and Crane's acceptances which were not transferred to TMs. The difficulty with this hypothesis is that it associates two stylistic alterations in lines 2 and 16 (the direction of which is not entirely certain, although that for line 2 seems to be a sophistication in Ph) with a censorship revision in line 11 and a correction (or, rather, correct reading) in line 19. A further difficulty is the time element, already commented on in "The Text: History and Analysis," for there was scarcely time for proof to be sent and returned between the typing of TMs, the release of the manuscript, and the publication from this manuscript in February, 1898. It would seem more plausible to take it that because of Crane's residence in England, Hubbard did not trouble to send him proof for this poem but altered it to suit his readers' sensibilities and his own taste. It may be that the request for proof marked on the manuscript of no. 79 resulted from Crane's objection to this cavalier treatment. At any rate, it is the present editor's working hypothesis that the *Philistine* has the correct reading in line 19 but the other variants result from Hubbard's unauthoritative tinkering. If as happened with nos. 72 and 79 Crane sent Hubbard the manuscript itself, no other conclusion seems so plausible.

89. A MAN SAID TO THE UNIVERSE

*WK

90. When the prophet, a complacent fat man

*TMs (NNC)
WK

Emendation: 6 grey."] WK; ~". TMs

Variants: 2 -top‸] ~ , WK
5 lands——] ~ , WK

TMs: Columbia University. Faint black typewritten carbon on unwatermarked wove paper (156 irregular × 202.5 mm.). Below the poem is an erased pencil line, now illegible but ending with four hyphens to represent a dash. The paper is the tail section and is torn across at the top. The upper part of the leaf has not been identified.

91. There was a land where lived no violets

*WK

92. There was one I met upon the road

*WK

Emendation: 12 he] He WK

Note: For an earlier version of the poem in *The Black Riders*, see no. 33. Although not consistent, the manuscript of no. 33 capitalizes 'One' in line 1 and in line 15 altered 'he' to 'He'. On the other hand, in the present poem the residual 'He' in line 12 contrasts with 'one' in line 1 and 'he' in line 17 and suggests less the possibility that manuscript capitals have been reduced in a lost TMs or in the setting of *War is Kind* than that the manuscript from which WK ultimately derived was irregular but had intentionally removed the capitals to alter the suggestion that the spirit was Christ. For example, in no. 53 of *The Black Riders*, in line 17 a 'one' appears who may be Christ but is not capitalized any more than is 'god' in line 1.

93. Aye, workman, make me a dream

*TMs
WK

Variants: 1 dream‸] ~ , WK
4 Breezes‸] ~ , WK

TMs: Columbia University. Black typewritten carbon on a section of torn-across unwatermarked wove paper (89–100 irregular × 202.5 mm.) from the top of a sheet. Two lines of hyphens are typed at the end of the poem. No. 94 was originally typed below.

94. Each small gleam was a voice

Ph (*Philistine*, 1 [Sept., 1895], 124, caps, signed, titled *A Lantern Song*)
S (*Souvenir and a Medley*, May, 1896, p. 28, caps, untitled text but titled *A Lantern Song* in Contents)
*TMs (NNC)
WK

Emendations: 2 lantern] Ph,S,WK; latern TMs
3 green,] Ph,S,WK; ~,, TMs
5 leaf-shadow] Ph,S(leaf-shadows),WK; ~ $_{\wedge}$ ~ TMs
13 soul's] Ph,S,WK; souls TMs

Variants:
1 voice$_{\wedge}$] ~ , WK
2 —A] $_{\wedge}$ ~ WK
4 water;] ~ , Ph,S
6 hills$_{\wedge}$] ~ , Ph,S,WK
7 silence$_{\wedge}$] ~ , WK
14 fathers$_{\wedge}$] ~ , Ph,S,WK
15 hymning$_{\wedge}$] ~ , WK
16 marvelous] marvellous WK
16 water$_{\wedge}$] ~ , Ph,S,WK

TMs: Columbia University. Black typewritten carbon on section from the bottom of an unwatermarked wove leaf (167–182 irregular × 202.5 mm.), credited to the *Philistine*. Originally typed below no. 93.

Note: An editor might as well flip a coin whether Ph 'leaf-shadows' or TMs 'leaf shadow' is the authoritative reading. It seems probable that revision is not involved and that one or other of these radiating documents is in error. However, since the very slight evidence indicates that TMs was not typed from a copy of Ph but from a manuscript (cf. 'souls' in line 13, for instance), the variant may go back to Crane himself, consciously or inadvertently. If, instead, the plural in Ph is a printer's error, it could be rationalized as a mistake caused by the plurals in lines 3, 4, and 6, But the case is wholly speculative. In Crane's second list the poem is no. 1 under the title 'The Lantern Song'.

95. The trees in the garden rained flowers

*TMs (NNC)
WK

Emendations: 23 "—The] V; — "~ TMs; "$_{\wedge}$ ~ WK
26 Lord,"] WK; ~ ", TMs
27 displaced] WK; misplaced TMs
28 wisdom."] WK; ~ ". TMs

Variants: 7 —Having] $_{\wedge}$ ~ WK
24 flowers?"] ~?$_{\wedge}$ WK
26 Lord] lord WK

TMs: Columbia University. Black typewritten carbon on unwatermarked wove paper (268 × 202.5 mm.).

96. "Intrigue": Thou art my love

*TMs (NNC)
WK

Emendations: 13 There] WK; The TMs
22,32 me.] WK; ~ $_{\wedge}$ TMs
45 For] From TMs,WK
68 welcome] WK; Welcome TMs

Variants: 1,7,16,23,28,29,33,37, 42,48,53,57,62 love$_{\wedge}$] ~ , WK
2 sundown$_{\wedge}$] ~ . WK
3 soothe$_{\wedge}$] ~ , WK
5 brooks$_{\wedge}$] ~ , WK
9 sky$_{\wedge}$] ~ , WK
11 tree$_{\wedge}$] ~ , WK
14 owl$_{\wedge}$] ~ — WK
17 thing$_{\wedge}$] ~ , WK
19 easily$_{\wedge}$] ~ , WK

21 sorrow$_\wedge$] ~ — WK
24 violet$_\wedge$] ~ , WK
25 -caresses.] ~ , WK
26 carelessly$_\wedge$] ~ — WK
30 ashes$_\wedge$] ~ , WK
31 them$_\wedge$] ~ — WK
35 face$_\wedge$] ~ — WK
38 temple$_\wedge$] ~ , WK
39 altar$_\wedge$] ~ , WK
40 heart$_\wedge$] ~ — WK
44,66 thee$_\wedge$] ~, WK
46 lies$_\wedge$] ~ — WK
49 priestess$_\wedge$] ~ , WK
50 dagger$_\wedge$] ~ , WK
51 surely$_\wedge$] ~ — WK
54 eyes$_\wedge$] ~ , WK
55,67 thee$_\wedge$] ~ — WK
58 thee$_\wedge$] ~ . WK
60 murder.] ~ — WK
63 death$_\wedge$] ~ , WK
65 black$_\wedge$] ~ , WK

TMs: Columbia University. Twelve leaves of black typewritten carbon on unwatermarked wove paper (202 × 142 mm.), one stanza per leaf. Lines 26–27, the last two in the fourth stanza, are typed in blue ribbon. On the versos the leaves are numbered, circled, 1, 2, 3, 4, 5, 6, 7, 8, 11, 10, 12, 9, presumably an earlier order that had been contemplated. The order of the present edition follows that of *War is Kind.*

97. "INTRIGUE": LOVE FORGIVE ME IF I WISH YOU GRIEF

*TMs (NNC)
WK

Emendations: 5 grief.] WK; ~ $_\wedge$ TMs
8 thus] WK; this TMs
12 scurvy] WK; scuroy TMs
17 love.] WK; ~$_\wedge$ TMs
23 shoe.] WK; ~ $_\wedge$ TMs
48 intention.] WK; ~ $_\wedge$ TMs

Variants: 1 Love$_\wedge$] ~ , WK
1 grief$_\wedge$] ~ , WK
3 breast$_\wedge$] ~ , WK
7 surrender$_\wedge$] ~ , WK
11 room$_\wedge$] ~ , WK
12 picture$_\wedge$] ~ , WK
14–15 *One line in* WK
21 gnash$_\wedge$] ~ , WK
22 shoe$_\wedge$] ~ , WK
24 medals$_\wedge$] ~ , WK
25 honors$_\wedge$] ~ , WK
26 sweetheart$_\wedge$] ~ , WK
28 —The] $_\wedge$ ~ WK
30 love$_\wedge$] ~ . WK
36 friends$_\wedge$] ~ , WK
37 civil$_\wedge$] ~ , WK
40 desires] desire WK
41 chosen$_\wedge$] ~ ; WK
44 stride$_\wedge$] ~ , WK
45 gesture$_\wedge$] ~ , WK

TMs: Columbia University. Eight leaves of black typewritten carbon on unwatermarked wove paper (202 × 142 mm.), one stanza per leaf. On the recto, leaves 1–4 and 7–8 have typed a roman number I–IV, VII–VIII at lower right below the last line. On the versos are the circled numbers 16, 17, 18, 19, 14, 13, 20, 21, presumably an earlier order that had been contemplated. The order here is that of *War is Kind.*

Note: Two variants in WK call for comment. In the first, the conflation of lines 14–15 of TMs to form one line in WK is quite unexampled elsewhere in this sequence; in the second, the change from TMs 'desires' in line 40 to 'desire' introduces a reading that superficially might seem superior. On the other hand, although both might theoretically have resulted from changes made in the ribbon copy for the printer but not transferred to the carbons, the phrase *mists of desires* is not clearly an oddity, especially since Crane was likely to use a plural idiosyncratically where a singular would ordinarily be the normal idiom. Moreover, the singular makes the allusion almost exclusively sexual, which does not seem to be the intention, given the context. Line 20 in no. 109 is probably a parallel: 'Behold, thou has moulded my desires | Even as thou hast moulded the apple.' Both WK variants, therefore, have been rejected as unauthoritative sophistications.

98. "Intrigue": Ah, God, the way your little finger moved

*TMs (NNC)
WK

Emendation: 4 [1]comb,] WK; ~ ‸ TMs

Variants: 1 moved‸] ~, WK
5 ‸Ah] — ~ WK

TMs: Columbia University. Black typewritten carbon on a leaf of unwatermarked wove paper (202 × 142 mm.). At lower right, below the last line, is typed the roman figure IX. On the verso is the circled figure 22.

99. "Intrigue": Once I saw thee idly rocking

*TMs (NNC)
WK

Emendation: 13 mourning.] WK; ~ ‸ TMs

Variants: 4 happy.] ~ , WK
5 womanhood‸] ~ , WK
7 it‸] ~ . WK
8 miserable‸] ~ , WK
9 head‸] ~ , WK
10 ogre‸] ~ , WK
11 castle‸] ~ , WK
12 cruelly‸] ~ , WK

TMs: Columbia University. Black typewritten carbon on a leaf of unwatermarked wove paper (202 × 142 mm.). On the verso is the circled figure 15.

100. "Intrigue": Tell me why, behind thee

*TMs (NNC)
WK

Emendations: 7 swinish] WK; swimish TMs
9 peace.] ~ ‸ TMs; ~ ! WK

Variants: 3 real‸] ~ , WK
4 thrice-damned] ~ ‸ ~ WK
5 dead‸] ~ , WK
6 alive‸] ~ — WK

TMs: Columbia University. Black typewritten carbon on a leaf of unwatermarked wove paper (202 × 142 mm.). At lower right below last line is typed the roman number XI. On verso is circled figure 23.

101. "Intrigue": And yet I have seen thee happy with me

*WK

Note: Although the language and subject indicate that the "Intrigue" poems continue to the end of *War is Kind* with no. 105, the typescript copies cease with no. 100 so that the last five poems have WK as their only authority. For a conjecture, see "The Text: History and Analysis."

102. "INTRIGUE": I HEARD THEE LAUGH

*WK

Emendation: 10 camp-fire] ~-|~ WK

103. "INTRIGUE": I WONDER IF SOMETIMES IN THE DUSK

*WK

104. "INTRIGUE": LOVE MET ME AT NOONDAY

*WK

105. "INTRIGUE": I HAVE SEEN THY FACE AFLAME

*WK

UNCOLLECTED POEMS

106. "I'D RATHER HAVE——": LAST CHRISTMAS THEY GAVE ME A SWEATER

*MS (Schoberlin)

Emendation: 8 street.] $\sim_{\wedge}$ MS

MS: Owned by Commander Melvin H. Schoberlin, USN (Ret.), who purchased it in Peabody's Bookstore in Baltimore, Maryland, about 1946, with other items belonging to Stephen's sister Agnes. He was informed by the owner of the store that Agnes had given these manuscripts to Clara Schmidt, and later he ascertained that this person could be identified as the 'Clara' mentioned frequently in Agnes Crane's diary. The manuscript is positively a holograph and is written in black ink on recto and verso of a torn and partly mutilated piece of wove paper (114 × 208 mm.). In the upper left corner, cut off by a diagonal missing piece, are the autograph letters 'ph.' (See illustration.)

107. AH, HAGGARD PURSE, WHY OPE THY MOUTH

*MS (NSyU)

Emendations: 8 smile] smilest MS
11 honestie.] $\sim_{\wedge}$ MS

MS Alterations: 1 haggard] *preceded by deleted* 'purs'
2 a] *preceded by deleted* 's'
4 wan] *preceded by deleted* 'br'
4 puffed] *followed by deleted* 'in many'

5 not] *preceded by deleted* 'th'
6 Why] 'y' *over* 'en'
8 do] *interlined*
13 names] *over illegible letters*
16 What] 'W' *over beginning of* 'A'

MS: Syracuse University. Two pages of wove pad paper (240 × 160 mm.), 28 red rules to the page. Two trials precede the poem: 'In a large vaulted hall that | blazed with light' | [space] | 'I'd sell my steps to the grave | at ten cents per foot, if t'were | but honestie'. Corwin Linson, who rescued this manuscript and preserved it, dates the composition as in December, 1892 (see *My Stephen Crane*, ed. E. H. Cady, pp. 13–14).

108. LITTLE BIRDS OF THE NIGHT

*MS (ViU), holograph

Emendation: 8 leaves.] ~ ‸ MS

MS Alterations: 2 Aye] *above is deleted false start* 'Flew'
6 groves] *interlined above deleted* 'lands'
7 at] *written over* 'by'
9 They] *above is deleted false start* 'And'

MS: University of Virginia. Two pages in Crane's Notebook (19v, 20v) written in pencil on ruled wove paper (218 × 129 mm.), 18 pink rules 11.5 mm. apart.

Note: In 1933 the poem was reprinted from this manuscript as *A Lost Poem by Stephen Crane*, New York, The Harvard Press, 100 copies printed for friends of Harvey Taylor. The next year it was reprinted in conjunction with "The Holler Tree" in the *Golden Book*, XIX (Feb., 1934), 189, advertised on p. 188 as 'The First Manuscripts by the Author of "The Red Badge of Courage" to Appear | since 1903: A Fable and a Poem from his Unpublished Intimate Notebooks', signed.

109. A GOD CAME TO A MAN

*MS (NNC), holograph
TMs[1] (NNC)
TMs[2] (NSyU)

Emendations: 6,8,9–16 *quotation marks supplied from* TMs1–2
19–34 *quotation marks supplied from* TMs1-2

MS Alterations: 6 eternities] 'ies' *over* 'y'
11 may] 'm' *over* 'c'
20 my desires] *possibly squeezed in later*
21 the apple.] *possibly added later*

Variants: 8+,21+ [*space*]] *no space* TMs1-2
16 But,—] ~ ‸ — TMs1-2
16+ [*space*]] *line of periods* TMs2
20 Behold,] ~ ‸ TMs1-2
22 How,] ~ ‸ TMs1-2
30 then] thou TMs2
30 splendor] splendour TMs1-2

MS: Columbia University. Written in black ink on two leaves of wove paper (179 × 114) watermarked DEXTER MILLS. On the verso of the first leaf, in pencil, is a scrawled 'C'; below it Cora wrote 91 (deleted) and to the right circled 100. To its right 100 is added to 525 for a total of 625. On the verso of the second leaf is the circled number 85 and then 85 added to 370 for a total of 455, all erased. In addition, an autograph expense list is written in black ink: '25 Break | 5 shine | 10 cigarettes & tob | 5 Elevated | 8 tin | 25 pillow case | 10 coffee-cake', these totaled to 88 to which is added 12 but no final total.

TMs[1]: Columbia University. Two leaves of black typewritten ribbon copy on laid paper (260 × 203 mm.), vertical chainlines 26 mm. apart, watermarked EXCELSIOR FINE. At the head of the page number 6 is deleted in pencil and 1 substituted in pencil and the number 7 on the second leaf is also deleted with 2 substituted in pencil.

TMs[2]: Syracuse University. Heads the third leaf of Cora's typescript collection "Lines," numbered 4.

Note: The preserved manuscript is a revision of the original submitted to Copeland and Day for *The Black Riders* but rejected by them. In their letter to Crane of October 19, 1894, they quote the opening lines as 'A god came to a man | And spoke in this wise.'

110. ONE CAME FROM THE SKIES

*MS (NNC), holograph
TMs[1] (NNC)
TMs[2] (NSyU)

MS Alterations: 3 band] *interlined above deleted* 'gold'

3 them] *added later*

4 A] *preceded by deleted* 'them' *run on from preceding line*

12+ [*omit*]] ' "For shackles fit apes. | He is not brave | Who leaves the iron on doves.' *pencil deleted and then partly erased*

MS: Columbia University. Written in black ink on wove paper (179 × 114 mm.), vertical watermark (partial) of DEXTER MILLS. On the verso is Cora's number 7 above a half circle; below this is her circled 70, and then 70 added to 455 for a total of 525.

TMs[1]: Columbia University. Black typewritten ribbon copy on laid paper (260 × 203 mm.), vertical chainlines 26 mm. apart, watermarked EXCELSIOR FINE. At head is the pagination number 8 deleted in pencil. On verso is Cora's notation, 'Sent to Truth || April 3rd | 1901. ||'. A search of *Truth* has failed to identify publication.

TMs[2]: Syracuse University. Typed on Indian & Colonial watermarked wove paper at the foot of the third leaf of Cora's collection "Lines," numbered 5.

Note: The paper used for the manuscript is the same as that of a revision of no. 109, suggesting that the present text is itself a revision of the version originally sent to Copeland and Day for *The Black Riders* but withdrawn at their specific request. The status of the pencil-deleted lines, and whether they were indeed intended to be revived by erasure of the deleting marks, is doubtful. The two typescripts are posthumous and thus have no authority. For what it is worth, Cora evidently thought the lines were intended for deletion. This would have been her decision, however, since it seems probable that her typescripts were made up not from a lost manuscript but from the preserved example. The deletion of the lines was not included in her word count of 70 (actually 69) on the verso of MS.

111. THERE IS A GREY THING THAT LIVES IN THE TREE-TOPS

*MS (NNC), holograph
TMs (NNC)

Emendations: 2,5 its] TMs; it's MS
7–8 [*flush*]] TMs; MS *outsets by an em or two*

MS Alterations: 5 branches] 'c' *over* 'p'
6 wail] *preceded by deleted* 'low'

Variant: 3 wilderness$_{\wedge}$] ~ , TMs

MS: Columbia University. Written in pencil on a section of legal-cap paper (140 irregular × 190 mm.), lines 10 mm. apart, tail space (inverted head space) 51–53.5 mm., pink, blue, pink rules 22.5–25 mm. from left margin. On verso, headed 5, is Cora's circled number 60, and then 60 added to 310 for a total of 370.

TMs: Columbia University. Black typewritten ribbon copy on laid paper (260 × 203 mm.), vertical chains 26 mm. apart, watermarked EXCELSIOR FINE. Paged 5.

112. INTERMINGLED, | THERE COME IN WILD REVELLING STRAINS

*MS (NNC), holograph

MS: Columbia University. A fragment starting with the turn-under of a line, written in pencil on rough wove buff paper (240 × 148 mm.).

113. A SOLDIER, YOUNG IN YEARS, YOUNG IN AMBITIONS

*MS (NNC), holograph

Emendations: 9 grey-beard] greybeard MS
24 its] it's MS
26 Its] It's MS

MS Alteration: 20 the] *interlined with a caret*

MS: Columbia University. Written in blue-black ink on a leaf of legal-cap paper (318 × 203 mm.), 28 rules, 9.8 mm. apart, extending only to the vertical rules at left; head space 49 mm., tail space 4 mm., 39 mm. from left margin to vertical pink, blue, pink rules. This poem is followed by five leaves of legal-cap paper paged 2–6 containing an essay given the courtesy title of "The Gratitude of a Nation" (reprinted in TALES, SKETCHES, AND REPORTS, *Works*, VIII (1973), 588–590. The first three leaves of this essay are written in blue-black ink on the same paper as the poem. The last two leaves, fols. 5–6, change the kind of legal-cap paper to one measuring 317 × 197 mm., 28 rules extending to the full left margin, 9.8 mm. apart, head space 49–50 mm., tail space 4 mm., vertical pink, blue, pink rules 39.5 mm. from left margin.

On the verso of fol. 6, turned about, in black ink is written a trial for no. 83 and some memoranda, for which see the Note to no. 83.

114. A ROW OF THICK PILLARS

*TMs (NNC)

TMs: Columbia University. Black typewritten ribbon on the upper section of a piece of laid paper (135 irregular × 203 mm.), vertical chain-lines 26 mm. apart, torn across at the foot. This is probably a section of a leaf of Excelsior Fine paper. The typewriter appears to be the same as that on which Cora's two collections were typed.

115. CHANT YOU LOUD OF PUNISHMENTS

*MS (NNC), holograph
TMs (NNC)

Emendation: 5 [1]strong,] ~ ‸ MS, TMs

MS Alteration: 4 the] *over* 'a'

MS: Columbia University. Written in black ink on legal-cap paper (293 × 200 mm.), 27 lines 9.5 mm. apart, head space 29 mm., tail space 9–10 mm., vertical pink, blue, pink rules 38 mm. from left margin. On the verso is Cora's circled pencil figure 60 altered from 61.

TMs: Black typewritten ribbon on laid paper (260 × 203), vertical chain-lines 26 mm. apart, watermarked EXCELSIOR FINE, paged 1. In the upper left corner at a slant Cora wrote in black ink 'not used in US.'; on the verso she wrote 'Lines' with an underline. The TMs is manifestly a copy of the preserved MS.

Note: In Crane's first list the poem appears as 'Chant you loud of punishments' in eighth place, written below a space and a double rule. The poem was first printed in the *Bookman*, LXIX (April, 1929), 122, headed 'II', under the general title *Three Poems by Stephen Crane.*

116. IF YOU WOULD SEEK A FRIEND AMONG MEN

*MS (NNC), holograph
TMs (NNC)

Emendation: 4,6,8 wares.] TMs; ~ ‸ MS

MS Alterations: 3 would] *interlined*

11 attention] 'at' *over* 'in'

13 as they cry] *added before* 'their wares' *as a turn-under; after* 'them' Crane *first wrote* 'when crying', *then deleted* 'when' *and* 'ing' *and interlined* 'to' *for* 'to cry', *which was then deleted and* 'as they cry' *added below*

MS: Columbia University. Written in black ink on legal-cap paper (304 × 200), 29 rules 9.8 mm. apart, head space 32 mm., tail space 7.5 mm., vertical pink, dark blue, pink rules 38 mm. from left margin. On verso paged 3, in pencil, is Cora's circled number 70 over 65, and then 160 to which 70 is added for a total of 230.

TMs: Columbia University. Black typewritten ribbon copy on laid paper (260 × 203 mm.), vertical chains 26 mm. apart, watermarked EXCEL-

SIOR FINE, paged 3. In the upper left corner Cora wrote in black ink, 'Not used in War is | Kind'. This is part of a broken-up posthumous collection that Cora made for sale.

Note: The poem is tenth in Crane's first list, as 'If you would seek a friend', this being the third of the poems added after a space and a short double rule.

117. A LAD AND A MAID AT A CURVE IN THE STREAM

*MS (NNC), holograph

TMs (NNC)

MS Emendations: 4 Oh,] *no indention* MS, TMs

10 turmoil.] TMs; ~‸ MS

MS Alterations: 2 a] *preceded by deleted* 'the'

3 moon-] *preceded by deleted* 'b'

6 shadows] *preceded by deleted* 'long'

6 adrift] *interlined above deleted* 'far'

7 sings] *preceded by deleted* 'pl'

Variants: 7 shore.] ~ , TMs

8 Oh,] *no indention* TMs

MS: Columbia University. Written in black ink on legal-cap paper (313 × 200 mm.), 29 rules 9.8 mm. apart, head space 33 mm., tail space 7 mm., vertical pink, dark blue, pink rules 38 mm. from left margin.

TMs: Columbia University. Black typewritten ribbon copy made by Cora on laid paper (260 × 203 mm.), vertical rules 26 mm. apart, watermarked EXCELSIOR FINE, paged 4.

Note: Entitled 'Oh night dismal, night glorious', this poem is given last in Crane's first list.

118. "LEGENDS": A MAN BUILDED A BUGLE FOR THE STORMS TO BLOW

*Bk (*Bookman*, III [May, 1896], 206, numbered I)

Note: Nos. 118–122 are printed, numbered I to V, the page signed, with marginal illustrations by Melanie Elisabeth Norton, puffed in the *Bookman* reprint in the same issue of nos. 9–10 with her sample illlustrations for those poems. The authority of the title "Legends" is unknown.

119. "LEGENDS": WHEN THE SUICIDE ARRIVED AT THE SKY

*Bk (*Bookman*, III [May, 1896], 206, numbered II)

Emendations: 1–2 When . . . asked] *one line* Bk

2–3 him . . . me."] *one line* Bk

120. "LEGENDS": A MAN SAID: "THOU TREE!"

*Bk (*Bookman*, III [May, 1896], 206, numbered III)

Emendations: 1–2 A . . . scorn:] *one line* Bk

2–3 "Thou . . . possibilities."] *one line* Bk

121. "LEGENDS": A WARRIOR STOOD UPON A PEAK AND DEFIED THE STARS

*Bk (*Bookman*, III [May, 1896], 206, numbered IV)

Emendations: 1–2 A . . . magpie,] *one line* Bk
2–3 happening . . . it.] *one line* Bk

122. "LEGENDS": THE WIND THAT WAVES THE BLOSSOMS

*Bk (*Bookman*, III [May, 1896], 206, numbered V)

Emendations: 1–2 The . . . age.] *one line* Bk
3–4 The . . . "why] *one line* Bk
4–6 sing . . . [1]idle] *one line* Bk
6 [2]idle . . . age?"] *one line* Bk

123. OH, A RARE OLD WINE YE BREWED FOR ME

*MS[1] (NNC), holograph
MS[2] (NNC), autograph Cora Crane transcript, signed Stephen Crane by her

MS[1] Alteration: 3 this] 'is' *over* 'e'

Variant: 7 babes$_\wedge$] ~ . MS[2]

MS[1]: Columbia University. Written in black ink on the upper section of a piece of thick laid paper (110 × 175 mm.), vertical chainlines 25 mm. apart. On the verso in pencil is Cora's circled 44 (the second digit over a 5). To the left 3280 is added to 625 for a total of 3905 to which is added 44 for a total of '3959 words sent' (the 59 written over 60). To the right 'Lines' and below this is 44 added to 625 for a total of 669.

MS[2]: Columbia University. Written by Cora in black ink on the upper section of a leaf of thin laid paper (189–195 irregular × 201 mm.), vertical chainlines 26 mm. apart, torn across at the foot but containing the blue carbon typewritten 'Of the < > d'. Cora signed this poem 'Stephen Crane' but in the lower left margin wrote 'Copy'.

124. TELL ME NOT IN JOYOUS NUMBERS

*MS (NNC), holograph

MS Alteration: 3 By] *preceded by deleted* 'W'

MS: Columbia University. Written in black ink on a piece of laid paper (264 × 195 mm.), vertical chainlines 20 mm. apart, no watermark. On the verso is the start of a draft in black ink, 'To the editor of the Gazette, Sir:— | [W *deleted*] I compelled to enter a feeble and tottering protest'.

125. WHEN A PEOPLE REACH THE TOP OF A HILL

*MS (NNC), holograph
Ph (*Philistine*, VII [June, 1898], 9–10, signed, entitled 'Lines')
SpA (*Spanish-American War Songs: A Complete Collection of Newspaper Verse Published During the Recent War with Spain*, ed. Sidney A. Witherbee [1898], pp. 182–183, signed)

Emendations: 16 censer] Ph,SpA; censor MS
23 clang]Ph,SpA; crang MS

MS Alterations: 4 comes] 's' *interlined above an ink blot*
5 shall] *interlined above deleted* 'will'
14 will come] *interlined above deleted* 'looms'
14 eyeless] *interlined above deleted* 'blind'
16 creed] *interlined above deleted* 'right'
17 At the head of the new] *interlined above deleted* 'March the new'
22 blue] *cap* 'B' *reduced by a slant*
23 Thy] 'y' *over* 'e'
25 feet] *interlined above deleted* 'ma'
26 another is] *interlined above deleted* 'and'
27 through] *interlined above deleted* 'toward' *and then* 'a shadow' *added with a caret*
28 The . . . battalions] *interlined above deleted* 'God lead the new battalions'
30 high. God lead them far] *interlined above deleted* 'new battalions'; *before* 'high' *is added* 'm' *to* 'the'

Variants: 0 omit] LINES. Ph; THE BLUE BATTALIONS. | STEPHEN CRANE. SpA
3 tongues,] ~$_\wedge$ Ph,SpA
3 lengthens] and lengthens Ph,SpA
3 arms.] ~, SpA
6 rise$_\wedge$] ~, Ph,SpA
7,18,29 —Blue battalions—] $_\wedge$~~. Ph,SpA
10,17,21,28,32 battalions$_\wedge$] ~, Ph,SpA (*at* 21 SpA: battalion)
11,22 —The . . .—] $_\wedge$~ . . . Ph,SpA
12 deep$_\wedge$] ~. Ph; ~, SpA
13 together$_\wedge$] ~. Ph; ~, SpA
14 eyeless,] ~ . Ph
15 beckon.] ~ , Ph,SpA
19 impulse$_\wedge$] ~ , Ph,SpA
20 right$_\wedge$] ~ , Ph,SpA
21 battalions] battalion SpA
23,24 Thy] thy Ph,SpA
23 wisdom$_\wedge$] ~ , Ph,SpA
24 Son's$_\wedge$] ~ , Ph,SpA
25 part,] ~ — Ph,SpA
26 —Aye] $_\wedge$~ Ph,SpA
26 son] youth Ph,SpA
27 Then$_\wedge$] ~ , Ph,SpA
27 through] thro Ph; thro' SpA
28 new] blue SpA
30 high.] ~ , Ph,SpA
30 far$_\wedge$] ~ , Ph,SpA
31 Lead . . . lead] God lead . . . God lead Ph,SpA
31 high$_\wedge$] ~ , Ph,SpA
33 — . . . battalions—.] $_\wedge$ . . . ~$_\wedge$.Ph,SpA

MS: Columbia University. Written in black ink on a leaf of laid paper (327 × 203 mm.), vertical chainlines 26.5 mm. apart, watermarked Britannia seated in an oval. On the verso, in Cora's hand, is the circled figure 178 and then 178 is added to 892 for a total of 1070. In pencil Cora wrote on the verso, vertically, 'Lines Unpub'.

Note: The substantive variants in the *Philistine,* lines 3, 23, 26, and 31 offer a problem, for they are either Hubbard's sophistications or Crane's second thoughts as he transcribed the preserved semidraft manuscript to make a copy to send to Hubbard. (Proof-alterations are not likely since Crane left England for the United States and Cuba before mid-April.) Although there is no bar to these variants being Crane's, and the Ph 'thy' for MS 'Thy' in lines 23, 24 seems to point to an inadvertence in the manuscript copied in the print, yet the differences in lines 3 and 31, particularly, are suspicious—the first as a smoothing and the second as a fancied improvement by literal repetition, which in fact is ungainly. If these two are not likely to represent authorial revision, the case against 'youth' in line 26 for MS 'son' may be strengthened as an outsider's attempt to avoid the comparison with 'Thy Son's' two lines before. It must be admitted, of course, that in copying out the manuscript Crane could have substituted this variation. The nonce word 'crang' in line 23 of the MS does not seem to be an uncorrected error caused by a change of mind from 'crash' to 'clang', for the change of mind would necessarily have come after the letter 'a' where there is no break between the letters 'a' and 'n'; a small break between 'r' and 'a' is characteristic enough not to have any necessary significance. The word 'clang' may be a correction by Hubbard in case the fair copy repeated it, although there are parallels enough, as in no. 1, line 2, 'There was clang and clang of spear and shield'. Otherwise one has the choice between regarding 'crang' as a simple inadvertence or else as a deliberate word that Crane thought existed. The text in *Spanish American War Songs* has been studied in Joseph Katz and Matthew J. Bruccoli, "Toward a Descriptive Bibliography of Stephen Crane: 'Spanish-American War Songs,'" *PBSA*, LXI (1967), 267–269. It has no authority, being a simple reprint of the *Philistine*. As 'Blue Battalions' no. 125 was added later to Crane's second list as number 11.

126. A MAN ADRIFT ON A SLIM SPAR

*MS^{1} (NNC), holograph, signed

MS^{2} (NNC), autograph copy by Cora Crane, signed Stephen Crane by her

Emendations: 10 cold.] MS^{2}; ∼ ‸ MS^{1}

23 spar.] ∼ ‸ MS$^{1-2}$

MS^{1} Alterations: 6 and] *preceded by deleted comma and* 'of of', *each independently*

12 may be] *interlined with a caret above deleted* 'are'

14 Because] *interlined above deleted* 'By the'; 'the' *having been deleted first*

14 babe.] *interlined above deleted* 'child.'

15 Oceans may become] *interlined above deleted* 'The seas turn to'; *on line above is deleted* 'God is cold.' *and a brace indicates that lines 14–15 should have no space between them*

20 a doomed] *interlined with a caret above deleted* 'an'

29 cold.] *followed by deleted* 'God is cold'

Variant: 20 assassin's] MS^{1}; assasin's MS^{2}

MS^{1}: Columbia University. Written and revised in black ink on laid paper (327 × 204 mm.), vertical chainlines 25–26 mm. apart, watermarked CARISBROOK SUPERFINE. On the verso in Cora's hand is the pencil circled figure 79 and then 79 placed below 3950 but not totaled; also 699 with 79 below for a total of '788 words lines'. Cora added vertically 'Lines | unpub', and there are various calculations in English money.

MS^{2}: Columbia University. Cora Crane's handwritten transcript of MS^{1}, paged 4, written in black ink on laid paper (258 × 201 mm.), horizontal chainlines 25–26 mm. apart, watermarked BROOKLEIGH FINE. In the lower left corner she wrote ':Copy:'

Note: As 'A man afloat on a slim spar' this poem is no. 12 and last in Crane's second list. This entry, and the preceding one for "Blue Battalions" (no. 125), were made at a different time and with a different pen and blacker ink than the first ten entries. Entitled *Three Poems by Stephen Crane*, the *Bookman*, LXIX (April, 1929), 121, reprinted the poem headed 'I', prefaced by a facsimile of MS[1] on p. 120.

127. THERE EXISTS THE ETERNAL FACT OF CONFLICT

*MS (NNC), holograph

Emendations: 16 Furious (*flush left*)] *indented* MS
19 infamy.] ~ $_{\wedge}$ MS

MS Alterations: 3 Afterward] *followed by deleted false start, perhaps a 't'*
11 practical] 'p' *over* 'P'
14 have] *interlined*
14 thousand] 'd' *over start of* 'f'
14 fields] 'e' *inserted*
15 record] *interlined above deleted* 'home'

MS: Columbia University. Written in black ink on laid foolscap (325 × 201 mm.), 35 rules 8 mm. apart, vertical chainlines 25 mm. apart, watermarked seated figure of Britannia in oval. On the verso are Cora's pencil calculations, a circled figure 140, then 140 added to 1070 for a total of 1210. In pencil Cora wrote 'Lines | Unpublished'.

128. ON THE BROWN TRAIL

*MS[1] (NNC), holograph
MS[2] (NNC), autograph transcript by Cora Crane, signed Stephen Crane by her

Emendations: 9 foreign] MS[2]; foriegn MS[1]
12,18 $_{\wedge}$Carts] (~ MS[1-2]
13,19 $_{\wedge}$Laden] (~ MS[1-2]
14 don't] dont MS[1-2]

MS Alteration: 10 We] *preceded by deleted* 'We'

MS[1]: Columbia University. Written in blue ink on laid paper (253 × 198 mm.), horizontal chainlines 26 mm. apart, watermarked E. BAYNES & C° | 120 CANNON STREET | E.C. On the verso is found Cora's pencil calculation 104 added to 788 for a total of 892. In pencil Cora wrote 'Lines | unpublished'.

MS[2]: Columbia University. Cora's transcript of MS[1], paged 2, made in black ink on cheap wove copy paper (265 × 207 mm.), 27 rules 8.5 mm. apart, head space 28 mm., tail space 9 mm. She signed the poem 'Stephen Crane' and to the left wrote ':Copy:'.

129. RUMBLING, BUZZING, TURNING, WHIRLING WHEELS

*Ph (*Philistine*, VIII [Dec., 1898], front wrapper recto, signed)

130. "THE BATTLE HYMN": ALL-FEELING GOD, HEAR IN THE WAR-NIGHT

*TMs[a] (NNC)
TMs[b-e] (NNC), blue carbons of TMs[a]

Emendations: 17 Thine] thine TMs
39 cane.)] ~‸) TMs

TMs[a]: Columbia University. Black typewritten ribbon copy on two leaves of wove foolscap (327 × 200 mm.), watermarked INDIAN | & | COLONIAL. The title is typed 'THE BATTLEHYMN. || BY. | STEPHEN CRANE. ||'. In TMs[a-b] the run-together title is divided by a black-ink stroke. On the verso of TMs[a] fol. 2 is written in vertically in black ink, 'The Battle Hymn | The'. Typed at the foot of fol. 2 is '(The ms., of above, has just been discovered in saddle-bags used by Stephen Crane during the late war with Spain.)'. TMs[b-c] are blue carbon copies of TMs[a] without notation except for the division of the title in TMs[b] but not in TMs[c]. In Cora's inventory made after Crane's death the title appears assigned with a query to the *Pall Mall Magazine*.

131. Unwind my riddle (Epigraph to "The Clan of No-Name")

*N[1] (*New York Herald,* March 19, 1899, sec. 8, p. 2)
N[2] (*Chicago Times-Herald,* March 19, 1899, sec. 5, pp. 1–2)
N[3] *San Francisco Examiner,* March 19, 1899, Sunday Magazine Section, p. 29)
BW (*Black and White*, December, 1899, pp. 13–16 italics)
A1 (*Wounds in the Rain* [Stokes, N.Y., 1900], pp. 42–73)

Emendation: 1 riddle.] BW,A1; ~: N[1]

Variants: 2 fly,] ~; A1
3 die,] ~; A1
4 high,] ~; A1
5 lie,] ~; A1

Note: The story was sent to Reynolds from Havana in late October, 1898. For details of its publication and the textual transmission, see Tales of War, *Works,* vi (1970), cxi–cxxv, 346.

132. A naked woman and a dead dwarf

*TMs (NNC)

TMs: Columbia University. Blue typewritten carbon on upper section of a leaf of unwatermarked laid paper (129–130 irregular × 202 mm.), vertical chainlines 26 mm. apart, torn across at foot. Typed on the Crane typewriter.

Note: *The Bookman*, lxix (April, 1929), 122, printed the poem from the TMs, headed 'III' under the general title *Three Poems by Stephen Crane.*

133. A grey and boiling street

*TMs (NNC)

TMs: Columbia University. Blue typewritten carbon copy on unwatermarked laid paper (258 × 202 mm.), vertical chainlines 26 mm. apart. Typed on the Crane typewriter.

134. Bottles and bottles and bottles

*TMs (NNC)

Emendation: 17 its] it's TMs

TMs: Columbia University. Blue typewritten carbon copy on unwatermarked laid paper (258 × 202 mm.), vertical chainlines 26 mm. apart. Typed on the Crane typewriter. The asterisks (four crosses) added by hand in black ink.

135. The patent of a lord

*TMs (NNC)

TMs: Columbia University. Blue typewritten carbon copy on the upper section of a leaf of unwatermarked laid paper (130 irregular × 202 mm.), chainlines 26 mm. apart. The lower part of the leaf is torn across. Typed on the Crane typewriter.

136. My cross!

*TMs[1] (NNC)
TMs[2] (NNC)
TMs[3] (NSyU)

Variants: 1 My cross!] MY CROSS! TMs[2]; MY CROSS. TMs[3]
5 francs] 'Francs' *altered by hand to* 'francs' TMs[2-3]

TMs[1]: Columbia University. Blue typewritten carbon copy on unwatermarked laid paper (258 × 202 mm.), vertical chainlines 26 mm. apart.

TMs[2]: Columbia University. Blue typewritten carbon copy on wove paper (158 irregular × 198 mm.), torn across at the top, watermarked INDIAN | & | COLONIAL.

TMs[3]: Syracuse University. Blue typewritten ribbon copy in Cora Crane's sequence "Lines," placed on first leaf of the text and numbered 2. Indian & Colonial paper.

Note: All typescripts were typed on the Crane typewriter. On the verso of TMs[1] of no. 88 *The impact of a dollar upon the heart* is the mirror-image offset of no. 136, apparently made from the oily ribbon copy of TMs[2] when no. 88 was placed on top of it with some pressure. Unfortunately this evidence has no bearing on the date of typing of either poem. The TMs of no. 88 is definitely one of the printer's-copy typescripts, made up probably in December, 1897. TMs[2] of *My cross!* is, just as definitely, not typed on the printer's-copy typewriter but instead on the Crane typewriter, and almost certainly as one of Cora's posthumous efforts to recover texts for sale. The TMs carbon of no. 88, in fact, was placed among these typescripts for sale, on the evidence of Cora's signing it *By Stephen Crane.* Thus it could readily have come into contact with the typescript of *My cross!* The confusion by which TMs[2-3] assigned the first line of the poem as the title, in caps, is unauthoritative. In fact, the first line—Crane speaking in the title about himself and then addressing the poem to Christ—is not inappropriate. But one would believe that the intention, instead, was to start with a line to be attributed to Christ, which Crane then answers. For a similar technique of a one-line beginning which is answered by the poem, see no. 15.

THE TEXT: HISTORY AND ANALYSIS

I. [NOTES ON MADAME ALBERTI]

A single leaf of cheap wove paper (249.5 × 140.4 mm., but with a vertical crease affecting the horizontal measurement by as much as 20 mm.), written in pencil and now partly illegible. The paper may be the same as that in no. II, "The Twelfth Cavalry and the Indian Wars," and a note on the verso 'Corporal O'Connor's Story' may refer either to an early form of this unfinished tale or else to some similar one, proposed or begun. The handwriting is early and shows the looped initial 'th' and 'to'. The material about Delsarte has been identified by Miss G. G. M. Kyles as notes referring to Madame Alberti, who taught at the Avon Seaside Assembly when Crane was assisting his brother Townley as reporter of local doings. On July 28, 1890, the *New York Herald Tribune* ran an account of the Avon Seaside Assembly that does not mention Madame Alberti but does refer to the classes in aesthetic physical culture that she taught (*Works*, VIII, no. 104); on August 4, 1890, these classes are specifically linked with her name although her master, Delsarte, is not mentioned (no. 105). Her teaching of the correct use of muscles in arm and wrist is mentioned in a report "On the Banks of the Shark River" (no. 135) printed on July 11, 1891, and in "The Seaside Assembly (II)," printed on September 6, 1892 (no. 116), is the description: 'The hall now rings with the merry voices of Mme. Alberti's pupils who come here to be taught Delsarte. Mme. Alberti is the dean of the School of Expression here. Dozens of young ladies come to this resort merely to attend her lectures. The "Delsarte Girls" are a familiar feature of the Avon-by-the-Sea landscape.' The notes on Delsarte in the present fragment might seem to apply best to this latter account, but the early handwriting and looped initial 'th' and 'to' do not permit so late a date. Instead, it would seem that the notes date most probably, from the hand, in the summer of 1890 and were possibly made for the preparation of no. 104 or 105 but not utilized. The text has been printed by G. G. M. Kyles in "Stephen Crane and 'Corporal O'Connor's Story'," *SB*, XXVI (1974), 294–295.

II. [THE TWELFTH CAVALRY AND THE INDIAN WARS]

Untitled story written in black ink on seventeen leaves of unruled wove paper (249.5 × 162.5 mm.) in the Special Collections of Columbia University Library. The pages are numbered except for the first without half-circles. The left lower corner of fol. 4 is torn off, excising a word or two. Various necessary words are omitted in the text and were never inserted on review. Folio 17 ends after four lines and perhaps in mid-sentence. The hand is an early one, with an invariable slope to the right, no circles about the periods, and the use of a V under quotation marks for superscript. In initial 'th' the ascender of the 't' is slightly looped on the upstroke and joined to the 'h' at the top; the same looped 't' is found in initial 'to' and initial 'ta'. One separated 'Th' occurs as well as joined examples. Both the fancy capital 'H' and the plainer 'H' but with a serif on the first ascender are found. One capital 'S' is in the early form. In its general conformation and the structure of variable letters this manuscript is almost identical with that of "Across the Covered Pit" (*Works*, VIII, no. 152), which can be dated in August, 1890. Not previously printed.

III. [MR. RICHARD EGREMONT]

This fragment appears without numbering on the verso of the first leaf of MS[1] of "Jack" (University of Virginia), and thus probably represents an earlier trial turned over and used to begin the inscription of the earliest manuscript of "Jack." The paper is a form of legal-cap (320 × 202.5 mm.), head space 37 mm., tail space 10 mm., vertical pink-blue-pink rules 35.5 mm. from the left margin, 29 lines per page extending from margin to margin, watermarked T. LEACH | 86 NASSAU ST | N Y. The writing in black ink slopes markedly to the right, uses plain periods, looped initial 'th' and 'to', and the fancy capital 'H'. The capital 'S' is in the early form. All signs point to a date no later than 1890; the paper has not been identified in other of Crane's manuscripts. Not previously printed.

IV. "JACK"

Three fragmentary manuscripts are preserved.

MS[1]: Untitled, three leaves of legal-cap paper (320 × 202.5 mm.), head space 37 mm., tail space 10 mm., vertical pink-blue-pink rules 35.5 mm. from left margin, 29 lines per page extending from margin to margin, watermarked T. LEACH | 86 NASSAU ST | N Y. Written in a black ink now faded to blackish gray. The first page is unnumbered; both the second and third are numbered '2' without half-circles; page 1 has Cora's inventory miniscule at lower left 'h' and pages 2 and 3 are numbered at lower left. First sentence reads, 'A party of campers on the Mongaup River in Sullivan County, New York had brought with them a large black mastiff called Jack.' Preserved in the Barrett Collection of the University of Virginia Library. All initial 'th' letters are looped except one, initial 'to' is looped, and six looped initial 'ta' formations appear as against one unlooped. The capital 'S' is in the early formation. The periods are uncircled. On the original recto of fol. 1 is the fragment of III, "Mr. Richard Egremont."

MS[2]: Untitled, seven leaves, numbered except for the first without half-circles, cheap wove unruled paper 250 × 161 mm., black ink. Second sentence reads, 'It was long ago before peaked hats and leather gun cases had invaded the grand old hills and fish and game were plentiful.' Owned by Commander Melvin H. Schoberlin USN (Ret.). In this manuscript the 'th' is no longed looped but has assumed its later form of a simple downstroke for the 't' joined with the 'h' from the foot. The 'to' is still looped, however, but the 'ta' is in an intermediate stage, with two simple downstroke 't' letters and one 'ta' that is looped. One capital 'H' is in its fancy form with a curved first ascender and a serif at its top; a second has a serif but a straight downstroke. The periods are uncircled.

MS[3]: Titled '"Jack"', nine leaves of unruled cheap wove paper (250 × 161 mm.) numbered except for the first without half-circles, original black ink now a brownish gray. Preserved in the Barrett Collection of the University of Virginia Library. Second sentence reads, 'It was long ago, before peaked hats and leather gun-cases and other paraphenalia of the modern sporting gentleman, had invaded the grand old hills.' The hand is generally similar to that of MS². The unlooped 'th' is consistent as is the looped initial 'to'; however, the only three examples of initial 'ta' are unlooped and in their later form. A fancy capital 'L' appears. The periods are uncircled.

The handwriting would appear to place MS¹ in 1890, close to "Across the Covered Pit." Something of a break seems to occur between MS¹ and MS², but little between MS² and MS³, especially as indicated by their similarity of paper. MSS²⁻³ might date from late 1890 to early 1891, probably the latter since there is some resemblance in the handwriting characteristics to the manuscript of "The Wreck of the *New Era*" (*Works*, VIII, no. 151), written on roughly similar but not identical paper. If the appearance of semicircles below the pagination in "The Wreck of the *New Era*" is significant, however, MS²⁻³ would date earlier than its inscription. All three manuscripts are definitely earlier than the inscription of the manuscript of "A Foreign Policy in Three Glimpses" (*Works*, VIII, no. 149) which has pagination with semicircles but also circled periods. Otherwise, this manuscript has the final form of initial 'th', but looped initial 'to', and a fancy capital 'L'. Initial 'ta' does not appear in it.

The order of MS² and MS³ is suggested not only by the title in MS³ where MS² has only a blank space left for one, but also by several alterations made during the inscription of MS² in which MS³ follows the later reading.

According to R. W. Stallman (*Stephen Crane: A Biography* [1968], p. 31), Crane offered a dog story entitled "Jack" to the magazine *St. Nicholas*, apparently in 1890–91, but it was not accepted.

Not previously printed.

V. [A SMALL BLACK AND WHITE AND TAN HOUND]

All four untitled fragments are preserved in the Special Collections of the Columbia University Libraries written in black ink on an unwatermarked laid paper (262 × 191 mm.), the vertical chainlines 25 mm. apart. MS³ consists of two leaves, the second numbered 2 above a semicircle; the others are single leaves. Each begins about half way down the leaf with room left for a title to be added later. The four trials can be ordered by the readings. In MS¹ the sun throws a 'pale yellow glance' upon the old house (98.4–5), but 'glance' has been interlined above deleted 'ray'. Thus it is significant that in MS² the reading is 'a pale yellow glance'. MS³ follows MS² in calling the house 'old, unpainted', whereas in MS⁴ the original inscription was 'old, unpainted' but 'old' has been deleted. Correspondingly, MS³ read 'stood wagging his tail enthusiastically', whereas MS⁴ originally had 'stood enthusiastically wagging his tail' but 'enthusiastically' has been deleted.

All four fragments have initial 'th' in its late form but looped initial 'to'. In MS³ occurs one looped initial 'ta' form but two later forms with a single downstroke; in MS⁴ the five appearances of initial 'ta' show the final formation only, including one word 'tatoo' which had been looped in MS³. MS⁴ contains one example of the fancy capital 'H' with curved first upright and serif, and one with straight first upright and serif. The four trials would seem to have been written within a relatively short time. It seems clear that they must be later than MS[1] of "Jack". Since they all circle periods, and MS[2] places a semicircle below the page number, it is probable that the four fragments come after MSS[2-3] of "Jack" but not by any lengthy interval. A date within 1891 would seem to be suitable.

MS[3] was reproduced by R. W. Stallman in facsimile on the verso of the cover of *Fine Arts Magazine*, VI (University of Connecticut, 1961).

VI. [APACHE CROSSING]

The two fragments of the untitled story are preserved in the Special Collections of the Columbia University Libraries. Since both are written on the same laid paper (259 × 195 mm.) with vertical chainlines 21 mm. apart, unwatermarked, the attempted revision must have been made relatively soon after the inscription of the first.

MS[1]: Three leaves, the first unnumbered and with space left for a title, the others paged 2 and 3 above semicircles. The late forms of initial 'th' and of 'ta' appear, but looped initial 'to' predominates over the unlooped forms. Quotation marks are set off with a V for superscript and the periods are circled. The capital 'S' is in the later form.

MS[2]: One leaf, unnumbered with space left for a title. The handwriting characteristics are the same as in MS[1].

The order of the two trial starts is suggested by the reading in MS[1] 'pointed to a small round hole in the door a little higher up than a man's head' whereas MS[2] originally read 'pointed a lean finger at a round hole in the door a little higher up than' before 'door . . . than' was deleted and the sentence ended 'top of the door.' The looped initial 'to' and the general characteristics of the handwriting make the usually assigned date of 1895 after Crane's Western trip quite impossible. Late 1891, or perhaps early to mid 1892 is more likely. The order of this piece and of "In the Country of Rhymers and Writers" is not to be determined, and each must have been written fairly close to the other. The changes in letter formation that take place by "A Desertion" and the poem "Ah, Haggard Purse" dated in December, 1892, on the authority of Corwin Linson make it certain that both "Apache Crossing" and "In the Country of Rhymers and Writers" were inscribed before that date.

First printed by R. W. Stallman in *Prairie Schooner*, XLIII (1969), 184–186.

VII. [IN THE COUNTRY OF RHYMERS AND WRITERS]

The two manuscript starts are preserved in the Special Collections of the Columbia University Libraries. Both are written in black ink on the same paper, laid unwatermarked sheets (264 × 195 mm.), with vertical chainlines 20.5 mm. apart.

MS[1]: Four leaves, unnumbered except for the first, which is paged 1 above a space left for a title. However, fol. 2 beginning ' "My name is Mr Rudolph Alfonso Moaner," ' is written on the verso, turned end-for-end, of a false start paged 2 above a semicircle, containing the same words except for some mistake in the word 'Moaner' which has been deleted by a large ink blot. The word may be 'Railer' but the reading is uncertain.

MS[2]: Nine leaves, 1–3 and 9 unnumbered, 4–7 numbered above a semicircle, 8 numbered without the semicircle. Space for a title is left on fol. 1.

Folio 8 is written on the verso of a leaf containing the start of a letter: 'To the editor of the Sun, Sir:– [¶] It has become fashionable among statesmen in this country to adopt a valiant and pugnacious foriegn [coun *deleted*] pop'. Folio 9 is written on the verso of a leaf that had had inscribed the false start of the opening of MS[1] in the form 'When little Mary Laughter awoke, the world had changed', which has been deleted by a large doodle extending down almost to the foot of the page.

In each manuscript quotation marks are indicated for superscript by a V and the periods are circled, as they are in all subsequent manuscripts reprinted here. Given the difference between sections that are largely copied, the hands are identical. The late forms of initial 'th' and 'ta' are invariable but looped initial 'to' letters predominate over the unlooped forms. The fancy capital 'L' appears; the capital 'H' has a straight downstroke for the first upright which is given a preliminary serif invariably in MS[1] and mostly in MS[2]. Late 1891 but more likely early to mid 1892 would seem to be an acceptable date.

The order of the two versions is subject to some conflicting evidence, but in the end there can be little or no doubt that the longer is the second. In favor of a reversal of the order assigned here and of a hypothesis that MS[1] is the later would be the curious hyphenated form 'un-rolled' in it at 101.28 which could be explained by a literal copying of 'un-|rolled' in MS[2] which is broken and hyphenated at the end of a line. If this were so, it would then be necessary to take it that the appearance of a rejected opening sentence on the verso of fol. 9 of MS[2] was not a case of Crane—as usual—saving a discarded leaf from an earlier version to write on its verso but instead a projected revision started on the turned-around verso of the last leaf of an original version. However, the textual evidence seems to confirm the assigned order, instead. Thus in MS[2] (102.3–4) Crane first wrote, 'making no Sign excepting defiant Tosses of the Head among Some and a greater Exhibition of Timidity by Others.' This follows roughly MS[1] (101.17–19) 'making no sign except a defiant tossing of heads among some and a great timidity upon the part of those who shrunk before.' Both read 'among' before 'some', but in MS[2] Crane deleted this 'among' that followed MS[1] and interlined 'by', thus apparently establishing the order. This order is confirmed by the change in the system of lower case in MS[1] to capitalized nouns in MS[2] which was irregularly managed in the inscription and needed to be corrected by revision when, evidently, MS[1] had been negligently copied in lower case. Finally, although MS[2] is extensively revised, no revisions except for a few of these capitalizations occur in the section where the two texts are parallel.

The manuscripts were first printed by R. W. Stallman in "New Short Fiction by Stephen Crane: II," *Studies in Short Fiction*, I (1964), 149–152. There would seem to be little evidence for his belief that the Little Mary Laughter introduction of MS[1] was intended to be retained before MS[2]; it seems much more probable that this original beginning was scrapped in the revision.

VIII. THE CAMERA IN A COMPROMISING POSITION

One sheet of laid unwatermarked paper (264 × 195 mm.), vertical chainlines 20.5 mm. apart, the same paper as "In the Country of Rhymers and Writers." The initial 'th' is in the later simple style, and the capital 'S' is also late. Presumably the date would be in early to mid 1892. Nos. VIII, IX, and X are preserved in the Special Collections of the Columbia University Libraries. Not previously printed.

IX. [LISTEN OH MAN-WITH-A-GIGANTIC-NERVE]

One sheet of laid unwatermarked paper as in no. VIII above, with space left for a title. The capital 'L' is fancy, the 'th' in the later style, and the quotation marks are drawn with a V for superscript. On the verso is a false start, ' "Listen, oh, gre'. The date is probably in early to mid 1892. Not previously printed.

X. [HEARKEN, HEARKEN, OH, MAN-WITH-A-COPPER-STOMACH]

One sheet of the same paper as in nos. VIII and IX, space left for a title. The capital 'H' has a straight downstroke but is introduced by a serif, the 'th' is in the late style, and the quotation marks are indicated for superscript. The date is probably within a short span of no. IX, since both appear to be starts on the same piece. The reference to a Zulu chieftain recalls Crane's narrative of Albert Thies's experience in "The King's Favor," printed in May, 1891 (*Works,* VIII, no. 148), and particularly ' "Hearken, oh warrior, son of many warriors, the fallen king loves you," said Cetewayo' (572.16–17), but the present handwriting is too late in its characteristics for a piece that may have been written in 1890 or early 1891, and the paper is wrong for such an early date. Moreover, Thies met a Zulu king, not a chieftain, and the epithets addressed to him do not fit a singer. It may be that Thies's experience lingered in Crane's mind so that he proposed some story about an old Zulu chieftain a year or so after "The King's Favor." It would be mere speculation that nos. IX and X are fragments from a part of "Dan Emmonds." Not previously printed.

XI. A FLURRY OF CONDENSED MILK

Three leaves of cheap wove unruled paper (218 × 141 mm.), titled, written in black ink, preserved in the Special Collections of the Columbia University Libraries. This appears to be the beginning and end of an otherwise lost early Sullivan County sketch, the first leaf titled but unnumbered, the second paged 2 without a semicircle, and the third 26 above a semicircle. Crane's typical grid ends page 26. The handwriting on page 26 tilts a little more to the left than that on pages 1–2, and it is only the similarity of paper that leads to the supposition that the third leaf is to be associated with the first two. The quotation marks are indicated for superscript, the periods are circled, and the formation of initial 'th' and 'to' is in the late manner.

That the similarity of paper may be uncertain evidence to associate page 26 with pages 1–2 is suggested by the preservation in the Columbia University Libraries of notes for Sullivan County sketches, and no doubt other pieces, some parts of which are associated with "The Octopush" in its early form as "The Fishermen" (*Works,* VIII, nos. 49, 49a) and these notes also contain the two lines 'Cast veils over their hearts. | —lofty heavens—'. The first phrase occurs on page 26; it is scarcely evidence that nothing from the first two pages is found in these notes. However, these notes are on the same paper as "A Flurry of Condensed Milk" and presumably so was the original manuscript of "The Octopush," now lost, and possibly other lost Sullivan County manuscripts. Since "The Octopush" was printed in the *New York Tribune* on July 10, 1892, the association between page 26, at least, of "A Flurry" and the notes behind "The Octopush," combined with the evidence of the paper, would date the manuscript fragment of "A Flurry" as about June, 1892. Since quotation marks are given superscript signs both in "A Flurry" and in the notes, this evidence is useful for dating manuscripts in which the practice has been abandoned. It is also useful to note a serif on the first upright of the capital 'H' but otherwise a straight downstroke, except that a curved downstroke occurs on an earlier fancy 'H' heading a false start 'Here come' below a page number 12 with semicircle that was subsequently used for the second leaf of the Sullivan County notes. For these notes, see *Works*, VIII, no. 49b.

Not previously printed.

XII. A DESERTION

Written in black ink on two leaves of cheap wove pad paper (240 × 160 mm.), 27 red lines to the page. No page numbering. The sentence above the title may be a note for some other piece. This manuscript is preserved in the George Arents Research Library of Syracuse University. The paper is identical with that used by Crane to inscribe the poem "Ah, haggard purse, why ope thy mouth" (no. 107), and heading the leaf on which the poem begins is a trial 'In a large vaulted hall that | blazed with light' which clearly is a false start for the opening sentence of "A Desertion." In *My Stephen Crane* (ed. E. H. Cady, pp. 13–14) Corwin Linson dates the poem as in December, 1892. The two leaves of "A Desertion" must be of the same date and were apparently rescued by Linson along with the leaf of the poem. On the verso of the first leaf is written in Crane's hand the note 'a ghastly, ineffaceable smile sculptored by fingers of scorn'.

In this manuscript the initial 'th', 'to', and 'ta' are all in their late and final forms, as is the capital 'L'. The several examples of capital 'H' all show a straight downstroke for the first upright. One has a serif, one a very elementary stroke intended for a serif, and one perfectly plain. Previously printed by R. W. Stallman and E. R. Hagemann in *New York City Sketches* (1966), p. 260.

XIII. [GUSTAVE AND MARIE]

This fragment is known only from the use of its blank verso to inscribe the cancellans leaf 137 of the final manuscript of *The Red Badge of Courage* in the Barrett Collection of the University of Virginia Library. The leaf is paged 3 above a semicircle and is a sheet of legal-cap paper (318 × 197 mm.) with the unusual feature that the space between the left margin and the pink, blue, pink vertical rules is unlined, whereas there are 28 blue lines to the right of the vertical rules. Although from a different lot, this kind of paper is similar to that on which Crane began the inscription of the final manuscript of *The Red Badge of Courage*, originally consisting of 52 leaves before another batch of paper was introduced (*Works*, II, 187). The paper would seem to place "Gustave and Marie" as part of a story started and then discarded or left incomplete in late 1893 or early 1894. First printed by

R. W. Stallman in *Bulletin of the New York Public Library,* LX (1956), 456–457. A facsimile of the page appears in *The Red Badge of Courage: A Facsimile Edition of the Manuscript,* ed. Bowers (1973), II, 263.

XIV. LITERARY NOTES

This titled fragment begins the Crane Notebook on fol. 1^{r}. This Notebook is made up of 59 of an original 76 leaves of cheap wove paper (220 × 130 mm.) with 17–18 red lines to the page, and is preserved in the Barrett Collection of the University of Virginia Library. The date at which the early notes were made is not to be established, but they would come before the Notebook inscription on fol. 19^{r} of the unpublished poem "Little birds of the night" which may date from early 1894. Nos. XIV and XV are followed in the Notebook by "The Art Students' League Building," which must have been written after the League had moved in April, 1894. Thus the early months of 1894 seem to be the nearest date that can be conjectured for these Notes. "Literary Notes" were first printed in *The Notebook of Stephen Crane,* edited by D. J. and E. B. Greiner (1969), p. 3.

XV. IN BRIEF

This titled fragment follows no. XIV in the Crane Notebook and must have been written with only a short interval, on fols. 2^{r} and 3^{r}. It has been printed in the *Notebook* (1969), pp. 4–5.

XVI. [MATINEE GIRLS]

The untitled sketch appears in the Crane Notebook on fols. $59^{r\text{-}v}$, at the point where the Notebook was reversed and Crane began to write on the versos. The date could well be in September or October, 1894. In the Notebook, "Matinee Girls" follows a draft of "The Duel That Was Not Fought," which was not printed in final form until the *New York Press* of December 9, 1894. However, beginning directly under its last line on fol. 59^{v} is a draft of "In a Park Row Restaurant," which the *Press* printed in revised form on October 24, 1894. "Matinee Girls" was first printed by R. W. Stallman in *Bulletin of the New York Public Library,* LX (1956), 459–460.

XVII. [LITTLE HEAP OF MATCHES]

One leaf of legal-cap paper (319.5 × 197 mm.) preserved in the Special Collections of the Columbia University Libraries. The vertical rules red, blue, red are 38.5 mm. from the left margin, the head space is 49 mm., and the tail space 4 mm. The paper has 28 blue lines extending from margin to margin. The writing is in black ink. The hand exhibits an even mixture of lower-case final 'e' with the curved upturn and the downstroke. The high proportion (6) of final 'r' with the curved upstroke in comparison to final 'r' with the downstroke (4) suggests that the date could be in the spring of 1894, not too long after the completion of *The Red Badge of Courage* manuscript. Not previously printed.

XVIII. [SIXTH AVENUE]

One leaf of wove unwatermarked paper (254 × 201 mm.) written in black ink and untitled but with space left for later insertion. This appears to be an uncompleted sketch for the New York series that Crane began publishing in late April 1894. The appearance in the single page of twenty-one final 'e' forms with the curved upstroke versus eleven with the marked downstroke suggests a date close to the completion of the manuscript of *The Red Badge of Courage*, and thus early in the series of New York sketches, say in the late spring of 1894. One final 'r' with the curved upstroke occurs but two with the downstroke. First printed by R. W. Stallman and E. R. Hagemann in *New York City Sketches* (1966), p. 117. The manuscript is preserved in the Special Collections of the Columbia University Libraries.

XIX. [A MOURNFUL OLD BUILDING]

Two fragmentary manuscripts are preserved.

MS[1]: A single leaf of wove legal-cap paper (317 × 218 mm.), head space 48.5 mm., tail space 5 mm., 38.5 mm. from left margin to the vertical pink, blue, pink rules, 28 blue lines extending from margin to margin. Written in black ink with space left for a title.

MS[2]: A single leaf of the paper from the same pad, written to the full page, and clearly within a very short time of the inscription of MS[1]. At the upper right of the space left for a title is the note in Cora's hand, 'to be looked | over'. Both manuscripts are preserved in the Special Collections of the Columbia University Libraries.

In the two manuscripts the final 'e' with curved upstroke occurs only a few times more than the final 'e' with the downstroke, and there are two appearances of the final 'r' with curved upstroke as against one of the 'r' with downstroke. Although the date is uncertain, on the whole mid to late 1894 would seem to be acceptable. There is no necessary reason to associate this abortive sketch with the abandoned Art Students' League Building. Printed for the first time by R. W. Stallman and E. R. Hagemann in *New York City Sketches* (1966), pp. 16–17.

XX. [THE TOY-SHOP]

A single leaf of wove legal-cap paper (316 × 202 mm.), head space 37 mm., tail space 4.5 mm., 37 mm. from left margin to two red vertical rules, 29 blue lines extending from margin to margin. Space has been left for a title; the leaf is not filled. On its verso, in Cora's hand, is the note 'Toy shop' underlined. In this brief fragment the evidence of the final 'e' and 'r' is opposed. The final 'e' with the upstroke is invariable; on the other hand, so is the final 'r' with a downstroke, appearing six times. The date would seem to be in 1894, and possibly late. The paper is an unusual form of the legal-cap pads, not otherwise encountered in Crane's manuscripts. The fragment has not previously been printed. It is preserved in the Special Collections of the Columbia University Libraries.

XXI. [MEXICAN SKETCH]

A single leaf of wove legal-cap paper (318 × 200 mm.), head space 35 mm., tail space 8.5 mm., 27.5 mm. from left margin to the vertical pink, blue, pink rules, 29 blue lines extending from margin to margin. Preserved in the Special Collections of the Columbia University Libraries. The final 'e' shows a similar proportion between examples with the curved upstroke and those not with a direct downstroke but with a stroke that ends on the line without an upward curve. The final 'r' without a curved upstroke is invariable. Since Crane did not return to New York until early June 1895, this fragment probably dates from the second half of 1895. The manuscript has not previously been printed.

XXII. [FRANKLY I DO NOT CONSIDER]

Begun in black ink on one leaf of cut-down wove legal-cap paper (243 × 200 mm.), without head space but with tail space of 7.5 mm., 37.5 mm. from the left margin to the vertical pink, blue, pink rules, 24 blue lines from margin to margin. Preserved in the Special Collections of the Columbia University Libraries. Whether this is the start of a draft of a letter or part of a proposed story or sketch is not to be determined. The final 'e' forms are mixed, varying between those with a curved upstroke, those with a stroke ending on the line, those with a distinct downstroke below the line, and several in the form of a Greek 'e'. The 'r' without curved upstroke is invariable. The date is most uncertain but is probably in 1895. The manuscript has not previously been printed.

XXIII. [HE TOLD ME ALL HE KNEW]

Two leaves of wove legal-cap paper (317 × 200 mm.), head space 33 mm., tail space 7 mm., 37 mm. from the left margin to the pink, blue, pink vertical rules (fol. 2 vertical rules irregular 34.5 to 30 mm.), 29 blue lines from margin to margin. On the verso of fol. 1 Cora wrote 'odd ms | [squiggle] | to be | examined | someday'. Preserved in the Special Collections of the Columbia University Libraries. The final 'e' forms are about evenly divided between those with a curved upstroke, those with a stroke ending on the line, and those with a downstroke below the line. The final 'r' without a curved stroke is invariable, and about half of these have a marked downstroke below the line. Two examples of capital 'H' with a serif appear versus one without serif. The writing begins on the second line, and it seems clear that this is not the start of a story although the unnumbered first page is succeeded by the second numbered 2 above a semicircle. The date is quite problematic but may be assigned to late 1895 or early 1896. It may be remarked that it is not impossible that this is an abortive fragment of the further adventures of Dan Emmonds, although the case can be only speculative. Not previously printed.

XXIV. DAN EMMONDS

The only document in which this text is preserved is a professionally made typescript consisting of 10 leaves numbered within parentheses at the foot of the pages prefixed by a title-page, 'DAN EMMONDS. | --------BY-------- | STEPHEN CRANE. | [double rule of hyphens]'. This is also the form of the headtitle on p. 1, except that 'by' is in lower case. The typescript is preserved in the Special Collections of the Columbia University Libraries. It is typed on laid paper (266 × 203 mm.) watermarked CONQUEROR | LONDON, with horizontal chainlines 28 mm. apart. Pasted at the foot of the titlepage is an identifying form from James B. Pinker's literary agency, which leaves the spaces for title and author blank but gives the length as

2,300 words and the price as '£10-10/- for serial rights.' Something of a mystery about how this manifestly fragmentary work came to be typed up for sale may be dispelled by an undated letter from Cora to Pinker that seems to be later than the correspondence about "Dan Emmonds" culminating in a letter of November 8, 1900. The present undated letter enquires, 'Will you kindly let me know to whom you sold the story "Dan Emmonds" & on what date. There is an item in your account for typing it—Dec. 1898. This may make it more easy to find in your books' (Syracuse typed transcript). One may conjecture from this that while Crane was away from England, Cora had had the manuscript typed by Pinker and put up for sale in an attempt to raise some money. It is clear from Pinker's notes about the serial rights that Cora trusted Crane would complete the story (for she could not have thought it a novel at the price for serial rights) on his return if some magazine could be interested by the sample.

The history of "Dan Emmonds" is one of the most debated matters in Crane's literary history. On March 26, 1896, Crane excused himself to Appleton's Ripley Hitchcock for giving *George's Mother* to Arnold:

> As for Edward Arnold, his American manager is an old schoolmate and ten-year's friend of mine and he conducted such a campaign against me as is seldom seen. He appealed to my avarice and failing appealed to my humanity. Once I thought he was about to get "The Little Regiment," when you stepped in and saved it. Finally I thought of a satirical sketch of mine—an old thing, strong in satire but rather easy writing—called Dan Emmonds and I gave it to him (*Letters*, p. 121).

In late May of 1896, in fact, Arnold published *George's Mother* and nothing further is heard about "Dan Emmonds" for this firm. However, the letter gave rise to the conjecture, held by Berryman and for a time influential, that in 1896 "Dan Emmonds" was the temporary title for *George's Mother*, but the discovery of the present typescript led to the contrary view that "Dan Emmonds" all along had been an unfinished short story.[1] However, more recently, George Monteiro has reopened the case.[2] He points out very pertinently the numerous references to a novel by Crane to be called *Dan Emmonds* and due for publication in the near future. Such references begin on March 16, 1896, and continue on April 18, later in April, and again in May. In June *The Bookman* noted: 'We understand that Stephen Crane's forthcoming novel, *Dan Emmonds*, which was announced for publication in June, will not be ready until the autumn. Mr. Edward Arnold will publish immediately, however, a new story by Mr. Crane entitled *George's Mother*.' Dr. Monteiro, indeed, lists an announcement from the Arnold catalogue in August 1896 that *Dan Emmonds* will be published in the fall of 1896, and quotes from a "New York Letter" by John D. Barry in *Literary World* on October 31, 1896, that 'Mr. Stephen Crane has abandoned the trip to England which he had planned to take this autumn. The novel which he began some time ago is not yet completed and will not appear this year.' The heart of Dr. Monteiro's argument is very likely sound insofar as Crane's

[1] R. W. Stallman, reprinting the text of the typescript, in "New Short Fiction by Stephen Crane: I," *Studies in Short Fiction*, I (1963), 1–7; T. A. Gullason, *The Complete Novels of Stephen Crane* (1967), p. 78.

[2] "Stephen Crane's Dan Emmonds: A Case Reargued," *The Serif*, VI (1969), 32–36.

early intentions were concerned: that is, Crane apparently had started work probably in 1895, but certainly by early 1896, on what he called a sketch in his letter to Hitchcock but which in his dealings with Arnold he seems to have hoped could be expanded to a novel if, indeed, it had not been begun with that expectation. However, the work had not progressed beyond his early attempt. (Some slight chance exists that no. XXIII "He Told Me All He Knew" is a part of Dan's later adventures, in which case Crane made some further sketches.) Dr. Monteiro conjectures that Crane would not try to persuade Arnold to accept a mere sketch when a book was wanted; but Crane's history is full of his attempts to secure advances and line up publishers for books barely started or even existing only as outlines. Thus it does not at all follow that there must have existed an early original manuscript for a novel, or part of a novel, now lost, and that the present typescript represents a redaction and rewriting started in short-story form. Dr. Monteiro takes very seriously the reference in *Book News* for October, 1896:

> Mr. Stephen Crane sails for England this month for a brief stay, returning probably a short time before the holidays. This will interrupt his work on his new novel *Dan Emmons*, and will probably postpone its publication until spring. . . . A few chapters of *Dan Emmons* have been written and they give promise of something quite unlike any of Mr. Crane's former work. Dan is an Irish boy, and the story as far as written deals with life in New York City.

A publisher's news item such as this cannot be taken too seriously. That is, the reference to Dan's life in New York City conflicts with the typescript, which after a relatively brief interval in New York puts Dan afloat. That Arnold had in its possession the manuscript is most unlikely. It is probable that Crane had shown the firm the start of the narrative and then required the return of the manuscript. The firm's publicity such as that in *Book News*, therefore, was very likely from memory and hence somewhat inexact. What was not inexact, however, was the statement that only a small part had been written—the 'few chapters' is, of course, publisher's inflation.

The unpublished letter from Cora to Pinker showing that the typescript had been made up at her instance in Crane's absence puts a different complexion on the whole matter, for there is no reason to suppose that Crane had continued the manuscript any further than its 1896 state before he left for Cuba in April 1898. The low price for serialization placed on the typescript by Pinker would seem to represent a misunderstanding on his and Cora's part that the typescript was the start of a short story, not a novel. In short, no evidence exists to prevent the natural assumption that the present typescript represents—without any rewriting—the state of the opening of a proposed novel in the spring of 1896 but one that was never continued. The naturalness of this hypothesis may be confirmed by a recently discovered letter (quoted in an added note by Dr. Monteiro) from Crane in Ireland on September 9, 1897, to his brother: 'The ms you mailed to me was not the one I wanted but I was glad enough to get it. Any odd bits of writing you find at H[artwood]; please mail to me. Some of them will come in handy. Have you noticed an ms devoted to the adventures of a certain Irishman? Try to get it' (Joseph Katz, "Stephen Crane to Edmund B. Crane: Two New Letters," *Stephen Crane Newsletter*, I [Spring, 1967], 8). That Crane wanted "Dan Emmonds" but that he rewrote the original start of a novel to its present form after he eventually received the manuscript at some unknown date is not supported by the fresh information about the origin of the typescript. There would seem to be every reason to date the present fragment as not later than March 1896, and no doubt—on Crane's word—earlier. The fancied resemblances of Dan's shipwreck to Cora's near shipwreck on her voyage to Constantinople in 1897, fused with Crane's experience in the open boat on 1 January 1897, are far from demonstrable for any rewriting.[3]

After Crane's death Cora, who had lost track of the typescript, but had some record of the existence of the work, bombarded Pinker with questions as she tried to turn Crane's literary remains to financial account. In an undated letter from Milborne Grove shortly before October 17, 1900, she wrote to Pinker: 'Have you a copy of "Dan Emmonds" and "The Reluctant Voyagers"? If not, please send me word where to address the Northern Syndicate who bought the last named' (Dartmouth). On October 17, 1900, Pinker returned that he did not have a copy of "Dan Emmonds" (Dartmouth) but on November 5 Cora wrote: 'I will be very much obliged if you will send me a copy of full statement of your account with my late husband, Stephen Crane, from Jan 1st 1899 to date. . . . P.S. What has become of the story Dan Emmonds! If you have it please send it to me to copy' (Dartmouth). A few days later on November 8 in a letter about Pinker's sales of some of Crane's stories, she again requested, 'Please send me Dan Emmonds' (Dartmouth). Pinker's accounting in response to her November 5 letter seems to have given her a clue, for in the undated letter from 6 Milborne Grove already mentioned she was able to point to the record of its typing in December, 1898. The presence of the Pinker typescript in the material from Brede now at Columbia University attests to her eventual success in retrieving the typescript.

XXV. [DURING A SESSION OF CONGRESS]

Three leaves of unnumbered wove paper (248 × 160 mm.), head space 45 mm., tail space 1 mm., 24 blue lines per page. The first leaf begins on the top line. The different items are separated by horizontal short rules. Preserved in the Special Collections of the Columbia University Libraries. On the verso of the second leaf is the scoring for some game between Cora, Stephen, and Camilla similar to that found on the foot of the recto of fol. 98, the first trial page of discarded Chapter XII of the manuscript of *The Red Badge of Courage* (see *Facsimile*, p. 185) later reversed and used to inscribe fol. 102 of the chapter. Crane was in Washington in March, 1896, re-

[3] There is one unsettling coincidence in this matter. Elbert Hubbard in the February 1897 issue of *The Philistine* (Vol. IV, no. 3), on page 87 made a stop-press correction to his premature obituary of Crane on page 84 of the same issue, the correction reading: 'LATER: Thanks to Providence and a hen coop, Steve Crane was not drowned after all—he swam ashore.' None of the preserved accounts of the sinking of the *Commodore* mentions a hen-coop and it is possible that Hubbard might have seen an early draft of Dan Emmonds, or the manuscript behind this present typescript, and confused the actual with a fictional account dealing with a similar subject, for Dan Emmonds makes *his* escape by hanging onto a dead pig and a hen-coop. However, even if the reference to a hen-coop is not merely coincidental, there still remains no reason not to date the piece prior to March 1896.

porting the doings of Congress; hence this series of notes should date from this time. The final 'e' is about evenly divided between the curved upstroke and the downstroke below the line, with a scattering of letters with strokes ending on the line. A Greek final 'e' appears. The final 'r' is invariably without the curved upstroke. Not previously printed in its entirety.

XXVI. [THE RIGHT OF ARREST]

A single leaf of legal-cap paper (316 × 202.3 mm.), head space 50.5 mm., tail space 1.5 mm., 37.5 mm. from left margin to the vertical pink, blue, pink rules, 28 blue lines extending from margin to margin. Preserved in the Special Collections of Columbia University Libraries. On the verso in Cora's hand is 'Right of arrest' with a short rule below, and then in an unidentifiable hand '#102'. Sixteen examples of final 'e' with a curved upstroke appear, versus two with a stroke ending on the line, and two Greek 'e' forms. The final 'r' is invariable and has a tendency for the downstroke to go below the line. This fragment, which begins on the third line and thus seems to have left space for a title, appears to be related to the Dora Clark affair, which would place it in September, 1896. First printed by R. W. Stallman and E. R. Hagemann in *New York Sketches* (1966), p. 259.

XXVII. [NEW YORK BOARDING HOUSE TALE]

Two fragmentary manuscripts are preserved.

MS[1]: Miscellaneous leaves from a draft of the story, written in pencil on wove legal-cap paper (316 × 200 mm.), head space 33 mm., tail space 7 mm., variable 37 mm. space between left margin and the pink, blue, pink vertical rules; 29 blue lines extending from margin to margin. Folio 1, unnumbered, is inscribed 'I.' in the head space and the text begins on the second line; on its verso is the underlined word count 195 and a column of fifteen chapter headings in roman, with word counts for the first seven: 400 (*following deleted* 500), 450, 300, 250, 375, 125, and 450. Folio 2, unnumbered, is headed 'II.'. On its verso appears the following dialogue: 'What name, please | Claxton | Haxton? | "No. Claxton." | Paxton | No Claxton'. Below, printed in angular letters is 'What the h' and below this, vertically, is 'What | thE HELL'. The third preserved sheet is paged 2 above a semicircle; on its verso appears the part page headed 'VI'. The fourth is unnumbered; on its verso appears the false start 'The five young men' and then, two lines below, the start of some text beginning 'During the meal'. The fifth and final leaf is unnumbered and contains only five lines of the last part of the text to be written, its verso blank.

MS[2]: Seventeen leaves of the same legal-cap paper as in MS[1], written in black ink. Except for the first leaf, the pages are numbered above a semicircle and on the backs in Crane's hand are pencil word counts for the recto inscription. On the verso of fol. 14, the leaf containing the brief Chapter VI, Cora wrote 'To finish' and added a large question mark below. No cumulated word count is present. Both manuscripts are preserved in the Special Collections of the Columbia University Libraries.

The similarity of paper indicates that the second attempt at this story was made very shortly after the first. The date is not to be determined with any exactitude. The legal-cap paper demonstrates that it was written in the United States, and thus before the end of 1896. The forms of final 'e' are mixed although the form with the downstroke predominates; the final 'r' with the downstroke is invariable, and various of these strokes extend below the line. The usual capital 'H' without serif appears, but there is a scattering of forms with the serif. Printed by R. W. Stallman and E. R. Hagemann in *New York City Sketches* (1966), pp. 8–14. These editors suggest that the date is 1893 since the story may reflect Crane's taking up residence in a boarding house at 136 West 15th Street, New York, in May 1893, the landlady of which was reputed to have a pretty daughter. However, the characteristics of the handwriting preclude a date in 1893, although any date in 1895 or 1896 would be possible.

XXVIII. [CHURCH PARADE]

A single leaf of laid paper watermarked CARISBROOK | SUPREME, vertical chainlines 27.5 mm. apart, lined in gray at intervals of 8.5 mm., preserved in the Special Collections of the Columbia University Libraries. Not much space is left for a title at the head of the page, and from the subject (and in part the paper) it is clear that this is an unused paragraph from the "London Letters," the writing of which occupied Crane and Cora between April and late September 1897. Since the London season ends in midsummer, the date is probably between May and July 1897. The paper does not show the char that appears in some of the preserved manuscripts of the "European Letters" (see *Works*, VIII, no. 170). Not previously printed.

XXIX. [AND HIS NAME SHALL BE CALLED UNDER TRUTH]

This unfinished sentence is scrawled in pencil on an English Post Office Telegraph message form preserved in the Special Collections of the Columbia University Libraries. What sort of a trial it is, and of what date, are quite unknown.

XXX. [PLAY SET IN A FRENCH TAVERN]

The manuscript of the first act is preserved in the Special Collections of the Columbia University Libraries, consisting of eighteen leaves of wove unwatermarked paper, fols. 1–11 and 18 measuring 255 × 202 mm. and fols. 12–17 of thicker stock measuring 252 × 201 mm. The first page is unnumbered; the remaining are paged 2–18 above semicircles. The first page may have been started with space for a title, but if so the opening stage-direction has been crowded in above the text in the space. The word count of the page is written in pencil on each verso; on fol. 1^{v} these are added up for a total of 3,280 words. On the verso of the last leaf Cora wrote 'Play', underlined, and below it 'Must be | finished' underlined, and below that two or three illegible words, possibly 'to be offered'.

A typescript of the manuscript is preserved of fifteen leaves, the first blank except for the note 'By | STEPHEN CRANE.', the others numbered 1–14. The paper is laid (261 × 203 mm.), watermarked EXCELSIOR FINE, the vertical chainlines 27 mm. apart. The typewriter does not appear to be the Crane machine; the typing is not Cora's and may be professional. The paper is that used by Cora for typing various of Crane's poems after his death. The typist has the characteristic of spacing a question mark after the final word of a sentence. The spelling is American.

It is probable that this typescript was commissioned by Cora after Crane's death. The date of the manuscript is completely uncertain, and no reference has been found in letters or memoranda to this play and its composition unless it is the one referred to in a letter from Cora to the agent Perris at some date after September 3, 1900, in which she states, 'I enclose four short things of Mr. Crane's, "Hartwood Park", "The Man from Deluth" and the little play can be sold both in England and U. S.' (Yale). In January 1898 Crane was urging Joseph Conrad to collaborate with him on a play, but Conrad's reminiscences give a quite different plot laid in the United States (*Letters,* ed. Stallman and Gilkes [1960], p. 167). Possibly it could be fitted in before Crane left England for Cuba, but it is barely possible, also, that it was a successor to the Spanish-American War Play in 1899. If one must flip a coin, the swashbuckling romantic style might seem to resemble what was to be found more skillfully managed in *The O'Ruddy,* in which case the date might be in the spring of 1899 when Crane was desperately searching for ready money. Even as early as 1896 he had been under the delusion that he could make money with a play.

In the present reprint irregularities in the punctuation of the speech-prefixes have been silently normalized. For the names of the four guardsmen Crane sometimes placed a dash after the initial, sometimes a period, a period and dash, but often a colon and dash. In the present text all are normalized to a form like 'G.—'. The other characters' prefixes are usually followed by colons, although sometimes by dashes; however, all have been silently made uniform to be followed by a colon. Ordinarily the punctuation is found in the manuscript after the prefix but before business enclosed in parentheses. This convention has been followed, and the few cases of colons placed after the parentheses have been silently normalized. (The typescript usually treats the prefixes as described.) Occasional missing punctuation in the manuscript found in the typescript is recorded as emendations, but manuscript periods missing after the initials for characters' names in the text are silently inserted without reference to the typescript practice. Other irregularities shared by both documents are either reproduced or else are recorded as emendations, but no attempt has been made in the stage-directions to secure uniform punctuation or capitalization. Since the typescript appears to have been posthumous and to have been typed directly from the manuscript, its few verbal variants cannot be authoritative. This play has been printed by L. H. Fine, "Two Unpublished Plays by Stephen Crane," *Resources for American Literary Study,* 1 (1971), 207–216.

XXXI. THINGS STEPHEN SAYS

Five leaves of cheap wove ruled paper (188 × 115 mm.), 22 rules to the page, in a notebook kept by Cora Crane preserved in the Special Collections of the Columbia University Libraries. Written in pencil, the items (not all written down at the same time) separated by short rules. Cora seems to have made these jottings shortly after Crane's return from Cuba to England in January 1899. This is a diplomatic reprint.

XXXII. [SPANISH-AMERICAN WAR PLAY]

The Special Collections of the Columbia University Libraries hold the three documents on which the text of this untitled and unfinished play can be based.

MS: A single leaf of wove paper (263.5 × 208.5 mm.), head space 29 mm., tail space 5.5 mm., 27 gray rules 9 mm. apart, containing the autograph dramatis personae headed '*Characters*'.

TMs[a]: Twelve leaves of a blue ribbon typescript containing Act I, wove unwatermarked paper (329 × 204 mm.), lacking the dramatis personae leaf. Autograph corrections are made in black ink later than a series of pencil corrections; the pencil also made exclamation points out of typed periods.

TMs[b]: Thirty-one leaves of a black carbon typescript on the same paper. The first twelve leaves are the carbon copies of TMs[a], the pencil corrections showing through the carbon, but the ink alterations have not been transferred. The carbon of a typed dramatis personae list is prefixed. As in TMs[a], the first leaf is unnumbered, but leaves 2–12 are paged within parentheses in the upper left corner. Act II, starting page 13, is unnumbered but thereafter 2–7 are paged within parentheses in the upper left corner and the notation '(Act II)' is placed in the upper right corner. Starting with the second scene on page 8 the leaves are not numbered but the right-hand notation changes to '(Act II) | (Sc: II)' on page 9, page 8 having only the act indicator. On the verso of the final leaf appears Cora's note, 'Copy of | Cuban Play | not finished'.

The date of composition is not known, but the earliest reference preserved is a letter from Crane's American agent Paul Reynolds dated January 9, 1900:

My dear Crane,–

I have offered your play to Nat Goodwin, but have a letter returning the play to me, saying that he does not think the play suitable for the kind of part he could play.

Who else do you wish me to offer it to? [Columbia]

If the attempt to interest a producer in the play followed close after its writing, or at least after the typing, late 1899 would seem to be a possible date for its completion even though it may have been sketched in earlier. Shortly before Crane's death on June 5, 1900, Cora must have written to Reynolds from Germany, for on June 14 he responded: 'I have received your letter of June 3d asking me to send Mr. Crane's play to Brede Place, registered, care of Chatters, and I accordingly do so. [¶] I enclose letter from Mr. Gillette in regard to the play. Mr. Nat Goodwin said that the play was entirely unsuited to the kind of parts he played' (Columbia). In a lost letter Cora must have changed her mind and asked Reynolds to try another producer, or at least to hold it for her arrival in the United States, for on June 22, 1900, he wrote: 'I have your letter of June 11th. I am sorry to say that I forwarded the play registered to your address in England some little time ago. [¶] I shall be glad to see you at any time. I am generally in my office between nine and ten in the morning, and at two and at five in the afternoon' (Columbia). Finally, on July 3, 1900, Reynolds addressed Cora at Port Jervis about Crane's affairs, and included the statement, 'In regard to the Cuban War play, as Mr. Gillette has read the play and declined it, I do not think he would be likely to be willing to finish it' (Columbia), reflecting a last desperate effort by Cora to get the play completed and produced.

In the present reprint of the text the copy-text for Act I is TMs[a], including its corrections, and the copy-text for Act II is TMs[b] since TMs[a] is wanting. A substantially exact transcript has been made with very little emendation.

Various decorations of colons and hyphens about the 'Characters' and the act-scene numbers are silently omitted. The typist's intention seems to have been to place a colon after speech-prefixes. In Act I these are present for the first thirteen prefixes but toward the foot of fol. 2 they stop for the rest of the act, only to resume for the first two prefixes of Act II. The evidence would suggest that these colons were present in the copy and that the omission was due to the typist; hence they have been silently added throughout for uniformity. When a direction in parentheses follows a prefix, the usual practice in the typescript is to put the colon after the name, a convention that has been observed and the few places where the colon follows the parenthesis have been silently emended. Perhaps reflecting a change in typist starting with Act II, the spelling 'Marjory' which was invariable in Act I changes to 'Marjorie' but as early as 148.14 the original 'Marjory' begins to appear irregularly. However, the manuscript spelling is 'Marjorie' in the *Characters* leaf, and hence this variant has been adopted throughout. The typescript was first printed by R. W. Stallman in *Bulletin of the New York Public Library,* LXVII (1963), 498–511.

XXXIII. PLANS FOR NEW NOVEL

One leaf of laid paper (331 × 203 mm.) watermarked Britannia in an oval, vertical chainlines 25.5 mm. apart, 34 gray lines 9 mm. apart, head space 23 mm. and tail space 9 mm. Written in Cora's hand from dictation. On the verso is written 'Plans for | Rev. Novel'. Preserved in the Special Collections of the Columbia University Libraries. In his Introduction to THE O'RUDDY (*Works,* IV [1971], xvi–xxviii) Professor J. C. Levenson has traced in detail the process by which Crane was lured back from Cuba by the promise of a Methuen contract for a novel, subject unstated, the contract being signed in late January 1899, on his return to England. But the completion of *Active Service* intervened and it was not until July, 1899, that Crane seems to have turned for the first time to planning what he had decided would be a Revolutionary War novel. The dictation to Cora comprising the present "Plan" probably occurred in this month. Not previously printed.

XXXIV. PLANS FOR STORY

Two leaves written in Cora's hand from dictation on laid paper (330 × 202.5 mm.), watermarked ECONOMIC | H M & S, vertical chainlines 25 mm. apart, 34 gray lines 9 mm. apart, the second numbered above a semicircle. Preserved in the Special Collections of the Columbia University Libraries. In his Introduction to THE O'RUDDY (*Works,* IV [1971], xxiv–xxviii) Professor J. C. Levenson traces the history of Crane's plans for the Revolutionary War novel from August, 1899, when Crane was writing to New Jersey and to his family for information. On September 22 he finally signed with Stokes a new contract that had been drawn up on July 12 to replace the January agreement and at the same time made arrangements for books that he needed for his research to be sent him on request. The present expanded "Plans for a Story" appear to date from this month of September, for by early October his failure to secure an advance without submitting copy had led to his abandonment of the project and his turning, instead, to writing THE O'RUDDY. Copy for the first two chapters of this romance was submitted on October 21 and Crane's agent Pinker was able to arrange advances on receipt of copy from Methuen, although it was not until February 13, 1900, that Stokes in the United States agreed to advance £70 against copy that was in the mail (Levenson, pp. xlii–xliii). The language of the letter from Stokes to Pinker is interesting, especially since it marks the last reference to the Revolutionary War novel: 'we take pleasure in sending you herewith draft of Brown Bros. & Co. to your order for £70. This payment is, we understand, in advance and on account of royalty for the new, historical romance by Stephen Crane, which is to take the place of the novel of the American Revolution that he was to write for us, the latter being postponed by him. We understand that a part of the copy proportionate to the payment we are now making, is on the way to us' (Dartmouth). Not previously printed.

XXXV. THE FIRE-TRIBE AND THE PALE-FACE: PLAY

The manuscript, preserved in the Special Collections of the Columbia University Libraries, consists of six leaves of cheap wove paper (265 × 208), with 27 gray lines per page, the first leaf unnumbered but the rest paged 2–6 above a short horizontal stroke. The versos are blank except for the offset on fol. 2v in a blue-black ink of Cora's inventory notation 'Cuban Play', and the vertical notation on fol. 6v in Cora's hand, 'Fire tribe | & the Pale face'. The only holograph writing occurs when Crane wrote in blue ink, 'For the high-priest mitred' in the upper right corner of fol. 5 above the text for 163.7–29. The play otherwise is inscribed in pencil and in an unidentified hand that wrote the three preserved manuscript pages of the Spitzbergen story "The Shrapnel of Their Friends." The inscription seems to have been made from dictation and the writing shows signs of haste. It is likely that the error *hearts* at 161.19 for *hearths* found in the manuscript of the story form is a mishearing. The irregularity of commas surrounding the vocative in this inscription contrasts with the regularity in Crane's own manuscript of the story, the inconsistencies very likely due to dictation. Whether the manuscript stopped in mid-sentence at the foot of fol. 6 or continued with lost pages is not to be determined. The title on the verso of fol. 6 written by Cora indicates sufficiently that when she inventoried Crane's papers this set consisted of only six leaves.

The relation of the dramatic to the narrative form of the story is not absolutely demonstrable, but several pieces of evidence point to the justness of the conjecture that the play was the earlier. The most striking is the fact that in the play Crane had not decided on the names of Rudin and Haryid but indicated Rudin as *Name* and Haryid as *Somebody*. Also, the Singer is not present in the dramatic text although he would have been useful. It may or may not be significant that the story manuscript at 173.36 describes Lean's freckles as *charms against being killed in battle* whereas in the play manuscript the inscriber first wrote *signs of*, from dictation, but then deleted this and continued with *charms against*. In general, the development of the language in the narrative form seems on a higher level than in the dramatic.

The events of the play take place after the conclusion of the war that had served as the subject of the four Spitzbergen tales (see *Works*, VI, for texts and introductions). It is a natural inference, therefore, that the attempt at a play for a fifth followed without delay on the completion of the four tales, which seems to have taken place in November, 1899; and this hypothesis is the more reasonable in that the amanuensis employed was the same as that for the manuscript of "The Shrapnel of Their Friends" and the paper the same as that found in "The Shrapnel" and also in Edith Richie's manuscript from dictation of "The Kicking Twelfth." Whether Crane thought he saw the story he had in mind as shaping into a better play than tale or whether he was making another abortive attempt at the quick money he thought there was in a play is anybody's guess. What does seem clear is that the play bogged down in short order and Crane turned to salvaging the idea by trying to turn it into a short story.

XXXVI. THE FIRE-TRIBE AND THE WHITE-FACE

The holograph manuscript in the Special Collections of the Columbia University Libraries consists of fifteen leaves written generally in an ink now turned brownish black. Folios 1, 7–15 are on a cheap wove stock (265 × 208 mm.), lined 9 mm. apart, the same paper as found in the play manuscript, in the manuscript of "The Shrapnel of Their Friends," and that of "The Kicking Twelfth." Folios 2–3 and 5–6 are written on a laid paper (325 × 202 mm.), vertical chainlines, watermarked MILTON FINE, and lined at intervals of 8.5 mm. Folio 4 is a sheet of laid paper (325 × 202 mm.), vertical chainlines, watermarked Britannia seated within an oval. Page and cumulative word counts mostly in ink but a few in pencil appear on each verso except for fol. 15^{v}, the total on fol. 14^{v} being 8500 words. On the verso of fol. 6 Cora wrote vertically, 'The fire Tribe & the | white face | £5.5– per 1000 wds'. On fol. 13^{v} she wrote, 'Fire Tribe | Copy sent to Frederick | Remington to see | if he would | finish it Feb 7th 1901'. On fol. 15^{v} she again wrote the title vertically, 'The Pale Face & | the fire tribe'.

Crane began to write in what is now the brown-black ink, making alterations in the same ink. On fol. 3 the two paragraphs beginning 'On the evening' (168.10) and 'The shoulders of the great hills' (168.5) had originally been written in this order but Crane wrote a marginal (B) before 'On the evening' and (A) before 'The shoulders' and wrote at the head of the leaf: 'Note to typewriter: | Change paragraph A | to place of [*ditto mark*] B.' The present text gives the paragraphs in the revised order Crane wished. On fol. 4 at 170.1 the name 'Benson' was changed in pencil to 'Harding' and thereafter occasional revisions appear both in pencil and in blue ink. The inscription changes to blue ink in mid-sentence starting with 'of the new pale-faces' (172.6), and some revisions in this part appear in black ink. This black ink reappears briefly with 'He had been bereft' (178.1) but gives place again to the blue with 'The man was certainly' (178.15). At the top of fol. 11 the black ink returns when after three lines by Crane in blue (182.4–6) Cora takes over the inscription from dictation, starting with 'The chieftains grunted' (182.7) and continuing through four lines on fol. 12 '. . . demanded Lean.' (182.37). Crane then picks up again in blue ink with 'They say——" rejoined the interpreter' (182.38) and writes the rest of the page and nine lines on fol. 13, whereupon Cora resumes from dictation in mid-sentence with 'sullenly took his nine dollars, bit them, and as he was being carried away' (184.24) also in blue ink, concluding with the end of Chapter 10 at the foot of fol. 14 (185.33). In blue ink, changing then to black, Crane started Chapter 11 heading fol. 15 but broke off in mid-sentence never to resume.

Three different typescripts are preserved in the Special Collections. TMs¹ consists of sixteen (of which thirteen only are true TMs¹) sheets of wove unwatermarked paper (330 × 204 mm.) starting with page 6 'The corporal eagerly fingered the sights of his rifle' (168.36) and ending on page 21 with 'We make' (182.18). Pages 6–13 are blue ribbon copies, 14–16 green carbon and are supplied from the otherwise missing carbon of TMs², and 17–21 blue ribbon. On page 7 the name was typed 'Serjeant Benson' as in the MS original, but was altered by Crane to 'Harding' in black ink, a change that indicates the late nature of the similar MS revision at this point. Crane made four corrections in the preserved pages of this typescript. On the verso of the final leaf Cora wrote 'Copy of | Fire tribe | unfinished'.

TMs² consists of the same pages 6–21 on the same wove unwatermarked paper (330 × 204 mm.) as TMs¹ but in a different typing. TMs² is a blue ribbon copy throughout but though it begins and ends with the same words as TMs¹ and is obviously typed from TMs¹ as its copy, it is only occasionally a paginal transcript. At 170.1 the name is given correctly as 'Serjeant Harding'. A few deletions and mendings of errors are made in ink and in pencil in an unidentifiable hand, which has also marked periods into exclamation points. Why only the same pages are preserved of TMs² as in TMs¹ is a mystery.

TMs³ is a blue-ribbon typescript on twenty-five sheets of laid paper (328 × 203 mm.), vertical chainlines 28 mm. apart, watermarked BRITANNIA | [helmeted head] | PURE LINEN. On the first leaf in Cora's hand at top left is written in black ink, 'from | Mrs Stephen Crane | 6, Milborne Grove | The Boltons | South Kensington | London', this address then deleted and 'Owensboro | Ky. | U.S.A.' substituted also in black ink. Corrections in the text are made by Cora in black ink but many serious mistakes were overlooked. The typing was almost certainly Cora's own and it is clear that her copy was the original manuscript. The departures from MS by TMs¹ and TMs² are not reproduced. Moreover, several occurrences of misreading the MS handwriting appear, prominent among them being the TMs³ error 'be' for unclear MS 'lie' (167.21) and the lower-case error 'singer' (170.31) where MS had read 'Singer' but with a not clearly drawn loop for the capital. Clinching evidence is present in the TMs³ reproduction internally in a line of the end-of-the-line dittographic MS error 'that | that' (174.28). Thus TMs³ was copied from MS, posthumously, and TMs² is merely a reproduction, with occasional errors, of TMs¹ copied from MS. Only the manuscript has textual authority.

Only a few references to the Fire-Tribe story have been preserved. On January 31, 1901, the Northern Newspaper Syndicate sent Cora a cheque for £2.12.6 in payment for her story 'Cowardice' and added, 'We will let you know about the late Mr. Crane's sketches when we have all in hand. We note that you are sending others. Have you a 3,500 words story by him?' (Columbia). On the back of this letter Cora noted: 'Northern Newspaper Syndicate ans. Feb 3. [¶] Offered the Fire tribe & white face at 5 guineas a 1000 words'. On February 26, 1901, Frederic Remington responded to a lost letter from Cora: "I have read the Fire-People M.S but it is utterly impossible that I should undertake what you suggest—for the reason that I could not imitate Crane's style and that I have a very pronounced one of my own. Again I am laborious in my writing—having little facility. I am not the man to do the work although from my regard for Mr. Crane I would do anything in reason for his widow. I have a great fear that you cannot find a man who can carry Cranes master hand through so mysterious a scheme as the Fire-Tribe story but thats however. [¶] I am returning the M.S.—registered—and am appreciative of your consideration" (Columbia). Finally, on May 25, 1901, the New York agent John Russell Davidson wrote to Cora: 'I return herewith the chapters of Mr. Crane's unfinished story 'The Fire-Tribe and the White Face.' [¶] In its present state the story creates no definite impression; I can not make out the author's purpose or his plot —so far there seems to be very little suggested, and I hardly know what to say in the way of advice. [¶] It occurs to me that the material would form the basis of a rattling good story, full of action and color; but it all depends upon yourself, with the knowledge of Mr. Crane's intentions, whether you can make anything out of it or not. It would be impossible to do anything with the manuscript, as it stands—it is so meagre. Should you wish me to help you sell it, later on, when you have wrought something out of it, I shall be very glad to do so' (Columbia).

APPARATUS

[NOTE: In this section all the apparatus for each fragment is presented together. The emendations listing is followed by the alterations in the manuscript(s) and the typescript only if the typescript is the copy-text. Variants from the copy-text of any additional documents are recorded. End-of-line hyphenation for the Virginia text and for the copy-text is listed at the end of each item. The symbols and practices used in this part of the volume otherwise conform with those in the poetry section; *see* Headnote to the Poems.]

II. [TWELFTH CAVALRY AND THE INDIAN WARS]

Emendations to the Copy-Text

[The copy-text is MS: untitled manuscript in the Special Collections of Columbia University Libraries.]

93.7 command] cammand MS

93.10 Eleventh] Elevnth MS (*incomplete alteration*)

93.25 again.] ~$_{\wedge}$ MS

93.25; 94.35 Twelfth] Twelth MS

93.26 hats] hads MS

94.10–11 head$_{\wedge}$trooper] ~,~ MS (*punctuation doubtful; possibly beginning of a hyphen*)

94.15 fatigue] fatique MS

94.18 up$_{\wedge}$ to] up, too MS

94.26 disorder, horses$_{\wedge}$] ~$_{\wedge}$ ~, MS

94.30 necks] neck's MS

94.34 commander] cammander MS

94.34 lieutenant.] ~, MS

Alterations in the Manuscript

93.7 [1]said] *followed by deleted* 'sir'

93.8 against] *preceded by deleted* 'on'

93.10 Eleventh] MS 'Elevnth' *with* 'v' *inserted*

93.11 as] *possibly inserted*

93.12 we] *interlined after deleted* 'they'

93.16 'Captain] *preceded by deleted double quotes*

93.25 Twelfth] *preceded by deleted* 'c[*and possible* 'o']'

94.1 colonel] 'c' *over* 'C'

94.1 caps] *interlined after deleted* 'hats'

94.5 as] *followed by deleted* 'we wou'

94.9 rise] *an* 'a' *before* 'i' *deleted*

94.13 decent] 'c' *over beginning of an* 's'

94.27 on.] *period inserted before deleted* 'an'

94.29 but] *preceded by deleted* 'an[*and the beginning of a* 'd']'

94.30 sorry] *first* 'r' *over* 'o'

94.31 we] *preceded by deleted* 'h'

94.31 down.] *period inserted before deleted* 'ourselves'

94.32 with] 'w' *over start of another letter*

94.34 commander] MS 'cammander' *with* 'c' *over the beginning of another letter*

94.34 lieutenant. Sixteen] 'enant,' *inserted beneath hyphen at right margin;* 'S' *over* 's' *but preceding comma not altered to period*

94.36 back to the column] *interlined above deleted* 'into camp'

94.38 lose his head and] *interlined with a caret*

94.38 scamper] *followed by deleted* 'as if a-lot' (*hyphen doubtful*)

95.2 stopped] 't' *over* 'p'

95.2 we] *preceded by deleted* 'he'

End-of-the-Line Hyphenations in the Copy-Text

93.14 sometime

93.24 someone

IV. "JACK"

[MS[1]]

Emendations to the Copy-Text

[The copy-text is MS: untitled manuscript in the UVa.–Barrett Collection.]

95.6 ¶ A] *no indention* MS

95.14 around] arround MS

95.15 pursuit] persuit MS

95.21 rapidity] rapidty MS

96.8 behind] hehind MS

Alterations in the Manuscript

95.7 called] *interlined above deleted* 'named'

95.10 jaws] *interlined above deleted* 'limbs'

95.13 tail] *possibly inserted*

95.14 He] 'H' *over* 'Th' *of original* 'The'

95.15 in . . . morsel] *interlined*

95.22 had] *possibly inserted*

95.24 thicket] 'c' *over beginning of another letter, possibly an* 'n'

95.24 fact] *preceded by independently deleted* 'dig' *and beginning of another letter*

95.27 [1]with] *preceded by deleted* 'at'

96.2 part] 'p' *over* 's'

96.2 curled] *preceded by deleted* 'coiled'

96.3 This] 'i' *over* 'e'; 's' *over* 'se'

96.5 Corps.] 'C' *over* 'c'; *period inserted and followed by independently deleted* 'though the' *and* 'For instance,' *of which comma undeleted in error*

96.5 signal] *possibly inserted*

96.7 gratitude,] *followed by deleted* 'from,'; *comma undeleted in error*

96.8 behind] *followed on next line by deleted* 'behind'

96.9 meant] *followed by deleted* 'tha'

End-of-the-Line Hyphenations in the Copy-Text

95.12 everybody

95.22 overturned

[MS[2]]

Emendations to the Copy-Text

[The copy-text is MS: untitled manuscript draft in the private collection of Cdr. Melvin H. Schoberlin USN (Ret.).]

96.11 ¶ We] *no indention* MS (*word heads page*)

96.21 miniature] minerature MS

96.32 guard's] guards MS

Alterations in the Manuscript

96.11 in] 'i' *over beginning of possible* 'o'

96.13 A] *over beginning of illegible letter*

96.15 with] *interlined above deleted* 'and'

96.16 scarcely] *second* 'c' *over* 's'

96.17 his] *possibly inserted*

96.22,29 always] 'wa' *over* 'so' *of original* 'also'

96.23 when] *preceded by deleted* 'with'

96.25 call] *followed by deleted* 'him'

96.26 whose] 'ho' *over* 'as' *of original* 'was'

96.27 and] *over* 'in'

96.30 ²at] 't' *over* 'n'

96.33 and] *followed by deleted* 'twice'

End-of-the-Line Hyphenation in the Copy-Text

96.32 mealtimes

[MS³]

Emendations to the Copy-Text

[The copy-text is MS: manuscript in the UVa.–Barrett Collection.]

97.3–4 paraphernalia] paraphenalia MS

97.14 boughs] bows MS

97.18 tired,] ~‸| MS

97.22 thoroughbred] throughbred MS

97.34 around] arround MS

Alterations in the Manuscript

97.3 hats] *possibly inserted*

97.4 gentleman] 'a' *over* 'e'

97.5 on] *inserted*

97.8 hunters] *preceded by deleted* 'shots'

97.9 I,] *followed by deleted* 'don't'

97.14 hemlock] *preceded by deleted* 'bed'

97.15 comes] *followed by deleted* 'ho'

97.17 flood-] *possibly inserted*

97.19 down] *possibly inserted*

97.20 and] *interlined with a caret*

97.34 us;] *semicolon over a comma*

End-of-the-Line Hyphenation in the Copy-Text

97.12 hoe-cake

[Complete collation of MS³ versus MS²]

97.2 ¶ We] *no indention* MS²

97.3 gun-cases] ~‸~ MS²

97.3–4 ²and . . . gentleman,] *omit* MS²

97.5 hills.] hills and fish and game were plentiful. MS²

97.5–7 were . . . two] camped along a little mountain river. Two MS²

97.8–24 sporting men . . . myself.] sportsmen and myself and a Mr Northcote with a little son scarcely seven years old. MS²

97.25 caused] brought MS²

97.25 bring] take MS²

97.25 Teddie] his son MS²

97.25 off] *omit* MS²

97.26 expedition were] expedition into the wilds of the Adirondacks were MS^2

97.26–27 but . . . them.] and have no connection with this tale. MS^2

97.28 But,] $\sim_\wedge$ MS^2

97.28 golden$_\wedge$haired] $\sim$-$\sim$ MS^2

97.28–29 with merry laughter] merrily MS^2

97.29–30 sailed . . . brook] played with pebbles and minerature boats in the brook. MS^2

97.31 left a guard] had to leave a man MS^2

97.32–33 made . . . camp. Teddie] went hunting or fishing and the boy amused himself readily. He MS^2

97.34 guard.] guard to the camp and then, a call would bring him back. MS^2

97.34–35 Bears . . . sign [*end of* "Jack"]] *see* MS^2 96.26–35 '¶ He . . . charge'

V. [A SMALL BLACK AND WHITE AND TAN HOUND]

[MS^1]

[The copy-text is MS: untitled manuscript in the Special Collections of Columbia University Libraries.]

Alterations in the Manuscript

98.2 made] *followed by deleted* 'the'

98.2 ^{2}the] *interlined with a caret*

98.5 glance] *interlined above deleted* 'ray'

98.5 the old house] *interlined above deleted* 'a little unpainted cabin,' *of which* 'cabin' *preceded by deleted* 'moun'; *comma undeleted in error*

98.5 gently] *interlined with a caret*

98.6 it.] *followed by deleted* 'From the ridge came the high-keyed methodical baying of a hound on the chase.' *of which* '-keyed' *inserted*

[MS^2]

Emendation to the Copy-Text

[The copy-text is MS: untitled manuscript fragment in the Special Collections of Columbia University Libraries.]

98.11 peeked] peaked

Alterations in the Manuscript

98.8 ^{1}the] *followed by deleted* 'doo'

98.13 if] 'f' *over* 't'

98.14 stretched] *preceded by deleted* 'rubbed'

[MS^3]

Emendations to the Copy-Text

[The copy-text is MS: untitled manuscript fragment in the private collection of Cdr. Melvin H. Schoberlin USN (Ret.).]

98.22 receptacle] recepticle MS

98.24 tattoo] tatoo MS

Alterations in the Manuscript

98.18 from] *preceded by deleted* 'of'

98.19 [2]the] *preceded by deleted* 'its'

98.20 unpainted] 'un' *inserted; preceded by deleted* 'crumbling and'

98.21 house,] *comma inserted before deleted period*

98.21 fore] 'o' *over* 'a'

98.21 a] *preceded by deleted* 'the'

[MS[4]]

Emendation to the Copy-Text

[The copy-text is MS: untitled manuscript fragment in the Sepcial Collections of Columbia University Libraries.]

99.8 tattoo] tatoo MS

Alterations in the Manuscript

99.1 wagging] *preceded by deleted* 'enthusiastically'

99.4 unpainted] *preceded by deleted* 'old' *and comma not deleted in error*

99.5 a] *final* 'n' *deleted and followed by deleted* 'old'

99.6 receptacle] 'a' *over* 'i'

99.6 bones,] *preceded by deleted* 'his'; *followed by deleted* 'at his meals'

99.7 speed,] *comma altered from period; followed by deleted* 'but'

99.8 but] *preceded by deleted* 'while'

VI. [APACHE CROSSING]

[MS[1]]

Emendation to the Copy-Text

[The copy-text is MS[1]: untitled manuscript fragment in the Special Collections of Columbia University Libraries.]

99.12 misshapen] mishapen MS

Alterations in the Manuscript

99.12 town] *preceded by deleted* 'city of'

99.14 a number] 'a' *interlined above deleted* 'some'; 'number' *inserted in margin*

99.15 It] *preceded by deleted* 'The al' *and followed by deleted* 'al[and the beginning of another 'l']'

99.17 who] 'h' *over possible* 'o'

99.20 [2]the] 't' *over* 'O' *or possibly beginning of* 'A'

99.22 Simerson] 'm' *altered from* 'n'

99.22 Blazers] 's' *added*

99.24 [1]in] *inserted*

99.24 cemet'ry] *second* 'e' *inserted*

99.24 we've] ' 've' *added*

99.25 and] *preceded by deleted* 'an[*and the beginning of* 'd']'

99.25 round] 'd' *added after an apostrophe not deleted in error*

99.25 hole] *followed by deleted* 'a little h'

99.27 then] 'n' *inserted after* 'the'

99.28 Jim] *followed by deleted* 'coul'

99.29 uv] 'u' *over beginning of an* 'o'

100.2 remarked] 'ed' *added*

[MS[2]]

Emendations to the Copy-Text

[The copy-text is MS: untitled manuscript fragment in the Special Collections of Columbia University Libraries.]

100.9 ¶ "Ol'] *no indention* MS (*but short preceding line*)
100.12 ¶ The] *no indention* MS (*but short preceding line*)

Alterations in the Manuscript

100.5 cemet'ry] *apostrophe inserted after being interlined after* 'm' *and then deleted*
100.8 ²a] *inserted*
100.8 hole] *preceded by deleted* 'wh'
100.8 top] *preceded by deleted* 'door a little higher up than'

VII. [IN THE COUNTRY OF RHYMERS AND WRITERS]

[MS[1]]

Emendations to the Copy-Text

[The copy-text is MS[1]: untitled manuscript fragment in the Special Collections of Columbia University Libraries.]

100.19 ¶ "Heigho] *no indention* MS (*but short preceding line*)
100.21 ¶ "My] *no indention* MS
100.22 fantastically] fantistically MS
100.24 ¶ "My] *no indention* MS (*but short preceding line*)
100.27 ¶ "No] *no indention* MS (*but short preceding line*)
100.29 ¶ "You] *no indention* MS
101.1 her.] ~, MS
101.5 ¶ "No] *no indention* MS
101.7 ¶ "Humph] *no indention* MS (*word head page*)
101.11 travellers] traveller MS
101.23 ¶ Mary] *no indention* MS (*but short preceding line*)
101.25 Guards] Gaurds MS
101.26 ¶ "Ho] *no indention* MS (*but short preceding line*)
101.26 villain] villian MS
101.28 ¶ With] *no indention* MS (*but short preceding line*)

Alterations in the Manuscript

100.16–17 When . . . changed] *false start on verso of* page [9] *of final version* 'When little Mary Laughter awoke, the world had changed'
100.21 Heigho] 'H' *over* 'h'
100.22 in] *followed by deleted* 'paper f' *of which a final* 's' *deleted from* 'paper'
100.24 My . . . Moaner] *false start on verso* page [2] '2 || My name is Mr Rudolph Alfonso Railer' *of which* 'Railer' *probably deleted and also beneath an ink blot*
100.25 poem,] *followed by deleted* 'Pitiless'
100.26 Wrath.'] *followed by deleted closing quotes*
100.27 ignorant] *period inserted before deleted* 'but'
101.1 scowling] 'c' *over possible* 'r'
101.1 now] *preceded by deleted* 't[*and the beginning of an* 'h']'
101.2 the] *interlined*
101.2 though,] *comma over a period*
101.2 musingly.] *period altered from comma*

101.3 anyhow?] *question mark made from period or exclamation point*

101.5 want] *preceded by deleted* 'come'

101.5 here] *followed by deleted* 'anyhow'

101.8 get] *preceded by deleted* 'ever'

101.9 never] *preceded by deleted* 'go'

101.11 numbers] 's' *added; preceded by deleted* 'any' *and beginning of another letter*

101.12 going] *preceded by deleted* 'all'

101.20 men?] *question mark made from a comma*

End-of-the-Line Hyphenation in the Copy-Text

101.16 Sometime

[MS[2]]

Emendations to the Copy-Text

[The copy-text is MS: untitled manuscript fragment in the Special Collections of Columbia University Libraries.]

101.31 ¶ Along] *no indention* MS (*word heads page*)

102.7 ¶ "These] *no indention* MS (*but short preceding line*)

102.8 *et seq.* Guards] Gaurds MS

102.9 ¶ The] *no indention* MS (*but short preceding line*)

102.9 whether] wether MS

102.13 Villain] Villian MS

102.13 Van.] ~, MS

102.15 ¶ With] *no indention* MS (*but short preceding line*)

102.24 ¶ More] *no indention* MS (*but short preceding line*)

103.5,18 Plum] Plumb MS

103.7 ¶ Good] *no indention* MS (*but separated by white space*)

103.7 furiously.] ~, MS

103.9 more——"] ~" —— MS

103.10 ¶ "Your] *no indention* MS (*but short preceding line*)

103.10 shrieked] shreiked MS

103.11 Lot.] ~, MS

103.15 well-known] well-know MS

103.27 the——"] ~"—— MS

103.32 Napoleon,] ~‸ MS

103.34 ¶ As] *no indention* MS (*but short preceding line*)

Alterations in the Manuscript

101.31 Road] 'R' *over* 'r'

101.34 their] ir *added*

102.1 Travellers] 'T' *possibly over* 't'

102.3 Tosses] 'T' *over* 't'

102.3 Head] 'H' *over* 'h'

102.4 [1]by] *interlined above deleted* 'among'

102.4 greater] *preceded by deleted* 'G'

102.4 Timidity] 'T' *over* 't'

102.4 Others] 'O' *over* 'o'

102.5,9,10; 103.38 Man] 'M' *over* 'm'

102.6 O] *over* 'Oh'

102.7 in Wrath] *interlined with a caret*

102.9 The] 'T' *over* 't' *and preceded by deleted* 'And'

102.9 young] *interlined above deleted* 'Young' *of which* 'Y' *over* 'y'

102.11,20 Valiant] 'V' *over* 'v'

102.14 You] 'Y' *over* 'y'

102.15 Bold] 'B' *over* 'b'

102.16,21; 104.1,3,5 He] 'H' *over* 'h'

102.17; 103.33 Their] 'T' *over* 't'

102.17 Faces] 'F' *over* 'f'

102.18 [2]Him] 'H' *over* 'h'; *followed by deleted* 'terrificially'

102.19 roared] *followed by deleted* 'alou'

102.19(*twice*); 103.26 They] 'T' *over* 't'

102.20 enraged] *followed by deleted period*

102.22 His] *preceded by deleted* 'h[*and the beginning of an* 'i']'

102.24 More] *preceded by deleted* 'And'

102.24 young] *preceded by deleted* 'Y'

102.24–25 investigating] *preceded by deleted* 'readin'

102.25,36; 103.38 His] 'H' *over* 'h'

102.25 Him] 'H' *formed from start of* 'h'

102.26 Road,] *comma inserted before deleted period*

102.27 [2]that] *preceded by deleted* 'w[*and the beginning of an* 'h']'

102.33 Fists] *preceded by deleted* 'Face'

102.33 Me] 'M' *over* 'm'

102.33 Poetry] 'P' *over* 'p'

102.34 [2]Me] 'M' *over* 'm'

102.35 Something] 'S' *over* 's'

102.36 Young] 'Y' *over* 'y' *and preceded by deleted start of* 'Y'

102.36 Knees] 'K' *over* 'k'

102.37 Scribe] *preceded by deleted* 'great Editor'

103.8 We] 'W' *over* 'w'

103.10 Who] 'W' *over* 'w'

103.11 Stupendous] 'S' *over* 's'; *preceded by deleted* 'Daring'

103.12 Syllable] 'S' *over* 's'

103.12 Originality] 'O' *over* 'o'

103.13 every] *followed by deleted* 'single work'

103.13 Word] 'W' *over* 'w'

103.13 Poem] 'P' *over* 'p'

103.14 The] 'T' *over opening single quote*

103.14 Phrase,] *comma over colon*

103.15 Epistle] *followed by deleted* 'C'

103.15 Calliopeans] 'o' *over an upstroke*

103.15–16 Hundreds of Years] 'H' *over* 'h'; 'Y' *over beginning of* 'y'

103.16,30 Works] 'W' *over* 'w'

103.17 was] 'wa' *inserted with* 'a' *over* 'i'

103.17 Author] 'A' *over* 'a'

103.17 Eating] *preceded by deleted* 'Pulle'

103.18–19 Language] 'L' *over* 'l'

103.19; 104.1 Words] 'W' *over* 'w'

103.19 copied] *followed by deleted* 'bodily'

103.20 Directory] 'D' *over* 'd'

103.21 Times] 'T' *over* 't'

103.21 Boy] 'B' *over* 'b'

103.23 wants] *preceded by deleted* 'w[*and beginning of an* 'h']'

103.23 on] *preceded by deleted* 'an'

103.25 Copyists] 'C' *over* 'c'

103.25 They] 'T' *over another letter*

103.28 He] *preceded by deleted* 'He' *of which* 'H' *over* 'h'

103.29 This] 's' *added after* 'i' *altered from* 'e'

103.31 [2]of] *inserted*

103.32 neither] *preceded by deleted* 'nor h'

103.33 Them] 'T' *over* 't'; *preceded by deleted* 'their doings'

103.33 Sayings] 'S' *over* 's'

103.34 It] 'I' *over* 'i'

103.35 He] *preceded by deleted* 'he'

103.36 He] *preceded by deleted* 'he'; 'H' *formed from* 'K'

103.37 [2]It] 'I' *over* 'i'

103.37 that] *followed by deleted* 'all Men'

103.38 Cases] 'C' *over* 'c'; *final* 's' *added*

104.4 As] 'A' *over* 'a'; *preceded by deleted* 'And'

104.4 [1]He] 'H' *over* 'h'

104.4 [2]He] *preceded by deleted* 'he'

104.5 Him] 'H' *over* 'h'

104.5 Little] 'L' *over* 'l'
104.5 Sights] 's' *added*
104.6 Each] *possibly inserted*
104.6 [1]Other] 'O' *over* 'o'
104.7 there] 're' *over* 'ir'
104.8 Them] 'T' *over* 't'
104.8 You] 'Y' *over* 'y'
104.8 [2]Man] 'M' *over* 'm'
104.9 Answer] 'A' *over* 'a'
104.9 [2]wrote] *followed by deleted* 'first, 'Fain' *of which comma possibly over a colon*
104.10 line,] *comma over colon*
104.10 a] *over* 'I'
104.10 Dogs] 'D' *over* 'd'
104.11 Poems] 'P' *over* 'p'
104.12 thus] *final* 'ly' *deleted*
104.12 Out-cry] 'O' *over* 'o'

End-of-the-Line Hyphenation in the Copy-Text

104.12 Out-cry

[Complete collation of MS[2] versus MS[1]]

101.31 Along a winding,] Little . . . again." [*see* MS[1] *version* 100.15–101.9] [¶] By this time, they had come upon a winding‸ MS[1]
101.31 Road] road MS[2](u), MS[1]
101.31–33 East, . . . Arms.] East. Upon this road were numbers of traveller going one way. They all carried huge manuscripts under their arms. MS[1]
101.33 Timidity; Others] timidity; others MS[1]
101.34 Heads] heads MS[1]
101.34; 102.16 They] they MS[1]
101.34 Step] step MS[1]
101.34–35 Intervals] intervals MS[1]
101.35 Men] men MS[1]
101.35 Woods at the Roadside] road-side MS[1]
102.1,2 Travellers] travellers MS[1]
102.1 Sometimes] Some- | time MS[1]
102.1 One] one MS[1]
102.2 out] aloud MS[1]
102.2 Blows] blows MS[1]
102.2 Most] most MS[1]
102.3 Way,] ways‸ MS[1]
102.3 Sign] sign MS[1]
102.3 excepting defiant Tosses] except a defiant tossing MS[1]
102.3 the Head] heads MS[1]
102.4 [1]by] among MS[2](u), MS[1]
102.4 Some] some MS[1]
102.4 greater . . . Timidity] great timidity MS[1]
102.4 by Others] upon the part of those who shrunk before MS[1]
102.4–7 (*no* ¶) A . . . Wrath,] [¶] "Oh, my goodness, who are those cruel men?" cried Mary. [¶] "They, my dear," said the author as his brow darkened, MS[1]
102.8 Guards] MS[1]; Gaurds MS[2]
102.8 ‸ of the great Emperor] , a band in the service of the King MS[1]
102.9–10 The . . . beaten.] Mary and her conductor walked along the road for some distance. MS[1]
102.10 And . . . marched] Ahead of them there went MS[1]
102.11 bold . . . Valiant.] bold man. MS[1]
102.11 Him] him MS[1]
102.11–12 Number] body MS[1]
102.13 Fellow] fellow MS[1]
102.13 Villian] villian MS[1]
102.13 Van] van MS[1]
102.13 What] what MS[1]
102.14 You] you MS[2](u), MS[1]
102.14 Bundle] bundle MS[1]
102.15 Smile] smile MS[1]
102.15 Bold] bold MS[2](u), MS[1]
102.15 un- | rolled] un-rolled MS
102.15–16 Manuscript] manuscript MS[1]
102.16 It Them. And] it them to read and MS[1]

102.16 They] they MS[1]
102.16 He] he MS[2](u), MS[1]
102.16–17 in Their Faces.] at them. [*end of* MS[1] *version*]

VIII. THE CAMERA IN A COMPROMISING POSITION

Emendation to the Copy-Text

[The copy-text is MS: manuscript in the Special Collections of Columbia University Libraries.]

104.18 Co.,] ~$_\wedge$, MS

Alterations in the Manuscript

104.17 a wild] 'a' *possibly inserted*
104.17 store] *preceded by deleted* 'story'

X. [HEARKEN, HEARKEN, OH, MAN-WITH-A-COPPER-STOMACH]

Alterations in the Manuscript

[The copy-text is MS: manuscript fragment in the Special Collections of Columbia University Libraries.]

105.3 aged] *preceded by deleted* 'ol'
105.4 the] *preceded by deleted* 'his'

XI. A FLURRY OF CONDENSED MILK

Alterations in the Manuscript

[The copy-text is MS: manuscript in the Special Collections of Columbia University Libraries.]

105.6 tin plates,] *a hyphen deleted; followed by interlined deleted* 'and'
105.7 cups] *followed by deleted* 'with some'
105.7 gesticulated] 'ed' *over* 'in'
105.10 [1]wash'em,] ' 'em,' *squeezed in at end of line*
105.11 meekly] *followed by deleted* 'and'
105.11 for] *followed by deleted* 'it was'
105.12 dishes for] *interlined above deleted* 'their'
105.12 returned] *followed by deleted* 'from was'
105.13 he] *preceded by deleted* 'the little man'
105.15 adieu,] *comma inserted before deleted* 'because'
105.15 [2]the] *final* 'ir' *deleted*
105.18 once more] *interlined with a caret*

XII. A DESERTION

Emendations to the Copy-Text

[The copy-text is MS: manuscript fragment in Syracuse University Library.]

106.5–6 mopping cloths] moping clothes MS
106.14 preceding] precedeing MS
106.18 thought.] ~$_\wedge$ MS

Alterations in the Manuscript

106.1 A Desertion.] *title added later*
106.2 large hall] *upstroke of* 'h'

deletes with intent comma following 'large'
106.3 Large] 'L' *over* 'l'; *preceded by deleted* 'Two'
106.3 slammed] *preceded by deleted* 'clan' *and followed by deleted beginning of a letter*
106.6 a] *possibly inserted*
106.10 A] *interlined above deleted* 'His'
106.11–12 the marks] *interlined above deleted* 'a look'
106.12 cheer] *final* 'fu' *deleted*
106.14 spoke] *preceded by deleted* 'had'
106.16 the] *preceded by deleted* 'his'
106.16 of] *followed by deleted* 'his cock-tail'
106.17 was apparently] *interlined above deleted* 'seemed to'

XIII. [GUSTAVE AND MARIE]

Emendations to the Copy-Text

[The copy-text is MS: manuscript page on the verso of page 137 of the manuscript of *The Red Badge of Courage* preserved in the UVa.–Barrett Collection.]

106.24 solemn] solomn MS
106.25 monsieur."] ~.‸| MS

Alterations in the Manuscript

106.22 He] 'H' *over* 'h'; *preceded by deleted* 'And'
106.22 rebuff] *interlined with a caret*
106.22–23 And Madame] *interlined above deleted* 'Your mistress'
106.27 about] *interlined*
106.30 slyness] *preceded by independently deleted* 'slyly' *and* 'slyness'
106.31 There] *preceded on line above by deleted* 'Ther[*and beginning of an* 'e']'
106.31 heavy] *preceded by deleted* 'the'
106.32 him] *followed by deleted* 'with the'
107.4 born] *interlined*
107.4 she] *preceded by deleted* 'her'
107.6 windows. A] *period inserted followed by deleted* 'and'; 'A' *over* 'a'
107.6 book] *interlined*
107.6 had] *preceded by deleted* 'she'
107.7 floor] *preceded by deleted* 'dark'

XIV. LITERARY NOTES

Alteration in the Manuscript

[The copy-text is MS: manuscript in the Crane Notebook in the UVa.–Barrett Collection.]

107.10 Jones] *followed by deleted* 'of the'

XV. IN BRIEF

Emendation to the Copy-Text

[The copy-text is MS: manuscript in the Crane Notebook in the UVa.–Barrett Collection.]

107.13 St.] ~‸ MS

Alterations in the Manuscript

107.13 963] '9' *over* '3'
107.13 East] *over* 'West'
107.15 -house] *interlined*
107.15 West] 'We' *over* 'Ea'
107.15 Street] 'S' *over* 's'
107.19 be] *interlined*
107.20 the] *interlined*

XVI. [MATINEE GIRLS]

Alterations in the Manuscript

[The copy-text is MS: manuscript leaves in the Crane Notebook in the UVa.–Barrett Collection.]

108.3 once] *interlined*
108.4 my] *interlined with a caret*
108.5 himself] 'him' *over* 'my'
108.9 true] *followed by deleted period*
108.9 began] *preceded by deleted* 'was'
108.11 they] *interlined*
108.11 likely] 'ly' *added; followed by deleted* 'as not'
108.12 Just] *preceded by deleted* 'The'
108.13 or] *interlined above deleted* 'and'

XVII. [LITTLE HEAP OF MATCHES]

Alterations in the Manuscript

[The copy-text is MS: untitled fragment numbered page 2 in the Special Collections of Columbia University Libraries.]

108.17 towel] *a final* 'e' *deleted*
108.17 mingled] *followed by deleted* 'with h'
108.18 space] *followed by deleted* 'and he had'
108.21 He] *preceded by deleted* 'He' *and the beginning of another letter*
108.28 so] *followed by deleted* 'from'
108.28 look] 'lo' *over* 're'
108.31 Later,] *followed by deleted* 'h'
108.31 caused] *preceded by deleted* 'm'

XVIII. SIXTH AVENUE

Alterations in the Manuscript

[The copy-text is MS: untitled manuscript fragment in the Special Collections of Columbia University Libraries.]

109.3 who,] *interlined with a caret above deleted* 'who in the sh'; *comma added on line below preceding* 'when'
109.3 pranks.] 's' *inserted*
109.4 doors] *preceded by deleted* 'great'
109.5–6 wonderful] *preceded by deleted* 'gre[*and the beginning of an* 'a']'
109.9 street] *a final* 's' *deleted*
109.10 remain] *a final* 'ed' *deleted*

End-of-the-Line Hyphenation in the Copy-Text

109.8 street-cars

XIX. [A MOURNFUL OLD BUILDING]

[MS[1]]

Emendation to the Copy-Text

[The copy-text is MS: untitled manuscript fragment in the Special Collections of Columbia University Libraries.]

109.26,27,28 its] it's MS

Alterations in the Manuscript

109.14 building] *a final* 's' *added then deleted*
109.18 awaiting] *followed by deleted* 'progress'
109.19 downfall] *preceded by deleted* 'pro'
109.20 avenues] 's' *added*
109.23 feet] *followed by deleted* 'lik[*and the beginning of an* 'e']'
109.24 supremely] 'ly' *added*
109.27 supremely] *followed by deleted* 'tall'
109.27 proud] 'd' *over possible* 'n'

[MS[2]]

Emendations to the Copy-Text

[The copy-text is MS: untitled manuscript fragment in the Special Collections of Columbia University Libraries.]

110.4,6,19 its] it's MS
110.5 pleaing] *query* pleading *but possibly a* Crane *nonce word*

Alterations in the Manuscript

110.4 building] *followed by deleted* 'wore an air'
110.5 neighbors] *preceded by deleted* 'comp'
110.7 side-walks] *final* 's' *added*
110.12 an] 'n' *added; followed by deleted* 'front'
110.19 a] *interlined with a caret after a final* 's' *on* 'ambition' *was not completed*

[Complete collation of MS[2] versus MS[1]]

110.1 between] *omit* MS[1]
110.2 In . . . was] it was, in a way, MS[1]
110.4 seemed . . . timidly$_{\wedge}$] wore an air of timidity, MS[1]
110.4–5 upward . . . neighbors,] as if it glanced upwards at its two companions. MS[1]
110.5–7 pleaing . . . buildings."] *omit* MS[1]
110.8 ¶ It] *no* ¶ MS[1]
110.9 progress, to] progress marching MS[1]
110.10 marching] striding MS[1]
110.10–11 Already, . . . see] Already$_{\wedge}$ one could see from the roof, MS[1]
110.11 buildings,] $\sim_{\wedge}$ MS[1]
110.12 an] *omit* MS[1]
110.15–17 At . . . down.] *omit* MS[1]
110.18 Once . . . proud.] And this mournful old building stood awaiting it's turn. MS[1]
110.18–20 It . . . side.] It had once been relatively tall and supremely proud with it's feet imbedded in ruins. And it's MS[1]

XX. THE TOY SHOP

Alterations in the Manuscript

[The copy-text is MS: untitled manuscript fragment in the Special Collections of Columbia University Libraries.]

110.21 As] *interlined above deleted* 'When'

110.23 and] *followed by deleted* 'said'

110.25 then] *interlined above deleted* 'began to'

110.25 swung] 'u' *over* 'i'

110.25 puffed] 'ed' *added*

XXI. [MEXICAN SKETCH]

Alterations in the Manuscript

[The copy-text is MS: untitled manuscript fragment in the Special Collections of Columbia University Libraries.]

111.3 weary] *preceded by deleted* 'mon'

111.4 tall coils] *preceded by deleted* 'curling'

111.5 plants] *interlined with a caret*

111.7 Four] *preceded by deleted* 'A group'

111.8 straight] *inserted in left margin*

111.9 eclipsed] *preceded by deleted* 'el'

111.11 rice!] *downward stroke of exclamation added over comma which was left unaltered*

111.12 tortillas] *preceded by deleted* 'tomales and'

XXII. [FRANKLY I DO NOT CONSIDER]

Alterations in the Manuscript

[The copy-text is MS: untitled manuscript fragment in the Special Collections of Columbia University Libraries.]

111.14 not] *interlined with a caret*

111.15–16 discouraged] *followed by deleted period*

111.16 when] *followed by deleted* 'you w'

111.17 Furthermore] 'F' *over beginning of an* 'a'

XXIII. [HE TOLD ME ALL HE KNEW]

Emendations to the Copy-Text

[The copy-text is MS: manuscript in the Special Collections of Columbia University Libraries.]

111.21–22 solemnity] solemity MS

112.4,9 don't] dont MS

112.5 acquaintance] acquintance MS

112.15 can't] cant MS

Alterations in the Manuscript

111.21 but he said] 'but' *and* 'said' *followed by deleted commas*

111.24 to say] *interlined above deleted* 'to have'

111.24 deal] *followed by deleted* 'to say'

112.3 notables] 's' *added*

112.9 don't] *followed by deleted* 'kno'

112.10 the] *interlined*
112.11 this] 'i' *over* 'u'
112.11 Am] 'A' *over beginning of* 'I'
112.13 I] *preceded by deleted* 'You'

XXIV. DAN EMMONDS

Emendations to the Copy-Text

[The copy-text is TMs: ribbon typescript in the Special Collections of Columbia University Libraries.]

112.27 properly."] ~.‸ TMs
113.10 Terwilliger,"] ~", TMs
113.19 directions] dirsctions TMs
114.16 bottle."] ~". TMs
115.10 hen-coop] hen-crop TMs
115.30 I was] it was TMs
116.23–24 fire|and the] fire and| and the TMs
117.4 harp.‸] ~." TMs
117.17 barbarians."] ~‸" TMs

Alterations in the Typescript

113.6 it] 't' *in ink over typed* 'f'
115.6 -coop] *first* 'o' *altered in ink from* 'r'
116.20 again] *interlined with an ink caret*

End-of-the-Line Hyphenations in the Virginia Edition

112.25 saloon-|keeper
115.36 well-|sailed

End-of-the-Line Hyphenation in the Copy-Text

114.9 quarter-deck

XXV. [DURING A SESSION OF CONGRESS]

Emendations to the Copy-Text

[The copy-text is MS: untitled manuscript fragment in the Special Collections of Columbia University Libraries.]

117.23 American] Amer-|can MS
117.31 Southerners.] ~‸| MS
117.31–32 approaches] approachs MS
118.7 New Yorker] NYorker MS
118.10 maintenance] maintainance MS

Alterations in the Manuscript

117.22 One] *preceded by independently deleted* 'P' *and* 'The'
117.23 life.] *period preceded by deleted period*
117.23–24 education] 'ion' *over* 'ed'
117.24 Yorker] 'er' *possibly inserted*
117.30 Yorkers] *followed by deleted comma*
118.8 Providence] 'P' *over* 'p'
118.11 bill] *followed by deleted* 'erection of a light-house'
118.15 cannot] *followed by deleted* 'feel'

End-of-the-Line Hyphenation in the Virginia Edition

118.10 unheard-|of

Hyphenated at the End of the Line in the Virginia Edition and also at the End of the Line in the Copy-Text

117.26 shrewd-|looking (*i.e.* shrewd-looking)

XXVI. THE RIGHT OF ARREST

Emendation to the Copy-Text

[The copy-text is MS: untitled manuscript in the Special Collections of Columbia University Libraries.]

118.25 its] it's MS

Alterations in the Manuscript

118.24 powers] *preceded by deleted* 'previleges'
118.26 is] *preceded by the deleted beginning of an* 'a'
118.26 people] *interlined above deleted* 'society'
118.27 caution. A] *period squeezed in;* 'A' *preceded by deleted* 'in'
118.28–29 Theoretically the] 'Theoretically' *interlined; capital* 'T' *of* 'The' *not reduced in error*
118.29 first result] *interlined above deleted* 'best function'
118.29 control] *preceded by deleted* 'po[*and the beginning of* 'w']'
118.30 nullify] *preceded by deleted* 'to'
118.30–31 criminals] 's' *added*
118.31 government] *followed by deleted* 'government'
118.32 this principle] 'this' *interlined above deleted* 'its first'; *a final* 's' *deleted from* 'principle'

XXVII. [NEW YORK BOARDING HOUSE TALE]

[MS[1]]

Emendations to the Copy-Text

[The copy-text is MS[1]: untitled manuscript in the Special Collections of Columbia University Libraries.]

119.7 No.] ~$_\wedge$ MS[1]
119.23 didn't] didnt MS[1]
120.7 its] it's MS[1]
120.14 don't] dont MS[1]
120.28 state.] ~$_\wedge$| MS[1]
121.5 loneliness] lonliness MS[1]
121.23 men] man MS[1]
121.24 ogled] ogleed MS[1]
121.26 smiles] smile MS[1]

Alterations in the Manuscript

119.2 rigging] *a final* 's' *deleted*
119.5 accentuating] 'ing' *over* 'ed'; *preceded by deleted upstroke*
119.12 old] *interlined*
119.14 for a time] *interlined with a caret*
119.22 them] *preceded by independently deleted* 'New York' *and* 'to'
120.1–2 original] *first* 'i' *over* 'e'
120.4 confidentially] *inserted*
120.4 tonight.] *period over exclamation point*
120.5 from] *preceded by deleted* 'back'
120.5 with] 'w' *immediately preceded by beginning of an upstroke*
120.6 am.] *period over exclama-*

tion point which was over a dash

120.6 was] 'w' *over* 's'

120.8 cheek] *preceded by deleted* 'round'

120.8 had] *followed by deleted* 'a pink flush.'

120.9 murmured] *preceded by deleted* 'having'

120.12 third] *preceded by deleted possible* 'u[*and beginning of a* 'p']'

120.16 "Well] *first stroke of* 'W' *over* 'I'

120.23 two] 'w' *over* 'o'

120.28 man] *interlined with a caret*

120.31 gulf] 'f' *over* 't'

121.3 mood] *preceded by deleted* 'lonely'

121.7 [2]the] *preceded by deleted* 'when'

121.7 he] *preceded by beginning of deleted probable* 'h'

121.10 roar,] *comma inserted before deleted* 'of the city'

121.10 passed] 'ed' *interlined above deleted* 'ing'

121.15 floor] *followed by deleted* 'with em'

121.15 embarrassment.] *followed by deleted* 'The shoe-clerk men of the'

121.16 young] *interlined with a caret*

121.16 women] *followed by deleted* 'had'

121.21 The] *preceded by deleted* 'Later'

121.24 he] *followed by deleted* 'seemed to'

121.24 ogled] 'ed' *inserted before deleted* 'in'; 'e' *of original* 'ogle' *not deleted in error*

121.26 would] *followed by deleted* 'have'

121.29 large] *interlined above deleted* 'far'

End-of-the-Line Hyphenations in the Copy-Text

120.1 shoe-clerks

120.22 gas-jet

[MS[2]]

Emendations to the Copy-Text

[The copy-text is MS[2]: untitled manuscript in the Special Collections of Columbia University Libraries.]

122.9; 125.11; 126.10 No.] ~‸ MS[2]

122.25; 123.17,23,25; 126.18 don't] dont MS[2]

123.2 ain't] aint MS[2]

123.16 tonight] ~-|~ MS[2]

123.21 Why——"] ~"—— MS[2]

123.35 least] last MS[2]

124.18 didn't] didnt MS[2]

124.29 its] it's MS[2]

125.17 isn't] isnt MS[2]

127.8 loneliness] lonliness MS[2]

127.22 men] man MS[2]

127.32 affected] effected MS[2]

128.5 receive] recieve MS[2]

128.5 smiles] smile MS[2]

Alterations in the Manuscript

122.8 part] *followed by deleted period*

122.9 their] 'ir' *over* 're'

122.11–12 house, prepared . . . age.] *comma inserted before deleted period;* 'prepared . . . age.' *interlined with a caret which is over the deleted period*

122.12 Thorpe,] *comma squeezed in beneath final* 'e'

122.14 in] *followed by deleted* 'the'

122.20 past him] *preceded by deleted* 'toward him'

122.23 making] *interlined above deleted* 'cutting'

122.26 one] *interlined with a caret*
122.28 Thorpe] *a final* 's' *deleted*
122.31 the] 't' *over* 'a'
122.31 And] 'd' *over* 'y'
122.32 could] *followed by deleted* 'give'
122.35 her?] *question mark over a period*
123.10 gazed] 'g' *altered from* 'sc'
123.11 way] *followed by deleted* 'and'
123.22 wrong] *preceded by possible deleted quote marks*
123.23 said] *preceded by deleted illegible letter*
123.29 street] *preceded by deleted* 'way'
123.29 expressing] *followed by deleted* 'thei[*and the beginning of an* 'r']'
123.32 There] 'r' *over* 'i'
124.11 it] *interlined with a caret*
124.12 which] *followed by deleted* 'is always'
124.12 chase] *preceded by deleted* 'sen'
124.13 in search of] *interlined with a caret above deleted* 'to seek'
124.22 it] *preceded by deleted* 't[*and beginning of an* 'h']'
124.22 drew] *followed by deleted* 'up'
124.29 power] *preceded by deleted* 'ener[*and beginning of a* 'g']'
124.36 In] *preceded by deleted* 'Before'
125.1 past] *followed by deleted* 'in'
125.2 At] *followed by deleted* 'anothe'
125.3 and] *preceded by deleted* 'while'
125.3 from] 'f' *over* 'o'
125.4 at] *preceded by deleted* 'by'
125.5 engaged] *preceded by deleted* 'expound'
125.9 numerals] *preceded by deleted* 'numb'
125.12 necktie] *followed by deleted comma*
125.13 Yorkers] 's' *added*
125.14 was] *preceded by deleted* 'd'
125.27 lit] *interlined above deleted* 'turned up'
126.7 virtue] *preceded by deleted* 'boarding-h'
126.12 he] *initial* 's' *deleted*
126.18 to] *followed by deleted* 'see'
126.23–24 and so] *inserted before deleted* 'but'
126.32 and] *followed by deleted* 'then'
127.14 entered through the] *interlined above deleted* 'came in at the'
127.14 unclean panes of the] *interlined with a caret*
127.24 retreating] *first* 'r' *over beginning of possible* 'g'
127.29 him] *followed by deleted* 'with'
127.30 water] *preceded by deleted* 'his'
127.33 she] 's' *inserted*
127.33 tipped] *inserted before deleted* 'held'
127.34 She] *preceded by deleted* 'She'
128.3 in] *followed by deleted* 'what the'
128.3 exasperatingly] *preceded by deleted* 'too bold' *and the beginning of an* 'a'
128.4 confident.] *period inserted before deleted* 'as if she would descend a'
128.4 It] *preceded by deleted* 'Ap'
128.12 His] 'is' *over* 'e'
128.13 him] *followed by deleted period*
128.14 recognize] *preceded by deleted* 'know'

End-of-the-Line Hyphenations in the Virigina Edition

125.2 hand-|organ
125.24 out-|lying
126.25 gas-|jet

End-of-the-Line Hyphenation in the Copy-Text

125.20 shoe-clerk

Hyphenated at the End of the Line in the Virginia Edition and also at the End of the Line in the Copy-Text

123.35 land-lady (*i.e.* landlady)

[Complete collation of MS^2, the final preserved manuscript, and MS^1, the early draft]

122.2 street$_\wedge$] $\sim$, MS^1
122.2 tiny] *omit* MS^1
122.2 riggings] rigging MS^1
122.2–3 grew like grass. They] *omit* MS^1
122.3 water] steel-colored water MS^1
122.3–4 which . . . Slanting] and slanting MS^1
122.4 southern side] southside MS^1
122.6 northern] northward MS^1
122.6–7 resplendent, . . . topaz,] resplendent$_\wedge$ MS^1
122.7–8 at . . . shadows] the sombre growing shadow MS^1
122.8 and . . . street] *omit* MS^1
122.10 Two] The two MS^1
122.10 shoe-store] $\sim_\wedge\sim$ MS^1
122.11 house,] $\sim_\wedge$ MS^1
122.12 an] the MS^1
122.13 took] came with MS^1
122.13–14 from . . . He] and MS^1
122.15 at . . . landing] *omit* MS^1
122.15 Trixell,] The four old ladies went at once to their rooms panting up the flights. Trixell, MS^1
122.15 ^{1}a] *omit* MS^1
122.15–16 flower$_\wedge$shop] flower-store MS^1
122.17 that$_\wedge$ perhaps$_\wedge$ the] , perhaps, that the MS^1
122.18–19 ^{2}and . . . ^{1}her] of going with her MS^1
122.19–20 Four . . . him.] *omit* MS^1
122.22–124.14 book-keeper . . . sentence.] *pages lacking* MS^1
124.15 III] II. MS^1
124.16 on] almost all over the city on MS^1
124.17 street$_\wedge$ . . . city.] street-car-lines. MS^1
124.20 There . . . Thorpe] It was the opening gun. Thorpe then MS^1
124.21–22 at . . . theory.] one of the shoe-clerks ventured some original theories. MS^1
124.22–24 Trixell . . . eloquence.] *omit* MS^1
124.25 A] The other MS^1
124.25 backward] back MS^1
124.27 lock] stray lock MS^1
124.27 temple] temples MS^1
124.28 foot] foot however MS^1
124.28 in] to and fro in MS^1
124.29 power] energy MS^1
124.30 pink.] pink. "Yes, I'm very tired!" MS^1
124.32 success$_\wedge$] $\sim$, MS^1
124.33 comrade] comrade clerk MS^1
124.34–126.15 On . . . smiling] *pages lacking* MS^1
126.16 answered] said MS^1
126.18 but] and MS^1
126.18 take] look for MS^1
126.19 a . . . mine.] my cousin. MS^1
126.20 reflected] reflected for a time MS^1

126.22–23 indifference$_{\wedge}$] ~, MS[1]
126.23–24 thief and so] thief but MS[1]
126.24 humbly and] *omit* MS[1]
126.24–25 gratefully:] ~$_{\wedge}$ MS[1]
126.25 She (*no* ¶)] ¶ MS[1]
126.26 in . . . words] *omit* MS[1]
126.27 there] then MS[1]
126.28 bed-room$_{\wedge}$] ~-~, MS[1]
126.28 grey$_{\wedge}$] ~, MS[1]
126.29 observed] said MS[1]
126.30–33 He . . . thief.] *pages lacking* MS[1]
127.1 thoug<[ht]>] reflected MS[1]
127.1 the dim] these vague MS[1]
127.5 tones] mellow tones MS[1]
127.6–7 he . . . wonder] in his mood he wondered MS[1]
127.7 could] if MS[1]
127.8 know] understood MS[1]
127.10 VII] *omit* MS[1]
127.11–12 [3]the . . . mind] a conviction MS[1]
127.12 overslept] over-slept MS[1]
127.13–14 Dusky . . . window.] *omit* MS[1]
127.14 The] From the streets came the MS[1]
127.15 came . . . streets] *omit* MS[1]
127.16 house,] ~$_{\wedge}$ MS[1]
127.16–17 its . . . cobbles] *omit* MS[1]
127.17 a] *omit* MS[1]
127.17 innumerable] *omit* MS[1]
127.17 Then at (*no* ¶)] ¶ At MS[1]
127.20 basement$_{\wedge}$] ~, MS[1]
127.21 paused] paused in the middle of the floor MS[1]
127.21 seeing . . . him] *omit* MS[1]
127.22 men] man MS[2]
127.23 plates$_{\wedge}$] ~, MS[1]
127.26–35 At . . . eggs.] *pages possibly lacking* MS[1]
127.36 ¶ During] ¶ The five young men | ¶ During MS[1] ('The . . . men' *possibly not deleted in error*)
128.1 clerks] man MS[1]
128.2 that . . . clerk] he MS[1]
128.2 ogled] ogleed MS[1] (*in error when* 'ed' *added to* 'ogle')
128.3 a . . . boarder] what was MS[1]
128.3 exasperatingly] a MS[1]
128.4 confident.] exasperatingly confident$_{\wedge}$ MS[1]
128.4 It . . . girl] manner as if she MS[1]
128.5 receive] recieve MS[2]
128.5 these] those MS[1]
128.6 soon] just MS[1]
128.6 bread$_{\wedge}$] ~, MS[1]
128.6–15 And . . . boarder.] *pages lacking* MS[1]
128.15 [*omit*]] The cousin who was expected to give him employment was said to live at one of the large hotels and so he started soon after breakfast to find him. He enquired until he came to the great structure towering above him in an MS[1]

XXVIII. CHURCH PARADE

Emendation to the Copy-Text

[The copy-text is MS: untitled manuscript fragment in the Special Collections of Columbia University Libraries.]

128.23 its] it's MS

Alterations in the Manuscript

128.18 in] *followed by deleted* 'driving'
128.19 ignoring] *followed by deleted* 'a'
128.21 left] *interlined with a caret above deleted* 'right'
128.24 is] *interlined with a caret*
128.24 A] *interlined with a caret above deleted* 'The'

XXIX. AND HIS NAME SHALL BE CALLED UNDER TRUTH

Alterations in the Manuscript

[The copy-text is MS: a fragment written on a British Telegram blank in the Special Collections of Columbia University Libraries.]

128.27 shall] 'h' *over possible* 'w'
128.27 truth] *preceded by deleted* 'the'
128.27 because] 'c' *over beginning of possible* 'g'

XXX. [PLAY SET IN A FRENCH TAVERN]

Emendations to the Copy-Text

[The copy-text is MS: manuscript in the Special Collections of Columbia University Libraries. The other text collated is TMs: typescript also at Columbia.]

129.2 L.] TMs; ∼, MS
129.3 R.] TMs; ∼, MS
129.5 eh?"] TMs; ∼?∧ MS
129.16 fighting?"] V; ∼?∧ MS, TMs
129.17–18 fighting?"] TMs; ∼?∧ MS
129.22 prayers] V; prays MS,TMs
129.23 guardsmen] TMs; gaurdsmen MS
129.27 villain] TMs; villian MS
129.33 privilege] TMs; previlege MS
130.6 gentleman] TMs; gentlemen MS
130.19 go——"] TMs; ∼"—— MS
130.24 villain] V; villian MS,TMs
130.29; 133.15 don't] TMs; dont MS
131.2 meditations."] TMs; ∼.∧ MS
131.8 shatters.)] TMs; ∼∧) MS
131.14 guards] TMs; gaurds MS
131.15 storm-king."] V; ∼-|∼.∧ MS; ∼∧∼."TMs
131.16 draw?"] TMs; ∼?∧ MS
131.28 insult?"] V; ∼." MS; ∼."' TMs
131.29 insult."] TMs; ∼∧" MS
131.36 churnfull] V; churnful MS,TMs
131.38 Coward!"] V; ∼!∧ MS,TMs
131.39 'Coward∧'!] TMs; '∼!'! MS
132.3 -eater?"] TMs; -∼?∧ MS
132.12 "'At daylight'!"] V; "'∼ ∼∧!" MS; "∧∼ ∼∧!" TMs
132.15 present] TMs; presnt MS (*doubtfully*)
133.5 have——"] TMs; ∼"—— MS
133.12 backs——"] TMs; ∼"—— MS
133.13 Say∧] V; ∼, MS,TMs
133.15 more——"] V; ∼"—— MS,TMs
133.18 G., B. and A.] V; G., B, A. MS; G.∧B. and A. TMs
133.28 eighth——"] V; ∼"—— MS,TMs
133.36 stranger.] TMs; ∼) MS
133.36 landlord.] TMs; ∼∧ MS
133.37 health!"] V; ∼!∧ MS,TMs
133.38 red.] TMs; ∼∧ MS
133.40 it.] TMs; ∼∧ MS
134.2 Flanders——"] V; ∼"—— MS,TMs
134.2 pantomime] TMs; pantomine MS
134.18 G.] TMs; G∧ MS
134.30 *et seq.* doctor] TMs; docter MS
135.2 its] TMs; it's MS
135.3 young!!"] TMs; ∼!!∧ MS
135.5 A.,] V; ∼∧, MS; ∼-∧ TMs
135.6 red.)] TMs; ∼.). MS
135.14 country."] TMs; ∼.∧ MS
135.15 Well——"] V; ∼"—— MS,TMs

135.16 truth——"] TMs; ~"—— MS

135.17 seems——"] TMs; ~"—— MS

135.33 accommodating] V; accomadating MS,TMs

135.33–34,37 acquaintance] TMs; acquintance MS

136.8 occasionally.] TMs; MS *punctuation unclear*

136.9 I——"] V; ~"——MS,TMs

136.21 them.] TMs; ~‸ MS

136.28 villainous] V; villianous MS,TMs

136.29 ‸Come] TMs; "~ MS

136.31 woman] TMs; women MS

136.38 ‸Sir——"] V; ‸~"—— MS; "~"—— TMs

137.4 Well——"] V; ~"—— MS,TMs

137.6 scrape] TMs; scrap MS

137.10 I——"] V; ~"—— MS, TMs

137.26 heaven——"] V; ~"—— MS,TMs

137.35 here‸to] TMs; ~-~ MS

138.2 (Exit . . . C.)] V; ‸~ . . . ~.‸ MS,TMs

Alterations in the Manuscript

129.1 Interior of] *interlined; followed by* 'A' *which was not reduced in error*

129.12,13 woman] 'a' *over* 'e'

129.17 right] *preceded by deleted* 'to'

129.19 A.] *inserted before deleted* 'B.'

129.19 is] *interlined above deleted* 'was'

129.20 fight?] *question mark over exclamation point*

129.21 'Who'] 'W' *altered from* 'w' *and also over a single quote; present opening single quote inserted*

129.21 question] *final* 's' *deleted*

129.23 rusting] *followed by deleted* 'away'

129.24 one] 'e' *followed by upstroke of possible* 's'

129.26 look! Perhaps] *exclamation point over comma;* 'P' *over* 'p'

129.27 will] *followed by deleted* 'dra'

129.29 thumbs?"] *question mark over beginning of* Crane's *circled period*

130.4 all] *possibly inserted*

130.5 landlord] *followed by deleted* 'since'

130.6 second,] *preceded by deleted* 'first,'

130.8 Generous] 'n' *altered from* 'r'

130.8 For] *preceded by deleted* 'Unselfish'

130.9–10 provincials] 's' *added*

130.10 sword-play] *followed by deleted* 'for miles'

130.12 a cudgel] *preceded by deleted* 'the use of'

130.12 [2]a] *interlined*

130.16 Landlord!] 'an' *over illegible letters and exclamation point altered from question mark*

130.18 [1]No,] *preceded by deleted* 'Nay'

130.20 travel] *final* 'led' *deleted*

130.23 have] *preceded by deleted* 'do you'

130.25 B.—] *dash inserted*

130.25 P—] *over* 'G' *or possibly* 'H'; *inserted over beginning of dash*

130.28 there] 'r' *over* 's'

130.31 loudly?] *question mark over period*

130.33 distasteful] *preceded by deleted* 'excee'

130.34 bottles] *interlined above deleted* 'crockery'

131.3 may] *interlined above deleted* 'can'

131.3 call] *preceded by deleted* 'the'

131.8 floor] *preceded by deleted* 'gr[*and beginning of* 'o']'

131.10 too much] *followed by deleted* 'to'

131.11 [2]turn!] *exclamation point altered from period*
131.14 mad?] *question mark over period*
131.14–15 'a man . . . peace'] *opening quote inserted*
131.19 now] *interlined with a caret*
131.21 courage?] *question mark over period*
131.24 can] *interlined above deleted* 'could'
131.24 with?] *followed by deleted* 'Do you think I have drawn my sword to reason with you?" '
131.34 I] *over* 'a'
131.34 admitted] *preceded by deleted* 'ad[*and upstroke*]'
131.37 sword?] *question mark over period*
132.2 landlord] 'o' *over* 'r'
132.3 me] *interlined above deleted* 'him'
132.5 (interfering)] *parentheses possibly inserted and followed by deleted opening parenthesis*
132.15 riding] 'in' *over* 'ng'
132.15 present] MS *doubtful* 'presnt' *with* 'nt' *added later*
132.16 am come] *interlined above deleted* 'am down'
132.18 horses.] *followed by deleted double quotes*
132.18 I] *over upstroke*
132.19 And] 'A' *over possible beginning of an* 'I'
132.19 that] *followed by deleted* 'I'
132.23 riding?] *question mark over period*
132.28 "My] *preceded by deleted* ' "Had I'
132.28 lord will] *beginning stroke of* 'w' *deletes with intent comma following* 'lord'
132.29 that] *preceded by deleted* 'for'
132.29 great] *followed by deleted* 'lor[*and beginning of* 'd']'
132.37 as] *interlined with a caret*
132.38 thrill] *preceded by deleted* 'join us'
132.39 your] *preceded by deleted* 'let us'
133.4 one of the] *interlined above deleted* 'the'
133.14 gentlemen] *followed by deleted closing double quotes*
133.18 "My] *preceded by deleted* ' "Doubtless'
133.21 no] 'o' *over illegible letter; followed by deleted* 'amount'
133.22 wasted] 'w' *over* 'm'
133.26 too,] *interlined with a caret*
133.29 shrivelled] 'led' *inserted*
133.30 indifference] *interlined above deleted* 'satiety'
133.36 eight] *a final* 'h' *deleted*
133.36 Exit landlord)] *interlined below* MS '(Drinks to stranger)' *with closing parenthesis not deleted in error*
133.37 Gentlemen] *third* 'e' *over* 'a'
133.39 Landlord] 'L' *over opening double quotes*
134.12 is] *followed by deleted* 'not'
134.15 bottle] *preceded by deleted* 'drop'
134.19 P—?] *question mark over exclamation point*
134.20 coin] *interlined above deleted* 'sou'
134.21 P—.'] *single quote over probable double quotes*
134.24 figure—] *followed by deleted closing parenthesis*
134.29 fellow.] *period over exclamation point*
134.29 Is he] *interlined above deleted* 'If he is'
134.30 doctor.] MS 'docter.' *with circled period over closing quotes*
134.34 man!"] *followed on the line below by deleted* '(Turns again)'
135.2 its] MS 'it's' *preceded by deleted* 'his'

135.12–13 gentlemen] *third* 'e' *over* 'a'
135.19 think] *interlined with a caret*
135.19 cutthroats?] *question mark possibly altered from an exclamation point*
135.21 surrounded] *followed by deleted* 'on'
135.22 careless] 'a' *over* 'r'
135.26 walked] *preceded by deleted* 'wa'
135.28 a] *interlined with a caret; preceded by deleted* 'his'
135.29 told] *preceded by deleted* 'had a'
135.30 it] *followed by deleted* 'to'
135.32 our] 'o' *over* 'm'
135.33–34 acquaintance] MS 'aquintance' *interlined above deleted* 'friend'
135.34 friend] *interlined above deleted* 'companion'
135.36 known] *interlined with a caret*
135.37 friend] *preceded by deleted* 'frien'
135.37 had been] *interlined above deleted* 'was'
135.38 king,] *comma inserted before deleted* 'bec[*and beginning of an* 'a']'
136.8 occasionally.] MS 'occasionally |' *followed by deleted closing double quotes; above* 'y' *is a mark possibly intended for a dash or a period*
136.10 us what] *followed by deleted* 'us' *and the beginning of* a 'w'
136.11 gentleman] 'a' *over* 'e'
136.14 gentlemen] *third* 'e' *over* 'a'
136.16 am] *interlined with a caret*
136.17 child.] *period inserted before deleted comma and* 'the real heir to [*followed by deleted* 'the'] my estate of E—.'
136.31 "Aye] *preceded by deleted* ' "Come' *with* 'A' *written over* 'C' *in an attempt to over-write* 'Aye'
136.32 Come] 'C' *over closing double quotes*
136.34 (Shrugging] *parenthesis over opening double quotes and beginning of an* 'I'
136.38 Sir] 'S' *over closing double quotes*
137.6 scrape?] MS 'scrap?' *followed by deleted closing double quotes*
137.7 sing!] *exclamation point inserted before deleted* 'us a'
137.13 me.] *period over an exclamation point*
137.17 [1]I] *over* 'a'
137.17 servingm'n] 'i' *possibly altered from* 'a'
137.25 "An] 'A' *over* 'H'
137.31 child] *interlined above deleted* 'thing'
137.36 Draws and] *interlined with a caret with following* 'A' *of* 'Advances' *not reduced in error*
137.37 man] *preceded by deleted* 'corpse or'

End-of-the-Line Hyphenations in the Copy-Text

130.24 Landlord
130.39 hail-storm
131.15 storm-king
132.10 hangdog
134.4 inn-keeping
134.35 gentlemen
135.38 somewhere

[Collation of MS versus TMs, substantives only]

129.2 before] and before TMs
129.24 where one] where one | where one TMs
130.3 you,——, I] ~,—— I TMs
130.6 gentleman] gentlemen MS

130.15; 131.6 (bawling)] (brawling) TMs
130.16–17 Landlord! . . . [2]Landlord!] *omit* TMs
131.15 peace] repose TMs
131.21 poisonous] poisoned TMs
131.26 any] my TMs
132.1 that] *omit* TMs
133.18 and] *omit* MS
134.12 Mon.] Mons. TMs
134.12 he] *omit* TMs
134.17 of] if TMs
134.25 can] *omit* TMs
135.22 Gentlemen] Gentleman TMs
135.29 friend] friend of TMs
136.31 woman] women MS
137.5 [2]Nonsense!] *omit* TMs
137.6 scrape] scrap MS
137.14 even] ever TMs
137.17 servingm'n] serving-man TMs

XXXI. THINGS STEPHEN SAYS

Alterations in the Manuscript

[The copy-text is Cora's notebook in the Special Collections of Columbia University Libraries.]

138.6 Leuitenant of Cavelry] *interlined with a caret above deleted* 'private'; 'v' *of* 'Cavelry' *over* 'l'
138.12 —his] *dash interlined*
138.16 because] 'b' *over possible* 'f'
138.28 A] *preceded by deleted* 'Picked up'
139.6 types] 'y' *over illegible letter*
139.10 &] *over period undeleted in error*
139.11 Printed] 'r' *over possible* 'i'
139.11 friends] *followed by deleted closing double quotes*
139.15 McCrady] 'C' *over beginning of another letter*
139.15 Three Sealers] MS *unclear*
139.16 all & each] *interlined with a caret*
139.17 thermometer's] *first* 'r' *and* 'm' *over* 'mo'; ''s' *inserted*
139.20 Open] 'O' *over* 'S'
139.23 of] *over illegible letters*

XXXII. [SPANISH-AMERICAN WAR PLAY]

Emendations to the Copy-Text

[The copy-text for lines 139.27–140.8 is TMs[b]: black carbon typescript in the Special Collections of the Columbia University Libraries. The other text collated is MS: manuscript at Columbia. The copy-text for lines 140.9–147.31 is TMs[a]: blue ribbon typescript at Columbia. TMs[b] is the copy-text for 147.32–158.22. The designation TMs without superscript indicates an agreement of TMs[a] and TMs[b] where both are present. Colons have been placed after the name of each character as in the first two pages of TMs; after that TMs lacks punctuation to a large degree, but occasionally has periods and once reverts to colons for half a page.]

139.27–140.8 *Mr.* . . . Troop. (*centered*)] MS; *flush* TMs[b]
139.27 *Mr.*] V; ~‸ TMs[b],MS
139.27 Cuba.] V; ~‸ TMs[b], MS
140.2 *Aguilar*:] V; ~,: TMs[b]; ~, MS
140.4 No.] V; ~‸ TMs[b], MS
140.8 *Brown*:] V; ~‸ TMs[b], MS

140.19 Linares."] V; ~.ₐ TMs

140.23 *et seq. except at* 147.35; 148.4,6,9,17,22,36 *Marjorie*] V; *Marjory* TMs

140.23 *et seq. except at* 145.17,21; 146.20; 150.18; 153.4; 157.17 dreadful——"] V; ~"—— TMs (*et seq. in this instance refers to the position of the closing quotes and the dash*)

140.29; 141.1,8 Patricio] V; Patracio TMs

141.4 "O] V; ₐ~ TMs

143.12 intention] V; imtention TMs

143.20 gradually more] V; gradu-allymore TMs

144.1,6 *Patten*] V; *Pattern* TMs (*not italicized at* 144.6)

144.4,7 *Stilwell*] V; Stilwell TMs

144.6 affair?"] V; ~?ₐ TMs

144.21 troop] V; tropp TMs

144.34 you."] V; ~". TMs

144.35 him] V; hom TMs

146.24 Thorpe] V; War Corres. TMs

146.25 deferentially] V; differen-tially TMs

146.30 *Thorpe*] V; *War Corres.* TMs

147.25 *Patten*] V; Patten TMs

147.25 interrupting] V; interupt-ing TMs

147.25 won't] wont TMs

148.13 welfare] V; wellfare TMs[b]

150.4,12,14,26 (*twice*); 154.14,25, 34; 155.15 Mr.] V; ~ₐ TMs[b] V; ~.—finally TMs[b]

151.13 dreadful, and] V; ~. and TMs[b]

152.28 immediately.— Finally] V; ~.—finally TMs[b]

153.35; 155.38; 156.27 won't] V; wont TMs[b]

154.25 me] V; mr TMs[b]

154.37 Use] V; use TMs[b]

154.38 Serjt.] V; ~ₐ TMs[b]

155.8 Krag] V; Craig TMs[b]

155.30; 157.19 coolly] V; cooly TMs[b]

156.16 (moves] V; (Moves TMs[b]

156.30 withhold] V; withold TMs[b]

157.3 (impatiently] V; (inpa-tiently TMs[b]

157.8 (turning] V; (Turning TMs[b]

157.12 (The] V; ₐ~ TMs[b]

157.28 to.] V; ~ₐ TMs[b]

157.29 amusing] V; ammusing TMs[b]

Alterations in the Manuscript

[For lines 139.27–140.8 there is a leaf in Crane's hand.]

139.27 *Stilwell*] *altered from* 'Stillwall' *though* 'a' *uncertain*

139.27 sugar-planter] '-planter' *interlined above a hyphen* (*which was not deleted in error*) *following* 'sugar'

140.7 *Sylvester . . .* Eclipse.] *in-terlined in* MS

Alterations in the Typescript

[There is a blue ribbon for lines 140.9–147.31 and a black carbon for the entire text. The carbon is not corrected as fully as the ribbon.]

141.11 scandalized] *interlined in ink above deleted* 'scandnlised' *of which* 'c' *over* 'a'; *carbon not marked*

141.15 in,] *comma inserted in ink; carbon not marked*

141.18 first] *interlined with a caret in ink; carbon not marked*

141.26 of] *interlined with a caret in pencil; comes through on carbon*

141.28; 142.18 insult'] *apostro-phe added in ink; carbon not marked*

141.35 he's] *apostrophe inserted in pencil; comes through on carbon*

142.1 convince'] *apostrophe added in ink; carbon not marked*

142.8 move] *interlined in pencil above deleted* 'war'; *comes through on carbon*

142.12 fight'] *apostrophe added in ink; carbon not marked*

142.19 C,] *interlined with a caret in ink, and* 'C' *over downstroke; carbon not marked*

143.15 in] *interlined with a caret in ink; carbon not marked*

143.16 Won't] 't' *typed over apostrophe in error*

143.27 "I] *preceded at margin point by* 'Patten' *deleted in ink; carbon not marked*

143.31 Sir?] *question mark added in ink over typed period; carbon not marked*

143.35 icily] *followed by ink-deleted* 'during some muffled sounds of a disturbance, L' *with period and closing parenthesis deleted in error; carbon not marked*

144.1 assaulting] *second* 'a' *inserted with a caret in ink; carbon not marked*

144.2 a muffled] *interlined in ink above deleted* 'the'; *carbon not marked*

144.3 begins . . . L] *interlined in ink above deleted* 'increases'; *carbon not marked*

144.8 him away] *preceded at foot of preceding page by pencil-deleted* 'him away'; *comes through on carbon*

144.13 done. That's] *period inserted in ink and* 'T' *over* 't'; *carbon not marked*

144.20 hope] *followed by type-deleted* 'you'; *deletion strengthened in pencil which comes through on carbon*

144.21 outside—] *typed dash over period*

144.33 Thorpe] *interlined with a caret in ink above deleted* 'war-correspondent'; *carbon not marked*

144.34 *Thorpe*] 'Thorpe' *interlined in ink above deleted* 'War Corres.'; *carbon fixed in strange hand*

144.34 (over] *pencil parenthesis over double opening quotes; comes through on carbon*

144.38 Thorpe."] *added in ink after deleted* 'war'; *carbon fixed in strange hand*

144.39; 145.4; 146.22,25 *Thorpe*] 'Thorpe' *interlined in ink above deleted* 'War Corres.'; *carbon not marked*

144.39 What's] *apostrophe inserted in ink and* 'i' *of* 'is' *deleted; carbon not marked*

145.2 *Thorpe:* (mystified)] *interlined in ink above deleted* 'War Corres.'; *carbon not marked*

145.15 see?] *question mark altered in ink from a period; carbon not marked*

145.26 people's] *apostrophe inserted in pencil; comes through on carbon*

146.1 superior] *followed by pencil-deleted* 'officer'; *comes through on carbon*

146.18 another] *followed by pencil-deleted apostrophe; comes through on carbon*

146.30 What? To] *ink question mark inserted and* 'T' *over* 't'; *carbon not marked*

146.37,40 battalion] *a second* 'l' *deleted in ink; carbon not marked*

147.8 mens] 's' *inserted in ink; carbon not marked*

147.10 —a few.] *interlined in ink above deleted* 'thirty six.'; *carbon not marked*

147.11 the] *interlined with a caret in ink; carbon not marked*

147.12 some] *interlined in ink above deleted* 'thirty six'; *carbon not marked*

147.15 proceedings] *followed by pencil-deleted period; comes through on carbon*

147.30 (CURTAIN)] *end of ribbon copy*

148.3 anybody] 'body' *interlined above deleted* 'one'; *carbon impression*

148.18 ²that] 'at' *over* 'e'; *carbon impression*

148.24 authority] 'u' *inserted with a caret*

149.4 *Marjorie*] TMs 'Marjory' *preceded on line above by deleted* 'Marjory' *at speech point*

149.28 hesitates;] *semicolon inserted after deleted closing parenthesis which was over a semicolon; carbon impression*

150.10 *Thorpe*] *originally typed without underlining at speech point, type-deleted and typed at margin point with underlining*

150.18 a] *interlined with a caret; carbon impression*

154.26 —er—] *interlined with a caret; carbon impression*

154.34 us] *followed by deleted* 'why'; *carbon impression*

155.16 "Er—] *preceded by type-deleted* ' "I don't' *of which quotes not deleted in error*

156.4 it] *preceded by type-deleted* 'that.'

156.16 (moves] 'o' *over opening double quotes at speech point*

156.22 Look] *followed by deleted comma; carbon impression*

156.23 than] 'n' *typed over* 't'

157.1 looking] *followed by type-deleted* 'out'

End-of-the-Line Hyphenation in the Virginia Text

149.32 picket-|shooting

End-of-the-Line Hyphenations in the Copy-Text

144.27 sugar-cane

148.20 something

150.13 cannot

XXXIII. PLANS FOR NEW NOVEL

Emendations to the Copy-Text

[The copy-text is MS: manuscript in the Special Collections of Columbia University Libraries.]

158.24 description] discription MS

159.2 house."] ~". MS

159.5 collection."] ~". MS

159.7 Agnes] agnes MS

159.8 Henry] Henery MS

159.10 etc.] ect. MS

Alterations in the Manuscript

158.27 Historical] 'H' *altered from* 'h'

159.8 to] *interlined with a caret*

159.8 the] 't' *over* 'T'

159.9 J.] *over* 'Y'

159.14 know.] *followed by deleted illegible capital letter*

XXXIV. PLANS FOR STORY

Emendations to the Copy-Text

[The copy-text is MS: manuscript in the Special Collections of Columbia University Libraries.]

159.16 ¶ Possible] *no indention* MS
159.16 Elizabeth,] ~‸ MS (*possibly* Elezabeth)
159.19 Shaw's] Shaws MS
159.19 Napoleon] Napolean MS
159.20 *World*] World MS
159.21 as] a MS
159.21 chief] *possibly* cheif MS
159.22; 160.12 Jonathan] Johnathan MS
159.23 appearance] appearence MS
159.25; 160.15 Monmouth] monmouth MS
159.26 Chatham's] Chatams MS
159.27 Cooper's] Coopers MS
159.30 familiar] familliar MS
159.32 benign] benigne MS
160.2 revolution] rovolution MS
160.7 imposing,] ~‸ MS
160.7 Find] find MS
160.8 handsome, alert] handsom, elert MS
160.10 Mention] Mension MS
160.11 incident] incedent MS
160.11 magistrate] magistrait MS
160.11 magnate] magnat MS
160.12 offended] offendid MS
160.14 Weir] Wier MS
160.14 Mitchell's] Mitchels MS
160.14–15 describing] discribing MS
160.17 excessively] exceisively MS
160.19 Cubans against] cubans and against MS
160.23–24 Henry Fleming's] Henery Flemings MS

Alterations in the Manuscript

159.22 Emphasise] *first* 's' *over* 'z'
159.23 appearance] MS 'appearence' *with a final* 's' *deleted*
160.19 Cubans] MS 'cubans and' *followed by deleted* 'the'
160.20 Americans] 'Am' *over* 'U.S.'
160.24 grand-father] *preceded by deleted* 'fathe[*and beginning of an* 'r']'

End-of-the-Line Hyphenation in the Copy-Text

160.12 simple-minded

XXXV. THE FIRE TRIBE: PLAY

Emendations to the Copy-Text

[The copy-text is MS: manuscript in an unknown hand in the Special Collections of Columbia University Libraries.]

160.27 squatting] squating MS
160.30; 161.2,5 Others] others MS (*doubtfully lower case at* 161.5)
161.19 hearths] *MS Tale* 171.10; hearts MS
161.20 myriad] meried MS
161.23 whitefaces] ~ | ~ MS
161.23 shone] shown MS
162.4 tell] Tell MS
162.8,13,19 woman] women MS
162.15–16 warrior's] warriors MS
162.20 widows'] widows‸ MS
162.28 see] See MS
162.30 O, Name.] ~‸ ~‸ MS
162.31–32 whitewoman] whitewomen MS (*second* 'e' *possibly altered to* 'a')
162.33 travail] Travaille MS
163.24 Catorce] Catorse MS
163.24 smiled."] Smile < > MS
163.25 Good!"‸] ~!". MS
163.35 blood)] ~— MS
164.7 [2]Fire God] Firegod MS

Alterations in the Manuscript

161.1,3,7 Catorce] 'c' *over* 's' *or mended* 'c'
161.8 god] 'g' *over erased* 'G'

161.10–11 whitefaces] *over erased* 'the white'
161.11 wrought] 'u' *over beginning of* 'g'
161.20 myriad] MS 'meried' *with second* 'e' *over* 'a'
161.22 sometimes] *final* 's' *added*
161.23 whitefaces] *final* 's' *added*
162.10; 163.12 And] 'A' *over* 'a'
162.13 says] *final* 's' *possibly added*
162.15–16 warrior's] MS 'warriors' *with* 'a' *over possible* 'o'
163.3 curious] 'c' *over possible* 'p'
163.10 Somebody] *over* 'Name'
163.17 young] 'yo' *over* 'm'
163.21 white] 't' *possibly inserted*
163.22 charms] *preceded by deleted* 'signs of'
163.22 battle] *a final* 's' *deleted*
163.24 chieftain] 'c' *over beginning of downstroke*
164.2 and] 'nd' *inserted*

End-of-the-Line Hyphenation in the Virginia Edition

161.14 flat-|wise

End-of-the-Line Hyphenation in the Copy-Text

162.7 bloodfriend

XXXVI. THE FIRE-TRIBE AND THE WHITE-FACE: SPITZBERGEN TALE

Emendations to the Copy-Text

[The copy-text is MS: manuscript in the Special Collections of Columbia University Libraries. The other texts collated are TMs¹: blue ribbon typescript comprising 13 pages, numbered 6–13; 17–21 (pages 14–16 are supplied in carbon and are from an otherwise missing set of carbons of TMs²); TMs²: blue ribbon typescript comprising 16 pages, numbered 6–21; TMs³: blue ribbon typescript comprising 25 pages, numbered 1–25.]

164.18 foreign] V; foriegn MS,TMs³
165.2 wasn't] V; wasnt MS,TMs³
165.15 commander] TMs³; cammander MS
165.19 *et seq.* don't] V; dont MS,TMs³ (*except* 'Don't' *with apostrophe inserted in ink at* 165.20,21,22)
165.28 preliminaries.] TMs³; ~‸ MS
166.5 tribe."] TMs³; ~.‸ MS
166.9 didn't] V; didnt MS,TMs³
166.13 isn't] V; isnt MS,TMs³
166.14 Forty] TMs³; Fourty MS
166.23 dominate] V; dominant MS,TMs³
166.30 understand——"] V; ~"—— MS,TMs³
167.12 doctor's] TMs³; docter's MS
167.12 *et seq.* doctor] TMs³; docter MS
167.14 doctors] TMs³; docters MS
167.33 guard] TMs³; gaurd MS
168.20 was] V; were MS,TMs³
168.26 appallingly] V; apallingly MS,TMs³
168.30 *et seq.* its] V; it's MS,TMs³ (*except* 'its' *for* MS [Cora] *at* 185.5, 185.16 *and for* TMs³ *at* 169.37, 185.5; *when present* TMs¹⁻² *read correctly* 'its')
168.35(*twice*) wouldn't] V; wouldnt MS,TMs³
170.20 wait!' "] V; ~'!" MS
170.22 Catorce!' "] V; ~'!
171.12 warrior's] TMs¹⁻²; warriors MS, TMs³
173.35 'freckles'] V; "~" MS+
174.21 have] V; has MS+
174.28 that] TMs¹⁻²; that | that MS; that that TMs³

174.29 tribe?"] TMs^{1-3}; ~?$_\wedge$ MS
175.16 and—"] V; ~"— MS+
175.16 "—And] TMs^{1-2}; —"And MS,TMs^3
175.21 log!] V; ~? MS,TMs^3; ~. TMs^{1-2}
177.5.1 [*space*]] V; *end of page* MS; *no space* TMs^{1-3}
177.16 halt——"] V; ~"—— MS+
178.19 seize] TMs^{1-3}; sieze MS
181.26 them——"] V; ~"—— MS+
182.2 wouldn't] TMs^{1-3}(TMs^3 *doubtfully*); wouldnt MS
182.7–37 The . . . Lean.] Cora's *hand*
182.17 between] TMs^{1-3}; betwen MS
182.18 destroy] TMs^{1-2}; distroy MS,TMs^3
182.19,36 shining] V; shinning MS,TMs^3
182.20 *et seq. for* Cora's *hand* receive] TMs^3; recieve MS
182.22 tribe's] V; tribes MS,TMs^3
182.29 killed.] ~$_\wedge$ MS
182.31 fire-tribe] V; Fire$_\wedge$ | Tribe MS; Fire-Tribe TMs^3
182.32–33 destruction] V; distruction MS,TMs^3
182.38 say—"] TMs^3(~-"); ~"— MS
183.1 "—They] V; —"~ MS,TMs^3
183.3 won't] V; wont MS,TMs^3
183.3 won't——"] V; wont"——; wont——" TMs^3
183.5 please——"] V; ~"—— MS,TMs^3
183.12 *et seq.* receive] V; recieve MS,TMs^3
183.17 can't] V; cant MS,TMs^3
184.12 He——"] V; ~"—— MS,TMs^3
184.24–185.33 sullenly . . . irony.] Cora's *hand*
184.25 [2]he] TMs^3(c); his MS,TMs^3(u)
184.36 chorus] TMs^3; chorous MS
184.39 serjeant] TMs^3; sargent MS
185.1 business." And] ~." and MS,TMs^3
185.2 fire-tribe] TMs^3(c); ~$_\wedge$~ MS,TMs^3(u)
185.4 fire-tribe] V; ~$_\wedge$~ MS,TMs^3
185.4 For] TMs^3; for MS
185.7–8 conceivable] TMs^3; concievable MS
185.8 fire-tribe's] TMs^3(c); ~$_\wedge$ tribes MS,TMs^3(u)
185.10 contempt] TMs^3; comtempt MS
185.12 controlled] V; controled MS,TMs^3
185.13 superstitions] TMs^3; superstiotions MS
185.13 immense] TMs^3; immese MS
185.14 Mexican] TMs^3; mexican MS
185.20 stiffly.] TMs^3; ~." MS
185.31 because] TMs^3; becaused MS
185.31 Lean's] V; Leans MS,TMs^3
185.32 whose] V; who's MS,TMs^3
186.13 -tribe's] V; -tribes' MS,TMs^3

Alterations in the Manuscript

164.19 streets. The] *period inserted before deleted* 'and'; 'T' *over* 't'
164.21 reaping] *preceded by deleted* 'slowly'
164.21 of everything] *interlined with a caret*
164.24 Line] 'L' *over* 'l'
164.29 of] *followed by deleted* 'it and'
164.30 it, wondering] *interlined with a caret*
164.31 district] *followed by deleted* 'the'
165.2 district] *followed by deletion of possible period*
165.3 the] *inserted*
165.5 beaten] *interlined with a caret*
165.7 white] *interlined with a caret*

165.8 pointed] *initial* 'ap' *deleted*
165.10 you to] *interlined with a caret above deleted* 'to'
165.15 adjutant] *preceded by deleted* 'captai[*and beginning of an* 'n']'
165.20 fingers!] *exclamation inserted before deleted period*
165.26 cot] 'o' *mended*
165.27 Sponge] 'S' *mended*
165.28 preliminaries] 'ies' *added with* 'i' *over* 'y'
165.29 annex] *preceded by deleted* 'an'
165.30–31 one part] *interlined above deleted* 'the nearest part'
165.31 all] *interlined with a caret*
165.34 me] *interlined with a caret*
165.35 It] 'I' *over possible* 'A'
165.35 contains] *followed by deleted* 'alone'
165.36 of] *followed by deleted* 'Indians'
165.37 Twelfth] 'T' *over* 'a'
166.3 celebrate] *a final* 'd' *deleted*
166.9 mean] *preceded by deleted* 'it'
166.11 one] *over* 'a'
166.11 what] *interlined above deleted* 'one'
166.12 hundred.] *period preceded by deleted* 'men" '
166.24 war-] 'w' *over another letter, possibly an* 'a'
167.1 The] 'Th' *altered from* 'H'
167.11 sound] *followed by deleted* '—they'
167.13–14 all doctors] 'all' *interlined above deleted* 'any'; 's' *added*
167.21 sharp direction] *both* 's' *and* 'd' *over* 'm'
167.25 impostor—] *dash over period*
167.27 Regiment] 'R' *over* 'r'
167.27 mountains] *preceded by deleted* 'hi' *and beginning of an* 'I'
167.28 [1]and] *preceded by deleted* 'an'
167.31 reflected] *preceded by deleted* 'mused'
167.34 [2]a] *over* 't'
167.34 [2]of] *preceded by deleted* 'mules'
167.36 soldiers] *final* 's' *added*
168.5 The] *preceded by* '(A)' *in margin and written in* MS *below paragraph at* 168.10 *which in turn is preceded by* '(B)'; *at the top of* page 3 *is* Crane's *note:* 'Note to typewriter: | change paragraph A | to place of [*ditto marks, beneath* 'paragraph' *on line above*] B. '
168.6 streams] *final* 's' *over* 'ed'
168.12 sense] *preceded by deleted* 'isolat'
168.13 home] *followed by deleted period*
168.14 felt] *followed by deleted* 'lik'
168.14 re-called] *followed by deleted* 'the'
168.15 mind] *preceded by deleted* 'his'
168.16 that] 'th' *over beginning of illegible letter*
168.18 were] *preceded by deleted* 'were' *and followed by deleted* 'by this ob'
168.19 but] *followed by deleted* 'now'
168.21 was] *preceded by deleted* 'were'
168.25 [2]upon] *interlined*
168.26 himself] *followed by deleted* 'up'
168.28 Lean] 'L' *over* 'H'
168.34 this thing] *interlined with a caret*
168.36 eagerly] *interlined with a caret*
168.36 fingered] *followed by deleted* 'it'
168.38 Lean] 'L' *over* 'h'
168.38 the corporal] *interlined with a caret*

169.11 all] 'a' *over beginning of* 'f'

169.17 It] 'I' *over* 'T'

169.18 failing] 'f' *over beginning of* 'u'

169.18 because of] *interlined above deleted* 'under'

169.19 on] 'o' *altered from probable* 'i'

169.23 it] *interlined after deleted* 'he'

169.24 [2]as] *followed by deleted* 'when'

169.29 rocks.] *preceded by deleted* 'cliff.'

169.30 at] *interlined with a caret before deleted* 'to'

169.32 [1]as] *interlined with a caret*

169.33 back] *interlined with a caret*

169.34 had] *interlined with a caret*

169.35 had been] *interlined above deleted* 'was'

169.37 destruction.] *period inserted before deleted* 'as'

170.1 Harding] *interlined in pencil with a caret above deleted* 'Benson'

170.3 thought] *interlined above deleted* 'said'

170.3 hit] *preceded by deleted illegible letter*

170.4 [1]a] *interlined with a caret*

170.7 Chapter III.] *preceded on the same line by* 'For' *deleted at paragraph point*

170.8 thirteen] *interlined with a caret*

170.8 warriors] *preceded by deleted* 'head'

170.9 their] 'ir' *added*

170.9 Some] *preceded by deleted* 'It'

170.10 [2]the] *interlined*

170.11 the] *interlined*

170.12 coiled] *followed by deleted* 'drearily'

170.14 chests,] *comma inserted before deleted period*

170.19 stirred; they] *interlined with a caret*

170.29 ye] 'y' *over* 'h'

170.35 Catorce] *preceded by deleted* 'named as'

171.1 -faces] *followed by deleted period*

171.3 warriors] *followed by deleted period*

171.5 of my people] *interlined with a caret*

171.8 [2]as] *followed by deleted* 'one of'

171.9 The] 'T' *over* 't'; *preceded by deleted* 'Low'

171.10 because] *interlined above deleted* 'when'

171.12 necklace] *followed by deleted period*

171.13 [1]they] *interlined*

171.18 warrior speaks] *a final* 's' *deleted from* 'warrior'; *followed by deleted* 'h[*and beginning of another letter*]'; *final* 's' *added to* 'speak'

171.18 two] 'w' *over* 'o'

171.19 of] *preceded by deleted* 'of'

171.20 stiffly.] *followed by deleted closing quotes*

171.20 tell] *interlined above deleted* 'speak'

171.22 [1]the] *interlined with a caret*

171.23 [2]the] 't' *over* 'p'

171.23 where] 'h' *interlined with a caret*

171.32 became] 'a' *over* 'o'

171.32–33 unable] *preceded by deleted* 'and'

171.39 great] *preceded by deleted* 'pale'

172.1 'Of] *single quote over double*

172.4 ye] *preceded by deleted* 'he'

172.7 [1]the] *interlined with a caret above deleted* 'a certain'

172.8 my] 'm' *over* 'h'
172.10 their] *followed by deleted* 'wh'
172.12 white] *interlined above deleted* 'pale'
172.14 warrior,] *comma inserted before deleted* 'with a face deeply'
172.20 enemies—] *dash over a comma*
172.22 even] 'ev' *over original* 'in'
172.22 warriors] 'w' *over* 'd'
172.27 scar] *a final* 'e' *deleted*
172.28 knife] 'f' *over* 'v'
172.30 spoke in] *beginning stroke of* 'in' *deletes with intent comma following* 'spoke'
172.31 learn] *preceded by deleted* 'know'
172.33 spring] 'i' *over* 'a'
172.36 interrupted] *followed by deleted period*
172.38 amid] 'ami' *over possible* 'amo'
172.38 arose] *followed by deleted* 'the'
173.2 fire-] 'f' *over* 'F'
173.4 Catorce,] *comma inserted after deleted period*
173.7 the] *interlined*
173.7 patch] *preceded by deleted* 'square'
173.13 paused] *interlined with a caret*
173.14 passion. Through] *period inserted before deleted* 'and'; 'T' *over* 't'
173.16 said] 's' *over* 'c'
173.20 die-away] *interlined*
173.21 is] *over* 'an'
173.23 of] *interlined*
173.23 to] *over* 'm'
173.26 young,] *followed by deleted closing quotes*
173.27 thoughtfully,] *comma preceded by deleted period*
173.33 sun. And] *period inserted;* 'A' *over* 'a'
173.34 nothing.] *period inserted before deleted* 'to nothing.'
173.36 battle] *a final* 's' *deleted*
173.39 chieftain.] *period inserted before deleted* 'and'
174.9 Singer] 'S' *over* 's'
174.12 we] *preceded by deleted* 'I'
174.15 We] 'W' *over* 'H'
174.17 meet] *second* 'e' *over upstroke*
174.17 them] *followed by deleted period*
174.18 [2]it] *interlined with a caret*
174.18 in] *interlined with a caret*
174.22 crows' chatter."] *apostrophe inserted before deleted period and double quotes;* 'chatter." ' *added*
174.25–26 at the stones] *interlined with a caret*
174.33 -machines] 'n' *over* 'e'
174.36 -faces do] 's' *added; final* 'es' *of* 'do' *deleted*
174.38 stayed] 'ed' *interlined; preceded by deleted* 'remained'
175.2 piercing] *preceded by deleted* 'flashin'
175.9 voice] *followed by deleted* 'to th'
175.16 tone] *preceded by deleted* 'voice'
175.22 that] 'at' *over* 'e'
175.23 IV] *over* 'III'
175.25 begin] *a final* 's' *deleted*
175.26 country.] *period inserted before deleted* 'and'
175.32 discussions] *final* 's' *added*
176.1 answered] MS 'an-|swered' *with* 's' *inserted and* 's' *on line above deleted*
176.2 sang] *preceded by deleted* 'prayed'
176.4 -priest] *preceded by deleted* '-place' *with hyphen undeleted in error*
176.6 speech] *interlined above deleted* 'words'
176.9 could] *over* 'can'

176.12 little] *interlined above deleted* 'nought'
176.13 [2]the] 't' *over* 'S'
176.16 meant] *preceded by deleted* 'mained'
176.17 faltered] *followed by deleted* 'and'
176.17 ground,] *comma inserted before deleted period*
176.22 dashed] *preceded by deleted* 'swept as'
176.25 bring] *interlined with caret above deleted* 'come thus with'
176.26 coming] *followed by deleted* 'of'
176.31 [1]the] *followed by deleted* 'news to'
176.38 them] *interlined with a caret*
177.3 Sinrival] *followed by deleted* ', the'
177.5 despair.] *interlined below deleted* 'sorrow.'
177.9 creatures] *interlined with a caret*
177.10 three] *followed by deleted* 'detail'
177.13 From] *preceded by deleted* 'A savag'
177.21 and turned] *interlined with a caret*
177.21 his great] *preceded by independently deleted* 'to' *and* 'over to his hands'
177.21 while] *preceded by deleted* 'wh'
177.25 do] 'd' *altered from* 'i[*and beginning of a* 't']'
177.27 It's] MS 'Its' *with apostrophe after* 't' *deleted and a close-up line drawn between* 't' *and* 's'
178.2 a] *interlined with a caret*
178.3 hope] *interlined with a caret*
178.3 that] *interlined with a caret; preceded by deleted* 'until'
178.3 would come within] *interlined with a caret above deleted* 'come near enough' *of which* 'come' *altered from* 'came'
178.9 I] *over beginning of a* 'w'
178.12 warrior] *a final* 's' *deleted*
178.15 certainly] *interlined with a caret above deleted* 'plainly'
178.16 they] *interlined with a caret*
178.19 and] 'a' *over a downstroke*
178.21 contract] *preceded by deleted* 'arran'
178.23 journey] *preceded by deleted* 'servic[*and beginning of an* 'e']'
178.24 occasions] *preceded by deleted* 'shou'
178.26 [2]we] *preceded by deleted beginning of* 't'
178.26 tie] *interlined*
178.32 him] *interlined with a caret*
179.6 guard] *followed by deleted comma*
179.10 figures] *preceded by deleted* 'in less time'
179.18 protecting] *final* 'ly' *deleted*
179.21 mule] *final* 'teer' *deleted*
179.23 interpreters stood] *beginning stroke of* 'stood' *deletes with intent a comma following* 'interpreters'
179.25 [2]face] *followed by deleted* 'to'
179.26 won for . . . moment.] 'for the moment' *interlined; period after* 'won' *undeleted in error*
179.29 with] *interlined with a caret above deleted* 'to'
179.33 them] 't' *over beginning of* 'm'
179.33 words] *followed by deleted* 'wi'
179.36 stride] *interlined above deleted* 'move'

180.10 me] *interlined with a caret*
180.11 are] *preceded by deleted* 'not' *which had been interlined with a caret, also deleted*
180.28 the] *interlined with a caret*
181.20 fore-head] *a final* 's' *deleted*
181.20 determined] *interlined with a caret*
181.22 despair.] *followed by deleted* ' "T'
181.26 them——"] MS 'them"——' *with quotes and dash inserted at end of line after dash on following line was deleted*
181.28 large] *preceded by deleted* 'grea'
181.31 The] *a final* 'y' *deleted*
181.34 they] *followed by deleted* 'true'
181.34 size] *interlined with a caret*
181.35 heavier,] *followed by deleted closing quotes and* 'replied the'
181.35–36 unflinchingly] *originally inscribed as* 'unflinchin' *at far right of line, as intended end of paragraph, but deleted and reinscribed at far left of same line*
181.37 give] 'i' *over* 'a'
182.4 chieftains,] 's' *added over an original comma*
182.7–37 The . . . Lean.] Cora's *hand*
182.14 O] *a final* 'h' *deleted*
182.14 and] *inserted*
182.23 she] *interlined with a caret*
182.27 moreover] 'm' *over* 'M'
182.29–30 And so . . . words] Cora's *hand possibly mended by* Crane
182.35 he] 'h' *over possible* 'c'
182.35 to Catorce] *interlined with a caret*
182.38 say——"] MS 'say"——' *with dash over comma*
183.1 will] *interlined with a caret*
183.2 afterward] 'ward' *inserted*
183.6 discovered] *followed by deleted* 'of'
183.7 was] 'a' *over* 'e'
183.10 he] *followed by deleted* 'he'
183.11 our] 'o' *over beginning of* 'w'
183.14 will] *interlined with a caret*
183.14 [2]the] *interlined with a caret*
183.15 stipulations.] *inserted before deleted* 'conditions.' *which had been interlined with a caret below the line;* 'stipulations.' *encircled with directional line to indicate position*
183.17 can't] MS 'cant' *preceded by deleted* 'don'
183.20 grinned] *followed by deleted* 'bl'
183.23 and food] *interlined with a caret*
183.24 -saddle] *a final* 's' *deleted*
183.27 consequence] *followed by deleted period and closing quotes*
183.28 Lean] *preceded by inserted paragraph symbol*
183.28 coins] *preceded by deleted* 'doll'
183.37 force] *preceded by deleted* 'emphasis'
183.38 unutterably] *preceded by deleted* 'unt'
184.5 your] *preceded by deleted* 'our peop'
184.5 fierce] *preceded by deleted* 'tribe'
184.8 I] *over* 'c'
184.9 two] *preceded by deleted* 'one'
184.13 confound] *interlined with a caret above deleted* 'damn'
184.14 Cajoles—] *dash over a comma*

184.14 know] *followed by deleted* 'what'
184.14 now] *initial* 'k' *deleted; preceded by deleted* 'is'
184.15 galaxy] *interlined with a caret above deleted* 'group'
184.17 forward] *followed by deleted* 'with did'
184.19 Lean] *preceded by deleted* 'Files'
184.19 man] *interlined above deleted* 'of these men'
184.20 moment] *followed by deleted* 'and'
184.20 bit] *interlined*
184.22 At] *preceded by deleted* 'Nea'
184.22 the released] *interlined with a caret*
184.23 litter] *preceded by deleted* 'lit'
184.24–185.33 sullenly . . . irony.] Cora's *hand*
184.28 Haryid] 'r' *over beginning of* 'y'
185.2 fire-tribe] MS 'fire∧tribe' *with* 'f' *and* 't' *over* 'F' *and* 'T'
185.19 asked] Cora's 'd' *mended, perhaps by* Crane
185.22 Lean.] *followed by deleted beginning* of 'T'
185.30 alarm] *followed by deleted* 'for'
185.33 rhetoric] *interlined with a caret by* Crane *above deleted* 'retoric'
185.35 was] 'a' *altered from* 'er'
185.36 company] *interlined with a caret above deleted* 'men'
186.5 loaded] *interlined with a caret*
186.6 this] 'i' *over* 'e'; 's' *added*
186.7 the] *over* 'a'
186.8 in] *followed by deleted* 'to'
186.9 garrulous,] *interlined with a caret*
186.10 time] *interlined above deleted* 'moment of silence'

End-of-the-Line Hyphenations in the Virginia Edition

165.25 head-|quarters'
170.24 death-|note
171.19 tree-|branches
173.4 blood-|friend
180.25 slave-|lord
185.36 over-|looking

End-of-the-Line Hyphenations in the Copy-Text

170.9 fire-tribe
174.34 white-face
178.30 half-hitches

Historical Collation

164.14–168.35 The . . . move.] *pages lacking* TMs$^{1-2}$
165.29 Eskelopo] Eskelope TMs^3
165.39 hills] hill TMs^3
166.15 Well] Will TMs^3
167.21 lie] be TMs^3 (*clearly a misreading of* MS)
167.33 rear] the rear TMs^3
167.34 mules] miles TMs^3
168.14 adventurers] adventures TMs^3
168.24 discerned] discovered TMs^3
168.38 noted] noticed TMs^2
169.3 blankets] blanket TMs^3
169.15 top] the top TMs$^{1-2}$
169.25 the chest] his chest TMs^3
169.27 *et seq.* its] it's MS,TMs^3 *except* 'its' *at* MS 185.5, 185.16 *and* TMs^3 169.37, 185.5)
169.29 clattering] chattering TMs^3
169.29 clinking] clanking TMs^3
169.32 at kirk] at at Kirk TMs^3
170.1 Meanwhile] Meantime TMs$^{1-2}$
170.31; 173.1,15; 174.9,30 Singer] singer TMs^3
170.35 Catorce] Catroce TMs^3

171.2,3,9(*twice*),10,17,18,23 Rostina] Rostana TMs[3]

171.4 earth] death TMs[2]

171.23 trails] the trails TMs[2]

171.25 altars] alters TMs[2-3]

171.26 -faces] -face TMs[3]

171.26–27 warriors . . . crystal] *omit* TMs[3]

171.27 these] those TMs[2]

171.36 has] had TMs[1-2]

172.1 [2]-friend] -friends TMs[3]

172.5 [1]bid] bade TMs[2]

172.5 I] *omit* TMs[3]

172.9 these] *omit* TMs[3]

172.12 [2]the] *omit* TMs[2]

172.13 spake] spoke TMs[3]

172.15 will] shall TMs[2]

172.16 widows'] widow's TMs[3] (*unclear*)

172.22 warriors] dead warriors TMs[1]

172.24–25 The . . . law."] *omit* TMs[3]

172.30 sad and grave] grave and sad TMs[2]

172.33 field] fields TMs[3]

173.2 slain] *omit* TMs[3]

173.13 around] round TMs[2]

173.14 passion. Through] passion. and Through TMs[1] (*period inserted and* 'T' *over* 't'; 'and' *not deleted in error*)

173.24 -devils] -devil TMs[1-2]

173.25 a very] very a TMs[3] ('a' *ink-inserted incorrectly*)

173.35 men] man TMs[3]

173.35 were] are TMs[2]

173.36 battle] battles TMs[1]

173.37 deference] difference TMs[3]

174.11 scars] scares TMs[3]

174.12 gasp] grasp TMs[3]

174.20 over-turns] over-turn TMs[2]

174.21 meetings] meeting TMs[1-2]

174.21 have] has MS, TMs[1-3]

174.22 crows'] crow's TMs[1,3]

174.28 that] that | that MS; that that TMs[3]

174.38 old] the old TMs[1-2]

174.38–175.1 other listeners] others listened TMs[3]

175.17 invent] invent new TMs[1]

175.28–29 chieftains] the chieftanins TMs[3]

176.4 buried] burned TMs[3]

176.6 Catorce's] Catorce TMs[3]

176.6 quieted] quited TMs[3]

176.8 wily] why TMs[3]

176.11 [1]of a] of the TMs[3]

176.12 strange] strong TMs[3]

176.17 again] *omit* TMs[1-2]

176.19,25 chieftains] chieftain TMs[3]

176.26 day] the day TMs[3]

176.36 disputes] dispute TMs[3]

176.37–38 They . . . deed.] *omit* TMs[3]

177.3,5 keening] kneeing TMs[3]

177.22 froth] forth TMs[3]

177.31 fired] had fired TMs[1-2]

178.3 within] in TMs[3]

179.21 in] *omit* TMs[3]

179.26 Subsequent] Subsequently TMs[3]

179.32 with] *omit* TMs[3]

180.20 a] *omit* TMs[3]

181.1 came] come TMs[1-3]

181.6 come] came TMs[3]

181.10 a] *omit* TMs[3]

181.21 for a] *repeated at head of next page* TMs[1-2]

182.2 are] were TMs[3]

182.8–11 line . . . minute!] *right portion of lines missing* TMs[2]

182.11 pled] plead TMs[1]

182.17 of] *omit* TMs[1-2]

182.18 make] *last word of* TMs[1-2]

182.27 aged] *omit* TMs[3]

182.28 councils] council TMs[3]

183.18–19 interpreter] interpreters TMs[3]

183.28 coins] coin TMs[3]

183.35–36 impulses] impulse TMs[3]

184.11 so] has TMs[3]

184.19 [1]man] men TMs[3]

184.32 the] *omit* TMs[3]

185.17 interpreters] interpreter TMs[3]

185.34 II] VI TMs[3]

TO USE IN STEPHENS LIFE

[NOTE: The following posthumous notes made by Cora for a proposed biography of Crane are presented here in a diplomatic transcript for their inherent interest. These jottings are inscribed in a shorthand notebook, on one side only, preserved among the Cora Crane papers in the Special Collections of Columbia University Libraries.]

A worshiper of everything beautiful in life, he could see rosy lights under the most sordid clouds and had the moral courage to write his true impressions he said: "The true artist is the man who leaves pictures of his own time as they appear to him." x A mind endowed for the highest artistic perceptions and sensuous joys: he was happy and prosperous giving to others of the visions clear to his own crystal mind x x His stumbles against the rough places in life made him the more tender to others x x an element of fraility there
June 4th day before his death he said to me: "I leave her[e] gentle, seeking to do good, firm, resolute, impregnable."

Write to Dr Skinner about Morphine—
—"Thats what strayed him"—
"You can cut them she cant."
"Little Butcher, I will tell Skinner how he came to Bali & stole me"—
To nurse: "Did you know Dr Bruce never heard of him?" Dr called
June 4th 8 P.M—Gave morphine injection—went at once to heart, I could see by muscular contraction Dr. saw too, tried to give champhor injection to revive action of heart. Dr said next day: "Can you forgive me?" What did he mean? don't dare to think.

Use Pass for Camp McCalla—among letters etc. to keep.

Stephen tought himself to read befor 4 yrs of age. Could read well at that age.

Did regular newspaper work before his mother died Dec 7–91—When first he spoke called himself "Tevie" one day when 2½ yrs of age some one asked him his name while his eyes fairly danced he said: "nome Pe-pop-ty" no one ever knew where he got it from; he evidently made it up—His sister Nellie used to call him by this name when he grew up

---

When at Claverick he was ashamed of being only boy without middle name so called himself Stephen *D. Crane

---

He never got in childish rages with people because they did not consider his work as good as he, himself considered it.

Fate sets its stamp upon the faces of those who are doomed to an early death.

Stephen said to me at Dover when Robert Barr was in room: "Don't you understand that men want to be alone together sometimes?"

Send "Wounds in the Rain" to Samkson——
He served up what was best in his heart and mind to his people. ['x they accepted it' *deleted*]

Souffredouleur (drudge)
Faith that his work was good his creed.
—Brilliant & generous nature.
Grave & melancholy expression x x possessed a sense of true delicacy x x "His thought changed often; but while it possessed him, he acts upon it with such ardor that others give away before him, fascinated by the ingenuity, the persistance of strong desire."

Bladen has observed like some catholic writers, the intimate resemblance between heavenly and human love, and in his lectures illuminated things divine by an imaging of erotic love. The piquant flavour of coquettish spice does not spur our affection so much as a gentle, tender sympathy.

One is bound to die by the laws of nature the same as men die on the battlefield for glory.

Karl Harriman states if he ever accomplishes anything in fiction writing it is due to talks and walks with S

Henley 1899

Modest, gentle, direct and unaffected. In character——modest to the point of diffidence x x Striving for no passing honors of audible applause. x x x x He would say after writing a paragraph: "This is good, by God its good!" One I said to him, "Why not write a popular novel for money something that everyone will read?" He turned on me & said: "I will write for one man & banging his fist on writing table & that man shall be myself etc etc——" x x He never thrust himself forward never posed for admiration. x x People were alway disappointed at his appearance—they always seem to have expected an old vetran. He was a delicate frail looking man with wonderful eyes. Dr. Frankel said they were the most wonderful eyes he ever

* Double underlined

saw: "They read the world" he said—— He spoke very slowly & distinctly and seldom—but when he did all conversation would cease; every ear would listen & they knew on whatever subject his oppinion would have been carefully thought out. It was only the last year that he overcame his bashfulness about hearing the sound of his own voice. x x at home always knickers —dress for dinner in England but sometimes would go unshaven— x Beautiful hands & glad his hair was cut during illness so he would not be a bald old man—Nose was straight & perfect—eyes deep grey at times blue at times green black—black brows & lashes hair a drab & very fine & thick long & carelessly worn—skin drab—Crane skin—mouth full lips, mustash golden brown. x x hated to write letters—loved to ride—play ball——

Played ball with Rectors children when delirious

Handwriting had a tendency to grow microscopic—ms. seldom corrected even puntuation & penmanship wonderfully neat x Sometimes misspelled & never kept papers neat—never cared for ms until married—wrote slowly forming each letter with greatest care x Intended writing memoirs as legacy for wife x Always more or less in debt x Thought O'Ruddy would free him—alway cramped for ready money x It was a condition which did not weigh upon him until last year of life x He was so used to it (? consider using this) Vulgar display impossible for him but condition of plain abundance—large household & free handed hospitality which welcomed all to his roof & board who visited him were of the necessaries of his life x A man's character is affected by Natural Surroundings x x Brede Place—etc discribe—photos—
Benifit of traveling x
Friendships x Influences x
young writers came to him—
journalists " " "
Posterity ?
ecclesiastical connections x
delicate & precocious—read as did William Morris at four years of age only he read Fennimore Cooper novels x
Emotional & imaginative psychology x Inspired eye for colour x
Pony—find out about pony's death x about camping at Hartwood x

---

Wanted to go to West Point—Will said no war in your life time & persuaded him to give it up x greatest play as infant boy buttons which he would call soldiers & would manuevre his armies—never picked up buttons after play x x
Hated gilding, mirrors & so called Empire furnishing x

Use the problem of heridity x

How he treated servants

Home life x Religion

Use sinking of Commodore Feb 97

Volo

Use old diary

Velistinio

Addenda to Volume VIII

NO. 7B. HOW THE OCEAN WAS FORMED

"O WISE ONE!" said the Youth, "how was the ocean formed?"

"Son," said the Sage, "once upon a time there was a man and a woman all alone in the vastness. And the woman said to the man: 'John, I prithee, get me some water that I may bathe my hands.' And the man went and came with water, and the woman dipped her hands in the water and withdrew them quickly, crying: 'Oh! John, it is too cold.' And the man went and fetched warm water and poured it in the water that he had brought in the beginning. And the woman dipped again her fingers and withdrew them, crying: 'Oh! now, it is too warm.' And the man fetched again cold water and poured it in with the waters. And the woman tried again, but cried: 'It is now too cold.' The man brought warm water and poured it in the other waters, but the woman cried: 'It is too warm.' And so the man went to and fro again, and again, and again. And the woman alternately cried: 'It is too cold,' and 'It is too warm.' Until at last, the waters which the man had brought, formed the oceans that cover the earth. Whereupon the woman cried with scorn: 'John, you can never do anything rightly. I ought to have gone myself in the first place.'"

THE TEXT: HISTORY AND ANALYSIS

It was fortunate that while this final volume of the *Works of Stephen Crane* was in the last stages of page proof, *American Literature,* XLVII (1975), 113–114 in "A New Stephen Crane Fable" by William L. Andrews, published the discovered text of the following fable, the earliest known, signed and printed in the humorous weekly *Puck,* 34 (February 7, 1894), 426. The text here is reprinted from the original correcting a single slip in transcription that appeared in *American Literature*: the addition of a comma following *John* in the penultimate sentence, and retaining the first three words of the fable in capital letters as they appeared in the original.

New York City Sketches

No. 76B. KELLAR TURNS MEDIUM

Kellar, the celebrated magician, occasionally performs feats in a private way that are no more wonderful perhaps than his stage performances, but which possess a singular quality of human interest. For instance, a young man came to him not very long ago and said that his father had fallen so completely under the influence of a certain spiritualistic medium that he would transact no business without advice from the spirit land, and it was feared that the old man was going to bring destruction upon himself through his serious attention to the ghosts. Some time ago the son stated the heavenly guides had advised their worshiper to invest in some mining stocks of doubtful character and he had declared that he would take the pointer. The son was greatly alarmed and he had come to Kellar to learn if by means of the magician's talent the venerable dupe's faith could not be shaken in these shades that come so good-naturedly from the land of the unknown to advise him in everything from the value of mining securities to the best type of bicycle. The possessors of the heavenly truths conveyed their meanings to the old man in messages written upon ordinary slates.

Kellar had exposed the notorious Dr. Slade at Philadelphia in some slate-writing phenomena before the Siebert commission and he knew the complete science of conveying messages from the abodes in the eternal stars to some weary pilgrim here on earth. The story of the young man gained Kellar's sympathy, and he arranged a scheme to thwart the spirits and deprive them of their pious old victim.

The son departed happy and upon meeting his father said: "Father, I have discovered a new medium who is a peach. All your friends are not in it with this one. He communes with the spirits every minute of his life and he knows every move they make.

Slate-writing? Why that fellow can just holler at a slate and the spirits will cover it with solemn advice in seven languages."

The father rejoiced at the discovery of his son and he gladly accepted an invitation to attend a seance for the new medium and get some more advice from heaven.

Thereupon the son simply informed Kellar that his father's name was Andrew, that his wife's name was Martha and that the name of his daughter was Susan. Equipped with this meager but satisfactory data Kellar prepared a campaign against the spirits.

An appointed hour found the old man, his son and a friend of Kellar's—there by special invitation to witness the performance—seated in the library of the magician's home. Across the knees of the old man lay a bundle of a dozen new slates which he had brought in his desire to defeat any ringing in of fake slates. Presently Kellar made his entrance and without any delay proceeded to the business of the occasion. Stripping the library table of its lamps, books and covering, he remarked casually that the moquette carpet of the room would probably interfere somewhat with the magnetic control of the spirits, but that he thought he could manage the ghosts all right. At his request, they examined the table and failing to find any satanic device about it, they took seats. Kellar instructed them to draw their chairs close to the table. The old man sat opposite the magician, the son and the friend were at either end. The room was brilliantly illuminated and remained so throughout the seance. After a pause, Kellar spoke in a low tone cautioning the others to remain perfectly quiet, to make no remarks and to ask no questions until after the spirits had had an opportunity to manifest themselves. In making these preliminary arrangements, Kellar's manner was solemn and mystic, his pale face was inscrutable, while his eyes swept from one to another of the party in those stern and challenging glances which somehow makes all victims of mediums feel meek and utterly incapable of doing anything so offensive as to expose a fraud. Presently he took the old man's slates from the table and carelessly inspected them. They were of many kinds and sizes, some in plain wooden frames, some in the decorated borders which school children admire. Picking up a small slate, the wood of which was stamped with figures, letters and drawings of animals, the magician asked the men to extend their hands one over the other, to the center of the table. A little stack of six hands having been made Kellar placed his long slim left hand on top of the stack. With his right hand, he thrust the slate under the table, keeping his thumb always in sight, however, just above the edge of the table. There was another moment of stillness. Opposite the magician sat the old man, motionless and awed, his eyes upon the pale expressionless face of the pretended medium. If some ghost had then arrived who was not used to serving mediums he could have found nothing in his ghostly experience to explain the meaning of these four still figures, seated in silence about the little table.

Presently Kellar drew the slate from beneath the table. All eyes were instantly upon it. However, it was still perfectly blank. Kellar eyed it wistfully and in a tone of disappointment whispered: "The spirits are a trifle slow this evening." Again he thrust the slate under the table always keeping his thumb in sight. In less than ten seconds he said: "Let us look again!" When the slate came into view it was found to be covered on both sides with writing, done in a hand too fine for any human being to have inscribed in such brief time. Moreover the writing was in seven languages—Japanese, Greek, Hindoostanee, Arabic, Chinese, Russian, and Navajo Indian. The old man had no knowledge of Japanese, nor Greek, nor Hindoostanee, nor Arabic, nor Chinese, nor Russian, nor Navajo Indian but this exhibition so paralyzed him that he didn't even ask for a translation.

"Thunder," he whispered excitedly to his son, "this beats anything I ever saw!"

"Didn't I tell you so," replied the young man. "He's a daisy! Shut up now and wait for the next act."

Kellar presently addressed the aged victim: "Please select a slate and write upon it the name of some friend who has passed to the other side of life."

The old gentleman picked out a slate and writing a name upon it laid the written side downward and slid it across the table to Kellar. Taking it between thumb and finger, the magician slid it under the table as before while the company again stacked hands in the center. Kellar said that the hand part of the program was a condition imposed by the spirits to perfect the magnetic harmony and concentrate the atmospheric thought currents which otherwise would seriously interfere with the travel of the shades and make a mobilization of any particular force of spiritual intellect next to impossible. "Gosh," said the old man.

The magician presently drew forth the slate but again it was blank. He murmured in chagrin and thrust it back once more. Immediately the scratching of a slate pencil could be distinctly heard, and in a very few moments three hollow raps sounded. When Kellar brought forth the slate, it bore these words: "Dear friends. We are happy to be able to send you a message through the mediumship of our dear brother. Tell Andrew that we are overjoyed in his faith, that his loved ones are guiding his every step. We are a powerful band and will not let him go astray. He can not feel us but we touch and embrace him every day. If he could only penetrate the thin veil there is between us he would see John, Martha and Susan standing over him. God bless you all."

The old man's emotion upon receiving this message was very great. He had not altogether expected that the medium could corral his own departed ones from the infinite spaces of the universe. In a voice hoarse with feeling he requested that this interrogation should be propounded: "Shall I mortgage the farm and invest in the mining stocks?" Almost at once the slate was brought back with this answer: "Do so by all means."

Transported, overcome by this proof of the care and devotion of the spirits, the old man leaned heavily against the table. But at this moment a vivid flash of lightning filled the room blinding the eyes with its white shivering brilliancy and stunning the company with astonishment. When the illumination became normal, there were but three men at the table. The medium had vanished.

All but one of the slates were gone. Upon this was written: "The flash of light which has just dazzled you will be the means of revealing within twenty-four hours that what you have seen and experienced here to-night is not the work of spirits but of a fellow mortal.

Harry Kellar."

At the door stood a grave servant who indicated the exit with one calm gesture. The company arose and groped their way toward the street. The old man went first and after him his son. As

Kellar's friend was about to step across the threshold the form of the great magician appeared motioning to him from an alcove and then over coffee and cigars Kellar told the story of the seance supply house, where he purchased a collection of the different kinds of slates manufactured in the United States. These slates he placed in the room underneath the trap, first covering several of them with writing in the seven different languages. The preparations were all complete with the exception of an hour's rehearsal with Barney, his chief assistant. The cues were thoroughly understood between the magician and his silent and cool-headed accomplice. The seance commenced. Kellar picked out a slate which was an exact duplicate of one of those upon which he had written. This he holds under the table as described. Withdrawing it to see if the spirits had written, he hastily pushes it back with the remark that the spirits were a trifle slow that evening. This is Barney's cue. Underneath on a temporary scaffold the counterfeit spirit unbolts the trap, thrusts upwards an arm and grasps the slate from his master's hand. Drawing it through the trap he picks out its duplicate from the collection which has been prearranged, and deftly, without a sound, places it under the fingers ready to receive it. Immediately the bogus medium exhibits the slate written in strange languages as described. The piercing glow of mysterious light was a magnesium flash operated by the magician's photographer hidden behind the curtains, who made an exposure of the scene at the moment when Barney was passing up the last slate. Kellar had all hands extended to the center of the table, not for the purpose of centralizing the magnetism, but to draw all eyes over the table and prevent any possibility of Barney's arm being seen.

Within forty-eight hours after this affair, a photograph was in the old man's possession. It was a very good portrait of Barney passing up a slate upon which was written holy advice from the sky.

THE TEXT: HISTORY AND ANALYSIS

Crane's various inventory lists contain six pieces that have not been identified either as known sketches published under other titles or else as published at all, even though there is a strong inference that each title represents a published work. These are "Wisdom of the Present" (650 words), "Croyden Tragedy" (595 words), "Crowds from the N.Y. Theatres" (2075 words), "From Our Scranton Correspondent" (1470 words), "Pursuit of the Butter and Eggs Man" (500 words), and "Kellar Turns Medium" (no word count given). The last of these has finally been turned up after a persistent search in the *Pittsburgh Leader* for July 12, 1896, and then in two other newspapers. The syndicating agent is not known, but since the item appears in a list of about August 1896 that includes five other 1896 sketches distributed by McClure, it is a reasonable conjecture that this was a McClure piece as well. The other mentioned works have so far defied identification. One reason for the overlooking of "Kellar Turns Medium" is that it was signed with a nom de plume, H. F. Jokosa, the only observed time that Crane thus concealed his identity. Since "Kellar" was discovered too late for inclusion in its proper place after no. 76 in *Tales, Sketches, and Reports* in WORKS, Volume VIII (1973), it may be identified as no. 76B, with 76 being assigned the number 76A.

N[1]: *Pittsburgh Leader*, Sunday, July 12, 1896, page 19, headlined 'KELLAR TURNS "MEDIUM." | [short rule] | THE CELEBRATED MAGICIAN BE-|FORE A PRIVATE AUDIENCE. | [short rule] | He Exhibited His Skill for the Pur-|pose of Undeceiving an Old Man | Who Had Been a Victim of a | Spiritualistic Medium—A Flash-|light Photograph Reveals the Se-|cret of the Seance. | [short rule] | By H. F. Jokosa.' No syndicate notice or signature is appended.

N[2]: *Portland Oregonian*, July 12, 1896, page 12, headlined 'Kellar Turns Medium | [short rule] | The Celebrated Magician Performs | His Magic and Then Exhibits His | Method to Undeceive an Old Man. | [short rule]'. A syndicate notice is wanting; the signature 'H. F. Jokosa.' is appended.

N[3]: *Denver Republican*, July 12, 1896, page 21, headlined 'KELLAR BECOMES A MEDIUM | [short rule] | How He Undeceived a Too Confiding | Spiritualist. | [short rule] | DID AN EXCELLENT SLATE TRICK | [short rule] | The Slate Brought by the Dupe Was | Covered in an Incredibly Short | Time with Messages Written in | Seven Languages—He Gave the | Old Man a Family Message and | Then Exposed the Whole Thing | by a

Flashlight Photograph. | [short rule]'. A syndicate notice is wanting; the appended signature takes the form 'H. T. Jokosa.'

Each newspaper prints a cut of the seance, initialed R. W., captioned *Kellar Performing the Slate Trick. From a Flashlight Photograph.*

Of the three examples, the *Pittsburgh Leader* (N^1) has been selected as copy-text on the basis of its apparent fidelity in its accidentals to what appears to have been a syndicate proof relatively faithful to Crane's manuscript. Indeed, the conventionalizing of the punctuation in N^{2-3} as against the appearance in N^1 of Crane's characteristically light punctuation as of adjectival series and compound sentences has encouraged the editor to follow its accidental readings in most places even against the joint variation of N^{2-3}.

TEXTUAL NOTE

349.9 his] The evidence suggests that by a misprint the proof here read 'is' (as reproduced by N^2) and that both the 'this' of N^1 and the 'his' of N^3 are compositorial interpretations. One or other is undoubtedly an authoritative reconstruction, but which one is undemonstrable. If 'these shades' of 1.14 may be taken as evidence, just possibly 'this' could be accepted. On the other hand, since something seems to have fallen out or been slipped in proof, it is simpler to conjecture that it was the single letter 'h' and not the pair 'th'.

EMENDATIONS TO THE COPY-TEXT

[The copy-text is N^1: *Pittsburgh Leader,* Sunday, July 12, 1896, p. 19. The other texts collated are N^2: *Portland Oregonian,* July 12, 1896, p. 12, and N^3: *Denver Republican,* July 12, 1896, p. 21.]

*349.9 his] N^{2-3}; this N^1
349.21 Siebert] N^{2-3}; Sibert N^1
350.2 spirits] N^{2-3}; spirit N^1
350.10 son$_\wedge$] N^3; ~, N^{1-2}
350.21 failing] N^3; fail$_\wedge$|ing N^1
350.22 instructed] N^3; istructed N^1
350.30 inscrutable,] N^{2-3}; ~$_\wedge$ N^1
350.31 to] N^{2-3}; *omit* N^1
351.2 left] N^{2-3}; *omit* N^1
351.12 Presently] N^{2-3}; President N^1
352.6 be distinctly] N^3; distinctly be N^1; be N^2
352.18 corral] N^{2-3}; call N^1
353.15 counterfeit] N^{2-3}; counterfelt N^1
353.24 last] N^{2-3}; late N^1

COMPLETE HISTORICAL COLLATION

349.9 his] this N^1
349.11 character$_\wedge$] ~, N^{2-3}
349.13 alarmed$_\wedge$] ~, N^3
349.20 Slade$_\wedge$] ~, N^2
349.21 slate-writing] ~$_\wedge$~ N^3
349.21 Siebert] Sibert N^1

349.21 commission$_\wedge$] ~, N^{2-3}
349.22 messages] message N^2
350.1 Slate-writing] ~-| ~ N^1; Slatewriting N^2
350.1 Why$_\wedge$] ~, N^3
350.2 spirits] spirit N^1
350.3 son$_\wedge$] ~, N^{2-3}
350.4 medium$_\wedge$] ~, N^2
350.7 Martha$_\wedge$] ~, N^{2-3}
350.10 son$_\wedge$] ~, N^{1-2}
350.15 entrance$_\wedge$] ~, N^2
350.16 to] to do N^2
350.16 table] *omit* N^3
350.17 books] book N^3
350.18 probably] *omit* N^2
350.20 request,] ~$_\wedge$ N^2
350.21–22 and . . . table] *omit* N^2
350.23 magician,] ~; N^3
350.24 illuminated$_\wedge$] ~, N^2
350.25 pause,] ~$_\wedge$ N^3
350.26 tone$_\wedge$] ~, N^2
350.27 remarks$_\wedge$] ~, N^2
350.29 arrangements,] ~$_\wedge$ N^3
350.30 pale] *omit* N^2
350.31 to] *omit* N^1
350.34 Presently (*no* ¶)] ¶ N^3
350.37 school children] ~-|~ N^3
350.37 slate,] ~$_\wedge$ N^3
351.1 , to . . . table] *omit* N^2
351.2 made$_\wedge$] ~, N^{2-3}
351.2 long$_\wedge$] ~, N^{2-3}
351.2 left] *omit* N^1
351.3 hand,] ~$_\wedge$ N^3
351.4 thumb] thump N^3
351.7 pale$_\wedge$] ~, N^{2-3}
351.10 these] those N^2
351.12 Presently] President N^1
351.16 table$_\wedge$] ~, N^{2-3}
351.20 brief] a brief N^3
351.20 Moreover$_\wedge$] ~, N^{2-3}
351.21 Japanese] Janapese N^2
351.21 Russian,] ~$_\wedge$ N^3
351.24 Indian$_\wedge$] ~, N^{2-3}
351.33 slate$_\wedge$] ~, N^2
351.33 and$_\wedge$] ~, N^3
351.34 it$_\wedge$] ~, N^{2-3}
351.36 before$_\wedge$] ~, N^{2-3}
351.37 program] programme N^{2-3}
351.39 currents$_\wedge$] ~, N^{2-3}
352.4 slate$_\wedge$] ~, N^{2-3}
352.6 slate pencil] slatepencil N^3
352.6 be distinctly] distinctly be N^1; be N^2
352.7 very] *omit* N^2
352.10 dear] dead N^3
352.12 band$_\wedge$] ~, N^2
352.13 can not] cannot N^3
352.13 us$_\wedge$] ~, N^{2-3}
352.13 touch] touch him N^2
352.14 us$_\wedge$] ~, N^2
352.18 corral] call N^1
352.19 feeling] feelings N^3
352.21 at] as N^3
352.25 room$_\wedge$] ~, N^2
352.31 twenty-four] 24 N^{2-3}
352.32 to-night] tonight N^2
352.32 spirits$_\wedge$] ~, N^2
352.33 fellow mortal] ~ - ~ N^2
352.38 first$_\wedge$] ~, N^{2-3}
352.38 him$_\wedge$] ~, N^3
352.38 As (*no* ¶)] ¶ N^3
353.1 alcove$_\wedge$] ~, N^2
353.12 table$_\wedge$] ~, N^2
353.15 Underneath$_\wedge$] ~, N^2
353.15 scaffold] scaffolding N^3
353.16 upwards] upward N^2
353.16 arm$_\wedge$] ~, N^2
353.18 has] had N^2
353.23 photographer$_\wedge$] ~, N^2
353.24 last] late N^1
353.29 forty-eight] 48 N^{2-3}
353.29 affair,] ~$_\wedge$ N^3

Subheadings
(N^3)
349.19.1 He Knew the Tricks.
350.9.1 The Seance Begun.
350.34 (fraud.) Selected a Slate.
351.25.1 Paralyzed the Dupe.
352.15.1 The Final Exposure.
352.38 (son.) How It Was Done.

Errata

Corrections and Revisions in Earlier Volumes

ERRATA
CORRECTIONS AND REVISIONS IN EARLIER VOLUMES

[NOTE: The publication of this final volume of the *Works of Stephen Crane* provides the opportunity to correct such errors as have been called to the editor's attention by the generosity of various scholars. On the publication of BOWERY TALES, Professor David Nordloh engaged himself to an extensive collation of the text and apparatus against the first edition and generously communicated to the editor the findings he had made of inconsistencies. Professor Thomas McHaney in a review also noted some discrepancies and queried readings. For a prospective article on *Maggie*, Professor Hershel Parker had an assistant, Mr. Brian Higgins, make a collation, and kindly permitted the editor to see the listing of inconsistencies and queried readings. From his close reading of Crane, Professor Masao Tsunematsu on leave of absence in Charlottesville from Shimane University provided some errata for other volumes, and an additional few were kindly communicated by Professor Henry Alden. However, research assistants for the Crane project independently made a double-checked fresh complete collation of all of the editions of *Maggie* so that the editor can take responsibility for the alterations now listed. In addition to the correction of error, the opportunity has been sought to anticipate a second printing of BOWERY TALES, volume I, by here making a few textual revisions, recasting certain features of the apparatus to agree with refinements introduced in later volumes, and correcting inconsistencies between the text and its apparatus on the basis of a fresh triple collation of all the documents. Although the system of distinguishing the accidental from the substantive emendations has been preserved (the two parts being amalgamated into a single list in subsequent volumes), the record of dialect emendations from normal speech of the same word has been unified in the accidentals section but the record of variation retained in the Historical Collation. (Dialect variants from dialect forms of the same word, such as *d'* for *deh,* are not listed in this Historical Collation.) Aside from textual revision, correction in the apparatus ranges from the setting right of misprints, of incomplete or faulty line-number notation, of omissions, and of simple error. However, the specification of the exact point of difference between original and correction proved to involve so many problems of identification that for the sake of uniformity all apparatus entries requiring alteration, for whatever reason, have been printed in full in their now-desired form as they will appear in any later printing.]

Volume I. Bowery Tales

The Text of the Virginia Edition

xvi.15 *for* fact the he *read* fact that he

Maggie

Textual Introduction

liv.15,18 *for* black-letter single quotation marks *read* roman
lxvi.39 *for* footnote 13 below *read* lxxvi.30–31
lxviii.4 *for* argue *read* argue (but probably with too much optimism)
lxviii.23 *for* omission. *read* omission. However, despite the literary reasons that may be suggested as possibly motivating a few of the A2 omissions or paraphrases of such detail, the A1 references to swearing are retained in the present text, the more especially since they cluster in the early chapters and in their inconsistency of revision may better be attributed to Crane's attempts to please his publisher.
lxviii.29–30 for *glittering . . . on* (15.13) read *eyes glittered on* becomes *glittering eyes fastened on* (15.3)
lxix.22 *for* 52.17 *read* 52.16,17
lxx.23 for *bouncer* at 57.10 read *bouncer* at 57.10; however, the latter is at least arguably editorial and has been so treated.

Text

7.6 *for* oaths *read* great, crimson oaths
7.23 *for* madness *read* cursing fury
9.6 *for* brag *read* swear
12.9 *for* struck *read* swore and struck
13.9 *for* lay *read* lay cursing and
13.11 *for* hips, *read* hips
13.29 *for* They *read* ¶ They
16.23 *for* said, *read* said:
23.17 *for* It *read* They
23.18 *for* a street car *read* street cars
24.10 *for* vicinity, *read* vicinity
26.32 *for* hell! *read* hell,
27.8 *for* damned *read* damn
27.25 *for* eart'! *read* eart',
32.27 *for* love, *read* love
34.3 *for* d'hell *read* d' hell
43.30 *for* again *read* agin
44.10 *for* out a *read* outa
44.26 *for* hell," *read* hell,'
48.4 *for* back *read* back,
49.23 *for* glass *read* glass,
49.37 *for* in hell have yeh *read* in hell yeh

52.15 *for* a collar *read* the collar
52.27 *for* Pete. *read* Pete,
55.3 *for* day *read* day,
55.24 *for* for *read* fer
56.2 *for* and *read* an'
56.4 *for* humor *read* humor,
56.20 *for* up, *read* up
57.10 *for* "bouncer" *read* bouncer,
60.30 *for* said *read* said,
63.21 *for* ha! *read* ha,
63.27 *for* putty *read* puty
66.39 *for* do me dirt *read* git me inteh trouble
67.4 *for* don't *read* don'
69.34 *for* replied, *read* replied:
70.3 *for* street *read* street,
73.1,5 *for* Sure, *read* Sure!
74.3 *for* Sure! *read* Sure,
74.7 *for* and *read* and,
75.10 *for* dan' *read* dan
76.2 *for* cried *read* cried,
76.14 *for* weeping loudly *read* loudly weeping

Textual Notes

Add:

63.27 puty] That this A2 change (in the form 'putty') from A1 'purty' was part of Crane's extensive revision of dialect speech in A2 is indicated by 24.10 'puty good looker'. Although 'puty' here in A1 (followed by A2) may be a misprint, the odds may seem to favor the A2 spelling 'putty' at 63.27 as the printer's mistaken reading of Crane's marking of 'purty'.

Editorial Substantive Emendations

Add:

34.29 that] A2; *omit* A1 [*place above* 34.29 should]
47.38 hands] A2; hand A1
*63.27 puty] V; purty A1; putty A2–E2

Delete:

7.6 oaths] A2; great, crimson oaths A1
7.23 madness] A2; cursing fury A1
9.6 brag] A2; swear A1
9.12 yehs] A2; yeh A1
12.9 struck] A2; swore and struck A1
13.9 lay] A2; lay cursing and A1
21.35 which] A2; that A1
24.12 er] A2; or A1
62.24 yeh'd] V; ye'd A1–2; yehs E1–2
66.39 do me dirt] A2; git me inteh trouble A1
68.24 was] *stet* A1

Alter to read:
18.9–10 a confused] A2; confusingly in A1
*19.7 into] A2; in A1
20.14–15 Once . . . What?"] A2; *omit* A1
22.23 that he] A2; *omit* A1
23.18 street cars] V; street-cars A1; a street car A2
29.3 prodigious] A2; prodigiously extensive A1
29.17 It would be an] A2; An A1
36.11 dazzling] A2; brain-clutching A1
63.17 at Maggie with] A2; in A1

Editorial Accidental Emendations

Add:
8.12 manhood] A2; manood A1
9.12 yehs] A2; yeh A1 [*place below* 9.12 d'] V; deh A1 (*omit* A2–E2)]
10.1 yeh] A2; you A1
16.23 em!"] A2; ~ ." A1
24.12 er] A2; or A1 [*place below* 24.12 t' hell]
24.18 collars‸] A2; ~ , A1
25.36,37,38 d'] V; deh A1 (*omit* A2–E2)
26.5,6 D'] V; Deh A1 (*omit* A2–E2)
27.25,26 d'] A2; deh A1 [*place below* 27.25 [1]an']
31.18 benefit.] A2; ~ ‸ A1
32.39 masses,] A2; ~ . A1
43.31 yerself,] A2; yourself. A1
44.32 d'] V; deh A1 (*omit* A2–E2) [*place below* 44.32 friend.]
44.39 d'] V; deh A1–E2 [*place below* 44.39 Gee!]
47.37 d'] V; deh A1 (*omit* A2–E2)
47.37 t'] A2; teh A1
62.24 yeh'd] V; ye'd A1–2; yehs E1–2
66.38 do] V; deh A1; d' A2–E2
72.26 ri'!] A2; ~ , A1
73.1,5 Sure!] A2; ~ , A1
73.22 no!] A2; ~ , A1

Delete:
23.18 street‸car] A2; ~ - ~ A1
57.10 "bouncer,"] A2; ‸ ~ , ‸ A1

Alter to read:
7.7 git yehs!] A2; get yehs, A1
9.36 dinner-pail] E2; ~ ‸ ~ A1–2,E1
14.1 I——"] A2; ~ "—— A1
20.16 ¶ While] A2; *no* ¶ A1
22.27 Foot‸passengers] A2; ~ - ~ A1
24.12(*twice*) t'] A2; teh A1
25.30,33(*twice*),34(*twice*) d'] A2; deh A1
25.34(*twice*) t'] A2; teh A1
26.4 But,] V; but‸ A1; but, A2–E2
27.25 [1]an'] V; and A1 (*omit* A2–E2)

27.28,29 D'] V; Deh A1 (*omit* A2–E2)
31.11,15 d'] A2; deh A1
33.26,28; 34.3 d'] V; deh A1 (*omit* A2–E2)
40.5 [1]me!] A2; ~ , A1
42.19–20 'Oh . . . yes,' . . . 'Oh . . . yes.' "] A2; "~ . . . ~," . . . "~ . . . ~." A1
43.7,13,17,19,34,36,37,38; 44.2(*twice*),10,11,12,13 d'] A2; deh A1
43.10(*twice*),29(*thrice*),30 d'] V; deh A1–E2
44.21,22,35(*twice*) d'] V; deh A1–E2
45.20 begrimed] A2; begrimmed A1
62.28,30; 63.3; 64.12 t'] V; teh A1–E2
71.10 An't'ing] A2; An'thin' A1

Word-Division

Section 2
Add:
14.15 frying-pan
23.12; 49.25 sidewalk
25.26 half-closed
28.9 dust-stained
31.18 high-class
32.30 self-contained
36.14 nickel-plated
36.23 granite-heartedness
38.25 curb-stone
45.24 foam-topped
48.18 Bowery-like
58.19 clear-eyed

Alter to read:
68.10 eyebrows

Historical Collation

Add:
13.29 ¶ They] *no* ¶ A2–E2
21.7 On] At A2–E2
23.17 They] It A2–E2
24.14 where] were E2
34.29 that] *omit* A1 [*place above* 34.29 should]
42.18 by] be A1–E2
43.30 agin] again A2–E2 [*place above* 43.30 damn]
47.38 hands] hand A1
52.1–2 danseuse] *danseuse* A2–E2
52.15 the collar] a collar A2–E2
57.10 bouncer,] "bouncer," A2–E2
57.11 an] a A1
63.27 puty] purty A1; putty A2–E2
76.14 loudly weeping] weeping loudly A2–E2

Delete:
66.38 do] deh A1 (*omit* A2–E2)

Alter to read:
7.6 great, crimson] *omit* A2–E2
7.23 cursing fury] madness A2–E2
9.6 swear] brag A2–E2
10.1 yeh] you A1
12.9 swore and] *omit* A2–E2
13.1 sat in] crouched on A1
13.9 cursing and] *omit* A2–E2
13.30–31 , in . . . frequence] *omit* A2–E2
17.10 throat] hairy throat A1
22.23 that he] *omit* A1
23.10 struck] would strike A1
23.18 street cars] street-cars A1; a street car A2–E2
24.8 disguised] disgusted E1–2
25.24 "elegant"] elegant and graceful A1
25.36,37,38 d' hell] *omit* A2–E2
26.35 ideal] beau ideal of a A1
27.8 damn'] *omit* A2–E2
27.24–25,25 go t' hell an'] *omit* A2–E2
27.28–29 D' hell I am] Yer joshin' me A2–E2
27.31 of a] of E2
29.17 It would be an] An A1
31.11 what d' hell?] what's eatin' yeh? A2–E2
33.7 leers] leers, or smiles, A1
33.17 With . . . orchestra$_\wedge$] When the orchestra crashed finally, A1
33.28 what d' hell?] go ahn! A2–E2
38.14,15–16 T' hell wid yeh] Go fall on yerself A2–E2
38.20–21 Wide . . . grins] A wide dirty grin A2–E2
38.24 over . . . to her] to her over their shoulders A2–E2
39.25 what d' hell's . . . yeh] What's wrong wi'che A2–E2
39.31 damned] *omit* A2–E2
39.34 frame] framed A1
39.35 T' hell . . . [2]yehs?] An' who are youse? A2–E2
42.19(*twice*),23 hell] gee—A2–E2
43.4 vaguely wonder] wonder vaguely A2–E2
43.31 Take . . . yerself] Go fall on yerself A2–E2
43.31–32 , an' quit dat] *omit* A1
44.13 damned duffer.] big stuff! A2–E2
45.21 all] *omit* A1
46.6 Oh, hell, yes,] Well, ain't he! A2–E2
49.37 yeh] have yeh A2–E1; have ye E2
51.19 to reach] *omit* A1
51.30–52.1 upon the stage . . . about] was flinging her heels about upon the stage A2–E2
55.33 wa'n't] wasn't A1
62.27,31 , fer Gawd's sake] *omit* A2–E2
63.17 at Maggie with] in A1

66.39 git me inteh trouble] do me dirt A2–E2
67.2 come] came E1–2
71.25 "Damn it," . . . time.] "W're havin' great time," said the man. A2–E2
72.15,19,22,27 damn] *omit* A2–E2
73.11,20 damn] *omit* A2–E2
74.9 damn it,] *omit* A2–E2
74.10,12 damn 't,] *omit* A2–E2
76.12 window] windows A1–2

George's Mother

Textual Introduction

111.33 *for* her *read* Her

Text

117.32 *for* Well *read* Well,
118.5 *for* the' *read* th'
120.23 *for* vine-line *read* vine-like
133.22 *for* It——*read* It—
141.11 *for* boys'll *read* boys 'll
158.5 *for* yound *read* young
175.6 *for* Kelsey *read* Kelcey

Textual Notes

181.26 *for* sing-sing *read* sing-song

Editorial Emendations

Add:
175.6 Kelcey] E1; Kelsey A1

Alter to read:
116.3 year!] V; ∼ ? A1; ∼ . E1–2
130.11 boy—"] E1 (∼ '); ∼ "— A1
143.25 Pig'!"] V; ∼ !' " A1, E2; ∼ ‸!" E1
173.12 not'in'] V; notin' A1–E2
177.17 [2]nothin'] E1; nothin A1

Word-Division

Section 1
Alter to read:
124.2 prayer-|meetin'
167.23 point-|blank

Section 2
Alter to read:
132.15,19 good-by
172.25 tin-pail

Delete:
127.11 sawdust

Add new section:
3. *Special Case*
[NOTE: The following word is hyphenated at the end of the line in the copy-text and in the Virginia edition.]
127.11 saw-|dust (i.e., sawdust)

Historical Collation

Add to headnote: Variant paragraph indention of dialogue in E1–2 is not recorded.

Add to list:
153.8;170.15 docter] doctor E1–2
173.18 Billee] Billie E1–2
173.24 don'] don$_{\wedge}$t E1; don't E2
174.27 was the] was a E1–2

Volume IV. THE O'RUDDY

Text

91.28 *for* Contess *read* Countess
154.4 *for* 'Tis is *read* 'Tis
271.20–21 for *revised* read *reversed*

Alterations in the Manuscript

93.38 for *papagraph* read *paragraph*

Volume V. TALES OF ADVENTURE

Introduction

xxiii.18 *for* the *read* these
lii.27 *for* us *read us*
lxxvii.10 *for* Press *read Press*
lxxxviii.22 *for* the *read* that

Textual Introduction

clvii.19 *for* LM,A1 *read* LM,E1
clxxvii.19 *for* nine *read* ten
clxxvii.25 *add* 135.5 concluded that] concluded BW, E1
clxxxv.2 *for* 1896 *read* 1898
clxxxvi fn. 88 *for* "A Tale of Mere Chance," *read* "The Squire's Madness,"

Volume VI. Tales of War

Introduction

xxx fn. 33 *for* 1912 *read* 1902

Textual Introduction

xxxvii fn. 1.3 *for* to see *read* to go see
xlvii.2 *for* to *read* for
cxi fn. 46 *delete; see Textual Notes below*

Text

115.38 *for* sputter *read* splutter

Textual Notes

324 *delete note to* 115.38 ('splutter' appears *The Red Badge of Courage* 106.13. See also Textual Note in *The Red Badge,* 89.1)

Editorial Emendations

Delete:
*115.38 sputter] McC; splutter WG

Historical Collation

Alter to read:
115.38 splutter] sputter McC

Volume VII. Tales of Whilomville

"The Monster"

Textual Introduction

5.19 *for* the leaves *read* all the leaves
5.21 *for* heap up *read* heap

Historical Collation

Delete:
62.3 heap] heap up MS

Whilomville Stories

Text

144.20 *for* staid *read* stayed
228.38 *for* Dalzel *read* Dalzel. There were not many boys in the school who could whip Willie Dalzel

Editorial Emendations

Add:
144.11 acquaintances] H; acquintances MS

Delete:
228.38–39 Dalzel and these] H (Dalzel,); Dalzel. There were not many boys in the school who could whip Willie Dalzell and these MS

Alter to read:
229.21–23 supremacy . . . tribe.] H; supremacy was fought out in the country of the tribe which had been headed by Willie Dalzell. MS

Historical Collation

Alter to read:
228.38 Dalzel. There . . . Dalzel] *omit* A1

Volume IX. Reports of War

503 No. 48, line 4, *for* 30 *read* 31
515 No. 68 *for* February 14 *read* January 25
591 No. 26 *for* 1899 *read* 1898

Index of Assigned and Variant Titles in the Virginia Edition

INDEX OF ASSIGNED AND VARIANT TITLES IN THE VIRGINIA EDITION

[NOTE: The first set of numbers after each item refers to the transcription of the text; the second set to the discussion of each item's textual history. First lines of untitled poems are indexed under first words, including articles; articles are ignored in the indexing of all other titles.]